ROMANCE McGregor
McGregor, Tim
Old Flames, Burned Hands
2013

DISCARDED

OLD FLAMES, BURNED HANDS

D1519333

Tim McGregor

Seymour Public Library
176 Genc   et
Auburn, NY 13021

Perdido Pub
TORONTO

Copyright © 2013 Tim McGregor.

All rights reserved. No part of this publication may be reproduced, distributed or transmitted in any form or by any means, including photocopying, recording, or other electronic or mechanical methods, without the prior written permission of the publisher, except in the case of brief quotations embodied in critical reviews and certain other noncommercial uses permitted by copyright law. For permission requests, write to the publisher, addressed "Attention: Permissions Coordinator," at the address below.

Perdido Pub
6 Lakeview Avenue
Toronto, Ontario, Canada

This is a work of fiction. Names, characters, places, and incidents are a product of the author's imagination. Locales and public names are sometimes used for atmospheric purposes. Any resemblance to actual people, living or dead, or to businesses, companies, events, institutions, or locales is completely coincidental.

Book Layout & Design ©2013 - BookDesignTemplates.com

Cover photo copyright © Cristina Otero

Old Flames, Burned Hands / Tim McGregor. -- 1st ed.

ISBN - 13:978-0-9920403-1-4
ISBN - 10: 0992040310

The saints are the sinners who keep on trying.

—Robert Louis Stevenson

1996

Love will tear us apart

WHEN TILDA PARISH OPENED her eyes, the world was all wrong. It was upside down. She had to blink twice before realizing that it wasn't, in fact, the world that was all wrong; it was her. The car had landed on its roof and Tilda hung inverted like some demented bat, tangled in the seatbelt.

Under her lay the remains of the windshield, a thousand pieces of shattered safety glass blown over the ceiling of the wrecked car. The engine still running. Something wet dripped up her nose and trickled into her eyes and when she wiped it away, her hands came away bloodied.

"Gil?" Her voice was cracked and parched. She turned to the passenger seat but it was empty.

Gil was gone.

She screamed his name but there was no response, no sound beyond the lapping of water against the pier.

Later in hospital, there would be great gaps in her memory about the accident itself and what came after but everything preceding it was sharp and crisp. Small details recalled with clarity about that last night they were together. The last night before Gil died, before her life was cleaved into to two halves; before and after. Her memory recall was a blessing at times and other times it was a curse. She clung to every detail, she wished she could forget the whole thing.

She had performed that night, standing on the black painted stage of the El Mocambo. Its stink of spilled beer and limes that should have been tossed the day before, the cloud of cigarette smoke boiling over the hot stage lamps.

The Spitting Gibbons was Tilda's fourth band in as many years. The band name had no significant meaning to anyone, having been dreamt up while high one night after practice. They just liked the way it sounded. Besides, Tilda had told her bandmates, they can always just make up some interesting story behind it for the inevitable interviews after they broke big. History would save them the trouble as the Spitting Gibbons wouldn't live to see Christmas.

So there was Tilda onstage, a stick figure of twenty-four years, lips to the mic and fingers curled around a Fender bass. A raw voice, like a choirboy who smoked unfiltered Navy Cuts. The guitarist was a hirsute trog who had schooled under the Robert Fripp academy before forgetting everything he had ever learned to find that low-fi amateur crunch. The drummer was a wiry octopus who banged for no less than four other bands at the time, this being one of those drummerless seasons where competent percussionists were scarce.

Neither boy was much to look at, which was just as well because all eyes were on her. Her head tilted to one side and her thin shoulders weighed down under that big Fender. Her voice cracking when she hit that high note but not caring, knowing it was masked under the wall of noise. Slow then fast, loud then soft. That kind of structure so many chased back then, the sound of the Pixies still ringing in their ears from the first time they heard it.

Coming down, her eyes dropped to the crowd (seventeen who'd paid at the door, another dozen who crashed). Peering through the footlights and smoke to pinpoint a certain face amongst all the others. His.

Gil Dorsey leaned against the bar at the back of the room holding a pint of swill that passed for draught. A smirk so big you would've thought the skinny dude just found a C-note sticking to the bottom of his glass but it wasn't that. It was her. The girl onstage was singing to him.

Something happens when your average human being climbs onstage and sings. Doesn't matter who it is, they transform up there under the lights and, admit or not, every warm body gets a woody. Even butt-ugly singers (look under Jesus Lizard, also Dinosaur Jr., too the Pogues) take on this strange magnetism when standing five feet overhead and bathed in sound.

Tilda Parish was no exception. On the everyday street, she was no traffic-stopper, no magnet for cat calls. Cute? Sure. A few freckles dotted the cheeks under her green eyes, her chestnut hair tinted black in a bad home-dye job. Someone you pass on the street and note the smile but could not recall the face five minutes later if your life depended on it. That was her. And yet she walks onstage, plugs in and starts singing? Everyone looked up, drinks frozen halfway to their lips. Even the near-comatose doorman plucked the toothpick from his scowl to take a look. Even the entrenched hetero girls clinging to their boyfriends responded with the flicker of a nipply hard-on.

Tilda and Gil were in love. Who wasn't in those days? And like the movie said; truly, madly, deeply. They had met fourteen months earlier at a dingy club where Tilda was gigging with her former band The Daisy Pukes. Loading gear out of the van, she was struggling to haul an amp inside when she heard someone ask if she wanted a hand. Looking up, Gil Dorsey was there.

Smiling, he reached down for the amp and tried not to strain under its weight. Tilda smiled back, grabbed a guitar case and led him inside. Neither of them believed in love at first sight but something sparked when their eyes met. She invited him to the show and when he saw her onstage that first time, he was a goner. Three songs into the Daisy Pukes' set, he was upfront with his eyes locked on the slight girl hammering a sunburst acoustic. Waiting for her after the gig, she asked what he thought of the show and he admitted to disliking cowpunk. 'You'll come around,' she declared. When he finally did, Tilda had already dissolved the Daisy Pukes to form a new band with a different sound. Didn't matter. By then they had both fallen off the deep end.

"This is kinda spooky," Tilda had said, and not for the first time. Hauling her gear back to his flat after the El Mo gig, they had uncorked a bottle of cheap Spanish red and shed their clothes. Seeing Tilda play had lost none of its power and left him aching to get his hands on her. For Tilda, she loved being wanted that much, that desperately. Like his life depended on it. There were more than a few times when they hadn't waited to get home and just went at each other in the club's grimy backroom.

"What's spooky about it?" he asked.

Lying next to him in the sweltering flat, waiting for each pass of the oscillating fan to cool her sweaty skin, Tilda kissed his shoulder. "You're all I think about now."

Gil patted the floor beside the mattress until he located the cigarette pack. Two left. He lit one for them to share. "You sound resentful."

"I am. I was perfectly happy before I met you. I'd sworn off boys. Too much trouble." She took the cigarette and blew smoke at the cheap fan. "But now? Jesus. We're in so much trouble."

"That's what I love about you. Such a romantic."

"The thing is, I don't remember feeling this way with anyone else. This strongly, you know? I can't imagine it being this strong ever again." Tilda sat up and flattened her palm on his chest. "I should just kill you now."

"Kill me?"

"Yeah. In your sleep. Then I'd kill myself. Your landlord would find us a month later, kicking down the door because of the smell. He'd find the two of us rotting into each other."

"Again with the romance." He leaned in and kissed her hip. She tasted salty.

Tilda stretched and went to the sink to fill a glass of water. Gil's place was small, a flat above a garage on Oxford.

The place smelled of solvents and oil. Stretched canvasses were stacked against the wall and paint of every colour dotted the scuffed floors. Gil was a painter and he wore it with pride. Every stitch of clothing he owned was splattered with it, more of it encrusted under his nails and embedded in the grooves of his fingerprints. Not untalented but no Picasso either. The work piled up in the corner.

Gil studied Tilda from behind as she stood at the small sink. There were times when, standing at the back of a club and watching her perform, he knew in his bones that, between the two of them, hers was the true talent. Raw and huge. She made it look effortless, all that sound crashing across the room to rattle your sternum. His own talents seemed trifling next to it and, in his weak moments, he sometimes resented her for it. Ashamed at its pettiness, he kept that secret. For now, he could afford to keep up this illusion that he was a painter. It was all he had ever wanted to do. The day of reckoning talents and facing the truth was far, far down the road. For now they had each other and, if he had his wish, he would have forever to reconcile the disproportion in their abilities.

He propped up on one elbow, still studying her figure. Her damp skin reflected red from the neon leaking in from the kitchen window. "I should paint you like that. All red from the glow."

"Like you need another nude of me. Paint something else."

"You're all I want to paint anymore."

"Obsessive much?" She turned around and let the cold counter press against her back. "Now *that* is romantic."

"You hungry? There's some eggs in the fridge." He nodded to the antiquated Kelvinator beside the sink. "Scramble us up a mess."

"Funny guy."

"Aw, come on, Til. Anyone can scramble eggs."

"Not me. I don't cook."

"Not even for me?"

"Gil, I love you but I'm not going to cook for you. Or any dude. The day you find me slaving in the kitchen is the day you can put a bullet in my head." She refilled the glass and came back to bed. "This is the extent of my kitchen skills. Water."

Gil didn't respond. His gaze stuck on the window, his eyes faraway.

"Hey," she said. "Where'd you go just now?"

He took the glass from her. "Sorry. Drifted off."

"You keep doing that. You okay?"

"Yeah. It's just... last night was weird."

"I noticed." She touched his knee where the skin was scraped raw. There were others cuts and bruises on his hands and shins. "You got banged up more than usual. What happened?"

"Nothing." He shrugged. "Just, uh, a close call."

There was more, she could read it in his eyes but didn't push the issue. He would either tell her or he wouldn't. In the last six months, Gil had taken up a strange and sometimes dangerous hobby; exploring abandoned buildings. He would break into deserted factories or condemned tenements to see what was inside. He would come home bruised and filthy, regaling Tilda with how he had crawled through tunnels or almost fallen through a rotten floor. She hated his hobby and didn't understand the appeal. Whatever close call he had must have been serious because he hadn't said a word to her about it.

"I wish you'd give that up. It's too dangerous."

"I think I will," he said.

That surprised her. He could be obstinate, just for the sake of it, and didn't take well to advice but something was different. He almost seemed humbled, she thought, which was something she'd rarely seen in him. Had he almost died last night, tumbling to his death in some rotting firetrap? She wanted to know but didn't want to ask. "Hey," she said. "I have something for you."

"You do?"

She couldn't stop smirking. "Yup."

"Is it breakfast?"

"No dummy." She prodded her toe into his ribs. "I wrote you a song."

He sat right up. "You did? Play it."

Tilda chewed her lip, stalling. She had written the song four days ago but kept mum about it. The melody had just popped up while noodling on the guitar. Stringing a few notes together, a verse and half a chorus dropping off her tongue like they had been waiting there all along. The rest of the song was teased out and cold-forged that afternoon. It was a love song; plain and simple. Worse than that, it was earnest. She hated love songs. There were just so many of them, all insipid and cruelly simple when there was so much more to craft a song around. Imagine her surprise when, innocently plucking notes on the old gut string, a love song of all things hiccuped from her throat. Her fingers working the fretboard like they already knew the chords.

It was unnerving how easily it came. She expected her roommate to burst in laughing and mocking her for such a maudlin tune. Tilda wouldn't have blamed her either. Yet here it was. She noodled and finessed it, this the fastest she had ever written a song. Simple chord changes, the words spare and direct. She blushed singing the lyrics out loud in her bedroom but she couldn't deny their accuracy. It was a love song about him.

"I want to hear it," he said when Tilda still hadn't moved. Gil swung off the bed, lifted her guitar from its case and placed it in her lap. An old Gibson Hummingbird, the varnish crackled over the sunburst body.

Tilda took a deep breath and plunged in. No point trying to describe the thing, the simple riff and words were meant for him and him alone. Leave it at that. She kept her head down, eyes on the strings. Chancing his eyes while playing it would have been too much.

She didn't look up again until she finished the song and the strings ran quiet.

His eyes were a tiny shade of red and painted with disbelief. "You wrote that for me?"

"Do you hate it?"

"God no. I absolutely love it." Now it was his turn to take a breath. "No one's ever written a song for me."

Tilda shrugged. "Well, I'm glad to be the one to pop your cherry."

"You should record that." He leaned in for a kiss, squeezing the guitar between them. "It's a beautiful song."

"No recording. That one is just for you."

"Don't be bashful. That could be a hit."

"It's too sappy. I'm glad you like it but you're the only one who's ever gonna hear it."

"Then you better get used to playing it a lot because I love it."

She returned the guitar to its case. "Sorry, lover. Special occasions only."

"Then record it for me. So I can hear it whenever I want." Gil went to the corner of the flat where her gear was stacked. Where most women left a toothbrush or a change of clothes at their boyfriend's place, Tilda left instruments and amps. Gil dug out the four-track she had stored in the corner, found the mic and the cables. "Please."

She demurred but he insisted, plugging a microphone into the track machine. He pressed the guitar into her hands again and sat still as a churchmouse while she recorded the song. When she was done, she popped the cassette out and drew three little hearts on the white strip label. "I'm not even gonna put my name on this. But listen, you can't play this for anyone else. Deal?"

"Deal."

She nestled tight into him until their skin grew slick in the heat of the small flat. "It's too hot in here," Tilda said. "Let's go up to the roof."

"Okay. Grab the wine." Then a devilish smirk broke over his face. "Hey, want to torch something?"

"Like what?"

He nodded at the stack of paintings. "I got some stinkers I wanna trash. But that's not the cool part. I want to show you what I made."

THE rooftop was a relief from the torpid sauna of the flat. A hint of breeze that cooled the sweat sheen of their skin. They hauled up the wine, two stretched canvasses and some strange contraption that Gil had cobbled together.

"What is that thing?" Tilda asked, leaning the frames against the low lip of the roof.

"This," he grinned, "is a homemade flamethrower."

The contraption consisted of a large can of butane slotted into the body of a caulking gun. A long barbecue lighter was fitted to one side and a rod extendeding from the undercarriage provided a wick. A click of the lighter lit the wick. Gil aimed the contraption at the sky and squeezed the trigger nozzle. A blast of flame roared into the sky in a seven- foot arc, brilliant and angry. Gil laughed as he sprayed fire at the stars.

Tilda scowled at the thing. "Why would you build that?"

"Because I can," he shrugged. "Here, set that painting against the wall."

"Be careful with that thing. You could hurt somebody."

"Yeah." He nodded at the painting. "Him."

The painting Tilda leaned up was a self-portrait Gil had done in acrylic. It wasn't his best work, Tilda conceded. Gil seemed to have gone out of his way to make his face look haggard and ugly.

"You want to give it a shot? It's fun."

Tilda stepped back. "No. It's your toy, you go ahead."

Gil held the homemade flamethrower at his waist like a machine gun. "Sayonara asshole," he said to the painting and fired. The flame blasted over the canvas until it rippled and burned, sending black smoke into the air.

He lowered the gun and grinned at her. "I'm a genius. Sure you don't wanna try?"

It did look like fun. Tilda clapped her hands. "Okay."

Slinging the strap over one shoulder, Tilda tested the weight of the contraption in her hands. Gil kicked away the smoldering pieces of framing and set the second painting in its place. Another self-portrait. He stepped back and said, "Fire at will."

She aimed, then chewed her lip. "Feels weird, torching your face."

"Just burn that son of a bitch, would ya?"

Tilda gripped the caulking gun tight and throttled back the nozzle. She squealed as the flame bellowed out in a

dragon's breath and incinerated the canvass. It felt powerful and dangerous but, she had to admit, it was fun.

He took the flamethrower from her, lit a cigarette off
the guttering wick before blowing it out. They watched the
greasy smoke billow from the torched painting. "I was
thinking about what you said. About killing your lover being romantic and stuff."

"Too corny?"

"No. But I think there's a better question to ask."

"What's that?"

"Would you die for me?"

Tilda took the cigarette from him and mulled it over.
"Hmm. Yes. I would. Would you die for me?"

"In a heartbeat."

Her cheeks flushed hot and something flittered deep in
her chest. "I love you."

"We should get hitched," he said.

Tilda reared back, as if burnt. "Easy, tiger. I said I'd die
for you, I didn't say I'd marry you."

"Such a bitch."

Tilda laughed then wiped the sweat from her brow. "I
think we just made it hotter with all this fire. Let's go
somewhere to cool off."

"You want to go pool-hopping?"

"No," she said. "Let's go down to the lake."

NEITHER of them were in any condition to drive but they were young and immortal. All those MADD warnings were meant for other people. Other drivers, other drinkers. Our parent's generation, who drove shitfaced as routinely as they brushed their teeth.

So off they went, bombing eastbound on Lakeshore Boulevard in Gil's dented Rabbit. Swerving onto the Cherry Street ramp, the rusty VW almost catching air as it hit that godawful bump before the lift-bridge. The stereo blaring, that old Joy Division tune that everyone knew, the one everybody loved singing to their beloved. Half the street lights were dark on that scabbed scratch of road, the place deserted. Gil opened it up, pushing the diesel stroke harder than he should have. The damp breeze from the lake blew in through the open windows.

Gil cursed, the brakes stomped. Tilda never knew what they hit or tried not to hit. One of the gaps in her memory of the accident. She remembered a thud, then the car spinning as it flipped. Driver and passenger tossed around like ballbearings in a can of spraypaint. Darkness.

The next flash was the world upside down. The Rabbit on its back like a carcass. Safety glass sprinkled like ice over the dome light. The blood. Tilda slung head down in the seatbelt.

Gil was gone. He hated seatbelts.

She called his name but all that issued forth was a wet rattle, like those nightmares where you want to scream but can't. Then a glimpse of him, there beyond the jagged teeth of the broken windshield. He must have been thrown clear. Staggering towards her like a wino and covered in so much blood that she thought he had dumped a can of candy apple red over his head.

He yanked on the door but it was crimped tight so he got onto his belly and reached through the window. Unclasped the belt as she ran her hands over his face and scalp for the source of all that blood. They were speaking, urgent and hurried, but Tilda could never quite recall what they had said. Which was a shame, last words and all. The only thing she remembered clearly was Gil saying that they had hit someone.

What happened next remained a fog of broken memory and conjecture. She had started to panic, screaming that she needed to get out of the car right away. There was something seriously wrong with her left hand. She couldn't feel it. He told her to slow down, not knowing if he should move her or wait for an ambulance.

Gil withdrew and Tilda remembered sensing someone was there. The person they had hit? Another driver who had stopped to help? When he turned back to her, his face was twisted up so bad it frightened her. Confusion via terror.

He whispered her name once and then he was gone. Gone as if the hand of God yanked him away, it was that fast. She lay there on the ceiling, crumpled over the dome light. Useless. Screaming his name until her voice gave out and all she could hear were the waves against the pier.

HOW terrifying is it to wake up in hospital? No memory, not a clue as to why you're there. A million questions that no one in the room will answer. The cloying masks of sympathy as someone runs to get the doctor. The doctor finally giving up some answers but not the ones you need. He listed off the broken bones and torn ligaments. The shattered wrist. After that, a police officer but all he had were questions of his own. Tilda withheld everything until he gave up some answers.

"Where is Gil?" she hissed. "Is he all right?"

The police officer's hands gripped the hat in his hand. "I'm sorry, Miss Parish. He's gone."

Gone. Imagine that. Gil Dorsey was presumed dead because they never found him. His blood on the pavement, that was all. The best the police could put together was that Gil had staggered away from the wreck, injured and losing blood, and had fallen off the pier into the lake. Although the officer didn't inform her of this, the police expected the remains to bob up further west along the breakers. Floaters always did, and once Mr. Dorsey made an appearance, they could pronounce him dead and close the file.

It didn't pan out that way. Obstinate in life, Gil remained so in death and the police never could close his file. He never bobbed up anywhere, remaining stubbornly on the muddy bottom of Lake Ontario.

So what of her? Tilda Parish sank to the bottom too, like an oceanliner ripped open by icebergs. Spiralling down into a grief so bottomless, few of her friends expected her to come up for air ever again.

Two days ago

I

Live through this

CATCH UP.

See Tilda? Same green irises but the edges of her eyes now hatched with a few crow's feet, those little mileage markers that get etched in if you make it this far. Hair swept back in a ponytail as she cracks eggs into the frypan and eyeballs the toast that will burn if left untended. Whipping breakfast together and wishing the coffeemaker would hurry up and brew so she could pour herself a cup. As much as she hated the morning rush, it was manageable once she had that first potent hit from the pot. A glance at the wall clock had her padding out of the kitchen to the bottom of the stairs.

"Shane! Molly! Time to hustle!"

While the eggs sizzled, Tilda diced fruit and popped the toast. Molly was finicky about her breakfast. Tilda had to prepare it just right or the kid wouldn't eat. A trait she got from her father. Tilda herself would eat anything, learning over the years to be satisfied with whatever she got onto a plate or the rejected dishes pushed aside by a fussy eater. With the eggs plated and Molly's fruit on the table, Tilda groaned at the prospect of packing lunches. A chore she detested. Doubly so for particular eaters.

Then the cat, a charcoal Russian Blue, brushed her leg as it padded to the center of the kitchen and threw up on the floor.

Shane came down first, tucking his shirt in as she was wiping up the regurgitated mess.

Thick and big-boned, Shane was built like a power lifter. All upper body strength but fighting the bulge in his gut that came with age. Sweeping in for a kiss, he scraped her cheek with stubble and made for the coffeemaker. "Morning, sweetheart."

"Are we not shaving today?"

"Got kicked out of the bathroom. Again. Did you sleep okay?"

"Best as I could." Tilda rinsed her hands under the faucet. Truth was, she rarely slept well, waking out of a deep sleep every night. Sometimes it was stress or her wrist was acting up and sometimes for no reason at all. Routine, as was his inquiry into her sleep every morning. Same question, same answer. Shane himself slept like the dead and Tilda's resentment of his narcosis could run hostile. But give him credit, he inquired about her rest every morning. Concerned, he just didn't know how to help her. Neither did she.

Tilda hunkered down to the task of sandwich-making. "Is Molly dressed?"

"Yup, but tread lightly." He raised the coffee to his lips and blew. "The monster has awoken."

Tilda blinked at the cup in his hand. How had he swiped the first hit off the pot like that? Grumbling, she poured herself sloppy seconds. May as well be the dregs.

Molly descended, parlaying her mood with each stomp of her heel against the wooden step. It was hard to believe that thirteen years and ninety-three pounds could make that much racket. The cat, reclining on a chair, leapt down and scampered for cover. He knew the score and if the two people left standing had any sense, they would have followed his lead. The cliché of the angry, hormonal teen was so tired and so played that even Molly was exhausted by it. But, like a genetic trait of hair colour or domestic lycanthropy, she was helpless before its curse.

"Morning, honey."

Molly slumped into her chair at the kitchen table. Outwardly, she was seraphic. The green eyes and slight frame inherited from her mom. Her father had contributed the sandy hair and toothy smile, rare as it was seen these days. As to whom she had inherited this hateful scorn and hair-trigger rage from was anyone's guess but each parent secretly blamed the other's family tree. A grandmother on either side was a safe bet but Shane suspected that, if not Satan himself, then some lesser demon. Baalzebub maybe.

Molly slumped forward, hair falling in a medusa's trap of tangles and sniffed at the bowl before her. She straightened up and pushed it away.

Tilda looked up, the big knife in her hand. "Eat up, honey."

"It has blueberries in it, " Molly growled.

"You love blueberries."

"When I was ten. God... "

Shane pushed the bowl back under nose. "Then pick 'em out. They won't poison the rest of it."

Wrong tactic, and everyone, cat included, knew it. "I'd sooner starve," said the girl. If Les Mis was holding auditions, the kid would have been a lock.

Her parents had neither the time nor the temperament for such accommodations so the kid got a pass. Press on, get on with the day. Shane wolfed down his eggs and Tilda scrambled to finish their lunches. She scooped down her own breakfast as she cut carrot sticks. It would be nice one day to eat at the table, seated and unhurried like any other adult. That was a weekend luxury.

Molly plucked blueberries from her bowl with dainty fingers. "The laptop blew up again last night," she said. "I think it finally gave up the ghost this time."

"I'll take a look at it after work." Shane mopped up the last of his eggs up with a wedge of toast.

"Can't we get a new one? That old thing is useless."

He shrugged. "Maybe I'll swing by Larry's. See if he's got a refurbished one."

"Does everything have to be used?" Molly groused. "Just once, can't we get something brand new?"

"Brand new just isn't in the budget this month, honey. Neither are used ones for that matter." Tilda slid a plate of toast under her daughter's nose. "Eat something."

"Sorry kiddo," Shane said. Watching Tilda return to the counter, he studied his wife's behind under the pajama bottoms and tried to remember the last time they had gotten friendly. Last Saturday? He straightened up and banged the table. "Hey, what day is it?"

Tilda froze, dreading what was coming. She'd half hoped everyone would forget but knew she'd be crushed if they did. To say she was uneasy about this one was putting it mildly.

Shane scooted down the hall for the closet. Came back with a poorly wrapped present. "Happy birthday, honey!"

Her green eyes lit up. Who doesn't like gifts? Even ones parceled up in Santa wrap in early June? "Shane, you didn't have to."

"Oh hush," he said. This back and forth was another part of the routine, had been since before they were married. Why upset the apple cart now? Shane looked at their daughter. "Did you make a birthday card for your mom?"

Barely a shrug. "Whoops."

He scowled at the kid but Tilda dismissed it with a wave. "It's okay."

"What'd you get?" said Molly, feigning interest to compensate.

The paper tore away and inside was a handbag. Retro airline style with a funky monkey logo.

"Do you like it?"

"This is the one I saw." Her face lit up, a quick kiss. She had mentioned it a few weeks ago after seeing it in a shop window. Shane must have been listening. "I love it. Thank you."

"Look inside," he said.

Opening the clasp, she saw black material. Lifting it out by the spaghetti straps revealed a silk teddy.

"Va-va-voom," Molly declared, eyeballing the garment dangling from her mother's hands.

"Shane!" Tilda blushed and stuffed it back into the bag.

"What? You'll look great in it."

Stealing another look at it now that it was safely inside the bag, she remembered a minor spat they had had last week. She reminded him that what was missing in their relationship was a little romance. He interpreted this to mean sex.

"Thank you."

Molly munched her toast. "When you guys have your birthday bonk, can you do it when I'm not here? No one wants to hear that."

"Don't be rude." He thwapped her shoulder. "Get your stuff, we gotta run."

With that began the scramble for keys and shoes, the envelopes to be dropped in the mail on the way. Shane running back inside for his Aviators. Molly dragging her feet like she had all the time in the world.

"Molly," Tilda said. "Your lunch."

Molly looked at the bag on the counter. A mesh weave bag with a picture of the Virgin of Guadeloupe on it. Tilda had to ensure that it looked nothing like a bagged lunch. God forbid her daughter should be seen with one.

"I don't want to bring that." Molly pushed it back across the counter. "I want to get pizza today."

"Honey, we've been through this. We're all tightening our belts now, so that means bringing lunch."

"It's embarrassing." The disdain on the girl's face was lethal.

"No, it's just food." Tilda turned away to clear the table, refusing to discuss it anymore. The sound of the car horn honking from outside spurred Molly out the door. When Tilda turned back to holler up a goodbye, she saw the Guadeloupe bag left behind on the counter. She blew her bangs out of her eyes. "Fine. Starve for all I care."

With Shane and Molly out the door, the kitchen settled into the quiet of a dripping faucet. Even the cat had fled, presumably to upchuck somewhere else in the house. Tilda took her coffee and sat down at the table to eat. Her gifts sat on the table and she pondered them while polishing off her daughter's breakfast. Birthdays, Tilda had discovered, become problematic the older one gets. Like a lot of things. Today she was forty-one and had, in fact, been dreading this all week. Contrary to cliché, turning 40 hadn't been a soul-wringing crisis. She knew it was coming but hadn't fretted it or broke down or tortured her loved ones with some mid-life crisis. No rash urges to tour Tuscany or cut her hair drastically short. No reinvention brought on by the cold fact that your life was, if you were lucky, half over. Being forty wasn't a problem.

Being forty-one was. If she could somehow stay on the big four-oh, she'd be okay but adding the one to it? Different story. And no, she didn't know why that was. Reaching forty had seemed like a goal, going beyond that number simply hadn't occurred to her. She scolded herself with the same logic we all do: it was irrational and silly, it was vanity and nothing more. None of it worked. Nothing had fundamentally changed in her world. She sat at the same table, eating the same breakfast, alone as usual, looking at the same mess. But now she was a 41-year old woman contemplating the teddy her husband had given her for a birthday present. The last thing she felt like doing would be to slip it on. Like so many of Shane's gifts, it was in fact, a gift for himself. The unthinking man's attempt to light a match under the marital bed.

The bag, at least, was practical. And kind of fun. She hooked it onto her arm and finished her breakfast, feeling coldly older than the forty-one years the calendar dictated.

2

Tower of song

BY HALF PAST NINE Tilda was out the backdoor and across the footpath, unlocking the door to the garage. A flick of the lightswitch and her studio popped into view. The furniture was old and the floor covered in threadbare Persian rugs. Old Christmas lights strung along the ceiling provided ambient light. Three acoustic guitars stood like soldiers at attention on their stands, flanked by a Telecaster with a B-bar at the end of the line. Hung from pegs on the east wall was a Fender Jazzmaster with a broken pickup and a black Rickenbacker 330 she rarely played. The sole bass she owned, an imitation Fender, remained in its case on the rack shelving like old luggage. Two microphones were set up in the middle of the room before a battered but sturdy wooden chair that didn't creak. The garage studio was cold in winter and stifling in summer but it was fairly soundproof and it was all hers. Most important of all it had a door, one that she could close, sealing off the outside world so she could concentrate on her work.

If there was a consistent thread stitched through Tilda's forty-one years, it was music. Where most floundered and squandered their youth over the impossible question of *'what are you going to do with your life'*, Tilda knew that answer from an early age. Where other people's youthful dreams of playing in the NHL or joining Médecins Sans Frontières were stomped by reality or lack of talent, Tilda blazed a path using a guitar for a machete. At seventeen she had formed her first group, the Tralfamadorians, which had lasted six months and played only one show, and that a house party. After the Tralfamadorians broke up (it was a stupid name anyway, the drummer spat, packing up his kit and going home), there had been an endless run of bands that Tilda formed, broke up, joined and reformed over the years. A quick glance at the egg-carton walls of her studio revealed an illustrated history of her musical trajectory. Badly photocopied handbills and silk-screened prints for all the gigs and all the bands that she had played in. A history, not only of Tilda's career but of the shifting landscape of Toronto's music scene. Clubs and venues that sprang up like dandelions over the city only to bloom and die and blow away. The glorious and grimy histories of indie music cast aside or buried under what was now a trendy cafe or yet another godforsaken condo.

Pinned over the soundboard hung a handbill for a Daisy Pukes gig at Sneaky Dees, Tilda's cowpunk band. To the left of that, a screen poster for the Spitting Gibbons Halloween gig circa 1995. The Gibbons had evaporated after the accident and Tilda's hospitalization, the downward spiral that followed. The blue years, as she looked back on it now. After her recuperation and the sham funeral for Gil (everyone knew the casket was empty but oh the looks his family cast her way, the blame) Tilda had collapsed inwards like a scarecrow with its stuffing ripped out and tried to drink it all away. Almost killed her. If it hadn't been for Shane, they would have buried her too. Along with the scars and broken heart, Tilda had been gifted with a lasting reminder of the accident that took Gil's life; a recurring ache in her left wrist that flared up in damp weather or when she was overly stressed.

Shane had pulled her out of her tailspin and put the brakes on her deathwish. No more passing friends during that blue period but when Tilda's friends began drifting away from her trainwreck of prolonged shiva, Shane remained one of the few friends left standing. God only knew what he saw in her in that state but she thanked

God he did. Despite his bruiser-looks, there was a gentle-
ness to Shane. Patience too, as if he knew Tilda would
come around if he just waited long enough without prodding. Tilda had looked up from her fog one day to see him
smiling at her and she realized that life wasn't so vile and
grey all of the time. That small beacons of light remained
where one could warm themselves over like a campfire on
a beach. Shane was one of them.

Two months into dating Shane, Tilda cleaned up her act
and took up her guitar again. Less than a month after that,
she had formed another band and attacked every stage they
let her climb onto. Gorgon consisted of two women (lead
guitar and drums) and a guy using Tilda's old Fender Bass.
Forming an all-girl band with a male on bass started as a
lark but something clicked in that formation. Tilda was
pumping out songs in her sleep, the result of a year-long
songwriting hiatus, and gigs got booked. A van was pur-
chased and Gorgon hit the road, knocking out clubs in
Hamilton, Montreal, Ottawa, Syracuse. Buzz grew and an
A&R guy from Pinko Records bought them drinks after a
show at the Horseshoe. Said he wanted to sign them. Over
the moon went the Gorgon trio. The holy grail had been
grasped. Shit got signed, a fancy studio booked for two
weeks and Gorgon banged out their first record. There was
an advance and everyone was cut a cheque. Tilda and Laura

(drums) put together the cover and sleeve art themselves and label guy got busy with the promotional push.

Shit happens. Two weeks before the record dropped, it all started hitting the fan. Pinko Records was bought out by Warner Music and the whole place went upside down. Gorgon's champion, the A&R guy, was fired as Pinko Records was subsumed and Warner trimmed the fat and cut the redundancies. Gorgon fell through the cracks, the CD release was pushed back two weeks and when it finally hit the streets, there was zero support. Crickets. When Tilda and crew watched their debut record squashed in the take-over shenanigans, they hustled to push it themselves but there was only so much force they could muster. There was a hardcore fanbase here on the home turf but outside of T.O., zilch.

Two weeks after the dust settled, Tilda saw the honey trap for what it was. No one in the band had read the fine print on the Faustian contract, no had had the foresight to get a lawyer to look it over. When their debut died a quick death, Gorgon was informed that the advance they had been cut was now owed the label. The heretofore fuzzy details of 'advance against royalties' suddenly became crystal clear. At an eleven percent royalty rate on each disc (of which the producer skimmed three percent), they would have to sell a bazillion copies just to earn out the cash they'd been handed upon signing. Added to the bill was the cost of the studio time, the producer and a whack of 'incidentals' that the band had assumed the label was footing.

Natch.

The salt in the wound was found further down the fine print. Signing the contract meant agreeing to a second record. Gorgon was barely out of the starting gates and already the balance sheet was killing them. Although Steve Albini's famous memo about how record labels routinely screwed bands was widely circulated at the time, it didn't fall into Tilda's radar until it was too late. She felt her heart crack reading it. If only.

They ate it. What choice did they have? They toured as much as they could, putting mileage through the Bermuda Triangle of Toronto, Montreal and Ottawa but it barely scratched the surface. No one at Warner gave a hoot or even remembered who they were. Nose to the grindstone, Gorgon sucked it up and attacked the sophomore record. The label wanted more of a pop sound and had the brilliant idea of trying to "sexy" up their image. The air inside the recording studio turned poisonous and the friction applied from above wore them down until the band cracked and fell apart. By the time the second record was in the can, the band was kaput. Contract fulfilled, they were free to go.

Tilda labelled that era as the brown period. Crude but it summed up her opinion of the whole fiasco. A painful education in bursting the big record deal fantasy. She and Shane were a solid couple at the start of that brown period and when Gorgon finally walked out of that sophomore recording session, she discovered the cause of the strange fatigue she'd been suffering; she was pregnant. It became one more nail in the band's coffin but by then she couldn't have cared less. Her whole world came to a screeching stop until Shane talked her through it and convinced her that having a baby wasn't the end of the world.

So, where did that leave Tilda Parish, former frontwoman of the now defunct Gorgon? At home with a baby girl christened Molly Grace, named after both of their grandmothers. Tilda and Shane were over the moon but, like first time parents everywhere, they were scared shitless most of the time. Adding to the stress was the urgency to buy a house. Pregnancy had brought out a ferocious nesting instinct in Tilda and, with the help of Shane's parents, they found a badly used but affordable three-bedroom Craftsman on a quiet street of Victorian bay and gables.

Those first two years, Tilda put music aside (along with sleep, friends, work, sanity) but after cake was served at Molly's second birthday, Shane whispered into Tilda's ear that he had a little gift for her too and led her out through the backyard to the garage. Since they didn't own a car in those lean years, the garage had become a repository of clutter. Shane threw open the door to reveal a completely empty space. All the junk was gone and the cobwebs swept away. Dead center of that clean floor space was her Hummingbird guitar laid across a wooden chair.

"It's not much right now," Shane grinned, "but we can fix it up. Soundproof it, insulate. What do you think?"

"This is for me?" Her voice cracked a little.

"You need somewhere to play where you don't have to worry about waking the baby. The baby monitor will work out here. I checked. You can thrash away all you want."

Overwhelmed to say the least. She threw her arms around him and dampened his collar with a few tears. As dopey as he could be to what she wanted sometimes, Shane had clued in to what Tilda needed. Together they converted the dusty old garage into a home studio (a fiasco in itself at times, and possibly the true test of a marriage) and since then it was Tilda's Fortress of Solitude. And she cherished it.

Coming back to music this second time, Tilda dismissed the notion of forming another band and struck out on her own. Gone were the crazy band names and frustrating power struggles, this time it was plain old Tilda Parish. This era she had dubbed the rose period. A little wiser and with a lot more at stake, Tilda took it slow and set about rebuilding her career a third time. She had to take it slow. With a baby at home, she had to pick gigs carefully, be more strategic in her planning rather than grabbing anything she could find. This allowed her time to craft and polish material in her new pared-down sound and each show went better than the last, drawing acclaim from club-goers and inquiries into a record. Applying the same methodology and patience, Tilda approached a smaller indie label named Meat Cleaver Records. Gun-shy but wiser from the previous fiasco, Tilda negotiated a smarter deal for herself with zero pressure from the label. What the Meat Cleaver gang lacked in deep pockets, they made up for in enthusiasm and a willingness to let their artists forge their own course.

It paid off. Her first solo record, *Lullabies and Wrecking Balls*, garnered praise in the local scene and rolled out from there. There was even, gasp, a really nice review in Pitchfork. Short mini-tours were arranged, two-day excursions here and there, allowing Tilda to gig without being away from home for too long. By the time Tilda was cutting demos in her garage for the next record, the label asked if she wanted to tour Europe. There had been an odd spike in record sales in Germany, Denmark and Ireland and the Meat Cleaver crew thought it would be prudent to get her over there. Tilda was overjoyed but dismissed the idea; four weeks away from home, away from Molly (who was four by this time) was impossible. It was Shane who changed her mind, telling her that they would all go. Cashing in all of his vacation time at work and saving every penny they could, they would all go as a family so she could gig Europe. He and Molly would be her roadies, he joked. So they went and Tilda was blown away by the reception she received on those winding roads through Europe. Small clubs in Deutchland, a church in Copenhagen and pubs in Eire, all welcoming and warm with applause. The case of CDs they'd brought sold out quickly and the label rushed more to them in Germany. The tour was hard, exhausting the three of them but it was exhilarating at the same time and when they boarded a plane at Gatwick for the flight home, Tilda had stoked a small ember of interest into a bonfire of new fans.

Back home, she put her nose to the grindstone recording the second record. Former band members and musicians from other groups offered to help out, allowing Tilda to put together an all-star roster of guest musicians, who dubbed themselves 'Tilda's Temporary Boyfriends'. Her second solo record, titled *Mermaid in a Gill Net*, got off to a solid start, gaining traction on college playlists and an ever increasing demand from Europe. For the first time in her life, she had been earning a real income from her music.

No temping or part-time massage therapist work to keep her afloat.

It hadn't lasted long. Just as her solo career was picking up steam, the whole music world had the rug pulled out from under it with the seismic shift of the intenet and file-sharing. CD sales declined globally and along with it went Tilda's income. Ditto her stability, ditto confidence, ditto career. The only way for musicians to earn a living now was through constant touring. Months away from home, criss-crossing Canada and the States. Fine if you were a 20-something kid with hunger in your belly but not so much for an over-thirty mom with a kid and commitments at home.

She redoubled her efforts, gigging where she could without travelling too far from home and trying to navigate the new paradigms of the music world along with everyone else. It fizzled out, leaving Tilda barely treading water and Shane now the sole income-earner.

Then the birthday, turning 40. Telling herself there was still time. Lots of artists broke through in their 40's. She just needed to try harder, want it more. But commitments and obligations nibbled at the edges, eating up her time and energy. It felt like an anchor lashed to her ankle just as she was cresting a wave and now sinking down to the bottom, her fingers rippling a little splash before the waters closed over her, leaving no trace she had ever been there. Morose and dramatic, sure, but that's what it felt like. Even if she never dared voice it out loud.

Today, another birthday. 41. The jolt of it biting into her marrow. Making a few hasty phone calls, she lined up a gig despite the fact that she hadn't performed in over six months.

All these posters and handbills smacked up on every wall. She had been so proud to put them up, a testament and reminder of her path to this spot. Now the damned things just gathered dust and mocked her for what she had become.

A has-been. An also-ran.

Tilda shrugged it off and reached for the guitar, eager to get back to the song she was working on. Her mouth grimaced when the cell phone went off. On the other end of the line was a recent contributor to her malaise. A creditor, ringing her up to rattle her cage about one debt or another and eat up the few precious work hours she had in the studio.

"Ms. Parish," the caller trilled. "I hope you're having a super day. I'm calling because I'm a little concerned over this balance here."

Tilda took a deep breath and scrambled her brains for an excuse that would get this creep off her back.

3

Rub til it bleeds

"OUCH," THE MAN ON the table said.

"That's really knotted up in there." Tilda eased off the pressure as she kneaded the man's rhomboid. "This is the same spot as last time, isn't it?"

"Yeah," he said. "Every time I play basketball, I yank it outta place."

"Muscles tend to do that as we get older. Can't take the abuse we put them through."

"Who you calling old?" Lifting his head from the table, he winked at her. The man's name was Jeff, a semi-regular client of Tilda's who played sports like he was still in his twenties and routinely pulled muscles as a result.

Three days a week, Tilda was a massage therapist at her friend's clinic. Massage therapy had been a hobby at first, helping out a drummer friend who'd suffered back pain at an early age. Later on she studied it properly, taking classes at Sutherland Chan during the downtime between gigs and recording. It evolved into a part time job flexible enough to work around her music.

"Put your arm up over here," she said. "We'll stretch this out a bit."

The man draped his right arm over the table and she dug into the problem area of his back. Jeff was the owner of a small cafe on Queen West who spent his free time on the court, no matter how bad it hurt. Always urging Tilda to come by the restaurant so he could repay her kindness for saving his game.

"Forget I cried uncle earlier," he said. "Dig in there hard as you can."

"It's going to hurt."

"Give it all you got." Another wink, then he laid his head back down. "The pain feels good."

Jeff was also a shameless flirt and, Tilda suspected, a closet masochist when it came to pain. It came with the territory sometimes.

She doubled up the pressure and seared into the muscles. Then a bolt of pain shot through her wrist, scooping her breath away and she backed off. The old break. It hadn't flared up like that in a while.

Jeff rose up on his elbows. "You okay?"

"I'm fine," she said, clutching the wrist. "Just an old injury."

"War wounds," Jeff said as he lay back down. "Sometimes those old injuries flare up to remind you of the past."

"Isn't that what photo albums are for?" She gingerly rotated her wrist, working the pain out. "You're all set. Remember to stretch your back properly before you hit the hardwood next time, huh?"

"Maybe it's time to take up golf." He swung his legs over the side and watched her rotate her hand. "Hey, you want me to rub that for you? I'm not too shabby with a rubdown myself."

The sly grin on his face. Tilda forced her eyes not to roll back. Dude never let up sometimes, the ring on his finger plain as hers. "Thanks, I'm good. I'll see ya outside." She went out and closed the door behind her.

Lippman Massage Therapy had four separate therapy rooms built inside its larger third floor loft space. The reception area flooded with sunlight from the floor-to-ceiling windows. Sara Lippman stood behind the counter, cribbing notes on a clipboard. Turning around, she smiled at Tilda. "How'd it go?"

"Fine," Tilda said. "Like always."

"I was about to make some tea. You want some?"

"Can't. I gotta run and get dinner on the table."

"What's on the menu tonight?"

"Don't have a clue. I'll figure it out when I get there."

Tilda had known Sarah forever, back when even Sarah was in a band. She had played drums in an all-female group that had, at the time, been erroneously lumped in with the Riot Grrl movement. An affiliation they couldn't shake until the band dissolved and Sarah sold her kit to study massage. Two years after opening her own space, Sarah had asked Tilda to join the studio and the two had worked together ever since. Two or three days, Sarah always accommodating about keeping her hours flexible to work around Tilda's career.

Sarah frowned at the schedule on her clipboard. "Are you in tomorrow?"

"I switched it. Two clients. I bumped them to Friday."

"How come?"

"I have a show tomorrow night. But my wrist has been acting up, so I don't want to wrench it out of shape before the gig."

"I forgot about that," Sarah said. "Been a while, huh? You ready for it?"

"Yup," Tilda lied. She was nowhere near ready for it. "Will you be there?"

"I'll try but I can't promise." Sarah's eyes dropped to Tilda's wrist. "That's weird about your wrist flaring up. I thought that only happened on rainy days."

Tilda slung her new bag over one shoulder. "Normally it does. I don't know why it's causing me grief."

"Stress," Sarah said. "You're anxious about performing again."

Jeff came out of the session room, buttoning up his shirt. "Hey, Sarah. How's business?"

"Gangbusters, Jeffrey." Sara took his credit card, swiped it through. "How's the back?"

"Tilda worked her magic." He punched at the keypad, took his card back and winked at Tilda. "Feels like a brand new me."

"Great." Sarah wheeled her chair to the computer. "Does the brand-new-you want to book your next appointment or should we wait until your next game?"

"Better pencil me in two weeks from now. I'll probably need it whether I play or not." He waved as he shouldered the door open. "See ya next time, Tilda."

"Remember to stretch," Tilda warned.

When the door clicked shut, Sarah shook her head. "The man is shameless around you. Winky-wink-wink. Jesus."

"He's harmless." Tilda adjusted the strap over her shoulder, ready to go.

"Hang on a second, honey. I need to talk to you."

"Sounds ominous. What is it?"

Sarah stood and leaned onto the counter. "I want you to reconsider being here on a more permanent basis."

"Sarah... "

"Hear me out," Sarah held up her hands as if calling a time-out. "I need to spend more time looking after mom. You know she's getting worse all the time and I'm stretched thin as I can get between here and her house. I'm not just asking for you to pick up more days in the box, I need help running this place. Scheduling and the books and the clients, all of it."

Tilda chewed her lip. The last thing she wanted was to let Sarah down, not after all this. "What about Chloe? She's always begging for more hours."

"Chloe's sweet as all getout but the girl's in outer space half the time. I need someone I can trust when I'm not here. Or called away at a moment's notice, which is happening more and more."

"Mom's that bad?"

"She's getting worse all the time. I got a call from her neighbour last night. She was in their backyard pruning the rosebushes, insisting they were hers. I don't know what I'm gonna do—" Sarah's lips pursed into a corkscrew.

Tilda squeezed Sarah's hand. "Aww, honey. I'm sorry. Must be hell to go through that."

"I'm not playing on your sympathies, honest. I'm just overwhelmed and I can't figure out what the right thing to do is."

Tilda contemplated Sarah's hand. Strong and ropey from years of digging into other people's flesh. Her hands looked old and hard to reconcile with the face. She wondered if her own hands looked like that too. "I think you know what the right thing to do is. But the guilt is clouding your decision. You'd be helping her, honey, not hurting her."

"I know, I know." Sarah took her hand back and quickly wiped away a lone tear. "Nevermind all that. Will you think about taking a bigger role here? Just think about it, talk to Shane. That's all I ask."

"I will." Tilda turned for the door. "Try and come to the show tomorrow, yeah? I could use a friendly face in the crowd."

"Won't Shane be there?"

"You know what I mean." Tilda winked as she disappeared out the door.

TEN minutes past eleven and Tilda tiptoed upstairs, looking forward to crashing into bed. Dinner had been spectacularly unremarkable. Molly morose and uncommunicative, Shane blathering on about work, the same complaints and gripes she'd heard a hundred times before. No one had inquired about her day. Which was fine, she had been far too distracted for much convo anyway. A knot slowly building in her guts about performing tomorrow night and the only relief was to get her butt out to the studio and practice. Re-ordering the set list for the sixth time, she put each song through its paces, flubbing lines or progressions on the first try but nailing it all by the second. Technically at least, every note was there but the delivery seemed off. Perfunctory and without warmth, like her heart wasn't in it. The lyrics just words that meant nothing. They rhymed, that was all. Chalking it up to worries, she put the guitar down and locked the garage door.

She slipped into bed physically exhausted but her brain still idling in overdrive, unable to gear down. Shane already asleep, dead to the world. The man never had trouble sleeping. He didn't even read in bed anymore, just dropped his head onto the pillow and he was gone. Sometimes she hated him for that. Snoring away in bliss while she stared at the ceiling and tried to cool her brain and unravel the knot in her belly. The numbers on the clock glowing red in the dark. 11:52.

She was not going to waste half the night trying to lure sleep in like a shy pony. It had been two weeks since the bed squeaked and there was always one sure-fire way to bring sleep on. Her hand slid down the waistband of her pajamas and between her legs. Kneading until she was wet. Shane snored on. Flipping back to a memory of them in a motel room somewhere, a wet and ragged session where they had almost eaten one another whole. The memory raised her temperature but it plateaued and the nagging thoughts infiltrated her concentration.

You're gonna screw up tomorrow's performance

Too rusty

Too old

Chasing the thoughts away, she reached down and slid open the bottom drawer on the nightstand. The vibrator was small and as innocuous looking as a tube of chapstick. Clicked to stealth mode, it was powerful but silent. Flipping through a back catalogue of scenarios, she imagined her eyes bound by a blindfold, hands tied at the wrist. An unseen lover clawing and biting at her, making her do things. The lover never said a word. She didn't even know if it was a man or a woman. All she felt was the hot breath on her skin and the sting of a palm as it smacked hard across her ass. Greedy hands and a hungry mouth.

You're wasting your time

You're in debt and going down with the ship

Take the job offer

Tilda gritted her teeth as the scenario in her head fizzled away. Few things were as much of a buzzkill as money woes. But she was getting close and desperately wanted to sleep afterwards. She conjured back the fantasy but it felt lukewarm, like she'd already worn out the high notes. Her wrist was getting sore so she switched hands, desperately scrounging for fire in her fantasies, memories, anything.

Her hair being tugged, a fist twisting it up around his wrist and pulling hard. The room dim and stale with the smell of beer and cigarettes. A band room, backstage somewhere. She had lost the skirt but still had her boots on. Those heavy black ones she adored so much, the heels lethal. He was on top of her, hammering her like his life depended on it. They shifted around on that disgusting old sofa and she straddled him. Gripping his cock and guiding him in. She was almost there when the door opened and a man walked in but he didn't retreat or even apologize. The faceless stranger just watched and Tilda didn't stop and then her muscles seized up rigid. It was only as she shuddered to a finish that she looked down to see who she was fucking in that old backstage room.

She shouldn't have looked. She should have kept her eyes closed until the fantasy faded away.

Tilda rolled onto her side and fluffed the pillow, feeling the tension unstring from her muscles as she tossed the chapstick back into the drawer. Sinking into the mattress, sleep crept in with promise. A slight unease lingered at what her memory had dredged up in those last moments.

So long ago. She was surprised she even remembered that night.

4

Hold on hope

IF SHE HAD BEEN PAYING attention, she could have predicted disaster. As it was, Tilda was distracted and on edge and missed every warning sign. It had begun at the breakfast table.

"Maybe you should take the job," Shane said. This after she'd woken to the same knotted guts she had bedded down with and telling Shane about Sarah's offer.

"It would be full-time," she'd replied. "Maybe more because of Sarah's situation with her mom."

"We could use the income."

Like she hadn't thought of that already. She flipped the eggs, letting the spatula bang off the counter a little too hard. "Of course it would, but I'd have no time to work in the studio."

He nodded his head, conceding the point. Molly said nothing, leaning over her breakfast with her hair draped over her face like a ghost in one of those Japanese horror movies. Her way of keeping out of the conversation.

She slid the plates onto the table and sat. He picked up his fork and said "We have to do something, honey. We're barely keeping current."

The debt load they carried. House upside down, even in this overheated market, the line of credit. An elephant that followed them from room to room, waiting to crush both of them under its sheer tonnage. A careless move and it could roll over the wrong way and flatten them all. Just thinking about it drove a swarm of panic into her belly. Ignoring it didn't help but arguing with Shane about it didn't seem to make a difference either.

"I don't know what to do," he said finally. "Business is still slow. I'm worried this year will be worse than last. We got to start knocking down the capital before it snowballs any further."

"Maybe you can sell some shit." Molly's voice issued from behind the tangle of hair.

"Language please," Tilda snapped. "And take your hair out of your breakfast." She stifled the urge to brush the girl's hair away herself. Molly excelled at finding new and inventive ways to drive them both bonkers. '*If you applied a fraction of that creativity towards school, you could win yourself a scholarship,*' she had scolded more than once. Parental platitudes rolled off her tongue with alarming ease, like she'd been waiting to employ them her whole life.

She looked down into the dark surface of her coffee. "What's left to sell?" she asked, to neither in particular. Shane's motorcycle was sold off long ago and their second car liquidated, the proceeds barely denting the capital. Like dropping a stone down a bottomless pit, there was no telltale ping that sounded bottom.

"What about some of your gear?"

"What are you talking about?"

"Just the stuff you don't use, like that old Fender amp that needs fixing. It's vintage, right?"

"We're not doing that."

"So it's just gonna sit there? Okay, then what about the spare mixing board that's out there? That Rickenbacker's gotta be worth a lot. And the Gibson SG, the one you never let anyone touch?"

Tilda backed off as if scorched by a hot element, unable to defend the gear hoarding in the garage. Shane wasn't a musician, he didn't understand. All of it was useful but to him it was just stacks of knobs and dials gathering dust.

Everyone bent to their breakfast, the clink of utensils against plates filling the vacuum of conversation. Maybe she was being too obstinate. The old SG she had picked up for a steal in Detroit about ten years ago. It was a beautiful guitar and made a hell of a racket whenever she wanted to crank it up and rattle the glass in the window panes but, practically speaking, she had little use for it. It would, without a doubt, fetch a good price. Looking up from her bowl, she shrugged a tiny shrug. "Maybe the Gibson could go."

He offered a shrug of his own. "Unless you wanted to start an AC/DC cover band. You'd look really cute in a schoolboy uniform."

"That's perverse," Molly said, munching away.

"Do you even know who AC/DC is?" Shane countered.

"All that old stuff in the garage," the girl said. "You're like one of those hoarder people."

"That's enough, honey."

Molly looked up, eyes barely visible through the fall of hair. "What are you clinging to? The glory days. Let it go."

Another spell of silence spilled across the table. Molly could do that, remain silent and detached until she fired one across the bow. A zinger that cut to the bone and killed all conversation. It was like living with a ninja assassin.

Tilda cleared the table as Shane scolded their daughter for being rude.

"I wasn't being rude," she heard Molly say. "I'm just being honest." The girl got up and left the kitchen, shuffling her feet across the floor like an octogenarian.

Tilda startled at Shane's touch as he came up behind her to set his plate in the sink. "Don't pay her any mind," he said. "The kid's crazy."

"I'm not clinging to anything."

"I know. That's just Molly. She sees a chink in your armour and strikes."

"Why doesn't she do that with you?"

"She has other ways to drive me up the wall." He swept her hair out of the way and kissed the back of her neck. "Are you ready for tonight?"

Another shrug. "I don't know. I guess so."

"I can't wait to hear you play again. It's been a long time."

"What does that mean?" A little too sharp.

"Easy. I just mean I love watching you onstage."

He squeezed his arms around her and she felt the length of his body along her back, pressing into her. She tried to remember the last time they'd had sex.

"You're not nervous about tonight, are you?"

"Nah, I'm fine." She turned her head to kiss him and he was off, a playful smack to her bottom. A total lie of course. She was petrified.

THE front bar of the Cameron was humming when Tilda and Shane arrived, bodies drifting by ones and twos to the backroom. Her gear was already back there, soundchecked earlier in the evening when the place was empty. Her jitters had ebbed off then, strumming to an empty room and waiting for the sound guy to nod but with the bar filled, the jitters roared back with a tingly vengeance. They all looked so young, this hipster crowd, and she felt out of place. Old. Past due.

And out of practice. She hadn't played a gig in over six months. She was rusty and nervous and could not get focused.

Despite dithering over what to wear for more than an hour, cursing her tired clothes and hating every pair of shoes, Tilda had to fight the screaming urge to run home and change one more time. Everyone in the room was so put together and so coiffed. Especially the men, primped and gussied as they were. When had that happened, she wondered, when men preened and fussed more than women? She felt frumpy and underdressed, an imposter waiting to be outed.

"Jesus." Shane tried to flag the bartender's attention. "Is it just me or do these people look like high school kids?"

"I think it's us." The wine did nothing to calm her gut but she ordered another quick. The sound guy waved at her from across the room. Time. Oh God.

She'd done this a million times before, she reminded herself. No big deal. Like that did any good. Strapping on her guitar and looking out at the half-filled backroom, she took a breath and broke into the first song without any stage banter. No one wanted to hear you prattle anyway, just hit 'em with what you got or get off the stage. Being in the song was breezy, it was the moment after that was killer. Performing, you were protected. Standing alone on stage between songs, well, you might as well be stark naked. No one but Shane clapped, no one but her husband even watched. Everyone in the room was either chatting away or staring wanly into their phones. She struck up the second number without a word. Then the third and the fourth. Shane sat at the back, giving the occasional thumbs-up. She tossed the set list she'd drawn up and broke into a couple foot-stompers she hoped would wake everyone up. Halfway through the seventh song, a buzz seemed to rise up in the room. More bodies drifted in and snatched up the few remaining seats. She thought she had finally broken through but when the song ended, she looked up to see the headlining act waiting at the wings.

Billie Rose and the Sidewinders were a rockabilly troop renowned for tearing the roof off clubs. Billie herself looked like she'd stepped straight out of a 50's juvenile delinquent movie. The bad girl in leopard print with a snarl to rival the King's.

Tilda unplugged and said 'thank you', her only address to the crowd, and then stepped off the stage. Shane was there with a big hug, effusing over her set but it felt empty. Forced even. The jitters that had soured her gut earlier curdled into a black poison. By the time Shane got her a drink, Billie and the Sidewinders kicked in and blew up. Even more people crushed into the backroom as Billie let out a rebel yell with her mammoth pipes. Girl could sing.

They sat through two songs. Tilda said she needed some air and squeezed through the crowd and pushed through the side door to Cameron Street. The night cool in her lungs after that humid room. She had just had her ass served to her on a plate by a girl half her age with twice the talent. Quadruple the stage presence and boatloads of moxy. All she wanted to do was leave but she'd have to wait until after Billie's set to collect her gear.

The world doesn't owe you a response, Tilda remembered. It was something that Chrissie Hynde had told her backstage at a festival years ago. It doesn't matter how much blood and sweat you put into a record, the world doesn't care. They don't have time. You got to make them care. It was wisdom that Tilda learned and relearned as she carved out her path in music. But it was exhausting and she wasn't sure if she was up for the fight anymore.

Driving home afterwards, Shane had filled the Pathfinder's cabin by complaining about parking like an out-of-town relative. Groused about spending so much just for the privilege of leaving your car on the precious street after dark.

"Honey?" she said, watching the lights of Queen pass through the glass. "Enough about the parking, okay?"

Little else was said on the drive back. Less arriving home and checking on Molly, whose door was shut. It wasn't until they were brushing their teeth that Shane told her she had given a great show but those kids were too sloe-eyed to appreciate it.

She didn't want to talk about it.

Crawling into bed. When Shane turned to her, she knew what he wanted but any of the heat generated that morning had gone cold. His arm snaked round her waist and his lips touched her collarbone. Already hard and pressing up against her hip.

"You okay?" he asked when she didn't respond.

"Just not in the mood."

"You might feel better if we do."

"I doubt it. Sorry."

"It's okay," He eased off, gave her cheek a kiss. "I thought you were fantastic tonight. I'd almost forgotten how beautiful your voice is when you belt it out like that."

She turned off the lamp. *That makes two of us.*

SLEEP was skittish and when the numbers on the clock clicked over to 5:00 AM, Tilda got out of bed and tiptoed downstairs. The sting from last night had lost none of its power, needling her like a thistle under her skin. Crossing through the mudroom, she went out the backdoor to the yard with her keys in her hand. It was quiet in that eerie stillness before the sun came up, before the city awoke. She unlocked the door to the garage.

The guitar case lay just inside the door where she'd left it last night. She'd almost thrown it across the room she was so disgusted. Not just with herself but with the entire thing. The nerves she had suffered, the self-doubt that nibbled constantly at the walls of her mind like woodmice chewing insulation. The frigid apathy of the audience, so typical of this city, their toddler-like attention spans and unquenchable need to be entertained. The audience, Tilda had thought more than once in her time in the trenches, were like a cadre of leeches, draining the performer dry before tossing aside its husk to demand another. Voracious and insatiable, fickle yet rapacious. And yet she, like so many others, threw herself willingly before its altar like a virgin sacrifice hurled into a volcano.

Why? Who in their right mind would chase such a cruel master? It was no surprise that musical pursuits were so often described as Faustian. Deals with the devil, haggled over at dusty crossroads.

Tilda stepped into the center of the room, feeling the threadbare Persian rug under her bare feet, and turned slowly in a circle. Surveying her little Fortress of Solitude from its epicentre where a chair and a mic were set up. The amp behind her, also miked. The soundboard at the back of the room, the guitars upright on their stands.

She stood perfectly still, hands over her mouth as if she was about to scream or smash something but she did neither. Her hands dropped and she popped her fists onto her hips in a gesture of defiance, nay resolve.

She knew what she had to do.

5

Rid of me

SHANE KNEW SOMETHING WAS WRONG by smell alone. Getting out of bed every morning had never been a problem for him because of the warm aroma of brewing coffee that drifted up from the kitchen. Like a promise, it lured him out of bed to chase the day but this morning was different. No yummy coffee smell, no telltale gurgling sounds of the coffeemaker. Something wasn't right.

Coming downstairs, he was greeted only by the stale tang of old java. The coffeemaker was still on but the coffee in the pot was a sludgy treacle long past due. The kitchen was empty. No sign of his wife anywhere.

"Tilda?"

For a moment, he wondered if she was still in bed. Had he woken up and stumbled downstairs without noticing her still asleep? No, her side of the bed had been empty. What the hell?

"Where's mom?" Molly shuffled into the kitchen, rubbing her eyes and looking around the quiet space. "Is she sick?"

He was about to say that he didn't know but thought better of it. Sorry sweetheart, we lost your mother sometime during the night. No clue where she could be.

A loud clatter from the backyard brought them both to the kitchen window. The door to the garage stood open, light streaming from inside. Piled onto the grass of the yard was a tumble of junk and debris. A milk crate flew out the garage door and crashed onto the paving stones, rolling over loudly. Shane looked at his daughter and then started for the door.

"Mom's finally having that big mental breakdown we've all been waiting for," Molly said, following him outside.

"Honey?" Shane called out.

There was no reply. He stood under the lintel of the garage door, about to call out again but decided to duck. A metal bookend bounced off the door jamb and tumbled onto the grass. "Tilda! What the hell are you doing?"

The studio looked like it had been ransacked by looters. Broken stands and bales of wire littered the floor, along with old notebooks and paperbacks. Guitar necks and tuning pegs and broken treblecleffs. Stray knobs and old vacuum tubes. Yards of cable coiled over the mess like a swarm of dead tentacles.

Astride the chaos was Tilda, her pajamas damp with sweat and her hands grimed from digging through the dusty mess. Her cheeks flushed, an odd light sparkling in her eyes. "Oh hi. How'd you sleep?"

"In bed." Shane looked for a bare patch of floor to stand in. "How long have you been out here?"

"A while. I couldn't sleep."

"Mom?" Molly crowded into the doorframe, eyes bugged at the mess. "Did you change your meds?"

"Molly, honey," Tilda smeared her forearm across her brow. "I really don't like that sarcasm of yours. It's mean and it's beneath you." She bent back to her work, pulling out boxes from under the bench.

Shane looked at his daughter then his wife again. "I think she meant to ask what you're doing in here."

"Cleaning out the studio. Getting rid of everything."

"Everything?" The girl looked sceptical.

Shane stepped over the amplifiers blocking the entrance. "Why?"

"I don't need it anymore," Tilda said, reaching into the box and plucking out an oddly shaped pair of sunglasses. "Hey look, my old bat-glasses. Catch, Molly. They're yours."

The girl caught the flying sunglasses and unfolded the bat-shaped frames. She put them on and turned to her dad. "I think this is what they call a moment of self-actualization."

"Again with the sarcasm." Tilda tossed the box onto the pile and reached for another. "It's a cheap shield, honey. If you got something to say, just be straight about it."

Shane took a step closer to his wife. "Why won't you need this anymore? It's your studio."

"The musical career of Tilda Parish is kaput. Last night was the farewell performance. I wish it had been more of a bang than a whimper but... so it goes. All that's left now is to snuff out the footlights and put up the chairs."

"Told you it was an Oprah moment," Molly reported from behind the bat-glasses.

It was then that Shane saw the studio's now bare walls. The posters were gone. He took Tilda's arm to slow her down. "Last night was just a bad show. They happen sometimes. You know that."

"Yeah. And?"

"And," he said, the frustration leaking out of his tone, "one bad gig is no reason to go nuclear and do something drastic."

"This isn't drastic. Neither is it rash nor spur of the moment or," a sharp eye on Molly, "an Oprah moment. It's been a long time coming. Last night simply underlined the moment. Nothing more."

Shane let his hands drop to his sides, unable to gauge her mood or formulate any response. He'd been in this spot before. A wrong word either way could set her off. Molly killed the subsequent silence. "This is has been real but when are we having breakfast?"

"You'll have to fix your own this morning."

Molly tilted her head, as if her mother had just responded in Lithuanian. "What?"

"Pour some cereal into a bowl, sweetheart. Add milk. Voila."

"God." Molly stomped towards the house. "Now who's being sarcastic?"

"Hey, come here." Shane studied his wife's eyes for some telltale cloudiness that would tell him what this was about but her eyes remained clear. When he slid his arms around her and pulled her in, he expected she would break down and sob onto his shoulder, letting out whatever was pent up inside. Just as she had so many times in the past. "Why all this? Why now?"

No sobs came, no shuddering of the shoulders or slow collapse into his chest. Tilda patted his back and pulled away, eyes lucid. "I'm done with it. I chased it long enough but now it's over. No more heartbreaks, no clinging to hope that there's still time." She turned away and pulled down the last of the handbills from the wall.

Shane remained stranded on the debris-strewn floor, unsure of what to do. With his embrace failing to bring on a gush of tears, his arsenal of responses was depleted and he couldn't even move without having to leap to a uncluttered space on the floor. A line from a song flitted across his brain, about finding no good place to stand in a slaughter. "So," he said, "you're just gonna quit playing music?"

"Not just playing. Writing, recording, performing, rehearsing." She balled up an old gig poster and lobbed it onto the pile. "Fretting about it, obsessing over it. All of it, over and done."

"Just like that?" He snapped his fingers. "What are you going to do?"

"I'm going to take Sarah's offer to help run the clinic. Earn a steady income, which will get us out from under the debt. As for this," she surveyed the room then settled her gaze back to him. "I'll sell the gear. Toss the junk. And then we can have a garage again. Maybe you can build that woodshop you've always wanted."

"Don't make this about me," he cautioned.

"Or, if our daughter's demeanour doesn't improve, maybe we can move her out here until she's nineteen." Tilda brushed the dust from her hands. "What time is it?"

"Just after seven."

"I need some coffee." She took his hand and leap-frogged over the mess to the door. "I'm going to drive you to work today. You can streetcar it home tonight, okay?"

"Why?"

"I need to load up the gear. Then haul all that other crap to the dump."

"It's not all crap," he said. "What about the records you made? The masters and the songbooks and all that stuff? You're not hauling all that to the dump, are you?"

"No. I have a plan for that stuff."

SHE lucked out snagging a parking spot right outside the door of Orbiter Music. The shop owners, two brothers that Tilda had known for years, helped lug her equipment inside for a closer look.

"You having a fire sale?" Travis said, kneeling over the gear assembled on the shop floor. He flipped the latches on the case holding the Telecaster. Next to it lay the Gretsch and two other acoustic guitars. Three more cases yet to be opened, then the two amps.

"Clearing up some floor space," Tilda said. She felt suddenly leery about revealing her decision to quit to two other musicians. Irrational, she knew, but there it was. "So what do you think?"

"These amps are sweet. They'll sell within the week." Matt said. "What else we got?"

Travis opened the last guitar case and whistled when he saw the Rickenbacker. "Bingo. This one you should put through consignment. The Telly too. You'd get more than what we could offer you for it."

Tilda watched the shop owners go over her equipment, checking each piece, talking quietly between themselves. She had expected this to be painful, wistful even, but it wasn't. Surrounded by all the guitars hanging on the walls inside the shop, her own instruments laid out on the floor were just more of the same. Gear. "Sounds good to me. What now?"

Matt stood and stepped over his brother towards the counter. "I'll start the paperwork."

SWINGING onto Lakeshore Boulevard, Tilda was seized by a sneezing jag so bad she almost sideswiped the Nissan into another vehicle. The back of the SUV was filled to the brim with the garbage and debris from the studio, and all that dust kicked up and roiled through the air. Even with the windows open, it would find her nose and bring on the sneezing. Wiping her watery eyes, Tilda wondered if there was a dustcloud trailing out from the back of the Pathfinder.

The pile of trash she had dislodged from the studio was too much to leave curbside, so she piled it into the truck and headed east. The transfer station on Commissioners Street was the only one open to the public today. Normally Tilda avoided the entire Portlands area but there was no getting around it if she wanted the junk gone.

Waiting in line at the weigh station, her gut rumbled uneasily being this close to Cherry Street, psychically urging the trucks before hers to hurry the hell up so she could get out of here. The queasiness dropped away when she drove up into the station and backed the Pathfinder up to the massive berm of trash. Hauling her junk out of the back and adding it to the massive pile, an idle thought flitted through her mind about coming back to this area later, to deal with the last remnants of the studio. A small stack of belongings remained behind in the garage that, until now, she didn't know what she was going to do with. Driving back down the ramp to stop on the weigh scale and pay her fee, the idle thought had resolved into a plan.

The plan wouldn't be easy but it seemed like a fitting end to her musical pursuit. A tad melodramatic maybe but, hey, sometimes the grand gesture was required.

Back home, she lugged the vacuum cleaner outside to hoover up all the grit left in the back of the truck. Shane would have a fit if he saw the mess in here. For a man who routinely could never locate a broom in the house, he was oddly fussy about the truck. With most of the day burned away, she had just enough time to shower before starting dinner. Towelling off, she got dressed with her back to the full length mirror. The day had been productive and her mood high, no need to spoil it by looking at herself naked in that big mirror.

Seeing the mess Shane and Molly had left behind for her to clean up dampened the high from her day's accomplishments. How can two people make this much mess pouring cereal? She had to hustle cleaning up first and the one thing she hated was having to rush dinner. Rushed to get dinner on time, she spilled and made messes of her own and that infuriated her. She should have gotten dressed after cooking. Cubing tomatoes, she had squirted juice on the sundress she'd put on, nearly ruining it. Peeling it off, she draped the dress over a chair and finished dinner in her underwear. Could the neighbours see? She decided she didn't care, then scalded her bare leg with splatter from the steam pot.

"WOW," Shane said as he came to the dinner table. "What's the occasion?"

The overhead was dimmed. Two tapers in fancy candlesticks enveloped the table in a warm ambient glow. Mussels al Diablo heaped into bowls, an uncorked bottle of red. And Tilda, back in her dress with her hair pinned up.

"Fresh starts," she said and poured the wine.

Molly flopped into a chair and took in the setting with a dropped lip. Her eyes hidden behind the bat-glasses. "Did we forget a birthday?"

"Take those off, please," Tilda said, passing her the salad bowl.

"Your mother's marking one era and beginning another." Shane took the bottle and splashed a finger into a glass before his daughter. "You can help us toast it."

"Shane?" Tilda protested.

"Her first taste," he said. "It's a special occasion."

Molly eyes goggled at the glass before her. "I get to drink? Chin chin. This is the music thingy, right?"

"Yes." Tilda raised her glass. "The music thingy."

"Jeepers, Molly." He shook his head. "You have no idea how talented your mother is. The songs she's written. Or seeing her onstage..."

"I've seen her play."

"In a crowded bar, up onstage belting it out? It's powerful."

Tilda swirled her raised glass to move things along. "Okay, let's keep it simple and not get maudlin. Onwards and upwards."

Clink.

Despite what her father assumed, this wasn't Molly's first taste of wine. She had snuck some at a wedding last fall and earlier this spring at her grandmother's place in Wasaga. For sure she had developed a taste for it now. She took a sip and tried her damndest to keep her lips from puckering but, in the end, lost out.

Shane threw his eyes at Tilda and they both laughed. He tucked into his mussels, said "This looks great, honey."

They ate in silence, the only sound that of the shells clinking into the cast-off bowl. Molly ignored the mussels, choosing instead to dip hunks of butter-slathered bread into the broth and slurping it back. Shane took her bowl, stole the untouched shellfish and gave the bowl back. He looked up at Tilda. "How's the garage looking?"

"Cleaner than it's ever been. Bigger too, with all the stuff gone." She rose and crossed to the counter where her bag lay. She came back, tossing an envelope at him. "Check it out."

He opened the envelope and his eyes widened at the sight of the bills. "Holy smokes. Where did this come from?"

"I sold the gear today. Not bad, huh?"

"How much is here?"

"Almost five grand." She found her glass and took a sip. "Plus there's more to come. The Telly and the Rick are up on consignment. They might fetch another five."

"You're kidding me?"

"Nope."

"Cool," Molly said. "Are we getting a flat screen?"

"No," Tilda said. Shane handed the envelope back and she tossed it onto the counter. "That, my dear, is going to get the jackbooted heel of debt off our necks."

Molly rubbed her belly. "Golly. That's exciting."

The meal ended and Molly drifted off before being excused. Shane poured a little more wine, took up both glasses and asked his wife to show him the garage.

"TA-DAA," She said, sweeping a hand over the decluttered garage space. "Not bad, huh?"

"Wow. I don't think it's ever been this clean." He turned around, taking it all in. The old couch was still there, along with the paint-splattered chair and the Persian rug. The workbench that spanned the south wall was clean. "I can't believe you got rid of everything."

"You should have seen the dust I kicked up. Half of it's still in my lungs."

His gaze fell to the bench, where two faded milk crates remained, crammed with material. "What about this? Keepsakes?"

"No. That's going too, but I have a plan for that."

"Are you sure you want to do this?" He poked through the crates. "Just wipe the slate clean?"

"I'm sure." Tilda set her wine glass down and plucked items from the trove. "Master tapes, the rest of the CDs. Posters. All must go."

"The masters? But then there's no record of any of this. Your songs."

Reaching behind the crate, she lifted up a vinyl record. The sleeve showcased her name overtop a photograph of Tilda leaning on an old cattle guard, guitar in hand. A vinyl pressing she had had done years ago. "CDs deteriorate, tapes rot. But vinyl doesn't die. I thought maybe... Well, never mind."

"No. What?"

She waved the thought away. "I thought Molly might want it one day."

"She will. When she grows out of this troll phase." He swept his glass over the crates. "So what's the plan for this stuff?"

"Just something I have to do."

"Okay," he said. Her tone telegraphed that she didn't want to discuss it any further so he let it go. Her breezy attitude to this sea change was too casual, too forced to be this easy. He'd simply wait it out. Whatever was churning inside would make its way out eventually. With Tilda, it always did.

Still, something about this seemed off. How Tilda could upend this all-consuming part of her life and just cut the strings and let it float down the river was mystifying. Music was everything to her. Maybe, he thought, the simple answer was that he didn't know his wife as well as he thought he did.

"I don't want to look at this anymore." Tilda drained her glass and moved to the door. "Let's go inside."

He was about to follow her out when one last glance at the crate buzzed further questions in his mind the way gunfire scatters birds from a tree. A bottle of lighter fluid stood inside the crate, crammed in alongside the tapes and notebooks and crumbling posters. The warning sign clearly stamped on its label;

FLAMMABLE

6

Five string serenade

THE SMELL OF THE LAKE wafted into the open windows as Tilda retraced her path east along Lakeshore but this time she swung onto the Cherry Street ramp instead of bypassing it. The tires droned across the metal grate of the lift bridge as her heart shot into her throat. Passing the concrete silo on her right, the old substation on the left. Headlights twinkled as one car passed her going the other way and then nothing, the road empty.

Her grip tightened on the wheel with the iron bridge coming up fast. She'd meant to pull over just before it, on that same spot where everything had gone wrong so long ago but her heart was clanging so hard she couldn't breathe so she kicked the accelerator and sped past it.

Cherry Street bottomed out just before the lake into an unpaved lot treacherous with potholes. The Pathfinder dipped and bounced along to the far end, parking well away from the only other car in the lot.

Tilda killed the engine, climbed out and listened to the sound of the waves rolling up the beach. That fishy reek that Lake Ontario exhaled, like something dead had washed up nearby. The impact was immediate as the tension ran out of her shoulders and her pulse slowed. She looked up and down the dark beach but saw no other pilgrims. She had the place to herself.

Unlatching the back door, she twisted on a flashlight and hauled out her gear.

THE firewood was scrounged up from the deadfall at the treeline; sticks and branches and stumps. The fire itself she cheated, dousing the tangle of wood with a squirt of lighter fluid to get it blazing quickly. She wasn't current with the rules about having campfires on this beach but she was pretty sure it was verboten. She'd have to do this quickly before the fire attracted some busybody, official or vagrant.

She rolled a stump before the flames, settling it next to the two crates she had lugged from the truck. The fire popped and cracked and when a wind blew up out of nowhere the flames sawed this way then that, singeing her knees. The gust died off and everything went still again.

She dug the bottle out of the box, along with a plastic cup, and poured the last of the wine. No toast this time, just business. This ritual. Hokey and maudlin? Sure, but not out of place. First into the fire was a silk-screened poster from the Spitting Gibbons days. A gig they'd played at Sneaky Dees and a big deal at the time, hence the silkscreening rather than the usual shitty-looking Xeroxed bills. The paper curled as the flames ate it and she reached for another. A handbill for her very first band, the Tralfamadorians, followed by a poster for the Daisy Pukes. A handful of glossy one-sheets for Gorgon, courtesy of the label. This last poster showed a photo of the band, all so young-looking and posing surly for the camera. So long ago now that it seemed like someone else's history, some other band. Last of all were bills of her solo career. Just her name in a fancy font, framed by a horseshoe or twinkly stars. Her last great hope. Tilda flung it all, one after another, into the flames. This illustrated testimony of her musical history, all of it consumed by the pyre.

Next were the notebooks. The frayed, smudged pages of song lyrics and poetry, random musings and doodles. She had kept all of them, going back as far as her first band, the garbly-named Tralfamadorians. She had held onto them not as mementoes but for reference, thinking she might go back to the pages and pages of lyrics scribbled down, crossed out and rewritten. She never did. Once filled, each notebook was tossed onto a shelf and she bought a new one. All that wordplay waiting for songs that would never come, like orphans left at the iron gates when no one came to take them home. The covers of the notebooks were plastered with stickers for other bands, each notebook conveying a snapshot of local history.

The paper burned hot and smoked grey. Tilda reached into the crate and came up with handfuls of Gorgon stickers. In they went. Two t-shirts, one stamped with a Daisy Pukes logo, the other with the Gorgons. These smouldered slowly, kicking up greasy black smoke that smelled of poison. Then a handful of music zines, the photocopied pages folded and stapled by hand. Each one had a band interview or a review and the fire ate them greedily. Next were two cassette tapes holding the only known recordings of the Daisy Pukes and the Spitting Gibbons respectively. Then two CDs, the two records that Gorgon had produced and only copies that she possessed. The plastic jewel case cracked as the interior cover burned with a blue flame.

The smoke from the fire boiled hot and toxic as it incinerated her history and that, she concluded, was appropriate. The devil had had his due and all that remained was this lingering stink of brimstone.

There were only a few items left but Tilda sat and watched the fire for a few moments more. Already the chittering teeth of doubt were eating her resolve. Do you really want to burn all of it? Even those broken, lost pieces of your heart?

Now or forever.

Reaching into the crate, she retrieved one last cassette tape and a dust-fuzzed tape player. She upended the crate to form a stand and set the player down and hit the eject button. The little gate flipped open, ready for a tape to be inserted into the heads. She looked at the cassette in her hand, tilting it to the light to see the label. No words, just three small hearts scrawled on that narrow strip of sticker paper. The small plastic wheels rattled inside the cassette and she startled at how badly her hand was shaking.

The song written for him. She had only performed it twice, the second time recording it at his request. He wanted it to listen to when she wasn't there to sing it for him but the tape was never played and she had never performed the song again. The lyrics were never written down, never documented in one of the old notebooks. This little strip of tape was the only record of its existence.

She slotted the cassette into the little gate and closed it shut. The play button flickered in the firelight, waiting to be pressed but she stayed her hand. The song hadn't been heard in seventeen years. Shouldn't she play it once before destroying all trace of it forever? Hearing it again would resurrect its sting and there would be tears. Was it worth it?

She downed the last of her wine, tossed the paper cup into the fire and hit the play button. A simple strum from G minor to A major, slow and rambling. Then her 24-year old voice drifting up like a phantom. The ghost of Tilda past. The lyrics were uncluttered and direct, the way all love songs should be, and the treble of the song bounced into her ear and hotwired straight to the pulsing muscle of her heart. She scolded herself not to cry but her throat constricted at the first verse and her eyes spilled by the chorus. That old old wound had scabbed over so long ago, the scar tissue hard as oak by now. Still, it split open so fresh and raw that she feared she might pass out from its sting. She punched the stop button, stabbed the eject and plucked the cassette free. Then she flung the cassette into the pyre.

It had been almost twenty years. How could it cut so sharp like it was yesterday? No one grieves that long. No heart hides a secret pain for that many seasons.

Enough

The crates were emptied but one last item remained. Tilda bent down and took up her old acoustic, the battered and beaten Hummingbird that she'd written so many songs on. Her fingers flourished a basic G chord but the strings were out of tune. She settled it onto the flames and a plume of sparks roiled up in a twinkling blizzard and blew down the beach. She watched the shellac on the wood blister for a moment and then she turned and walked away.

She startled at the explosion, spinning around to witness a spume of flame geyser straight into the sky. Comets of flaming embers arced through the darkness, one singeing her dress. Something combustible in the guitar or the tapes or an alchemical mix of everything must have set it off. She ran for the truck, heels digging into the sand until her soles flapped to the hard-packed sand of the lot.

The headlights popped on as she turned the ignition. The brake pedal felt odd against her bare foot and she realized that she had left her flip-flops at the campfire. Add it to the sacrificial fire, she thought as she backed up and pulled away. She wasn't going back for them now.

UNDER an overpass in the west end are a handful of broken headstones so old that the few remaining markers were cemented into a wall to preserve them. A military graveyard near an old fortress, the bones of British and

Canadian and American soldiers jumbled together in a forgotten graveyard under the roar of the traffic above.
Ghosts are said to walk the footpath here and after sun-
down, the dark is so disquieting that even the vagrant and
the reprobate avoided it.

Just not this night. Two figures broke from the tree
cover into the open meadow, inky silhouettes under the
light of a crescent moon. The first lurched and stumbled,
falling to his knees and begging to be left alone. The second followed six paces behind, tall and lean like a coil of
rope, advancing on the bedraggled first. He made no move
to help the lurching figure, watching it flail and crawl away
through the grass.

In two strides the tall one advanced and flattened the
other to the earth with his heel. He knelt down over the
other and whispered something to him but the prone figure
flailed and pleaded, repeating the word 'no' over and over.

Sobs sounded as the figure curled up and wept, accept-
ing the inevitable but the dreaded sting never came. The tall
figure stopped and turned as if startled by some interloper
but there was no one there. He tilted his head at a faraway
sound rolling downhill into the forgotten graveyard. He
shook his head like a dog trying to dislodge the sound but
it was still there. Rising up, he stepped away with his ear
cocked to catch the faint noise. Trying to pinpoint its direc-

tion. East by southeast. A glance at the splayed body at his feet and then he strode away quickly, his footsteps vanishing along with him into the darkness under the overpass.

THE night was warm but Tilda came home chilled and damp from the beach. She stripped out of the dress that now reeked of woodsmoke, its hem ruined from burning embers, and tossed it into the corner. Inching in close under the blankets to catch his warmth, she spooned up tight into Shane's back. Her guts would not stop churning from what she had done and her brain refused to gear down. She pressed closer to Shane, flattening the length of her body against his. Her hand roamed and she put her lips to the hollow between his shoulder blades. He stirred, became hard without waking and rolled onto his back. She slid out from under him and climbed on top, grinding hard against him until she was wet enough. Her hand reached down and took hold, guided him in. He blinked his eyes in confusion. By the time his sleepy brain twigged what was happening, Tilda was picking up steam and grinding fast in the one position she knew would make her come. Her mouth froze into an oval shape and her muscles seized up tight in a spasm and then she collapsed onto him. He rolled his wife onto her back and hammered away until he too collapsed.

Seymour Public Library
176 Genes   Street
Auburn, NY 13021

He could smell the smoke in her hair but was too groggy to make any sense of it.

In the morning, he asked Tilda if it had really happened or had he dreamed the whole thing.

7

Center of Gravity

ONE ASPECT OF THIS new phase of her life Tilda hadn't anticipated was the chaos thrown into their morning routine with all three of them rushing to get out the door. Until today, the routine saw Tilda in the kitchen while Shane banged on the bathroom door, hollering at Molly to hurry the hell up. Now all three scrambled for the shower until Shane capitulated, deciding to forgo it altogether.

Breakfast was a shambles, the lunches thrown together with nary a thought to nutrition nor taste. Tilda scowled at the mess of dishes left in the sink but there was no time for it now. Few things were as loathsome as coming home to dishes left to petrify all day. The new morning routine would have to be tweaked. Maybe Shane could pack lunches while she made breakfast, instead of sipping his coffee and staring out the window. Maybe Molly could help out too for that matter.

The clinic was only a twenty-minute walk if she cut through Bellwoods park. The sun was bright but the humidity had yet to take hold. The park busy with dog-walkers and joggers and the old man who asked her for a cigarette every time she passed the John Gibson House. The same question every time and always the same polite reply. You'd think the geezer would remember by now but no. And yet, every time she saw him, Tilda wondered if he would survive another winter. So, she supposed, she was no better.

Padding along the footpath, she watched the young people on the grass. Tossing their Frisbee or sitting around in chatty circles, the whole day to themselves. A few already tipping back tall boys. Didn't they work? How does one live like that? She caught the resentment in her blood and hated how old she sounded. Grousing about the youth of today. She was no different at that age, frittering away the day simply because she had the option to. No responsibilities, zero obligations. Nothing to kill but time.

Sarah was on the phone when she walked into the clinic, eyes lighting on the tall tray of coffee in Tilda's hand. Sarah ended the call and shot to her feet. "Look at you," she squeed. "Bright and early, with coffee. I told you this was gonna work out great."

Tilda draped her new bag onto the back of a chair. "Is everything okay?"

"Just Olga again. Intent on throwing my day out of whack."

Olga was one of Sarah's oldest clients, and as such expected Sarah to cater to her most arbitrary whims. A princess, despite the fact that she was old enough to be either of their mothers. "What did her highness want today?"

"Same as usual," Sarah shrugged. "Wants to switch her morning appointment to the afternoon."

"When's she scheduled?"

Sarah looked at the clock. "In thirty minutes. But I gotta be at the hospital this afternoon and get the banking done and this just screws my entire day."

The deposit book was sitting on the desk. Tilda gathered it up, pressed it into Sarah's hand and shooed her towards the door. "Go to the bank now. I'll take care of her highness . Go."

"Are you sure?"

"Yes." Tilda waved her away. "That's what I'm here for now. Are there any other fires that need putting out?"

Sarah bit her lip. "Do you want to take a crack at the schedule? Ann-Marie called in sick again and Chloe wants to trade days with Sandy and so on and so on."

"I'm on it. Take your coffee and shoo."

Alone in the studio, Tilda got on the phone to sort the problem with Olga. Music filtered from the speakers and it burred in her ear. She toggled the dial over to CBC Radio. A discussion about teacher unions and government clawbacks. Safe and dull with no chance of hearing anyone sing. She took a ten-thirty appointment and spent the rest of the morning wrestling the schedule to the mat. It took a number of calls to the other therapists in Sarah's roster but by noon, she had finalized next week's schedule in blue ink. Sarah returned to the clinic an hour later with take-out from Terroni.

"YOU burnt everything?" Sarah's eyes widened as Tilda unpacked the events of her excursion to the beach.

"All of it. Up in smoke."

"The Hummingbird too?" Sarah leaned forward, as if she had missed a detail. "Burned?"

"It wasn't really worth anything in its condition. But that didn't matter, it had to go. Part of the ritual."

Tilda fished two more slices from the box and handed one to Sarah. They ate in silence for a moment.

"The bonfire at the beach, I can see," Sarah declared. "But quitting music altogether? What does that even mean? You're never gonna pick up a guitar or sing a song?"

"Exactly. Haven't you ever felt that way?"

"No. But I didn't pursue it the way you did. The Smash-Cans were sort of a lark. We thrashed and had fun but it wasn't the be-all-and-end-all for me. You know? But I still play once in a while. Goofy reunion shows or even campfire nights. You can't just lock that stuff in a box and pretend it never was."

"I beg to differ." Tilda tossed the crust back into the box. "I gave it all I had and now there's nothing left to give. There's more to life than music."

Sarah wiped the grease from her fingers. "Why Cherry beach?"

"It's close to where the accident was. I wanted to do it there, right at that spot but... " She waved the thought away. "I couldn't even pull over. So I drove on to the lake."

Sarah mimicked a head slap. "Oh my God. I totally forgot about that. I'm sorry, honey."

"It's okay. It was only like a million years ago."

The two of them went back that far. Part of the same scene, gigging together. After one of the many band break-ups, they had even talked of forming their own group but nothing ever came of it. Sarah had visited her in the hospital, a stalwart during the dark period that followed. She had watched Tilda sink into a black hole of grief so deep that there were whole days when Tilda hadn't spoken. Not a word. Shambling about like a zombie, drunk a lot of the time. Friends drifted away like dandelion spores, unable to endure the sick house any longer. Sarah had toughed it out, waiting for Tilda to come back to the world. Helped her find her legs and walk again. For that, Tilda remained fiercely loyal.

"I can see why you chose that spot," Sarah said after a moment. "Do you still think about it a lot? The accident or the depression?"

"I try not to but it's always kinda there, you know?"

"Sure." Sarah touched her hand. "A campfire at the beach sounds nice."

"A funeral pyre."

"You should have made S'mores." Sarah cocked her ear, listening to the drone of the radio host. "Ugh, how can you listen to this blather? The Ceeb puts me to sleep." Reaching across the desk, she tuned the radio back to an internet station. A twangy surf tune sprang up.

Tilda glanced at the clock. "What time's your mom's appointment?"

"Ah, damn." Sarah shot out of her chair and flung her bag onto her shoulder. "I should be back by four but you never know with her doctor."

"Don't rush back here. I'll close up today."

"Are you sure?"

"Yes. Go."

Sarah squeezed her shoulder on her way to the door. "I'm so glad you're here. Love ya."

With that Sarah was gone and Tilda folded the pizza box into the blue bin. She checked the schedule, wondering if she had time to fix the tempermental printer before the next client showed. No one wanted to be worked on by toner-stained hands.

The surf tune wound down and an old Blue Rodeo song drifted up and Tilda felt her guts clench up tight. She di-alled the radio back to the previous station. The host sleepwalking through an interview with some drip of an author droning on about his latest book. Dreary and dull but safe, without the risk of getting snagged on some song.

God bless the CBC.

MUSIC, as it turned out, was difficult to avoid. Every shop she stopped in had music throbbing underneath, so bland and constant it became white noise. Walking home was a sonic gauntlet as every business seemed compelled to pump music through their doors or amp it outside through speakers. When had this become the norm? Why did every business insist on providing a cloying soundtrack for her shopping experience? Why did paying for any purchase require shouting over a dance beat or the goddawful torture of Auto-Tuned vocals?

It wasn't that she suddenly hated music or shunned it altogether, she simply needed a break. What she wanted now was a little silence to clear her head but that, it seemed, was too much to ask. Silence was a pox that the world would not tolerate, filling every empty space with music or chatter or tawdry sound effects. Any quiet pause in a conversation saw one or the other conversant blather on in a panic to fill the dead air.

Had it always been like this? Even walking home through the park, there was music from three different blasters among the picnicking hipsters or a heavy bass rumbling from cars trawling along Queen. This constant, incessant music, and if music was absent, then jackhammering or honking. Not a shred of silence anywhere. Was it any wonder there were so many crazy people in this city?

Tilda's eye caught sight of a missing persons poster plastered to a lamp stand near the playground. A young man last seen three weeks ago in the park. These homemade missing persons posters had become common in the last few years. A runaway kid or refugee from another city living in the park. Tilda wondered if the noise had simply gotten to this young man, driving him out of the city without notifying his friends.

Home should have been an oasis of quiet but that was not the case. Not with a teenager at home who seemed to think that every radio, computer, sound system or television was there to be switched on, dialled to full volume and then forgotten about as she moved on. Tilda marched from room to room, turning off every squelching device. Molly was in the den, flopped upside down in a chair with the phone to her ear. The TV flickering and the stereo booming overtop.

Molly flipped upright as her mother switched it all off. "Hey!" Molly flattened the phone to her chest. "What gives?"

"It's too loud in here." Tilda marched out of the room. "How can you talk on the phone with all that noise?"

"Jeez Louise. Who peed in your cornflakes?"

"Don't be rude."

The girl's jaw fell open. "Me?"

When she marched into the kitchen, she heard the stereo flip back on but the volume was toggled back a notch. Small mercies, she thought as she opened the fridge and then pondered the workaday torture of what to make for dinner.

Working full days, dinner proved to be another pillar of routine that needed tweaking. Tilda was rushed getting it ready, late getting on the table. She thought of asking Molly to help with the prep, since she was the first one home but that was a fool's errand. The girl was repulsed by domestic chores, often refusing to perform what she termed 'woman's work'.

When she finally sat down to eat, a deep exhaustion settled in so heavy that it was difficult to keep up with the dinner conversation. Not that there was a lot to speak of. Shane inquired about their day, politely nodding as he listened but impatient to be asked in return how his day had proceeded. What followed was a longwinded saga of suffering a sea of idiots who, to all empirical observations, had nothing better to do with their time than to find ways to waste his. It was a running theme with Shane, waxing over the ineptitude, foibles and calamities of his co-workers with an almost poetic sense of grace. Sometimes, after a few beers, he would scale it biblical and often describe his workday as Job-like in its testing of his patience. Wife and daughter both listened without interruption, knowing that any question or request for clarity on some point would only prolong his discourse .

With his oration complete, Shane looked at Molly. "So honey, what's going on with your friends these days? Any new kids in your social circle?"

"There's this new kid at school. He's from, like Bosnia or Botswana or Butt-something. Doesn't speak a word of English, he's in a wheelchair and he's got, like, this nasty drooling problem. And poof, suddenly he's everybody's new B.F.F." Molly blurted out in a rapidfire cadence. "But then these underprivileged kids, like in a gang, they rolled him for his lunch money."

Shane scowled. His idea of keeping the lines of communication open with his teen was to fire direct questions at her concerning peer pressure, drugs, eating disorders and the perils of teen sex. Molly used to meet this line of questioning with stony silence but had recently begun fabricating elaborate tales designed to offend him. "Well, good for you, honey. Even Botswanian Bosnians need a friend."

The clink of forks against plates filled the silence. Shane looked at Tilda "You okay, sweetheart?"

Tilda nodded slowly, as if her cranium was weighted down with lead ballast. "Just tired."

"The new job not agreeing with you?"

"No. It's good. Just need to adjust is all."

"No kidding," Molly snorted. "Dinner's stone cold."

"You know," Tilda said, dropping her hand over her daughter's arm. "I was thinking you could start helping with dinner now. You're the first one home now, maybe you can start the prep."

Molly's jaw hung open, exposing a mouthful of half-masticated food. Then she laughed.

AFTERWARDS, Molly barricaded herself in her room and Shane withdrew to his woodshop in the basement. The burr of the tabletop router vibrated through the floor as Tilda cleaned the kitchen. Her somnambulist attendance at dinner brought a second wind and once she was finished with the dinner mess, she fetched up a garbage bag from under the sink and went out the backdoor to sweep up the mess in her studio.

Garage, she reminded herself. The studio was gone. It's just a garage now.

Crossing the unmowed yard with the broom in hand, something didn't look right. The garage door was ajar. It should have been locked, something she always double-checked given the equipment inside. A habit that hadn't changed even now, with all of her gear stripped out. Had Shane been in here?

Stepping inside, she hit the switch plate. The interior looked as she had left it; stripped and bare save for the ratty couch and wooden chair. One small thing out of place. On the bench where the mixer used to be lay a guitar.

Not one of hers, she could see that immediately. An old six string, hollow body. Moving closer, she saw that it was a Hummingbird. Not her old one but close. The colour was right, sunburst, but the fretwork was rosewood, not the ebony of her old instrument. She took it up and ran her thumb down the strings, surprised to find it tuned.

Where had it come from?

She turned around, scanning the empty space as if the guilty party was still present. Bare walls and a dirty floor, nothing more.

Shane, she thought. Who else would have put it here? But what did it mean? Was this his way of telling her that he didn't agree with her decision to quit music entirely? No one had been more encouraging and supportive of her pursuits than her husband. Of course it was him. It was oddly sweet, this gift with no accompanying note or hint during dinner. Time for her to surprise him.

Hurrying back into the house, she heard the whirr of the sander and tiptoed down to the basement. Shane had his back to her, bent over the table. She worked the frets, picking out a flamenco flourish.

He spun around, blinked a few times in confusion. "Hey. I thought you sold all your stuff."

"I did." She blew a kiss. "Thank you for this."

"What?"

"This." She raised the instrument. "This was sweet of you. But just so you know, you could have just told me straight out that you thought I was making a mistake. You didn't have to go buy me a guitar."

"Buy you... ?" Shane slipped the safety glasses from his nose. "Honey, I didn't get you a guitar."

"You left it in the studio for me to find. It's very sweet."

This time he didn't blink. "Tilda, I didn't buy you that guitar. Where did you find it?"

8

Teenage spaceship

"THE LOCK WAS JIMMIED."

Tilda stood in the grass holding the suspect instrument in her hand as Shane examined the lock on the garage door. He ran a finger down the splintered wood of the door-frame. "Here. You can see where somebody dug into it with a knife and popped the lock."

"Why would someone do that?"

"Dunno." He shrugged and stepped into the garage. "Was anything stolen?"

"There's nothing left to steal." Tilda stayed close to him in the cool space. "Besides, they didn't steal anything. They left something behind."

"What kind of thief breaks in only to leave stuff?"

"Santa Claus?" She set the guitar down onto the bench and popped on the swing lamp, taking a closer look at the thing. "Maybe we got a dyslexic burglar."

He stood at her elbow. "This isn't your old guitar, is it?"

"No. It's the same make, maybe the same year but it's not mine." She examined the neck, peered through the strings at the label inside the body. Nothing personalized, nothing unusual. "This is nutty. Who would do this?"

Shane snapped his fingers. "Some crazy fan of yours."

"That's ridiculous."

"It's happened before. You remember that weird guy, McFly? He was practically stalking you."

She'd forgotten all about him. Kevin McNab or MacInnes. Mac-something. He used to attend every show, bring her gifts and write her letters. Bad poetry scrawled inside homemade cards. Shane used to refer to him as Marty McFly, and he wasn't far off the mark. "That was years ago," she said. "And he was harmless."

"Maybe he's at it again. Did you check inside the body? Maybe he left you more shitty poems."

"He never came around the house. It's not him."

Shane took up the instrument and shook it, as if she hadn't checked it properly for a clue. "Then it's someone like him. A stalker."

"That doesn't make any sense." She examined the damaged doorframe. "I haven't played a show in over six months. Or put out anything new. Hell, I would have welcomed a stalker-fan then."

"That's not funny." He set the guitar back down. "We'll have to replace that lock tomorrow."

She looked back over her shoulder. "What's the point? There's nothing left to steal."

"I don't want your fanboy bringing you more surprises. Or before you know it, he'll replace everything and we'll have a garage full of crap again."

"Crap?"

"That's not what I meant, honey." He killed the light and they stepped back into the yard. The Hummingbird was left inside. "Doesn't this worry you?"

"Of course." She folded her arms. "Should we call the police?"

"What are they gonna do? I don't want to wait five hours for some cop to show up only to tell us there's nothing he can do."

He followed her back inside and together they went through the house, setting the dead bolts and locking every window.

THE mystery guitar remained in the garage, untouched and unplayed. Aside from its strange appearance, Tilda had no interest in it. She did, however, purchase a new lock and spent an hour replacing the old one on the garage door.

Work remained busy as she took on more of Sarah's duties and began learning some of the basic bookkeeping. Grateful for the relief, Sarah seemed less tense than she had in months. During a slow stretch between appointments, Tilda wrote up some classifieds ads on Craigslist to sell a few last pieces of gear.

With that accomplished, she wandered over to her Facebook page and skimmed through her friend's updates. The mystery instrument was still nagging at her and she wondered if Shane's hunch about her old fanboy was true. If only she could remember his last name. Was it McNab or MacGivens? She searched both names but the Kevins that popped up looked nothing like the man she remembered. She tapped her nails on the desk, wondering if any of her friends remembered him. She clicked up the pages of a few friends and began searching through their list of friends. A blur of profile pictures scrolled by and then bingo. Kevin McQuibbin. A horse-faced man throwing up a Vulcan hand signal. Clicking the thumbnail, she scanned through his details. Her old fanboy was living out west in

Vancouver, working for a marketing firm. He was married and had three children.

Crossing his name off the sole list of suspects in her head, Tilda frowned. Who did that leave? She had no idea. For a moment she wondered if Molly had done it, playing some prank on her but quickly shunted the notion aside. The girl was insulated in a bubble of her own world and, despite being told, Tilda didn't think her daughter was even aware of her decision to quit music.

So the mystery was backburnered as the days rolled forward with Tilda trying to keep pace with the new routine. She was forever looking up at the clock and wondering where the hour had gone, the day. Her first week and already she was chomping at the bit for the weekend to hurry up and arrive. She had become a statistic, another parent struggling to balance work and family, exhausted by both.

Friday, Shane had plans with people from work and Molly was staying over at a friend's house. Tilda had no plans but relished the thought of not making dinner and having the house to herself to do whatever the hell she wanted to. In all likelihood, that meant she'd be asleep in front of the TV by ten 'o clock.

"I need a ride," Molly announced as Tilda staggered in the door.

"I thought Zoe's mom was picking you up?"

"Their car's in the shop. And I'm late."

Tilda sighed and kicked off her flats. "It's only five-thirty. Can't you take the bus?"

"No," the girl bristled. "I got my bag and I'm bringing all this food." She chinned at two plastic tubs on the counter, loaded with cookies. Molly had recently discovered baking and, Tilda had to admit, she was getting pretty damn good at it. Even if it was woman's work. The kid's caramel toffee snaps were deadly. "Please."

Tilda sighed once more and scooped the car keys from the bowl on the hall table.

TURNING onto Harbord Street, Tilda clamped her molars together. Whenever they were in the truck, Molly commandeered the stereo like it was her birthright and became a complete radio fascist. Tilda had no one to blame but herself. When Molly was little, Tilda would play songs they could sing together, fun stuff like *Yellow Submarine* or *Ring of Fire*. As her daughter grew, she'd craft playlists for car drives, slyly guiding her daughter through a history of music from big band swing to rockabilly and Motown to New Wave. She got a kick out of hearing her six-year old shout the chorus to *Sheena is a Punk Rocker* or croon along with Sam Cooke. Like most parental contrivances, this too came back to bite her in the ass as Molly felt it was her godgiven right to wield the tuner with an iron fist.

Molly toggled through the stations, a rolling sample of dance music or cloying pop tunes before settling on one and leaning back in her seat. And Tilda almost drove off the road as an early 80's anthem thumped up through the cab like a swarm of angry ghosts. To make matters worse, her daughter sang along.

Why is the bedroom so cold?

Turned away on your side.

Tilda stabbed the power button, killing the radio.

"Hey!" Molly startled as if slapped. "I was listening to that."

"I hate that song," Tilda muttered.

"I don't care." Molly flicked it back on, cranked the volume. "I love this tune. You should be happy I like one your old fogey songs." Molly, like every young person before her, adored the tragic gloom of that old standby. Who didn't, really?

Tilda's cheek clenched as she bit down and her foot stomped the pedal, racing to Zoe's house just to end the torment. When the chorus returned, something snapped. She killed the radio a second time and when her daughter reached to turn it back on, she barked.

"Leave it."

Awkward. Molly flung herself out the door when they pulled up before a semidetached Victorian on Roxton Road. "Have a nice time!" Tilda called as her daughter stomped away with her bag and trays of cookies. Molly didn't even look back.

LEFTOVER biryani in front of the TV. With the weight of the week pressing down on her, Tilda forced herself to get up before she nodded off. The television winked out and the house became silent. The odd creak or tick of an old home. "Run a bath," she said to no one. "Before you pass out completely."

The glass of wine balanced on the side of the tub was cornball but so what? The house was empty and she damned well wanted one. Once the tub was full, she let her clothes drop to the bathroom floor and slipped into the water, bracing against that odd inbalance of scalding water and cold porcelain against her back. Sinking to her chin and looking at her toes, she mused over the idea of falling asleep in a hot bath. Soothed to death as her nostrils dipped below the tideline and she drowned. Was that even possible?

She closed her eyes only to shoot them open again. A noise, from downstairs. She held her breath but it was already gone.

"Shane?"

No answer, no sound beyond the soft slur of bathwater. Settling back into the tub, another sound came but this time from outside. A scraping noise like tree branches blowing against the clapboard but there was no wind. The bathroom window was open, the night air absolutely still.

Bolting up again, she had the sudden creeping sensation of being watched. The bathroom was on the second floor, the window free of any neighbouring house. Still, her imagination sprinted along goosed by fear. She was alone in the house and naked in the tub, a scenario straight out of every slasher movie she'd ever seen. Michael Myers hiding in the closet. Jason Voorhees waiting under the stairs, face hidden behind the vacant expression of a goalie's mask.

Water puddled on the floor as she got out and towelled off. The gooseflesh sensation of being watched jacked up five notches, every dark window a lecherous eye as she dropped the towel and snatched her robe from the back of the bathroom door. Every time she froze and held her breath to listen, there was no odd sound or strange noise. *It's just the house*, she scolded. *The cat traipsing over the fence in the yard.*

Or the person who had broken into the garage was back.

The old steps creaked impossibly loud under her feet, her eyes darting about as she crossed into the kitchen. Touching the switchplate near the backdoor, the outside bulb popped on and cast a glow over the backyard.

The door to the garage stood open.

Call the police. Call Shane. Run to the neighbour's house. Three simple options that she ignored. The icy tang of fear in her belly soured into anger at the sight of the breached garage. Who does this bastard think he is? To just break into their home and leave his unwanted crap behind? Did he think he was being cute? Enigmatic? An image of Kevin McQuibbin flashed up in mind's eye, writing his stupid poetry and those simpering eyes he used to moon at her with. Her knuckles turned white at the thought of bashing his stupid face in with a brick.

The baseball bat stood in a tall bucket of umbrellas near the door. Her husband's macho idea of home security. She plucked it from the bucket, threw open the door and marched onto the lawn in her bare feet. She hoped it was Kevin because the urge to hurt somebody juiced her veins like dope.

She stopped before the garage entrance. "Who's in there!"

No answer. The door remained ajar. She put the tip of the bat to the door and pushed it open. Thrusting a hand inside, she bashed at the interior wall until she found the switch. Light winked on and lit up the empty garage. There was nowhere to hide but she checked behind the couch just to be safe. Nothing.

Something new snagged her peripheral eye. Small and dark, next to the guitar. Approaching it cautiously, she couldn't decipher what it was. An odd shaped hunk of plastic, spooled with dark ribbon. She blinked twice before realizing that it was a cassette, partially melted into a blob with the tape spilling loose. The label was dark with soot and she wiped a thumb over the thin strip.

No words. Just three little hearts scrawled in blue ink.

She dropped it like it was poison, the warped plastic clacking against the floor.

A sick joke. Who would do this to her? With her nerves peeled raw and too many contradictory thoughts shouting in her brain, she tried to parse what it meant. She had been stalked, plain and simple. Whoever did this had followed her out to the beach that night, watched her burn her trove and then retrieved the cassette from the fire before it melted completely. And then left it here for her to find.

Why would someone be so cruel? How did they know? There were only two people who knew what was on that old tape, and one of them was dead. Shane didn't even know.

With adrenaline doping her blood, fear tipped all the way over into a deep rage boiling her guts. This asshole, this creep, had not only broken into her home but plucked out this painful shard from her past and threw it in her face. The clammy sensation of being violated and exposed became gasoline on her kindling rage and she gripped the baseball bat with both hands and stomped out the door.

Standing in the grass, she scanned the shadows of the yard for the bastard who had done this. She screamed at him to come out. She knew the perpetrator was male. Only a man would do something like this.

"What do you want from me?" she barked. The bat held high, her knuckles white over the grip. "Step out, you coward! Let me see your face!"

The crickets in the grass fell silent but those in the neighbour's yard chirped on. The warm night ignoring her rage and shrill tone.

"You got something to say, then come out and say it! Now!"

The crickets at her feet dismissed her shrieks and resumed their chirping. Tilda lowered the bat and her fury spilled out with nowhere to go. Her arms were trembling and, with the adrenaline burning off, a sharp ache stung her wrist. The old injury, flashing hot in her duress.

Don't cry, she scolded. Already the tremors spread and her hands were shaking badly.

Do. Not. Cry.

A noise behind her, sharp against the lulling crickets.

She spun, peering into the darkness near the willow tree, where the light of the patio bulb failed to penetrate. Nothing there, just shadows and her imagination. Then another sound, something scraping against the brambles.

Two pinpricks of light hovered in the inky darkness. Like fireflies moving in tandem, the small lights tilted and swayed. The bat fell from her hands when she saw that these sparks were eyes, twinkling at her from the dark.

The fireflies came forward and a dark silhouette bled from the shadows under the willow. He stepped into the faint reach of the patio light, his oddly refracting eyes zeroed in on hers and Tilda felt her heart seize up in her chest. His face made no sense. It was all wrong, as if a Polaroid had come to life and stepped whole and complete before her.

Gil.

And somewhere in the red meat of her heart, she knew it would be him. But he was dead, had been for almost twenty years and in this moment, she hated him for that. She didn't like this dream, this nightmare she was having.

She must have fallen asleep in the tub after all. This dream was cruel and it was sick and she wanted to wake up. Now.

She also wanted to know why the earth was suddenly rising up fast to smack the grass into her face.

9

Pushing up the daisies

"TILDA? WAKE UP."

The voice was far away, like an echo calling to her from the end of a storm culvert. A hand shaking her. Fingers tapped her cheek. She opened her eyes and blinked against the nova of a naked bulb on the ceiling. No clue where she was or what was happening. Or why someone was shaking her. Couldn't they see she was sleeping?

"Honey, look at me. Right here."

Shane's face took shape, hazy and out of focus. She felt his hands grip her biceps, pulling her up into a sitting position. His face swam away as her eyeballs rolled back but the snapping of his fingers brought them round.

"Shane..?"

"Are you hurt?" He looked her over, searching for some injury. "Jesus, you really scared me. What happened?"

"I don't know." His face was too close, her depth perception all wrong. Looking beyond him, all she saw were blank walls. "Where..."

Answering her own question, Tilda took in the interior of the studio. No, not studio anymore. Just the garage now, stripped bare of everything except the ratty old chesterfield she lay on. How did she get here? Flashbulb images popped through her memory. The garage door open. The melted cassette on the bench. A figure bleeding out of the shadows.

"Try to focus, honey." He knelt before her, searching her eyes like he'd misplaced something within them. "Do you remember what happened? Did you fall or hit your head on something?"

"No. I don't think so."

"Did you fall asleep out here?"

"No. I was in the yard... in the grass, I think."

"Are you sure?" He ran his fingers through her hair, searching her scalp for a cut or a bump. "I found you in here, lying on the couch. I thought you were asleep but then I couldn't wake you. Your eyes had rolled over white. Scared the hell out of me."

She tried to piece it together but everything was jumbled and out of place. The tape in her hand, the fireflies in the yard. Then other images flashed up, misplaced snapshots of being upside down in the car, blood on her hands and the smell of the lake. A hospital bed. Her wrist throbbing under a cast. A noise from the yard.

"Someone was here," she mumbled. "They broke in again. There was a cassette on the bench. I heard something in the yard. Then someone—"

A snapshot of the figure sklathing into the ambient light.

Him

"Someone was here?" Shane's mouth dipped into a scowl. "Who was it? Think."

"I don't know. It's all messed up." She pulled the bathrobe tight and rubbed her eyes. "I don't know what it was."

"Okay, just take it easy." His hand came up and touched her temple, crimping her hair between his fingers. He whistled. "What did you do to your hair? Did you bleach it?"

"What are you talking about?"

"This." He lifted a lock of her hair for her to see. "Here at your temple. Your hair's gone completely white."

BACK inside the house, she stood before the cool glare of the bathroom mirror. Her face was pale and drained but it was nothing compared to the shock of white in her hair. Straying from her left temple, the hair ran hot white from root to frayed ends like a crooked blaze of snow against the dark chestnut. A Bride of Frankenstein lightning bolt stamped into her follicles.

Stupidly, her next thought was wondering if the white could be dyed over. She had prided herself on passing forty with so little grey but now this, this zap of white. As if her age had held its breath all this time only to blow it all out in one shocking gush.

"Are you sure you don't remember anymore?" Shane sat on the edge of the tub, watching her transfixed by her own reflection. "Walk me through it."

"I came home after dropping Molly at Zoe's. Ate leftovers in front of the TV and had a bath."

"That's it?"

"That's all I remember. I was so tired when I climbed into the tub." It was a reach but she grasped at it anyway. "Maybe I fell asleep. Sleep-walked out to the garage."

"You don't sleepwalk." He rose and brushed his fingers through the streak of white. "It's like you had a huge shock. Maybe you should see a doctor."

"I'm okay. Really. I just need some sleep."

"Are you sure?"

She reassured him that she was fine, which was a lie, and crawled into bed wondering if she was losing her mind.

SLEEP was skittish and broken. She jerked awake before sunup, startled out of a bad dream and unable to find her way back to slumber. Tiptoeing downstairs, she made coffee and thumbed through the Saturday paper without digesting a word of it. Last night's events seemed ridiculous, almost comical, in the bright glow of a sunny morning. Maybe she had dreamt the whole thing. And yet that image of Gil stepping out of the shadows was so clear and sharp it made her dizzy even recalling it.

Gil. Why had she dreamt of him after all this time?

Then she remembered the tape, the melted cassette left on the bench. She padded out to the backyard with the keys and unlocked the garage. The guitar lay where she had left it but there was nothing else on the bench. She searched the floor and looked under the couch but no half-burned cassette turned up.

With no tangible evidence, the logical argument skewed to the fact that it had all been a dream or some kind of hallucination. Then why was her gut telling her otherwise?

"IT'S stress," Sarah declared. "Plain and simple."

They were folding towels when Sarah called a time-out and told Tilda to spill. She'd been distracted and clumsy all morning and did not want to discuss the bizarre shock of white in her hair. Sarah couldn't take anymore. Out with it, she'd said so Tilda went over the events of Friday night. Sarah had shrugged, as if this was some common problem like a case of the sniffles. "It's post traumatic stress. It comes out in weird ways."

"Don't you need a traumatic event first?" Tilda countered.

"You made a huge change in your life. Same thing." Sarah watched Tilda's lips twist with scepticism. "You've been pursuing music since you were a kid. And, with the exception of becoming a mom, it's been the biggest thing in your life. Your sole reason to get up in the morning. Now it's gone. It's no different, really, than going to war or suffering a death in the family. You're mourning."

"Maybe." Tilda shrugged but remained unconvinced. "But what does that have to do with Gil? Why would I see, or imagine I saw, him?"

"Easy. This grief period you're going through now got all mixed up with your grief for him. An actual death in the family." Sarah puffed her cheeks, blowing out a sigh. "Do you remember how far down the rabbit hole you went when Gil died?"

Tilda hated remembering that awful time. A whole year lost. It was embarrassing and shameful. She clutched at her hair, waving the white shock at her temple. "Then how do you explain this?"

"I can't," Sarah said, leaning in for a closer look. "But you've been pretty lucky, getting to forty-one with so little grey. I think it looks cool."

"So this blast of white hair and seeing Gil and the melted tape with his song, all of that I dreamed up? Or hallucinated?"

"I don't have an answer for that, honey. What does Shane think about this?"

"I didn't tell him."

"Why not?"

"I dunno. It just seemed so crazy."

Sarah fixed her with a sharp look. "Does Shane know about Gil?"

"Yeah," Tilda blustered, a sudden blush of shame on her cheeks. "The basic facts. I never bored him with the details."

"You need to. Do you know why? Because you looked really guilty when you admitted that just now. Like it was a secret you've been keeping. Tell him all of it. Flush it out and get shed of it. Do that and I doubt you'll have anymore dreams about dead boyfriends."

Tilda rubbed her eyes. "And if that doesn't work?"

"Then we'll burn some sage and toss around some holy water. Exorcise the ghost and send him on his way." Sarah patted her shoulder and laughed. Tilda tried to force out a laugh in response but it came out all wrong.

"THAT'S A really bad highlight job," Molly said upon seeing her mother's hair. She climbed into the passenger bucket and pulled the seatbelt around. "Did you pay for that?"

"It's not highlights," Tilda put the stick in gear and pulled away from the curb. "It just went like that over-night."

"Yeah, right." Molly reached for the radio. "I'd change stylists if I was you, cuz you got robbed."

Tilda turned into an alley to avoid Bloor Street and cut across to Shaw. Molly settled on one of her stations and ticked the volume up. Tension leftover from their previous spat lingered inside the cab like a bad smell. Molly pushing the issue with the radio again. Tilda let it go, forfeiting this round to the kid. "How was the sleepover?"

"Lame."

"That's nice." Tilda shot a glance at her daughter but the girl's face had already settled into a grimace of disdain. Dance beats thumped from the speakers and Tilda bit her tongue as the saccharine lyrics grated every nerve. "Are we still fighting?"

"I don't know. Are you still being a music nazi?"

"I really wish you wouldn't use that term."

"Great," Molly huffed. "Now I can't use certain words. Is there any small detail of my life you don't want to control? Jesus."

Tilda raised a hand, waving a white flag, and they drove on in silence. Turning onto their street, Molly darted a glance at her mother's hair again. "That's not a dye job?"

"Nope."

"It just went like, shazam, hello grey?"

Tilda wheeled to the curb, shrugged. "Pretty much."

"Wow. " Molly popped the door latch and flung herself out. "Getting old sucks."

Tilda killed the engine and watched the girl drag her knapsack across the flagstones and on into the house. "Pretty much."

ALONE in the kitchen, Tilda couldn't shake the tingle on the back of her neck. She kept looking over her shoulder, expecting to see someone there but the kitchen remained empty. It's just fatigue, she told herself, but logic did little to dispel the prickly feeling of being watched. She closed the curtains on the picture window and avoided the curtain-less window over the sink.

For company, she lit up the radio and endured a talk show host canvassing mindless opinions until the news came on. She turned to set the salad bowl on the table and startled at the figure in the doorway. The bowl exploded against the tile and greens shot everywhere.

Shane startled too. "Whoa. What happened?"

"Don't sneak up on me like that." Tilda's hands quaked.

"I wasn't sneaking up on you."

"Well... Jesus." She looked at the mess at her feet and went to get the broom.

"Slow down." He took her arm, held her still. "You've been jumpy all day."

"I know. I'm just tired." She shrugged off his hand. "Let me clean this up."

He bent and gathered up the broken pieces of the bowl. "Have you given any thought to what I said? About seeing a doctor?"

"I'm not sick."

"Something happened to you last night," he said. "You don't remember what it was, or you don't want to talk about it. And you've been weird and skittish all day."

She fixed him with a harsh look. "And? You think I'm going crazy?"

"I'm worried." He dumped the shards in the trash. "Maybe there's something physical going on. Stress or high blood pressure or something."

"There's nothing wrong with me. Life is just hard sometimes and the doctor can't fix that." Sweeping up spilled salad proved useless, the dressed greens clung to the floor like tape and the broom just flattened them more. She leaned the broom against the wall. "I'm going to lie down."

Shane brushed the grit from his hands and watched her walk away. Turning to the stove, he lifted the lid off a pot and looked inside.

CONVINCING herself that what she had seen was a bad dream or the result of stress didn't help. Staring at the eternal crack in the ceiling did nothing to soothe the fever in her brain. That left two options; she was losing her mind or what she had seen was a ghost.

Terrific.

Her eyes snapped open at every tiny sound, lifting her head from the pillow to catch it again but there was nothing more. The sound of Shane's breathing, her pulse thumping her ears. She flung the blanket away and swung her legs over the side of the bed. A change of venue, she thought. Curl up on the sofa and let the TV dull her to sleep but when she got to the landing at the bottom of the stairs, she walked past the living room into the kitchen and unlocked the back door.

The air was humid and it clung to her with no breeze to push it away. Standing on the flagstone pathway, Tilda folded her arms and surveyed the yard. Nothing out of place, no rustling shadows near the old weeping willow. The garage door firmly closed. Was she expecting to see something? She realized she had and suddenly felt foolish standing here in the backyard in the middle of the night.

Still, the keys were clenched in her fist and she padded across the footpath to turn the key in the garage door. Hitting the lights, her stomach notched a measure of disappointment that the space was empty.

The guitar on the bench.

The concrete was cool against her feet as she slid onto the bench and folded her legs. Seating the foreign Hummingbird in her lap, she tested the strings and tuned them up. She already knew what song she was going to sing and wondered if she had known before she had even gotten out of bed.

She strummed the chords in that simple progression and sang the words she had written so long ago. Her voice soft and low, this the fourth time she had ever sang the finished song. A seventeen year gap between performances.

The song hadn't dated or grown hoary. If anything, it bit hard and hooked strong.

The last note hummed around the empty garage until she dampened the strings, ending it. Propping her arms over the guitar shell, she leaned back into the wall and told herself to go back to bed. There was no purpose to this. She was wallowing, plain and simple, so she laid the guitar back onto the bench and pushed it away.

That's when she heard a sound outside the door, like someone trampling through the rose bushes.

10

And no more shall we part

A FIGURE SAT HUNCHED on the picnic table in the yard. Elbows perched on his knees, head bowed as if studying the ground. He didn't look up when she stepped out of the garage, didn't move at all.

Tilda stopped cold. The two of them like statues planted in the yard, waiting for the other to blink first. She knew it was him. Even backlit, turned away from the patio light with his features blacked in shadow, she knew. She would know his frame anywhere.

He still hadn't moved. She was unable to, paralyzed like the nightmares that steal one's voice, her mouth open but no sound spilling out. Even the old willow tree held its breath.

"Gil..." she whispered in a dry voice.

His head tilted by a fraction, the way a dog does at a strange sound.

She tried again. "Look at me."

His words hushed across the grass in a low rumble. "I shouldn't be here."

She winced as if snakebit at the sound of his voice. So familiar yet so absent it parched her throat. "Look at me. Please."

"You played the song," he said.

"What?"

"Don't play it again. I can't be here."

She gripped the doorframe to steady herself. "I'm dreaming this, aren't I?"

"Yes. This is just a dream."

She let go of the door and took one small step forward. "Why won't you look at me?"

"I can't. If I look at you, I'll never go."

"Then don't go."

He looked up, tilting his face into the weak light. Gil Dorsey. Exactly as she remembered him. Not the terrible image of his bloodied face that she had carried for so long but the way he had been. Beautiful and terrible at the same time. Gaunt and hungry.

A thousand questions tumbled through her mind but all of them bottlenecked at her throat trying to get out. One little word squeezed past the rest and fell from her lips.

"How... ?"

He looked away, as if shamed by her question. She wanted to rush forward but feared he would vanish like a mirage at her touch or she would wake and the dream would be gone. Then his eyes swung back, landing on her bare feet in the wet grass and travelling up. Measured and unhurried, drinking in every inch and every detail until his eyes drew level with hers.

The impact was physical. She thought her knees would give out.

She gambled another step. He didn't vanish in a wisp of smoke. "This is crazy," she stammered, choked. "You died. Why did you—"

"No questions," he said. "I can't answer them right now." His eyes locked onto hers and would not let go. His mouth tilted, almost smiling. "Look at you. I'd almost forgotten how beautiful you are."

She flinched as if punched in the gut and the earth went lopsided under her feet. She was going to collapse but couldn't stop it, didn't care. The only word she could utter was his name, whispered in a church voice.

"Sit down, Tilda. Before you fall over."

She was already pitching forward like she was drunk, the ground zooming up fast to smack her like it had the night before. She was dreaming all this, that's all there was to it. She teetered but the impact never came, something clamped down hard and held her. His hands, gripped so tight that it hurt and she knew it would leave bruises on her arms even as she was scooped up and settled onto the picnic table. Seasick, she gripped the edge of the bench seat until the earth stopped pitching under her.

When the pain slackened she realized he had let go and her hands shot out to pull him back. It didn't matter if it hurt. She caught his wrist and his skin was cold in her hot palm but it was solid and didn't dissipate under her touch like she had expected it to.

He hovered over her with his arm thinned out in her grip. "Let go."

She wasn't going to do that. Not now, not ever. How could he even ask that? "No."

The tables turned and now he swayed as if unsteady, his height ready to timber down like a felled tree. She tightened her grip on his cold wrist, pulling him back and his resistance evaporated. Gil dropped to his knees in the dewy grass as if strings had been cut. "Stop. I can't be here."

"Yes, you can." Any moment now he would vanish like smoke so she held tight, forcing the illusion to remain through brute force. "Gil. Where did you go? Why did you leave me?"

He said nothing. A slight shake of his head as if she had asked the wrong question.

She held her breath and tried again. "Why did you come back?"

"The song. I heard you play the song." He pried her grip loose then he pressed her hand flat between his. "I couldn't stay away anymore."

Her bones were already scorched, her insides melting into slag and now this. What was she to make of that? Her brain steamed into vapour, unable to catch any of the thousand and one questions that swarmed up like a cloud of bees. She was let off the hook when he looked at her with a question of his own.

"Why did you burn your guitar?"

Her mind blanked, unable to remember anything in the moment. Why had she burned it? Why hadn't she thrown herself onto the pyre like grieving widows were expected to?

"I gave it up."

"You gave it up? What does that mean?"

She had to claw her eyes away from his long enough to slot words into the right order. "I can't do it anymore."

"Why would you do that?" His head dipped, trying to hook her eyes again but she held her gaze to the ground. The dry grass slowly turning brown from lack of rain. "Your songs, your voice. You can't hide that away."

"I'm not hiding anything. I burned it. I don't know how to explain it." She smoothed her palm over the back of his hand, feeling every joint and contour. Scratching up friction but no heat came. Her eyes rose. "Why are you so cold?"

"You know why."

"You died."

He nodded his head.

"You died," she repeated, "and left me all alone."

He slid forward until his chest bumped against her knees and his grip traced up her leg until his fingers clamped over her hip bone. The chill from his hand seeped through the thin pajama material, goosing her flesh.

Tilda studied his face. Paler and more gaunt than she remembered but otherwise the same. Striking and angular. Her fingers stretched out involuntarily to touch his face, the pad of her thumb running the length of his bottom lip. His clock had stopped while hers wound on, marking every

minute on her flesh. The contrast of her hand against that
face was unsettling so she withdrew her hand and looked
away.

His grip bit into her hip. "Don't turn away."

"You haven't changed. You're still twenty-six for God's
sakes. And beautiful."

"Your eyes have gotten greener." Leaning in, he smiled.
"I've missed their colour."

Chilled as she was, a rose of warmth bloomed over her
cheeks. She felt dizzy again, her balance knocked from her.
"What happens now?"

"I'm not sure."

She tore her eyes from his face to look up over the
trees. The rim of the sky was turning pink. "We could
watch the sun come up. Like we used to do."

"I can't."

She knew he would say that, even before asking the
question. This was how fairy tales worked; ghosts vanishing
at dawn, carriages turning back into pumpkins. Tilda lowered her eyes but avoided his face. She needed to think
straight for a moment. "You're going to disappear on me
again, aren't you?"

"For now." His hand squeezed down on hers, as if she
was the one to vanish this time.

"Will you come back?"

"Yes." He rose to his feet and turned to the eastern sky behind them. "Tomorrow. If you'll have me."

"Yes. Come back."

She stood and her heart began knocking hard. How was she supposed to say goodbye to him? A handshake was out of the question but an embrace would leave her clinging to him. A kiss and she would open her mouth and swallow him whole.

His hand came up and touched her cheek. She could feel his fingers trembling. "Goodbye, Tilda."

"Don't say goodbye."

His eyes creased as he smiled. "Goodnight then."

He stepped back into the shadows beyond the cast of the patio light until she lost sight of him. The wooden fence creaked and swayed and he was gone.

She shivered violently. The air was humid but she was frozen to the core and once it began, the shivering wouldn't stop. Hurrying back inside, she tiptoed into the bedroom, holding her breath the whole time until she heard Shane sawing logs. Slipping back into bed, she pulled the covers to her chin but could not lose the chill no matter how tightly she curled up.

II

Goodbye's all we got

OVERSLEEPING IS A LUXURY that comes with a price. Tilda jolted out of bed when she saw the time and staggered downstairs on stiff legs. She was greeted with the sight of her husband and daughter destroying the kitchen in an attempt to make breakfast. Eggs slimed across the counter and dark smoke rising from the toaster. Molly's attempt to dice fruit resembled an attempt to make smoothies without a blender. Tilda swayed, unsteady on legs that were still asleep. "What have you done to my kitchen?"

"Well look who's up." Never a morning person, Molly's tone dripped venom. "Nice of you to join us this morning."

"Why didn't you wake me?"

"I tried," Shane said. "You were dead to the world so I let you sleep."

Tilda unplugged the toaster and waved the smoke away. The chill that had followed her into sleep returned and she folded her arms around her ribs. "I was?"

"Dad had this brilliant idea that we could handle the morning shift," Molly moaned. "Too bad it all went tits-up."

"We're doing fine," Shane admonished. He splashed coffee into a mug and shooed her into a chair. "Sit down. I'll get your breakfast."

Folding her hands over the steaming mug, Tilda brought the coffee to her lips and recoiled. The liquid may have been brown and hot but coffee it was not. "It's okay. I'm not hungry."

He stopped and took a second look at her. "Are you all right? You look really pale."

"I'm fine," she lied. The chill would not let up, the shivering unstoppable. "Just didn't sleep well, I guess."

"Maybe you're getting sick." He touched her brow but the skin felt cool.

"We're gonna be late," Molly interrupted. She abandoned her destroyed fruit altogether. "And we still got lunches to pack."

Tilda rose from her chair and chased them out. "I'll get it. You finish getting ready." She hoped neither of them noticed her clutching the counter to stay upright.

"Sit back down," Shane said. He peeled a few notes from his wallet and jammed one into Molly's pocket. "We'll buy lunch today."

Molly rolled her eyes at the bill. "Wow. Mickey Dee money."

Father and daughter ran pell-mell to get out the door on time. Tilda, spurred by guilt and obligation, located misplaced keys and the shoes Molly just had to wear that day. By the time the door banged shut behind them, Tilda was spent. She flopped into a chair, unable to face the collateral damage that was her kitchen.

Running the shower, she dialled the tap to full heat until the bathroom steamed up and left her pajamas in a heap on the floor. Slipping under the jet stream, she waited for the heat to scald the chill from her bones.

Gil.

He had appeared to her last night. He had come back. How, she didn't have a clue. She didn't care. Every rational question was shouldered aside by the twanging tremolo deep inside her belly. A sharp intake of breath when she recalled the contour of his lip against her thumb.

Was he a ghost, dredged up from whatever watery grave had claimed his remains or, more pedantically, just a figment of her imagination? An elaborate fabrication induced to life by her recent crisis and flailing attempt at soulsearching? Scalding her face under the hot water, she decided that it ultimately didn't matter. He said he would be back. Had practically asked her permission to return. Later, when the sun went down on this day and the house was quiet and still, Gil Dorsey would come back to her.

Towelling off, she opened the window to vent the steam. When the fog cleared from the big mirror, she noticed two purpled blotches on her upper arm. Fingerpaint bruises left when he stopped her fall. That or she had somehow done it to herself.

THE day rolled out as slow as a snail and Tilda forced herself to stop checking the time because the clock didn't move at all. The slow burn of anticipation and dread made it difficult to concentrate and she kept making silly mistakes. Sarah commented on her lack of colour, wondering if she wasn't coming down with something and Tilda had to lock her jaw to keep from spilling everything that had happened the night before. She was desperate to tell Sarah, to relive every detail and obsess over the tiniest nuance with a fellow conspirator but she kept her mouth shut.

It sounded insane, delusional, psychotic even. How else would Sarah, or anyone, respond? Tilda pushed her secret down to where all the butterflies swarmed and wondered if it was possible for a human being to explode. It got so bad at one point that, saying she needed some fresh air, she jogged three blocks west and three back just to burn the edge off. Wilting in the midday humidity, she hoped it would just sweat itself out like a fever.

SHE hated all of her clothes. Every drawer in the dresser pulled out and the wardrobe open, Tilda could not find a single thing to wear. Everything was either worn out or frumpy, dowdy or stained. When had she become a slave to casual comfort?

Dinner had been a complete washout. Distracted and pent up like a volcano, she charred the asparagus in the pan and overcooked the trout. Splattered hot oil on her hands, which stung like the devil. When she had finally joined her family at the table, Molly asked, with a condescending sneer, if she was dieting again. Asking what she had meant, the girl nodded at her mother's empty place setting. Tilda had completely forgotten to fix her own plate.

When the house had quieted, she ran upstairs to change her clothes only to be stymied by her options. Loads of clothes but not a thing to put on. She pulled on one top only to peel it off immediately and try another and throw it aside a moment later. She could already feel the nagging little doubts and recriminations that stung like nettles anytime she got too close to a mirror.

The streak of white in her hair was still a shock to see in the reflection and her opinion of it waffled constantly. One minute it looked bold and almost punk but other times it just made her look old. Older than forty-one. Her hand went reflexively to the little pot belly she'd gained after having a baby and the lines around her eyes looked deeper than ever. She had to push back the shrill urge to crawl into bed and never come out.

Why would Gil come back to her? She was almost twice his age now while he had somehow remained the same, flashfrozen at 26 years. What would he see in her now? She's not even a singer anymore. Just a wife and mom, a working schmuck with worry lines and tired feet.

Pounding footfalls boomed up the stairs. Shane sauntered into the bedroom, sweaty and blowing hard after his jog. He stripped out of his gear and tossed his damp clothes across the room into the hamper. "You feeling any better?"

"A little," she said, making an effort to keep her tone breezy. And feeling shitty about that. "How was your run?"

"Good." Shane watched her from behind as he peeled away the last of his clothes, his eyes drawn magnetically to the shape of her ass in those jeans. He came up behind her and wrapped his arms round her waist. "You should come jogging with me sometime."

"Not my thing." She shrugged out of his arms. "You're all sweaty."

"So? Let's get more sweaty."

"Too tired." She peeled off the shirt and reached for another. She didn't know what it was about jogging but Shane often came home red-faced and randy, pawing at her like he was starved for sex. Maybe that was why he was always encouraging her to jog with him.

He frowned. Seeing her topless didn't help matters either. His eye caught something and he touched her arm. "What happened?"

She looked down to see his thumb stroke the purpled bruise on her bicep. Her mind blanked. "That? I just bumped into something."

"Like what, a Mac truck? When did you do that?"

"Not sure." She pulled another shirt over head, the sleeves covering her arms. "I must have done it cleaning out the garage."

"Looks nasty." He checked to make sure the hallway was empty then sauntered into the bathroom, his erection bobbing the air before him.

The strain in her neck relaxed when she heard the shower thrum to life. What was she doing? Had Shane sensed her tension, her stilted replies? It made her feel a little sick to her stomach but it didn't stop her from digging for something else to wear. Trying on another top, she was pleasantly surprised by what she'd chosen in her haste. It fit nicely at the waist and plunged recklessly down the neckline.

SUNSET, according to the weather channel, would fall at 8:58 that night. It was four minutes late. Tilda slipped out to the backyard and unlocked the garage and frowned at the empty space. She had expected him to be waiting for her but the only thing that greeted her was the smell of old concrete. She flopped onto the sofa and stewed, remembering acutely how he used to always make her wait. It drove her crazy, and she realized with a slight hitch of panic that it still did. Death tends to smooth the rough edges of the deceased's flaws, transforming the departed into something of a saint. Gil Dorsey was no exception, his infuriating shortcomings and tics forgotten and forgiven by the bereaved. Now that he was returned from the land of the shadow of death, she revoked her amnesty. She seethed at his tardiness, his inability to arrive within any reasonable timeframe. In the old days (old days!), it had been a power issue, to make her wait like this. Maybe it still was.

Desperate for some distraction, her eyes fell to the alien guitar on the bench. Taking up the old gut string, she slipped back out to the yard and plunked down on the picnic table and tuned the strings.

She strummed and picked, a guitar in her hands as natural as breathing. Thrumming through one of her songs, she remembered a jumble of notes she'd last worked on, the crude rootling of some tune she'd tried to hammer out. Having gone days without playing or even thinking about music, the rough draft of song she had frittered at now came out whole in two passes. No second guessing, no doubts; the melody was just there. With no ready lyrics, she simply hummed the vocal, nailing it dead to rights with little effort. All she needed now were the words and, given the bizarre events of the last few days, finding something to write about would be a cinch. She was already matching couplets in her head.

She laid the Hummingbird down and sprang to her feet, eager to rush to the kitchen for pen and paper but she stopped herself. She had given this up, hadn't she? This was the past and it was behind her. No diving for the notebook to capture lightning in a bottle or fighting past clichéd phrases for some accurate way to pinpoint an idea or feeling and wrestle it to the mat. No more music.

And where the hell was Gil? He said he'd return but she'd been out here for an hour with no sign nor hint that he was coming back to her. How stupid was she? Waiting in the grass for an old boyfriend who'd been dead almost two decades. There was no Gil Dorsey. She'd dreamed the whole damn thing. Was in fact still dreaming as she stood out here waiting for something that wasn't going to happen. A prom date stranded on the porch, hoping against hope to spot the headlights of her date's car even as the clock ran out. A fool. Miss Havisham at her cobwebbed wedding banquet under the light of the moon.

Moon

June

Croon

It was hard to turn off the lyric-crafting. Even the clichéd tripe. Second nature.

"What's that one called?"

She flinched and spun around to see Gil perched on the top of the fence, watching her. "How long have you been sitting there?"

"I just got here."

She meant to level her tone but the sting of being abandoned was too fresh. "I thought you weren't coming."

He dropped to the ground but remained just outside of the cast of the patio light. He looked dishevelled, like he'd woken late and ran out the door. He nodded at the guitar on the picnic table. "I liked what you were playing."

"It's nothing." Her reply was too curt and she scolded herself to get over it. Having anticipated this moment all bloody day, this wasn't how she wanted it to play out. Gil remained on the far side of the yard. "Come here. I won't bite."

"Take a walk with me."

She hesitated but didn't know why. "Where?"

"Nowhere. Does it matter?"

It didn't. She crossed the yard towards him, suddenly uncertain of how to greet him. She wanted to embrace him, even a quick hug, but he turned and unlatched the gate. Pushed it open for her. "After you," he said and they proceeded without any greeting at all.

The gate fed into the garage alley behind the house. Battered roll-up doors on both sides, a webbing of power lines overhead. The lone streetlight flickered as if dying, its light reflected in the puddles of stagnant water that rainbowed with a skein of oil.

Gil didn't say anything or even look at her, content to simply walk the length of garages and ramshackle sheds. Striding beside him, it was all Tilda could do to not stare at him or reach out for his hand. To touch him to prove that he was real. Had something changed? He seemed unaware of her, as if he was alone and she just happened to be travelling in the same direction. Maybe this was a mistake? Her stride chased her thoughts and she walked faster, outpacing him as if in a hurry to get there although no destination lay ahead.

"Where are you rushing to?"

"Sorry." Tilda slowed and he came alongside. "I tend to walk fast when I'm antsy."

"You do? I don't remember that." Passing into a shadow so deep she could barely see him, he said, in lieu of nothing, "You look beautiful tonight."

"Thanks. I look my best in the dark" she guffawed. "I can't even see you in this gloom."

"You haven't changed."

"What does that mean?"

"You brush off every compliment. Or dismiss it with a joke. Why do you do that?"

"I don't know." It was the truth, a habit so ingrained he may as well have asked her why she breathes. When had it started and why did it persist? Why does the sun come up?

She looked at him. "You've changed a little. You never used to say things like that."

"Then shame on me. I should have told you that every day." They came out of the alley, onto the quiet street. No cars or pedestrians. They crossed and he led the way into another alleyway. "If I had, maybe you'd realize it was true."

"I doubt it." Passing under the available light, she stole whatever glances she could without outright staring before they ducked out of the hazy wash of streetlight and back into the gloom. "But saying it too often waters it down and it becomes meaningless. It's like saying 'I love you' too many times. It just becomes words after a while."

As she uttered those three words, she saw him flinch and look her way but Tilda couldn't read his face. His eyes narrowed as if offended. He wagged his chin forward. "Come on. Now you're lagging behind."

Cutting across another street and into a deserted laneway, they wound their way west without ever hitting the lights of College Street and she realized Gil was avoiding the streets altogether. A stroll down a maze of back alleys and service lanes, sightseeing the metal fencing and plankboard gates. She thought she knew most of the alleys in her neighbourhood but Gil led her into so many niches cut between buildings and gaps in fences that she became disoriented. "Where are we going?"

"How about the park?"

Coming out of another lane, the houses looked familiar. Across the street was the soccer pitch and old oaks of Dufferin Grove. They popped over the low fence and walked through the grass. The trees looked spectral, backlit as they were against the hazy park lights.

On their right, a clutch of people congregated around the cold fire pit, tipping back beers and smoking weed. Gliding back and forth on their skateboards with nothing to do and nowhere to go. Gil wagged his chin in their direction. "The young ne'er-do-wells."

Tilda watched the boys and girls roll away and glide back. "That used to be us."

"Neither of us were any good on a board."

"No," she said. "I meant just hanging at the park, doing nothing and spending all night doing it."

"You sound wistful."

"Sometimes I am."

"Don't be," he said. "We're here, aren't we?"

They moved on but now Tilda led the way, guiding them past the wooden posts of the playground. She beelined to the swings and plunked down in the vulcanized seat, kicking her feet against the sand. Gil leaned against the pole, watching her swing towards him and then swing away.

She looked over the play structures. The metal run of the slide buffed shiny from a thousand little keisters. "I miss this place."

"The park?"

"The playground. We used to come here all the time when Molly was little. We practically camped out here in the summertime."

Gil stepped in front of her, like he meant to be walloped by her upswing but then sidestepped at the last second, making Tilda laugh. He dropped into the empty swing next to her. "Molly. That's a pretty name. How did you choose it?"

"It was my grandmother's name."

"I don't remember that either."

Tilda tucked her feet on the backswing. "You never met her."

"What's Molly like?"

"At the moment, she's a bit of a pill but in her defence, she's thirteen. Something happens to girls around that age. All those changes produce this weird rage and everybody's a target."

"I'm sure she'll grow out of it."

"Oh I know. It's just exhausting when there's no let-up from it." Tilda sat up, letting her momentum fade. "She's crackerjack smart. Too smart sometimes. And hilarious and sweet when she allows for it. I really miss that side of her."

He whistled. "You have a daughter. That blows me away."

"Why does that surprise you?" she asked, a tad too quick and a shade too defensive.

"Never saw it back then. I know it was a lifetime ago but... I guess it just never came up." He grinned, teeth flashing in the light. "Does she look like you?"

"A little. She has my nose but the rest is all her dad."

"Her dad." Gil traced a divot in the sand with his heel and stared at it for a long while. Somewhere in the park, a dog barked and its yap cracked through the still air. He looked up at her. "What's he like?"

"Shane? He's a good man. Sweet and supportive. He's a really good father."

His head bobbed in a slow nod. "That's important. How did you meet him?"

"What's with all the questions?"

"I want to know everything."

She threw up a frown. "But I can't ask you any questions? That hardly seems fair."

"Nothing's fair."

"Gosh. That's deep, Gil."

"And you wonder where your daughter gets her snarkiness from?" He laughed then. "I'll fill in some blanks, I promise. Right now I want to know about you. You've lived a life and I'm a nosy bastard hungry for details."

"You make it sound like you've been asleep all this time."

"I got locked in a deep freezer, missed everything." He swayed back and forth. "So. Shane. How did that happen?"

Tilda kicked off her shoes and dug her toes in the sand. She didn't want to talk about her husband or how they had met or any of that. She crunched the details into the briefest summary. "I met Shane about eighteen months after you... vanished. I was at the bottom of a very dark hole, determined never to sober up or crawl out. For reasons I still can't decipher, Shane helped me climb out of that awful place and come back to the world. We became really close friends. And then more. A year later, Molly was born."

The chains of his swing stopped creaking and Gil became still. "I'm sorry, Til."

"Yeah, well... You suck, Gil Dorsey." She kicked off and swung again. "What was it you used to say? Life's a bitch and then you die."

"I was wrong. And stupid as dirt. Life isn't a bitch."

Tilda dipped back to boost her momentum, anger rising up out of nowhere. "What do you know about it? You up and died or disappeared or whatever you did."

"I used to think I knew everything back then. I didn't know shit. Just a loudmouth covering up his ignorance with braggadocio."

"Please don't get all sullen with me. I can't do sullen anymore." Tilda swung, disliking this route the conversation had suddenly taken. Not what she had imagined or scripted in her head. "You weren't all bad."

"Your hindsight has been coloured rosy, my dear. Do you know that I used to resent you sometimes?"

"Resent me?" A surprise. It threw her rhythm off. "For what?"

"Your talent. It was real." He leaned his back against the chain and watched her swing. "I wanted to be an artist so bad but I knew deep down I didn't have it. But you did. It just rolled out of you so effortlessly. And, being a twenty-something shithead, not only did I resent you for it, sometimes I blamed you too. For holding me back."

"Did I?"

"No. That was just my ego getting in the way."

"Your paintings were great," she protested. "Creepy but great."

"They were mediocre. Less than that." He pushed off and swung to catch her momentum. "It was petty. I've had a lot of time to think it over so don't argue with me. I should have been more supportive, instead of trying to drag you down sometimes. Shame on me."

She stopped kicking and fell out of rhythm. Up when he was down, his expression a flash on the bypass.

His heel plowed the sand, slowing his pace. "How could you just give it up? Music means everything to you."

"I just can't do it anymore. The cost is too high."

"Touring I can understand. I remember how tough it was on you. But to never play again? Or write a song? You write songs the way other people breathe. It's a part of you."

"I won't do it halfway. I can't just fool around with the guitar sometimes, play the odd show. Get all maudlin about what coulda been. It's all or it's nothing."

Gil watched her sway. "Can I tell you something?"

"Anything."

"I think you should reconsider. All of that stuff, the performing and the songwriting, it's who you are. Stopping cold turkey would be like amputating a limb. You need it."

"I don't know about that," she said. "What's done is done."

"What you do, Tilda, it moves people. I mean it physically moves them. People dance, they tap their feet, they sing along. It's almost a religious experience, the way people respond to music. No one reacts that way to a painting. I would have killed to have that kind of response to my stuff." He lifted his gaze to the sky but not a single star was visible. "I wonder why that is."

"That's easy," Tilda shrugged. "Music doesn't go through your brain, it goes for the guts first. No other art does that."

"How do you figure that?"

"Just a theory. Do you want to hear it?"

"Yeah."

"Almost every form of art is visual. It goes through your eyes and then into your brain. Painting, sculpture, books, poetry. Film or photography. Because you have to see it to process it. And if it's good or if it has meaning, then it reaches down and touches your heart. Music bypasses the brain altogether and goes straight to your guts, to your heart. It either moves you or it doesn't. You dance or you don't. But it's only after it hits your heart that it travels up to the brain. Does that make sense?"

"Yeah, it does. I never thought of it that way."

"It's a primal thing. Your body reacts to music, the brain gets it afterwards."

Gil rose out of the seat and looked out over the deserted playground. "I miss seeing you play. There was something almost spooky about watching you onstage. I'd give my left arm to see that again."

She drifted to a stop. The rubberized seat felt suddenly uncomfortable so she launched out of it. They were designed for little kids after all, not over-forty ex-musicians with a habit of talking to dead boyfriends.

She bent to retrieve her shoes and found him staring at her again. His gaze never fell far, watching her every move. It was unnerving and, for reasons that escaped Tilda, it sparked a wick of anger in her. "Where have you been all this time?"

It broke the spell, the query snapping the glaze from his eyes. He turned aside as if to deflect the question. "Here."

"Here?" Her tone sharpened. Was that a joke? "You've been here in town this whole time?"

"Yes."

The wick glowed brighter. "So you thought, what the hell, it's been twenty years. Maybe I'll stop by and say hello?'"

Zero response. His silence more infuriating than any answer he could have uttered. *Give me something*, demanded the scream inside her skull. "Do you have any idea what it was like when you... left? What I went through? Why didn't you come to me then?"

"I couldn't."

"Why not? How could you let me go through that?" The rage, when it came, immolated her. Years of it, catching fire like a match dropped into gasoline."Why did you do that to me?"

"Stop."

But she couldn't stop. The levy broke and it was all pouring through the breach and she hurled the question at him over and over and still he gave no answer.

Stop

The voice was unnatural, an octave below eerie, but the fire burned out of control and Tilda swung, striking his face. His cruel, stupid, emotionless face. Then his hands locked around her arms so hard she thought they would snap.

Stop, said that awful voice.

Tilda felt her throat constrict and then realized that her feet had left the ground. Suspended in his grip, she feared he might shake her to pieces like a child.

"I couldn't." His voice trebled back to normal. "Do you think I wanted you to go through that?"

Her feet touched ground again and she stepped back. "That doesn't make sense. Why couldn't you come back to me then? What happened that night when the car flipped? Jesus Christ, did you fake your death?"

"No."

"Tell me." Tilda clenched her molars to bottle up the scream inside. "The police thought you fell into the lake and drowned. But after a while they gave up looking for you and that was the worst. Not knowing. I spent weeks down on the water, walking around Cherry beach hoping to spot you floating in the water. So at least I would know."

"I'm sorry."

Tilda stood her ground but all the rage she had stomped down pushed its way back up and found her eyes. The world went blurry. "You have to give me something here, Gil. You owe me that much."

"Don't do this."

"No. Tell me what happened or I will walk out of here and I never want to see you again."

A breeze rustled the treetops overhead but other than that, dead silence. *My God,* Tilda thought, *he won't do it. He won't give even that much. Fine. Twenty years of mourning was enough. She couldn't give anymore.*

"I didn't fake my death. And I didn't drown." His voice was a whisper notched just above the sound of the trees. "I was tossed from the car when it flipped. There was blood everywhere, I could barely move. I tried to get you out but my hands didn't seem to work. Then I was dragged away from the car, away from you, and I was killed."

"Killed how?" The questions dropped faster than she could lob them. "Dragged away by who?"

"Do you remember why we crashed the car?"

"You were wasted. We both were. You were going too fast."

Gil reeled back. "You don't remember that... *person...* stepping into the road? Swerving to avoid him?"

What was he going on about? "No. The road was empty. You were driving too fast."

His eyes narrowed at her. "What do you remember about that night?"

"Everything. I remember every goddamn detail of that night. I wish I didn't because it's always there, every moment of it and I've spent every day since regretting it. I knew you were too wasted to get behind the wheel. You refused to let me drive or turn around and go home. I should have been stronger but you always got your way and then—" Her voice snagged as it came bubbling up. A volcano threatening to erupt. If it did, words would become useless and she'd be reduced to simply wailing like a banshee. She took a breath.

"You did," he said.

"I did what?" Tilda snapped.

"Insist I pull over. So I did. You got behind the wheel." He bent forward, trying to lock onto her eyes. "Don't you remember?"

She shook her head. "No. That's not what happened..."

"I pulled over after the lift bridge and then you drove. I remember thinking it wasn't a great idea either because you gunned it down that big empty road no more sober than I was."

That's not how it happened...

He kept talking. "And then out of nowhere, something lurched out right in front of us. You swerved to avoid it and the car spun and flipped. You had buckled up but I hadn't. I was thrown from the car."

Why was he making this up? It's not true.

"I hit the ground, couldn't see anything because of the blood running into my eyes but I could hear you screaming my name. I crawled back to the car. You were slung upside down and your hand was twisted all wrong. I've never forgotten the look on your face, the terror of it."

Stop—

"I tried to pull you out but my hands were useless. And then something grabbed my legs and dragged me away from you. The thing that had run out in front of the car. It pulled me down off the pier. There were more of them. Waiting."

The lie he was telling, about her being behind the wheel, was shunted aside. Drowning in all the questions and lies, Tilda bobbed to the surface long enough to spit up a question. "Who? Who dragged you away?"

Whether he didn't hear it or ignored the question, she couldn't tell. Stuck on his narrative track, he barged on. "I died that night, Til. And then I came back. But I couldn't go to you. That was the deal. If I had, if I had even looked at you from a mile away, they would have killed you too."

She repeated her question. "Who?"

"The dead ones," Gil said. His timbre fell flat, a dampened fret buzz. "The coven. I became one of them."

The ground under her began to list. She looked for something to hang onto. "I need to sit down."

His hands were on her, keeping her propped up. Why had she cast about for something to hang onto when he was standing right there? She fell into him, her cheek against his sternum and her hands locking around his back. Her body remembered his, the way it folded into his frame like a cast refitted into its mould.

She felt him kiss the crown of her head, heard his voice whispering that he was sorry. Other things he shushed into her hair; about how he had had to stay away from her and how it was the hardest thing he had ever had to do. He said that he had never stopped loving her. She kept her cheek pressed into his chest because she knew that if she looked up at him it would be all over. That she would tell him to shut up so she could kiss his mouth and then she would be in a world of hurt and trouble but even now it was too late because she was tilting up and pulling him down until she forced her lips onto his mouth so hard it hurt and she thought her lip was bleeding but she didn't care and didn't stop and how she would not ever come up for air.

It wouldn't be a bad way to die, asphyxiating with her mouth clamped onto his. Let it come and never let it end.

The police spotlight was harsh. Even with her eyes closed, its hot light blasted through her eyelids. They broke off, Tilda sucking back air and they saw the police cruiser rumbling along the footpath as it trolled through the park like a shark. The uniform on the passenger side blasted the searchlight over the grounds and people fluttered up and scrambled away like birds flushed from a hedge. The skate-board kids and the bench drinkers and the lovers strolling the grass, all the nocturnal park people swam away from the great white cruiser rumbling through their midst.

They weren't doing anything wrong but Tilda already felt convicted under that spotlight and wanted to explain but Gil was moving away, leading her by the hand back into the darkest spans of the park grounds. Circling around the fence to put the playground between them and the prowl car.

The police unit rolled out of the park but Gil didn't stop to look back, hurrying them into the gloomy alleys and laneways. So fast that at times she felt lifted and carried along, feet barely scraping the gutters. When the blurred momentum stopped, her feet were planted solidly in the parched grass of her own backyard.

She heard him whisper goodnight and felt his lips tap her cheek but she must have blinked because when she opened her eyes, he was gone.

12

Some velvet morning

SHE HAD KILLED GIL DORSEY. She had been be-hind the wheel that night. She had crashed the car and killed the man she loved and her own memory had be-trayed her. There was little else that Tilda Parish could think of as she sleepwalked through the day. Shane asking if she felt okay and Molly sneering at her for being a space cadet. It was all just noise in her ear, their banter and ques-tions and unending griping. Why couldn't they just shut their mouths for once and be quiet? Why couldn't the two of them get themselves out the door without the harried rush and need for her to ensure they had everything they needed?

It was the same story at work, unable to focus on anything other than the thought that she had killed Gil Dorsey. Had she really remembered it wrong all this time? She sifted through her memory of that night and had to admit there were gaps. Most of that night was solid in her memory; the gig at the El Mo, fooling around in the back room and then later at Gil's flat. Torching the paintings and getting in the car. Beyond that, the snapshots grew dull. There were gaps, as if someone had taken scissors to the spool of film and cut whole scenes out and spliced it back it back together at the moment she opened her eyes to see the upside down world from within the totalled VW.

Hoping music might shake something loose, she went to the computer and dug out that old Joy Division tune from one of Sarah's playlists and listened to the one song she never wanted to hear again. Nothing shook loose, no hidden memory of pulling over and getting behind the wheel. Certainly no recall of anyone stepping out onto the road and forcing her to swerve so hard she rolled the car. And what was she to make of what Gil had told her? That someone had intentionally stepped in front of the car, causing the crash and then dragged him away? Down the pier where there were more and they killed him. But he had come back somehow and had been haunting the streets of the city all this time without ever coming to her. Until now?

None of it made sense. Who would do such a thing? Why did they want Gil? What had he done? And why hadn't they come after her? Why had he shown up now? Skulking around her house every night, waiting for her to come to him—

"Tilda!"

She startled, saw Sarah crossing the lobby. "Can you turn that down, honey? It's too loud." Sarah leaned on the counter and scrutinized her face. "Are you feeling okay? You seem kinda out of it right now."

"Sorry." Tilda shook her head, forcing herself back to the present.

"Another bad night's sleep?"

"Something like that." She looked down at the deposit book on the desk before her. The page only half filled out. How long had she been doing this?

"You should pay attention to that. Too many sleepless nights, your body's telling you something's wrong."

Tilda nodded, scrambling for something else to talk about. "I think I just need to eat something"

"HAVE YOU ever had an old boyfriend look you up?"

They were sitting at a wobbly table in the back patio of La Hacienda. Even in the shade it was almost too hot so they splurged and ordered sangria. It would do nothing to clear her head but Tilda didn't care.

"Oh yeah." Sarah leaned back and stretched. "All of them."

Tilda's eyebrow shot up. "All of them?"

"Facebook," Sarah shrugged. "It's impossible *not* to look up old flames."

"Of course." She hadn't thought of that, concurring that the site seemed practically invented for that purpose. "But all of them?"

"Yup. All of my old flames have gotten in touch." Another quick shrug and then Sarah raised her glass. "Or I looked them up. Whatever."

"So it was nothing." Tilda paused when the food came, waiting for the surly waitress to move out of earshot. "Just a hello-how-are-you kinda thing."

"Pretty much. I mean, you've done it, right?"

Tilda honestly hadn't. Of course she had been reunited with old friends but no old boyfriends. There was only Gil and she was pretty sure the dead didn't maintain an FB page. Although, given recent events, who was to say he didn't? "But nothing beyond that?"

"No. Well..." Sarah leaned in and lowered her voice. "Do you remember Frank Vittorio?" When Tilda shook her head, unable to place the name, Sarah leaned in further. "Frankie Vomit? From the Vomiteers?"

That Frankie. Tall, dark and nasty. Handsome as hell but a vicious disposition, hell bent on antagonizing everyone in sight. Sarah had dated him for about six months back when Tilda was still fronting the Daisy Pukes and it had damn near almost killed her. She and Frankie Vomit were volatile and left a path of destruction in their wake. Tilda never did learn why or how they broke up but given Mr. Vomit's disposition, any reason would do. "Didn't he go to jail?"

"A long time ago. Do you know what he's doing now?"

"Living under a bridge?"

"Get this, Frank's a photographer now." Sarah tucked into her salad. "A successful one too. He specializes in shooting product. Like glamour shots of blenders or laptops for ad agencies. Consumer porn."

"Jeez. I thought for sure that guy would be dead by now." Tilda sipped her sangria, feeling it cold and bittersweet on her tongue. "So what happened? Did you meet in person?"

"We did. And it was a lot of fun. For someone who put himself through a crapload of abuse, he looks really good."

Tilda guessed where this was headed. "Tell me you didn't hook up."

"Almost," Sarah flushed, looking sheepish. "There was tons of flirting and he looked great and that old spark was still there. I felt twenty-two all over again. It was such a high, you know?"

"Sure. But what about Billie?" Sarah's partner of the last five years. Billie was a tall woman with a tough exterior, whom Tilda had always been a little intimidated by. "Or Frankie for that matter? Is he married?"

"Yeah. Didn't matter to him though. He was all for hooking up, having a fling. He gave me that old song and dance about his loveless marriage and how the heart wants what it wants. Said it was wrong to deny ourselves."

Tilda leaned in further. "So? Did you?" Sarah's cheeks burned red and her gaze bounced around, unable to meet Tilda's eye. Guilty as charged and Tilda hissed. "Sarah Lippman! Why didn't you ever tell me?"

"Because it was awful." She swigged back the sangria and set the glass down. "He showed me his studio one night after we'd met for a drink. But all that spark and flirting just fizzled when we started fooling around. It was awkward and weird and he couldn't get it up and then he started crying. Telling me he couldn't go through with it, couldn't do that to his wife even though they hadn't had sex in over two years."

"Two years?" The idea of it sent a shudder down Tilda's spine. How could a married couple go two years without ever having sex? She watched Sarah's face wither in shades of shame. "What a shitty thing to do. You must have felt awful."

"You have no idea. I was lying there naked, ready to do this and he starts blubbering that he can't. I felt like a piece of dirt because I was ready to go through with it."

Tilda took Sarah's hand and stroked her thumb over the knuckles. "Don't beat yourself up over it. I can understand it."

"It's not that I don't love Billie anymore. That's never changed. But we go through these phases. Lesbian bed death. And with Frankie, all that flirting and carrying on, it got to me. It's not like I wanted an affair or anything, I just wanted to get laid. A real down and dirty bout like we used to. And then he pulls that shit on me, jumping the moral high ground and leaving me feeling like a piece of dirt."

"Ah honey, I'm sorry." Two tables over, a young couple were watching their exchange. Tilda shot them a look so harsh it sent both their eyes zooming back to their plates. She turned back to Sarah. "Did you tell Billie about it?"

"Jesus, where's the waitress?" Sarah had finished her glass and wanted another. "I wasn't going to. Nothing had really happened so I convinced myself nothing was wrong.

But the Catholic in me couldn't manage the guilt and I spilled. Told Billie everything."

"And?"

"I'm still paying for it," Sarah said. "Whenever we have an argument, she stops the show by bringing that up again and throwing it in my face. After that, there's nothing I can say. It's like her silver bullet to win every fight." She blew out her cheeks like she'd just run a quarter mile. "It's awful."

Tilda scrambled for something to console her with, some silver lining that her friend hadn't thought of but she couldn't find one. The story bit a little too close to the bone, leaving Tilda's guts queasy.

"So?" Sarah caught the attention of the waitress across the floor and swirled a finger over her empty glass. The waitress sneered and turned away. "Who's the old beau?"

"What?"

"I'm assuming you asked me this because some old boyfriend has gotten in touch. Who is he?"

"Oh, no. It's not that."

"Bullshit. What's his name?"

Tilda groped for a lie. "Someone from high school. Back before I knew you. No big deal."

The waitress clunked a fresh drink before Sarah and walked away without asking if Tilda wanted another. "My advice?" Sarah said. "Whatever you do, think it over first."

SARAH'S cautionary tale stayed with her the rest of the day. Leaving work, she cut east and headed into Kensington to pick up a few things. The market was in full summer swing, stinking to high heaven in the broiling heat and the layabouts everywhere. Kensington was like its own little time zone where everything went slower, a 'ya mon' feel of eternal siesta, sealed off in a bubble from the frenzied pace that infested the rest of the city. With its retinue of middle-aged punk rockers chugging back tall boys on stoops, the market existed in its own alternate universe and Tilda loved and hated it with equal measure.

It was still hard to believe that Sarah had never told her about her secret fling with Frankie Vomit. It almost stung that she hadn't shared it with her, as if Tilda was some blabber-mouth who couldn't be trusted. That was too harsh, she reconsidered. She had clearly been humiliated by the whole thing and was living with the consequences. Who wouldn't keep the sordid mess to themselves?

Was she headed down the same road to ruination with Gil? Nothing had happened (yet) but it was going to sooner or later. Holding Gil's hand and, more so, kissing his mouth had shocked her system so hard she thought she might spontaneously combust. But she had wanted more. She was starved for more and wanted it all. Moreover, this was Gil she was talking about and the circumstances were different, if not downright otherworldly. Logic had taken a vacation so the regular mores of social conduct didn't apply. She was on her own and Sarah's sad experience was no signpost she could use to navigate her own path. Or was she simply justifying her own selfish actions?

After picking up chicken on St. Andrews and greens on Baldwin, Tilda stopped in front of The Porthole, a narrow defile of a bar that was considered decrepit during the Mulroney era. The grimy marquis over the door displayed the shows for the next two days; *The Dum Shags* tonight and tomorrow *Tox1c Tuesday*, an open stage night for surprise acts. Her own name had appeared in that marquis more times than she could remember, albeit spelled haphazardly as the bar was eternally short of all the changeable letters for the sign. She had often been billed as Tilda Parsh or Tlda Parish.

She pushed through the door into the dark interior. The chairs and stools were still propped upside down on the tables, the floor waiting to be swept. A man stood behind the bar with his back to the door, counting the fridge inventory.

Tilda crossed the floor. "Ivan?"

The man shot around, reading glasses half down his nose which looked out of place with his black Viletones tee. "Tilda! How are you?"

"I'm good." She cocked a thumb at the door. "I see you're still missing the 'i' for the marquis."

"It'll show up the day I retire." Ivan pushed his glasses up into his hair and came around from behind the bar. "Say, a little birdie told me you quit the biz. Is that true?"

"Yup. I retired on all my millions."

"Good to have a back-up plan. So what brings you to my stoop today?"

"I wanted to ask about Tuesday night. Is the bill filled out?"

Ivan scratched his head. "I had one band cancel out. And there's always some dipshit who forgets what day it is and doesn't show. Why, you coming to see the show?"

"No. I want a slot in the line-up. Just me, no band."

The bar owner leaned back in surprise. "Huh?"

13

No Aloha

LASAGNA NIGHT. Tilda was reluctant to run the stove in this heat but it was one of Shane's favourites so she sweated through it to keep him happy. Shane wasn't a complicated man, as he was fond of declaring. His needs were simple and his wants were few. She couldn't argue with that and, she had to admit, it made life easier.

Concentrating on the task at hand was the difficult part. She had checked the forecast. The sun would set at 8:51 PM. It was nigh impossible to stop glancing at the window to see if it was getting dark yet. Dinner conversation was slippery as she kept falling behind the topics and Molly rolled her eyes at her distraction.

When he asked if she was feeling all right, she deferred to the usual answer of being tired from a bad sleep. He suggested going to bed earlier and went back to grilling Molly about her schoolwork and her friends with all the tact of a sledgehammer. Firing direct questions at her, he didn't seem to understand that Molly's one-word answers signalled that she was shutting down. He seemed satisfied with replies of 'good' or 'fine' and let the conversation die quickly as if his parental obligations had been met and he was now relieved of duty. He finished off his lasagna and went back to the stove for seconds.

Along with her utter disgust with absolutely everything, Molly's easy retreat into silence was disquieting. The grunts or disdainful sighs were as close to conversation she came and it worried Tilda. The only strategy Tilda knew to get her daughter talking was through subterfuge. Indirect questions about one of her friends or mentioning a certain band that they both liked (there were actually a few). It was like fishing, tossing bait into the water and hoping for a bite on the line. A parental sleight-of-hand that, thank God, her daughter hadn't clued into yet.

"Hey," she said, turning to Molly. "Guess what I found when I cleaned out the studio space?"

"Friskers?" Molly replied in a droll reference to their old cat who had disappeared when she was eleven. "Was he all dried up like a mummy?"

"No, miss negativity. The pink ukulele! Remember?"

"Oh. Wow."

The pink ukulele was an eyesore of an instrument that Tilda had found in a thrift shop in Winnipeg. Despite its hot pink finish it played well and Tilda had brought it home to add to her collection. Molly, who was eight at the time, had fallen in love with the thing right away. She and Kisha Tremblay (Molly's neighbourhood BFF between the ages of eight and eleven) had adored the ukulele and bashed away at it in the studio. The two of them spent hours out there, singing into cold mics and strumming that pink instrument. The Labour Day before Molly started grade five, the ukulele had gone missing and both Molly and Kisha were inconsolable. Tilda had spent hours tearing through the clutter trying to find it but the pink instrument had clearly sprouted legs and run away. By Halloween of that year, Molly and Kisha were not even friends anymore.

"Have you spoken to Kisha lately? I wonder how she's doing?"

"She moved away," Molly said.

"Moved away? Where to?"

Molly shrugged. "Her parents split. She and her mom moved to Whitby. Her dad's a real asshole."

Shane's eyes shot up at the word *asshole* but he was unsure of who had uttered it. Seeing Tilda unperturbed by the obscenity, he assumed everything was fine and tucked back into his lasagna.

Tilda sat up, this was news to her. "When did this happen?"

"Over Christmas. Her mom finally clued into the fact that Mister Tremblay was cheating on her."

"Whoa!" Shane jumped back into the conversation. "I knew there was something shifty about that guy. Who was he snogging? Was it that Argentinean woman across the street?"

"Does it matter?" Tilda fired a look across the table.

"Worse," Molly sneered. "A mutual friend. They'd been doing it for like two years."

Shane shook his head in mock solemnity. "Jesus. What an asshole."

"I know, right? She was friends with Kisha's mom the whole time." Molly pushed her plate away. "People suck."

Shane snorted. "He's French. What do you expect?"

Tilda rose and gathered up the plates. "That's enough."

"What are you so upset about?" Shane said. "You never liked the guy."

"That doesn't matter." She snatched the plate from under her husband's nose. "It's not a joke. That family was torn apart."

WHEN the sun finally went down, Molly retreated into her room and Shane went down to his workshop. Tilda made tea and took her book out to the patio and pretended to read. Ears cocked for sound, her heart leapt at a rustling in the rosebush but all she saw was a plump raccoon waddling precariously along the fence. It looked at her as if irritated at her presence before clambering down into the neighbour's yard.

She couldn't wait to surprise Gil. He had said that he wished he could see her perform one last time and, despite her resolve to end her career, she would play one last show. Just for him. Which was only a day away. Christ, she thought, maybe she should practice.

The guitar waited on the bench where she had left it. It was a bit heavier than her old Hummingbird but it had a stronger resonance to it and she meant to ask Gil where he had gotten it. She couldn't picture him perusing instruments in a shop. Had he stolen it? She had so many questions like that, details that dropped away the moment she saw him. They returned in the moments he wasn't there, in the anticipation of seeing him again.

Where does he live? Was it close by or across town? Does he have a home at all? What does he do when he's not haunting her? How does he live? Is he even technically alive? All of these nagging queries would drop out of her head the moment he appeared so she stopped listing them all and strummed the guitar, launching into an old song from her Daisy Pukes days, just to see if she could remember the chords.

An hour ticked by and she had warmed her way through a dozen songs, the melodies and the lyrics coming back easily. Scrounging up pen and paper, she drafted up a rough set list for tomorrow night. She'd start with some of the more recent tunes, toss in an older one from the Spitting Gibbons that she remembered Gil liking and then alternate between the old and the new. Or new to Gil anyway. Toxic Tuesdays at the Porthole could easily turn busy. She might only have about thirty minutes to play and already her set list was too long.

She took the pen and crossed out a few titles, trimming and reordering the songs to crunch the set to thirty minutes. A noise outside startled her. The guitar banged onto the bench, strings humming as Tilda leapt to the floor.

Shane stood in the doorway, a prybar and a crate of tools in his hands. He sauntered in and set the heavy crate onto the bench. "It's nice to hear you playing again. I miss that."

Her eyes zeroed in on the tools. "What are you doing?"

"Thought I'd tear out some of the soundproofing on the far wall where the squirrels got into it over the winter."

"Do you have to do it now?"

He shrugged. "Thought I'd get a head-start. The sooner I can move the woodshop out here, the sooner we can free up some space in the basement."

Something close to panic clenched up inside her at the idea of Shane invading her space, eager to claim it as his own. It was her refuge, her only retreat where she could scrape out some small peace of her own that didn't involve him or Molly or anyone. He already ruled the house, at times leaving her no place to breathe and now he wanted this too? "No. It's too soon. I'm still using it."

Shane cast his eyes over the garage. Aside from that ratty old sofa and a single wooden chair, the space was empty. "For what?"

"I just need it."

"But we agreed we'd move stuff out here. The house is so cluttered you can't turn around without knocking something over. We need the space, honey."

"Not now. This is still mine."

Her raised voice bounced over the sound-proofed walls and Shane took a step back. His hands went up, crying uncle. "Okay, okay."

"It's too soon. That's all."

"Fine. Whatever." He turned on his heel and went out the door. "Take all the time you need." Stomping back into the house, he took his anger out on the screen door by letting slam shut, something he was constantly barking at everyone else to quit doing.

Tilda leaned back against the bench. She must have come off as crazy just now. So what? Shane should have warned her before barging in like that, ready to take this away from her. Didn't he know how hard all of this was for her? Of course he didn't. Subtlety and nuance never worked for Shane. He had to have everything spelled out for him. Let him sulk. He'd get over it.

Chuffed, she snatched up the guitar but her mood had curdled so she set it back onto the bench. Where the hell was Gil? It was getting late and the waiting was jagging her nerves.

Her tea had gone cold so she went back into the house to make more. The roar of the television boomed from the living room, the sound of gunfire and explosions from some action movie Shane was watching. Even that irked her. She reached for the kettle but decided against it. The night was too hot so she rifled through the fridge for a beer and headed back outside.

He would show up before she finished the beer, she wagered. Settling onto the picnic table, she took small sips to stretch it out but nothing stirred and nothing rustled. Before long, she was tilting back the last of the pilsner. Maybe he wasn't coming after all. Had she done something wrong, said something harsh the night before to keep him away? Maybe Gil had changed his mind and didn't want to see her anymore? What if—

Stop

The doubts and recriminations swarmed up faster than if she had kicked a hornet's nest. Shut it down, she scolded herself, before you drive yourself buggy. She had downed the beer too fast, that's all. It was a hot night.

She took her time with the second one. Back in the garage, she reordered the set list again and played through a few more songs before making the mistake of settling onto the sofa. It was old but deep and hard to get out of once you were on it. She closed her eyes, declaring to herself that she only needed a few minutes. When she jerked awake, the clock read three minutes past 2:00 AM. She killed the light and shuffled back to the house. To hell with Gil Dorsey.

AS much as she tried, TIlda couldn't stop fretting over Gil's no-show the night before. Scolding herself to stop overthinking it the entire workday proved useless. It was impossible not to speculate on what had gone wrong and from there it was a short hop to panicked obsession. He had said before that this was a mistake. Maybe he had resolved that it was and vanished for good. Or had she said or done something to turn him away? Maybe she had changed too much for him. There was, after all, almost two decades between them.

And so it went for the rest of the day and the walk home and the hustle of getting dinner on the table. Over-analyzing every moment, scrutinizing every awkward pause and projecting drama into every nook and cranny until she thought she would scream. This is what it feels like to go insane, she concluded. Brains frying from internal arguments, each wild speculation adding more fuel until her grey matter boiled up inside her skull.

When dinner was over and Tilda sat alone at the messy kitchen table, a wave of smothering exhaustion blanketed her so hard she thought she might keel over onto the floor. Molly and Shane had both scampered once the meal was over, wary of her snapping remarks and short fuse.

Zombie-shuffling into the living room, she found Shane and Molly watching an orange-fleshed TV host prattle on about celebrities. She stepped in front of the screen and asked the two of them to take care of the kitchen. She needed to lie down, she declared. They groused.

Ignoring their kvetching, Tilda dragged her sorry bones upstairs and laid down on the bed. Too wired to nap and too anxious to distill her thoughts, she stared at the spiderwebbed crack in the ceiling. She still had a gig to perform tonight and, Gil or no Gil, she was going to play. It was too late to cancel out and simply skipping it was not an option. She may have given up her career but the work ethic remained firmly locked in place. She remained absolutely still for twenty minutes, grasping at nirvana, before she rose and crossed into the bathroom. Turning the shower on, she dialled the temperature valve to its hottest setting and slipped out of her clothes.

MOLLY sat on the floor of her room turning the pages of an art book about Frida Kahlo. With a school project due next week on the life of an artist, she had been drawn to Kahlo's strong but bizarre imagery. She had meant to be taking notes about Kahlo's life but her notepad sat idle as she turned the pages, lost in the paintings.

This was going nowhere. She pushed the book aside and sat up. She needed something to drink. Something cold and caffeinated so she could get back to work before she frittered the whole night away. She opened her door and made for the stairs.

"Honey," her mother's voice called from the bedroom. "Can you come in here for a second."

Molly groaned and shambled to the door of her mother's bedroom. "Yeah?"

Tilda stood before the mirror, smoothing a hand down the front of the vintage cocktail dress she wore. "Does this look okay?"

"I dunno. What's the occasion?"

"I'm playing a show tonight." Tilda adjusted the bustline. The fit was tight and flattened her chest. "Is this too, you know, showy?"

"I thought you quit playing."

So the kid had been paying attention, Tilda thought. "One last gig." Tilda smoothed the material again. "So? Too much?"

Molly tilted her head, as if to see better. "Is that new?"

"No. But I've never worn it."

"I wouldn't go with that," Molly shrugged. "Maybe if you were taller."

"Taller?" Tilda spun, craning her neck to see the mirror. "You mean I look fat in it? Be honest."

Molly sensed her mother's anxiousness and was puzzled by it. Most of her mother's moods were puzzling these days but she chalked it up to some mid-life crisis, which would explain the dress. For once, she went for diplomacy. "I think twenty-year olds would have trouble with that dress."

Tilda's face darkened. "I'm too old to pull it off."

"No. You look like you're trying too hard. Know what I mean?"

Tilda took another sweep of her reflection, cocking a fist onto her hip. "You're right. Okay, what do you think of these?" She nodded at the clothes laid across the bed and then shimmied out of the dress.

Molly surveyed the choices on the bed and chewed her lip. "The club you're playing. Is it fancy?"

"God no. It's the Porthole."

"Easy." Molly took two pieces and put them together then tossed them aside. She dug through the closet and came back with a pencil skirt and a tank top. "Try that."

Tilda looked over the clothes. She never would have thought to put them together. "You sure?"

"Vintage chic."

Tilda slipped on the clothes, checked the mirror and liked what she saw. "It's perfect. Thanks honey."

"Sure." Molly smiled then and sauntered off down the stairs.

The smile almost startled Tilda, so seldom did she witness it anymore. Recruiting Molly's help in picking outfits had been the nicest five minutes spent with her daughter in ages and she wanted to call her back, not wanting it to end. She kept mum and let the girl go. Better not to spoil the moment.

She went to the window and looked down into the yard. Nothing different, nothing out of place. She pressed her brow against the cool glass and willed him to simply appear in the grass under the willow tree. Nothing happened. She collected her shoes and hurried down the stairs.

Shane was washing his hands at the kitchen sink. He glanced up then snapped back for a second look. "Wow, look at you." His face dropped. "Is it date night? Did we make plans?"

"No." Tilda gathered up her bag, scrounging the contents for her keys. "I'm playing a gig tonight."

His face dropped a little more. "A gig? TIlda, what the hell? You don't want to give up the garage and now you're playing a show? I thought you let all this stuff go."

"I've been doing this my whole life, honey. Cold turkey is harder than I thought." Her keys jingled up from the bottomless pit of the bag. "The gig just came up. Thought I'd give it a shot."

"Are you sure? The last one didn't go so well."

"I know. That's why I don't want that to be the last gig. This one will be better. I'd like to go out on a better note."

"Fair enough. Where's the show?"

She told him where it was and he made a face, as if tasting something sour. "Let me clean up," he said. "I'll go with you."

"No, it's okay. This one's just for me. To say goodbye."

"Okay." His eyes went up and down her a third time and he came up behind her, kissing the back of her neck. "Shame to let you go off alone all dressed up like that. You look hot."

She tried to slip away but he pulled her back in tight against him, his hands running down her hip bones. "Slow down, cowboy."

"Can't. You feel too good."

She felt his lips on her bare shoulder, the warmth of his frame pressed up against her back and, despite everything, felt herself respond. Letting his hands go where they wanted to. Angled up against the sink, facing the window that looked out over the backyard. A shadow stretched across the yard, blocking the patio light momentarily before vanishing again.

"I have to go." She slipped out from his grasp and towards the backdoor.

"Why do you always do that? Pull away from me?"

"I'm late. I gotta run."

The disappointment on his face was palpable. "Hurry back after your set. Feels like forever since I touched you."

She gave him a wink as she went out the back. "I have to get my guitar."

The crickets shushed as she stood in the grass and let the heat of the moment pass away. Nothing moved nor stirred. Maybe it was nothing.

Ducking into the garage, she folded the set list and tucked it into the guitar case. Tearing a page from the notebook, she scrawled out the name and address of the club, along with the time, in big letters and left it on the bench. Maybe Gil would see it. Lugging the guitar outside, she waited again but no form stepped from the shadows. A scowl clouded her features as she marched out the gate towards the street. The Pathfinder was parked at the curb. She unlocked the back and loaded the guitar in.

"Where are you going?"

Gil sat on the hood of the adjacent parked car, feet up on the bumper.

"Jesus. Don't sneak up on me like that." Tilda swung door closed. "Where were you last night?"

"I couldn't make it."

Tilda stepped closer, wanting to touch his hand but he seemed cool and wary. "I thought I scared you off."

"That's my line isn't it?" He wagged his chin at her vehicle. "Where are you going?"

"Remember the Porthole?" When he nodded, she said "I'm playing there tonight. For you."

"What?"

"It's just a short set, no big deal. You said you wanted to see me play one more time, so this is it. My last show."

She hoped he'd be surprised. A smile at least but there was nothing. His face drew cold and he slid off the car. "Tilda, that's very sweet of you to do that for me. But I can't go."

"Why not?" Expectations popped like birthday balloons. This didn't need to be difficult. "I know the place is a bit skeezy but it's all I could finagle. I did this for you."

His palms turned up, as if it was beyond his control. "I can't go."

"Why?"

"I just can't. Don't ask me why."

Tilda watched him take a step back, as if she was contagious. A sickly wash of shame flooded over her and she felt ill. Arranging the gig, overturning her vow to give up music, wanting to make him happy; all of it thrown back in her face. Was he playing a game here? Another power issue? "Your loss," she said and reached for the door handle.

"Tilda, don't go."

"I have a set to play. Be there or don't. Your call." She climbed under the wheel and turned the ignition. In the rearview mirror Gil flared red in the glow of taillights and then receded in the distance as she pulled away.

14

Turn on the bright lights

SHE DIDN'T WANT TO BE HERE, standing on the sidelines in a narrow bar with people half her age. Nursing a glass of the house plonk, Tilda considered leaving. Pulling a no-show in a smelly hole-in-the-wall, what a fitting cap to her failed career. But Ivan had already spotted her, waving to her from behind the bar. Hightailing it now was out of the question.

Why did Gil refuse to come? Yes, his circumstances were weird (if not bizarre beyond comprehension) but he knew how gloomy and grim the Porthole was. Easy enough to find a dark corner and stay out of sight. Maybe all that talk about wanting to see her play was just that; talk.

"Hey Tilda!" Ivan appeared at her side and touched her arm. "I'm glad you're here. How do you feel about going first?"

"I feel ill about it." She hated going first, warming up an apathetic crowd. "I thought I was going third?"

"Yeah well, the first two bands dropped out. I know you hate opening but you're the strongest of the bunch. Start it off right, then play a second set later on." He clapped his hands together in mock prayer. "Please."

Tilda looked at the stage, already set up with another band's gear. "Okay."

She took her guitar to the stage, adjusted the mics and dove into the first song without an opening word to the crowd. *Fisher Wife* was an old tune originally performed with the Daisy Pukes and tweaked over the years to suit a solo performance but it still had a stomping honky-tonk vibe. The crowd shushed momentarily then the hum of chatter slowly crept back up. She had about half the crowd, the other half were a thousand miles away.

Kicking into the second number with no preamble or intro to the audience, she was surprised at how good it felt to be onstage. No expectations meant no reservations. She simply didn't care what the audience thought. Part of the crowd she had captured with the first song began to drift away, chatting up their friends or staring stupefied into their phones.

Not bad for an opening slot but if this was her last show, she wanted all their attention. On the stage behind her sat another band's gear, set up and presumably sound-checked. Including that Fender Strat on its stand. Shrugging off her acoustic, she picked up the Strat and slung it on. She signaled to the sound guy, who suddenly looked confused but reached for the board to turn up the guitar.

The set list she had redrafted three times lay abandoned at her feet as she switched it up again. The guitar was crunchy and twice as loud, jarring the crowd to attention. That was better, she thought, as she launched into a song from the Gorgons era called '*Kicking out the footlights*'. It was a venomous tune and she let it rip. The anger felt righteous and most of the crowd sat up, giving her their eyes and ears. That was good but she wanted them all. And there was a song in her arsenal that just might do that.

A wicked thrill zapped through her at the thought of performing the one song she had never played to a crowd. Adapting the chords of Gil's song from acoustic to electric was simple enough but she wanted it dirtier so she kicked the fuzz pedal at her feet. The patter of the crowd evaporated as everyone in the room sat up and turned to see what was happening onstage. Just a girl and a guitar. The simple love song, warped by buzz and distortion, forced even the most sullen-faced and self-absorbed to pay attention. It was startling to behold and so distracting that Tilda closed her eyes to lose herself in the moment.

He was here.

In the darkness behind her closed eyes, she could feel him in the room.

It took a moment to locate his face amongst the crowd. Way at the back, in the darkest corner of the bar. The expression on his face was hard to decipher. Was it awe or shock? One moment joy, a pulse later frigid grief. He didn't seem to register that she was looking right at him, his gaze taking in everything too fast to focus on any detail.

It didn't matter. The others melted away and she sang only to him. The song was almost twenty years old but right now, in this moment, no time had passed and she was sitting on the mattress in his dingy flat, singing it for the first time. Her heart knocked against her ribcage the same way it did then, she had to keep it strapped down before it choked off her voicebox. Everyone in the room held their breath. Bashing out the last note, she turned the guitar to the amp and let the feedback murder everyone's eardrums.

The stinging squelch faded and the sound of clapping rose up. Someone whistled. Redemptive? Maybe. Exhilarating and heady? Without a doubt.

She squinted against the low slung stage lamps, trying to keep Gil in her sights. Wheeling the volume knob to nill, she unslung the guitar and set it back onto its stand and stepped down. Winding through the cramped tables, vaguely aware of people praising her set and asking about that last song. She moved past them towards the back of the room but lost track of Gil in the crowd. Swimming through the bodies, he appeared again. A blasted expression in his eyes.

She pushed aside the last of the interlopers to get to him, hands reaching up to grip his collar and pulling him down to get at his mouth. His lips were cold but he pressed against her hard, hands pulling her in like he wanted to swallow her up.

Voices murmured, someone cracked a joke. All of it white noise. Gnats.

Tilda came up for air. "Change your mind?"

"Do you know how often I dreamt about this?" He pinched her bottom lip between his teeth. "Thank you."

The buzz in the room died away as a band stepped into the footlights and took up their instruments. The wild-haired young man whose guitar she had borrowed leaned up to the microphone and cracked a joke about following a tough act.

Tilda settled in to watch. Ivan swung past with a glass of the bad house red as a thank you. He asked Gil what he was drinking but Gil said he was fine and Ivan darted back behind the bar. She felt his hand mesh into hers and they watched the band. She leaned into him, feeling dizzy. It all felt so familiar; standing in the dark and watching someone play. It was now, it was twenty years ago.

It didn't last long. Something shifted in the room. Faces in the crowd turned back their way, craning their necks to look at them. No, she thought, not them. Gil. One woman after another stealing glances back at the man by her side. A few brazenly flashing him sly smiles or boldly waving at him to come talk to them. A few of the men too, bold and even more shameless than the women. Tilda felt her back go up and clenched his hand tighter, as if Gil would drift away, pulled into the tractor beam of those come-hither looks.

It didn't take long before other men were looking back too. The boyfriends or hook-ups started swivelling their heads to see what the hell all the fuss was about. Their eyes clocked Gil and turned instantly venomous, hateful even. Any threat, no matter how small or imagined, is hard to dispel once lodged in the male eye. A challenge to the overweening sense of their own status, a menace to be quashed and beaten down and humiliated.

Gil squeezed her fingers. "We should go."

"Not yet." Her hand responded with another squeeze to calm him. "Never mind them."

The band was halfway into their second number when the first woman slunk forward, batting eyelashes at Gil and asking his name. He didn't even look at her and the woman rushed off, pretending she hadn't said anything at all. The second woman cruised past with pretty much the same lack of tact. She received the same response. Tilda pretended not to notice but couldn't help feeling some small thrill as her date brushed off these graceless advances. When, she wondered, had young women become so bold?

"What the fuck, Romeo?"

Tilda startled as a big man with a shaved head swung up into Gil's face. The man's bull neck was cabled up with tension, his whole frame tensing up and ready to spring.

Gil tore his eyes from the stage to the man blocking his view. "What do you want?"

"You, pretty boy. Making fuck-me eyes at my woman. Just how fucking stupid are you?"

Gil cleared some room in the crowd to pass through and nodded to Tilda. "Time to go."

The man shoved the heel of his hand against Gil's chest. Wide shoulders and thick arms, he outweighed Gil by a hundred pounds. "That's right, nancy-boy. Run off and take your old whore with you."

Boom.

Everything went to hell at that point. The sound of breaking glass ripped Tilda's ears. The front window exploded and the muscled man lay sprawled over the sidewalk, shrieking as he rolled against the shards of broken glass. The crowd backed away in confusion.

Gil was already pulling her out, tugging her towards the door, her guitar case clenched in his other hand. They stepped over the screaming man on the pavement and muscle-head cursed Gil as a faggot and vowed to kill him. Gil spun around and stomped his bootheel to the man's throat and advised the man to shut his mouth before he got his skull pulverized against the curb. They were running down Baldwin and shooting up Augusta before Tilda could catch her breath.

A figure stepped onto the street and blocked their path. An old woman with matted hair, clad in a heavy parka despite the heat. Tilda had seen her before, haunting the market and muttering to herself about Jesus and how everyone was going to Hell unless they repented. In her grime-stained hand was a cross fashioned out of sticks and duct tape with which she would wheel about as she warned sinners in broken English that Jesus was coming.

Even at a distance, Tilda could smell the woman. A ripe tang of soured sweat and stale urine that only got stronger as they almost ran the woman over. The woman waved her cross and told them to repent but when her eyes fixed onto Gil, she cringed back and hissed. "Devil!" she shrieked, thrusting the splinterwood cross at Gil. "The devil here! The devil here!"

Gil cut left, pulling Tilda away. The woman was still shrieking full volume and people about were turning this way, alerted to her screams. Tilda glanced over shoulder and saw patrons from the Porthole spilling out onto the puddles of the street.

"Gil, stop." She tugged at him to slow down. "This is crazy. We can't run."

"We can't stay. Come on."

"My car is here."

"We'll come back for it." He gripped her hand tighter and hurried on. A figure tottered out of the darkness and lurched towards them. Gil shoved the man away without breaking stride.

It was all happening too fast. She pulled on his hand again. "Where are we going?"

"Just keep up."

It wasn't easy. Gil moved quickly, cutting down a lane-way and then into an alley so dark she could barely see the pavement. Completely disoriented by the fourth turn, Tilda had no idea in which direction they were travelling.

"Watch your head," he said as they ducked through a break in a fence and emerged onto another alley. Buildings loomed before them, brick monoliths that were old in the Victorian era. Every window was dark. Past a loading dock to an unlit portico, a metal door squealing as Gil yanked it open and pulled her inside. The worn steps of the back stairwell creaked under each step, winding up three floors. He let go of her hand to dig into a pocket, producing a key that he slotted into the lock of a door of faded green paint.

Tilda followed him inside but when the door closed, she was left blind in total darkness. "I can't see anything. Where's the lights?"

"What?" His voice somewhere in the pitch. "Hang on."

Her knee knocked into something hard so she remained still, listening to his footfalls in the dark. The rattle of something being jostled, something else falling to the floor. A match was struck and Gil's face floated in its glow as he lit a number of candles. "Is that better?"

She took a cautious step forward. The candlelight was too soft to reveal anything of the space she was in. The outlines of some furniture, objects stacked against the walls. "Where's the light switch?"

"There's no power here." He blew out the match and stepped away into the gloom. "Maybe this will help."

A drape was pulled aside to reveal a tall window, letting in the glow of city lights. Tilda scanned her surroundings. The space was vast, with tall ceilings like a loft, and it smelled of dust and old wood. A few mismatched pieces of furniture formed a sitting area in the middle but the rest of the room appeared to be haphazard storage. Metal shelving rose from the floor like towers, crates stacked here and there with no organization or reason. The wall to her left reflected the light of the candles in what she thought at first to be mirrors. A closer look revealed a bank of old aquariums running the length of the wall, the glass greened with desiccated algae, the inhabitants long gone.

She took a step forward. "What is this place?"

"Just a quiet spot," he said, searching through the drawers of a desk.

"Do you live here?"

"Sometimes."

She crossed the floor and looked out the smudged window. The garish neon of Chinatown glowed up from below, the noise of the street leeching through the cracked panes. Her breath fogged the dirty glass.

Gil leaned against a table in the center of the room, watching her.

Tilda wandered, taking in the place but the candlelight only travelled so far and the space remained dim and obscure. She clocked a lumpy sofa but no bed or kitchen of any kind. "Where do you sleep?"

He shrugged. "I don't really sleep much."

Her knees bumped into things she couldn't see. The adrenaline had burned off, leaving her hands shaky and guts a little queasy. Her wrist was aching and she wondered if she'd knocked it against something during the run. "Do you think that guy's okay?"

"Who?"

She stopped and looked at him. Was he joking? "The guy you put through the window. He was cut pretty bad."

"He got off easy."

The coldness of that startled her. "I don't remember you being so violent."

"What was I supposed to do? Let that asshole run his mouth?" He looked away, shaking his head. "He isn't worth worrying about."

Tilda regarded him from across the room. Back at the club, it had felt like nothing had changed as she held his hand but now, everything had changed. It had been almost two decades. Maybe she really didn't know him at all anymore. She slid a book down from a stack and tilted it towards the candle but the spine was frayed raw, the title lost.

Cracking it open, she found the book was in a foreign language, its pages mouldy. "What happened back there? All those women kept looking at you. Some of the men too, like they couldn't keep their eyes off of you."

His eyes narrowed but he said nothing.

The silence was maddening. "I mean, I can't keep my eyes off you but that's me. Those other women, they were so bold, practically coming on to you right in front of their boyfriends."

He watched her knead her wrist. "Did you hurt your hand?"

"No. It's just the old injury."

"From the accident?"

"It's never been the same since."

Closing the distance between them, he reached for her hand but Tilda hesitated, almost retreated. She didn't know why. He frowned then took her hand, wrapping his fingers around her wrist.

"Does it always hurt?"

"Not always."

He studied her forearm, as if he could see through the tissue and determine what was wrong with the bones. The flesh on the back of her neck bristled as this backdrop bore down around her. They weren't skulking around in her backyard anymore, whispering against the rustle of the weeping willow. This was his turf. They were here alone and no one knew where they were.

Even she couldn't pinpoint exactly where they were.

He was close enough that she could smell him and her heart was clanging. Her entire being existed only in that slender patch of skin where his hand touched hers.

Unbidden and unwanted, a wheezy nag of a voice crawled inside her ear. *What now? You knew where this was going all along. What are you thinking?*

Shut up.

You know what they call it, the voice ragged on. *You know the wreckage that follows. There's a name for women like you.*

I don't care.

All it takes is a match. But know this, the fire takes all. Everything burns and nothing will be left. Cinders. Less than ash.

What was she supposed to do? Stop? Now, after all this time?

"Gil," she said, partly to squelch that awful voice. His grip tightened on her wrist as she spoke his name.

"Tilda," he said, and his eyes lifted to meet hers. She felt his hand slide over the small of her back and pull her in. "I think we're in trouble."

She let go and fell into him, like a daydream or a fever. All or nothing. She felt his hands on her, greedy and demanding, and she pushed into him, wanting to swallow him up. Eat him alive and in turn let herself be gorged on. Torn apart and rent asunder. Burned to nothing.

She felt her clothes pushed down and pulled off, her own hands ripping at his. A tug at the back of her head as he pulled her hair to tilt her chin up. His mouth scraped down her neck to her collarbone. To her breast, his teeth clamping onto the nipple so hard she jerked and flinched. His hand tightened on her hair to keep her still as his teeth tugged her raw.

Then a sharp prick of precise pain. Another and another, like stings, until it crossed wires and she reared back. She pushed him away but he wouldn't let go, his teeth clamped over her nipple.

"Stop. You're hurting me."

Another, sharper sting. She pushed his face from her breast and Gil stumbled back like he was drunk, his gaze walleyed and unfocused. There was blood on his lips, more of it smeared over his chin.

"Gil." She looked down, saw her breast slathered with blood. Pulsing out in a sluice from thin cuts. "What did you do?"

Staggering back, he knocked hard into the wall of aquariums. His mouth twisted up and his eyes flickered between regret and horror. "Tilda. I didn't mean to hurt you."

Her palm slapped wet as she cupped the wound. "I'm bleeding."

She moved towards him but he scrambled backwards like a magnet on the reverse pole. "Wait," he said.

"It won't stop." She watched the blood dribble through her clenched fingers. "Oh shit, Gil. It won't stop."

He came back to her, a length of cloth in his hand from God knew where, clamping it against the wound. Enough pressure to snap a rib. "It's okay. It'll stop."

"I think you nicked an artery." She clutched his wrist. "Why did you do that?"

"I didn't mean to hurt you. I thought I could keep it clenched." He hovered over her, keeping the pressure on the wound. "Bad call."

"Keep what clenched? What are you talking about?"

"You haven't figured it out yet?"

"What am I supposed to figure out?" The anger flashed up hot and quick. She slammed her palm into his sternum and turned away. "I can't figure out anything about you!"

He stayed where he was, watching her gather up the cloth to reapply the pressure over the lacerated nipple. "Do you remember the night before I died?"

She wanted to scream that she remembered everything but, recalling the last time she'd made that claim, she held her tongue.

The hum from the street below leaked into the room.

"Tell me," she said. "Tell me all of it."

15

Nocturnal me

GIL WIPED THE BACK of his hand across his blood spackled chin. "Do you remember my old hobby? The one you hated."

Tilda kept her distance. "Creeping around abandoned buildings?"

"That's how it started."

There was a name for it, Tilda recalled. Urban exploration. Infiltration. Breaking into abandoned or forbidden sites, trespassing where you weren't supposed to go. A subculture of crawling through condemned buildings, closed down properties and urban ruins. There was even a zine, published irregularly by one of the movements founders in the city. Ninjalicious? Something cute like that. The mysterious author would go off exploring these verboten spaces and take photographs and write up each adventure in his zine. Gil devoured every issue he could find.

They were both avid zine readers at the time. These crudely laid-out, hand-stapled, missives were the primary modes of communication for a dizzying array of subcultures. Where Tilda read zines about music, Gil's tastes ran a gamut of body modification to confessional sexcapades, Nordic Satan worshippers to the prison art of convicted serial killers.

He had taken to urban exploration with the same passion brought to his painting. Breaking into shuttered factories near the old stockyards or the tomb-like silos along the waterfront. Gil would come home at dawn with his clothes filthy and torn, his hands and arms scraped raw with the threat of tetanus. Exhilarated and triumphant after each dive-bomb into these forbidden zones, he'd regale her with what he'd seen. Tilda begged him to be careful but never tried to stop him. Only once did she tell him to quit these dangerous outings, and that was the night he'd stumbled upon a corpse in a vacated warehouse near the railyards. An intransigent who, as far as Gil could tell, had taken shelter in the building only to freeze to death during a frigid winter night. He'd placed an anonymous call to the police about the remains but never learned anything more about the lost soul.

She suggested he find a new hobby but Gil wouldn't listen. Said he was just getting to the good stuff now, the hidden secrets sealed up behind every 'Do Not Enter' sign. Tilda suspected that he continued his adventuring because he wanted to make her sick with worry and, in retrospect, he admitted that there was some truth to that. But it was so much more. Infiltrating verboten ground was a high that made his pulse spike like nothing before.

"It was like a drug," Gil said. "The more I indulged, the more I craved it. Until I went too far." He leaned back against the table and folded his arms. Looking up at the smoggy sky in the high windows, Gil told Tilda his story.

Two nights before the accident is when it began.

Shimmying through a gap in a boarded-up window, Gil dropped to the floor of a dryrot warehouse near the butt end of Parliament Street. One of the oldest structures he had ever broken into, some last vestige of old Corktown. Scavenging through the debris, the floorboards snapping under his feet, he picked through bottles and awls and hammers from over a century ago. Down a flight of stone steps, into the cold cellar, was where he stumbled across the blood.

At first glance it looked like oil, splashed so dark and thick over the flagstones. More of it spattered against the walls, dried to a blackened skin that flaked away into sand against his fingers. Handprints of the stuff on the cool wall and footprints tracked through the pool on the floor. Sitting smack in the center of that mass of blood was a single running shoe, the inside sole strangely free of the red stuff as if its owner had kicked it off to tramp barefoot through the gore.

A chill passed through him as he realized that the blood and the stray sneaker must have belonged to the same person. There was so much blood it was hard to conceive of it coming from one person. Throwing the beam of his flashlight over the gore, Gil could pick out older stains of blood speckled amongst the new stuff. A killing floor. Roaming the light across the bloodied handprints stirred images of some satanic cult to his mind. The stuff he'd read about, the weird rituals and blood ceremonies. The thrill of discovery vaporised and cold fear took its place, shrivelling his balls back to reality.

This is fucking freaky, he thought. Don't panic. Just the get the hell out of here.

Gil halted his story, shaking his head as if he didn't believe his own tale. Tilda didn't move, waiting for him to continue.

Gil took a breath. "When I turned for the stairs, I realized I wasn't alone. I couldn't see anyone but I could hear them. I thought maybe it was rats or something but it wasn't. The sound was weird, like a hissing noise. But more than that, I could feel them in the room with me. I'd never felt so scared in my life."

"Them?" Tilda didn't want to interrupt but couldn't help herself. "There was more than one?"

He bobbed his head. "I got a look at one of them. That's when I ran. Like I'd never run before."

"Who were they?"

"Not who. What. I got no more than a glimpse of it, Til, but it wasn't..." His voice withered and he looked away.

Tilda stifled her questions. This clearly wasn't easy for him to get out and he needed room to unpack it all. So she waited.

"I cut my hands to shit crawling back out of that window. I could hear them coming up behind me, hissing and making all kinds of awful sounds. One of them caught my boot and I panicked and kicked like a son-of-a-bitch. Left the boot behind. Do you know how hard it is to run for your life with only one boot? The car wasn't that far away. I jumped in and booked it out of there, laying on the horn the whole time."

"Hold on. When did this happen?" The question just blurted out and she scolded herself to shut up and let him speak.

"Two nights before the accident," he said. "I called you when I got home. Do you remember?"

"I do. You weren't making much sense. You just kept saying that you loved me, over and over." She bit her lip, not wanting to confess something but felt the need to. "I had no idea, Gil. I thought you were high."

"That's okay. I must have sounded like a babbling idiot."

"That's why you were in such a weird mood that day," she muttered, thinking back to the eve of the accident. He'd been so moody and erratic with her, snapping at any perceived slight, acting paranoid. "I just assumed you were coming down off a bad night. I'm sorry."

"I kept telling myself that I'd imagined it. That they were just vagrants squatting in an empty building. I should have called the cops, about the blood at least, but I didn't. I didn't do anything. If I had, maybe none of this would have happened."

"What wouldn't have happened?"

He wiped his hand across his mouth again. Looked up at her. "That was what stepped out onto the road that night. They caused the accident. They came looking for me."

She still didn't remember that part, someone running out in front of the car. Or the fact that she was driving. None of this made sense. She held up a hand to slow him down. "How did they know where to find you?"

"They were following me. Waiting for the right moment. The minute we hit Cherry, it was a done deal. They caused the car to flip and then they dragged me away."

The wail of a police siren leeched through the window, growing louder until it crested and faded.

Gil stared at the window long after the siren had dissipated. "There was five or six of them, dragging me down to the water's edge. Where it was dark. Too dark for me to see them. Small mercies. They tore into me, like I just did to you. All of them, ripping me with their teeth. I never thought anything could hurt so bad. When the pain faded I knew I was going into shock. I knew I was going to die. At that point, I didn't care anymore, if it meant the pain would stop.

"But then one of them withdrew, losing interest in me, and it crawled up the embankment. It was looking for the car. Looking for you. I panicked. I begged them not to touch you. I swore I would do anything if they left you alone. I didn't know if they even understood what I was saying."

His voice trailed off again. Tilda felt her fingernails cutting into her palms. "What happened?"

"I died," he shrugged, as if the point was obvious. "Then I came back."

She tried to let that sink in but it refused to settle anywhere. How could it? It made no sense. She reached out for his hand. "Gil, who were these people?"

"They weren't people, Tilda. They bled me dry with their teeth. They hide in the darkness. A long time ago they were people but not anymore. They're not even human."

Tilda exhaled, she had been holding her breath the whole time. Had she expected some other answer? Was she disappointed? Was there a response to this story that didn't sound absolutely fucking crazy?

"Vampires? Is that what you're trying to say?"

"I know. Insane, right? But there it is." His eyes dropped to the bloodied cloth cupped to her breast. "Has the bleeding stopped?"

"I think so." She tilted the makeshift bandage away to find the blood congealed into dark lumps. Taking in another deep breath, she tried to organize her thoughts. "So you're one of them now? That's where you've been all this time?"

"Yes. They understood what I pleaded for that night. A bargain was struck. They left you alone." He watched her eyes cast about the room, as if looking for something to latch onto and hold steady. "You're not buying anything of this, are you?"

"I'm trying to. I am. But Jesus, Gil... it sounds absolutely insane." She almost laughed. "Vampires? Sleeping in coffins and turning into bats and all that?"

"It's not like that. These things are monsters. And they hold to one sacred abiding law, which is to be unseen. They hide in the darkness. They don't mingle or associate with people in any way. They hide their tracks. That's why they came after me. I'd stumbled into their nest and gotten away. A loose end. And they would have taken you too but they needed something from me."

"What did they want?"

"Someone new. The coven is kept small, which is one of the ways they manage to stay hidden. They hadn't allowed an initiate in a long long time but they needed someone new to keep them safe. Someone who understood the outside world.

"You gotta understand, they're not human. They don't even speak English anymore. The world moves on and changes while they keep to the shadows but they need someone new from time to time to help the coven stay hidden. Someone who understands the current world. That's what they needed from me."

"They don't speak English?" she asked.

"They barely speak at all. It's hard to explain but they communicate with sounds or body language. Smells even. It's almost telepathic. It took a while to understand what they wanted from me."

It was too much to absorb. Too fast and too fucking insane. She felt her chest pounding. "What happened when you... you know, woke up?"

"You don't just wake up. You scream your way back from death. It's like being born again but you're conscious the whole time, and the birth canal is made of sharp teeth. When I stopped screaming and when the pain levelled off, they were standing over me. Watching me come through. It was terrifying. To go through that and then to open your eyes to those awful faces.

"Only one of them could still speak. Barely. He told me what they were. What I was now. That I was part of them and my place was to help them. If I refused, they would hunt down the woman in the car."

The weight of it settled like ash, covering Tilda whole. "So you agreed."

"It's a rare event when they turn someone," he went on as if he hadn't heard her. "They just kill and feed and dispose of the body. Even when they do turn someone, it rarely takes."

"Why?"

"Most people can't take it, the change. Coming back from the dead, understanding what they've become. Most people go insane, and I mean completely apeshit. They're destroyed on the spot. But the ones that make it through and join the coven? For them, the real test is still to come. The true test is to cut off all ties to humanity, and more importantly, to everyone you ever knew.

"Rule number one, their most sacred law, is to never be seen. Never expose the coven. That means you can't ever see your loved ones again. You can't go back to your folks or your kids or siblings. Your spouse. You can't even go peek in the window to see if they're okay. Because the coven will know if you do and then they'll destroy you. And then they'll kill your loved ones just to be safe."

"Stop," Tilda said. There was no oxygen left in the room. "Please."

"I wanted to come back to you so bad, Til. Even just a glimpse through a window but I couldn't risk it."

She clapped her palms over her ears. "I don't want to hear anymore."

"Do you know what it's like, living like this? Existing like a cockroach. Hiding down in the filth, scurrying from the light. What you once were keeps slipping away. You start doubting your own memories, unsure if they were ever real. It's like a dream you barely remember or a story someone once told you."

"Shut up!" Her hands became fists. "What am I supposed to do with that? Am I to blame? If I am then I'm sorry but, Jesus— just stop. Please."

"Tilda, I'm not blaming you. I brought this on myself but you need to know what happened."

"No. I don't care. Even if it is the truth." She rose, pacing back and forth. "I have to go."

He snatched her elbow. "You can't go. Not now."

"Don't touch me!" She jerked her arm free and stumbled on, knocking into a bank of filing cabinets. Unable to see a damn thing. "Where's my guitar?"

She felt her feet leave the floor and her back slam into the wall, pinned there like a butterfly to a corkboard. His face a hair from hers. "You can't just leave," he spat. "You're the only thing that kept me sane. The only part of me that didn't fade away. You can't go."

"Don't do that. Don't make me your saviour. Because I'm not." She pushed him away and he backed off. "You died and left me alone. I went to hell because of it but it was a lifetime ago. I have a husband and a child and... and a life without you. You can't just pop back from the past and lay this at my feet."

"I know this is hard. But you brought me back when you played that song. I've been good all this time, shutting you out." His fists bunched his hair and he stomped into the shadows. "But you played that song and I couldn't stay away. You can't leave now."

She still couldn't see anything in this light. Neither him nor the way out. "Where's the door?"

Silence. All she could make out in the wan light were the aquariums, bouncing back the neon splash from the window. She couldn't see or hear him anywhere. "Gil?"

A rusty squeal tore the silence and a wedge of light broke against the black as the door swung open. The guitar case lay bare in the dilating band from the hall. She ran for it, crossing over the threshold and descending the steps two at a time. A glance over her shoulder. He didn't follow her, didn't fly down the stairs to stop her. Winding round and round to the ground floor, then she looked up through the banister railing. "I'm sorry."

The same metal-on-metal squeal was the only reply, punctuated by a low thud of his door slamming home.

The alleyway was another labyrinth, cutting left and now right. The only breadcrumb trail was the noise of the street that she followed back to safety. Passing between gateposts of garbage mounds, she popped onto the red-tinged lights of Spadina Avenue. She marched south and then swung west onto Baldwin where she'd left the Nissan. She stopped when she saw the commotion up ahead.

Red and blue lights blinked against the shop windows, alternating from a police cruiser and an ambulance. A crowd lined the walk further down, fanning across the street before the Porthole club. Three uniformed officers held the gawkers back as paramedics wheeled a gurney into the back of the twinkling ambulance.

Two stragglers ambled away from the chaos, thumbing their phones as they passed Tilda on the sidewalk. Coiffed with slick hair, their mustaches waxed to fine points, they resembled some hipster version of a barbershop quartet. Tilda stopped the nearest one. "What happened?"

"Dude got stomped," the young man said.

"Is he okay?"

The other one resembled an effete lumberjack. He sneered under his waxed moustache. "Game over. That guy was dead before five-oh even got here."

The pair moved on, dropping their faces to their little handheld screens. Tilda darted for the parking garage, scampered up one level and tossed the guitar into the back of her vehicle. She roared down the ramp, fumbled her card into the automated teller. The liftgate took forever but when it finally went up, she raced south down Kensington and west onto Dundas. One eye on the rearview mirror but when no police unit appeared after her, she gunned the engine for home.

16

Fuck and run

SHE COULDN'T GO HOME. Too wired up and too close to tears, Tilda drove without destination or purpose. Sifting through the story he had told, she tried to make sense of it but there was no sense to be had and as the odometer clicked over another digit, she simply went numb. Letting her mind go blank, she drifted north then east then back west again.

The Pathfinder found its own way back to Spadina, past the El Mocambo where she had played countless times and into a parking spot on Oxford. Killing the engine, she listened to the vehicle tick as it cooled and mulled over her own capacity for delusion. Did she really think she was going home after all this? The moment she stormed out of his place, hadn't she known all along that she would come back?

Exhausted by the endless questions she let her gut lead her, retracing her steps back through the alley and up the creaking stairwell. The door to his space was unlocked and the candles fluttered as she pushed inside. No response when she called his name and as her eyes adjusted to the gloom, the space appeared deserted.

Drawing back another of the heavy drapes to let in more streetlight she was surprised to see an easel emerge from the darkness. It stood alone in a cleared stretch of floor. A table nearby was cluttered with paints and brushes, jars of solvent. The smell of the turpentine and linseed oil lit old memories.

Gil still painted.

The easel stood empty in the center of the clearing but she found stacks of paintings pushed into the corner. There were dozens of them, faced to the wall so all she saw were the backs of each stretched canvas. She hesitated, thinking it would be rude to look without asking but curiosity won out and she lifted out the nearest one.

Her windpipe constricted. It was a painting of herself. Not an exact portrait (that wasn't Gil's style), the brush strokes heavy and almost haphazard but it was clearly her. It wasn't the hair or the eyes that startled her but the tilt of the head, the slant of her shoulders. Her body language was what rang true. He had captured the way she held herself and that, more than the eerie expression of the face, prickled the tiny hair on her arm.

Setting it aside, she pulled up the next painting in the stack and then the one after that. They were all of her. Different poses, different settings or no settings at all. Some full length, some portraits, a few nudes. All different moods but the subject remained the same in every one.

A frame at the end of a stack caught her attention and she stood it on the easel to study it. Like all the others, a painting of her yet different from the rest. Where the other paintings showed a younger version of herself (what Gil would have remembered from the past) this rendering was of how she looked now. The glaring streak of white hair fell from her left temple. She touched the frame and found the oil still wet, the pigment staining her fingertip.

"That one's not very good."

His voice rumbled up behind her somewhere but she didn't startle or turn around. Had she known he was there all along? "I can't believe you painted all of these."

"Kind of stalker-ish, huh? You're still my favourite subject."

She flipped through more of the frames, stacked ten or twelve deep against the wall. "How many paintings have you done?"

"Dunno. Never counted them," he said. Then, "I'm surprised you came back."

She still hadn't turned around. "No you're not."

She felt his breath on her ear, his arms locking around her. Pulling her hard up against him, he swept her hair aside to kiss the back of her neck.

"Gil." The word no more than breath. "I don't know what to do."

"Yes you do."

Of course she knew. She just needed to vent the thought, a stray sense of propriety that needed to be aired. He was hard up against her and she pushed back into him. She felt his hand cup her breast. "Does it still hurt?"

"A little." She turned about and kissed his mouth, then pulled back. "You can't bite me anymore. Can you do that?"

"Yes."

Folding her hand in his, he led her past the stacks to a clearing near the back. A bed hidden away, crowded with piles of books. He knocked the books away and threw back the bedcover. Turning back to her, he smiled and took two steps backwards. "Take off your clothes. I want to see you."

"Bring a candle," she said. "I can't see anything back here."

He came back with two, setting them on a high shelf. Reclaiming the space he'd vacated, he kept a good three paces between them. His eyes were hungry as they took her in.

Tilda hesitated, frozen by a sudden shudder of self-consciousness. "I'm not twenty-four anymore, Gil. You might want to lower your expectations."

"Take them off."

She couldn't help the smirk on her lips as she pulled the shirt over her head. Hooking her thumbs into the waistband of the skirt, she shimmied her hips and let it all drop to the floor and stood naked before him.

What she heard was a low growl as his gaze scrolled down to her toes and slowly back up to her eyes. Yanking his shirt over his head, he undressed quickly. He looked the same as ever, wiry muscles stretched over his lanky frame. Another twinge of doubt nagged her looking at that unchanged body but it dissipated the moment she felt his chest flatten against her, his skin cool on her warm flesh.

They fell onto the bed and Gil stayed true to his promise not to bite but Tilda found she couldn't do the same.

She bit into him between kisses, sinking her teeth into his bottom lip and curve of his shoulder, his ribs. She wanted to eat him as much as fuck him. She tore into him and he pushed her down, pinning her arms above her head and tasted every inch of her. She did things she hadn't done in a long time. She let him have her in ways she'd thought were long over with and their skin smacked together in the sweat.

The candle glowed on the shelf, its taper blurring in her eyes afterwards. Nestled up against him, their skin slicked together felt right. A puzzle piece that had been missing for so long. He pincered the lobe of her ear in his eyeteeth and whispered that he loved her.

Was there any other response to that? She pulled his arm tighter around her and tilted her head up to touch his lips. Her words barely a whisper. "I love you too."

He felt Tilda nestle against him even closer and Gil smiled until he felt her tears fall hot onto his arm tucked under her neck.

17

Hardcore UFOs

MOLLY LOOKED DOWN AT THE PLATTER of pancakes her mother set onto the table. "What's this?"

"Pancakes," Tilda said.

"I can see that," Molly groaned. "What's the occasion? Did you think it was Sunday?"

Tilda slid bowls of sliced bananas and fresh blueberries next to the platter. "I just thought a big breakfast would be a nice break from the usual."

"Looks good to me." Shane said as he took his chair, interceding between mother and daughter as he so often did. "Let's eat."

Tilda slugged down another belt of coffee and turned back to the last two flapjacks in the frypan. Her hands were shaking from being so tired and she tried to hide it from the two at the table. Mornings were tough under the best of circumstances, mornings with only a few hours sleep were punishing. Tilda had spilled and splattered the kitchen in her clumsy stupor as if drunk. She didn't know what possessed her to make an elaborate breakfast this morning.

That was a lie.

"Pancakes always come with bad news," Molly said drolly. "What is it this time?"

"If you don't want it, then don't eat it. I guess I shouldn't have bothered." Tilda winced at how quickly the retort came. She sounded so much like her own mother in that moment. Molly, who delighted in popping the balloon out of any pretence in the room, had simply called her out. The nauseating guilt that was churning in her belly had spurred Tilda to make pancakes for her family. Like that would excuse what she had done and make everything okay. It was pathetic.

Shane nodded to her chair. "Sit down. Eat."

"Soon as these last ones are finished."

"Let me get it. You look exhausted" Shane guided her to a chair, setting her mug before her. He darted to the stove and flipped the last two flapjacks in the pan. "I didn't even hear you come home last night. Did you get in late?"

"Yeah. After midnight."

Molly looked up from her plate. "It was way later than that."

Tilda stiffened as Shane came back to the table and flipped the last cakes onto the platter. He looked at Molly. "What do you mean, honey?"

"It was after three in the morning when I turned out the light. You weren't home yet."

Tilda's knuckles clenched white over her fork. "Why were you up so late?"

Shane's gaze ping-ponged from Molly to Tilda. "You were out till three? Geez."

"I don't remember what time it was. I just went straight to bed."

"Glory days," Molly sneered.

"No wonder you're zonked," Shane said. "You should have slept in this morning. I coulda made breakfast."

Tilda's stomach soured, killing her appetite. Why was he being so nice? It was unbearable. She took her plate to the counter. "I'm okay. You two eat up before you're late."

Molly poked at her breakfast. "This one's burned."

"Maybe it's time you started helping with breakfast." He pointed his fork in his daughter's direction. "You and I could take turns on the morning shift. Give your mom a break."

Molly laughed out loud. "Yeah right."

Tilda turned her back to them, afraid she was going to scream. Why was he torturing her like this? Did he suspect anything? She blocked out their banter and rushed to finish up. She set their packed lunches onto the counter, refilled her mug and hurried to the stairs. "I need to hop in the shower. Leave the dishes."

Reeling up the steps, she heard Shane cajoling their daughter into clearing the table. Then the clatter and bustle of getting them out the door. A workday Laurel & Hardy routine. Standing under the spray of hot water, she didn't relax until she heard the front door bang shut behind them.

SHE looked like she'd been beaten. Purpled bruises on her arms and red scrapes along her ribs. Tilda stood before the foggy mirror, scrutinizing her naked reflection. She was still raw from last night and it showed on her flesh. Turning to one side revealed more marks on her back and buttocks. Worst of all was the angry looking wound on her breast where Gil had bitten her. A dark scab over her nipple, the surrounding breast mottled purple. How was she to explain this? Could she keep covered long enough to heal? How long would that take?

Her stomach knotted up thinking back to last night, a seasick push-and-pull between exhilaration and shame. The giddy rush she had felt being with him churned up alongside the sickening regret over what she had done. All of it punctuated harder by Shane being so kind to her this morning. Did he know? Did he possibly suspect anything?

No. Shane wasn't one to hide his mood or mask any bitter feelings. He didn't store away his hurts to use as ammunition later. He gave immediate vent to whatever he was feeling no matter what the circumstances. If he suspected anything, he simply would have said so.

So what? Tilda challenged the naked woman in the mirror. Does that make it okay? Does that mean you got away with it?

It can't happen again, she vowed. Simple as that. Yes, the circumstances were weird as weird can get but that was no excuse. She'd had her fun and scratched that itch but it could not continue any further. Not like this. She and Gil would have to set some hard and fast boundaries because the lines were too easily blurred. They could still be close. Still see one another but they could not be lovers. She simply couldn't do that to Shane. Or Molly.

Gil would not be happy about it but he'd simply have to deal with it. It was this or it was nothing. Take your pick.

She laughed at the stern crinkle in her eyes. It was so easy to talk tough when she was alone, so determined while scripting the imagined confrontation. The real test would be saying this to his face and she could already feel herself bending.

"What am I gonna do?"

The woman in the mirror had no answer. With her bruised and scraped flesh, she looked like a battered woman.

She touched the tender flesh of her breast, brushing the puncture marks that had scabbed over with black blood. The tale Gil had told her resurfaced along with the memory of his teeth biting into her.

What if it was infected?

What would it do to her?

She fled the mirror and hurried to get dressed. She was already late for work.

SHE shouldn't have bothered. Typing the term 'vampire' into a search engine produced an onslaught of results that were overwhelming in number yet completely and utterly useless. The volume and variety of information dedicated solely to the subject of the undead proved Gil's claim to be contradictory. He said that they stay hidden from the world. According to Google, they were absolutely everywhere. A spook from a child's tale had become a cultural joke.

The idea, once uttered aloud, was hard to shake, lodging in her brain like a dirty thought that wouldn't go away. It was ridiculous, preposterous and delusional. Maybe that's why it stuck so fast and refused to be scrubbed away by the reassuring warmth of daylight. Its very absurdity made it real. And then there was Gil himself. Aside from being a little gaunt, he hadn't aged at all since the day he died. How to explain that?

There was nothing to be learned from the search results. Nothing useful anyway. She ticked off a few points she knew about the subject; avoiding sunlight, sleeping in coffins, turning into bats. Hokum. She killed the search and turned away from the computer. The banking needed to be done and a fresh stack of bills needed sorting before her eleven-thirty appointment arrived. Yet no matter how hard she threw herself into the task, that one little word kept nibbling the edges of her consciousness, clawing its way back to the center.

Sarah blew into the clinic an hour later and a steady rotation of clients kept everyone busy until the late afternoon. Sarah stole Tilda away to get something cold at a nearby cafe.

"How's your mom?" Tilda asked once they settled onto a picnic table that overlooked the street.

"Getting worse." Sarah stirred the straw in her glass. "It's hard watching her drift away like this."

"I can't imagine how hard that must be."

"Sometimes I wonder if it wouldn't be easier if she had a stroke and passed quickly, rather than this slow fade."

"That's an awful dilemma to face."

Sarah's eyes glassed over, faraway and lost. "I'm tired of thinking about it. About death, what comes after."

Tilda patted her friend's hand but said nothing. Sarah looked at her. "Do you ever wonder about it? About what happens after death?"

Despite a Catholic upbringing, none of the spookshow stuff ever clung to Tilda. She understood the need to believe in an afterlife but had always considered it a pleasant fantasy. Recent events had spun that certainty on its head. "I don't know what I believe anymore. I guess anything's possible. What about you?"

"I want to believe in it," Sarah said. "I honestly do. If only for her sake."

They settled into silence and watched the seagulls float over the meatpacking yard. Sarah squinted across the table, as if trying to solve a riddle. "Did you cut your hair?"

"No. Why?"

"You look different. Kind of radiant actually but I can't figure it out. Did you colour your hair?"

Tilda took hold of her white streak of hair and flapped it. "I think I would have covered this up if I had."

"Then I give up. What is it?"

Tilda shrugged. Her clothes were old, her hair unchanged and, if anything, needed washing. There was nothing new. "Maybe you finally need glasses, girl."

Unwilling to give up, Sarah tilted her head. "Did you get lucky last night?"

Tilda felt her cheeks burn hot but tried to mask it under a laugh. "You're hilarious. I played a show last night."

"I thought you quit."

"I did," Tilda said. "This was just spur of the moment."

"Maybe that's your secret; playing gigs. You shoulda told me. I would have gone."

Tilda reached for her drink but the glass was empty. Her insides steamed at having to keep it all bottled up. She wanted to blurt it all out and glush over every detail. To admit to Sarah that her guess was correct and that she had gotten lucky last night. More than that, she needed to talk through the predicament she was in, this moral and ethical corner she had painted herself into. About Gil and about Shane. It was too much to hold inside, to keep to herself.

Tilda looked at her friend across the table. Maybe Sarah would understand.

No. There was simply no sane way to explain it. Or, she rued, she was just too ashamed to try. Would her friend pat her hand in empathy or would Sarah recoil at her actions and wag an accusatory finger in her direction?

They went inside to settle up and when Tilda reached for her bag, Sarah insisted she put it away. Playing hooky had been her idea. The television over the bar was blaring the midday news. Sarah nudged Tilda's ribs and nodded at the screen. "Did you hear about this?"

The news footage showed a police cruiser on a narrow street, a few onlookers hovering beyond the yellow caution tape. A uniformed officer standing before a broken storefront window. It took a moment before Tilda recognized the scene as the Porthole on Baldwin.

The flat voice of the newscaster reported that an assault in Kensington Market had been upgraded to a murder investigation. The victim, who had been thrown through a window during the assault, later died in hospital. Police were continuing their investigation, urging anyone with information to come forward.

"Holy moly," Sarah sputtered. "The Porthole? How many times have we played there?"

Cold ice sluiced down Tilda's spine. All she could muster was a hushed blasphemy.

"That's just effed-up." Sarah shook her head and turned for the door. "The Port isn't like that. Dope-smokers and dealers, yeah. But violent dudes? What's the world coming to?"

Tilda stammered, as if her friend had suddenly twigged to the fact that she was involved. She set her jaw and outright lied that she had no idea what the world was coming to.

18

Little trouble girl

SHE COULDN'T BELIEVE THE MAN was dead.

It didn't seem real or even possible. It was all she could think about on the walk home, trudging through a humid soup as the heat of the day rippled up from the sidewalks. The park offered little relief and when she emerged from the footpath onto Dundas, her shirt was sweat-plastered to her back.

The sound of shattering glass kept exploding in her mind, the sight of the man hurtling through the window. He didn't seem badly injured at the time. How could he have died? Then she remembered Gil stomping the man's neck. There was nothing accidental about that. The thought of it, mixed with the sticky humidity, made her feel sick.

Molly was in the kitchen when she arrived home, her friend Zoe beside her. The two of them were eating popsicles, dripping sticky juice all over the floor.

"Hi Mrs. P" Zoe said, a wide toothy smile on her face. Unlike Molly, Zoe was always cheerful and chatty with adults. She was so much the opposite of her sullen daughter that Tilda wondered how the two of them got along so well.

"Hi Zoe." Tilda beamed, genuinely pleased to see the girl. "How have you been?"

"Scorched." The girl raised the popsicle in her hand. "Sorry about the mess. We'll clean it up."

"Why don't you girls set up the sprinkler in the backyard and cool off."

Molly rolled her eyes. "We're not six, mom."

"Ah, come on." Zoe nudged Molly's ribs. "It'd be fun."

"Don't encourage her," Molly spat back.

Tilda ducked out of the conversation, making for the stairs. "Do what you want. I'm going to rinse off."

Standing under the shower, Tilda let the jets punish her shoulders. A bone-deep exhaustion set in and she wanted nothing more than to flop onto her bed and just lie still. To cool her brain from a hot and endless loop of questions and worries. The window was notched open at the top to vent the steam and she watched a seagull float by in a cloudless patch of blue sky. The sun would set in a few hours. When it was dark, Gil would come back.

She turned the water off, flung back the shower curtain and startled. Shane stood at the toilet. "Hey sweetie."

"What are you doing?" She hid behind the curtain.

"Sorry. My teeth were floating. Couldn't wait."

She stretched to get the towel without stepping out from the curtain. "You couldn't use the downstairs bathroom?"

"The girls are using it. God knows what they're doing." Seeing her groping, he scooped the towel up and passed it to her. "Here."

She snatched it up and flung the curtain closed as she dried off. Shane watched her blurry figure through the plastic screen, surprised at the sudden modesty. Tilda would often dry off by parading around naked after her shower and Shane rarely missed an opportunity to see her in the raw. It didn't matter that they'd been married for fourteen years and he had seen her body a million times over, it still entranced him. He felt robbed when Tilda stepped out of the shower with a towel cinched under her arms and another coiled up over her wet hair.

She fanned the fog from the mirror. "Why are you home so early?"

"Knocked off early." A sly grin creased his mouth. "Hoping to catch you in the altogether."

"Too late, mister."

His hand slid round her waist. "Least you can do is flash me. It'd be like, the highlight of my day."

"You're sweet but I'm bushed. Can you start dinner tonight? I just need to lie down for a while." He didn't answer. She turned. "Ten minutes. That's all I need."

Shane's eyes bored into the back of her bare shoulder. "Where'd this nasty bruise come from? Looks painful."

"What? Oh it's nothing."

He touched her arm. "There's another one here. What happened?"

Her cheeks flushed hot. "Nothing. I took a spill last night. Tripped over some cable."

He blanched. "How high was the stage? Look, there's one on your leg too. Jesus, you look like you got beat up."

"It looks worse than it is. Really." She brushed her hair vigorously, hoping to shoo him from the narrow bathroom. Watching him in the mirror, she saw his eyes darken with something she could only guess was doubt. Suspicion maybe. It hurt to see it, whatever it was.

The ring of the doorbell broke the spell. Shane stepped out into the hallway. "What now?"

"Probably one of Molly's friends." She hoped he would go see, so she could dress in private.

He hollered down the railing. "Who is it, Molly?"

Tilda stopped brushing, listening for the reply.

Molly's voice echoed up the stairs. "It's the police. They want to talk to mom."

THERE were two of them, plainclothes detectives with neutral faces and chill manners. Detective Rowe was puffy-faced with sweat beading his upper lip. Invited to have a seat at the kitchen table, he thanked Shane and then asked if he could trouble them for a glass of water. Detective Crippen declined a seat and hung back. He was lanky and tall, leaning back against the countertop with a bored air like he had someplace better to be.

Tilda wanted to bolt for the door but she took a seat and forced a smile like she couldn't be happier than to chat with two policemen.

Shane placed a glass of ice water before Detective Rowe. "What's this about?"

"Thank you," Rowe said. "There was an incident on Baldwin Street last night. We just have a few questions that Mrs. Parrish might help us with."

"What kind of incident?"

Rowe wiped his lip. "A bar fight. Turned ugly and one poor man died."

"Died?" Shane shot a look at Tilda, then back to the policemen. "Why do you want to talk to Tilda about that?"

"Sir?" Detective Crippen's voice boomed off the tile, impatient and to the point. "Could you let your wife answer the questions."

Tilda bristled at his tone. "I'm sorry. Was there a question?"

Rowe smiled at her. "Did you see anything that night? The fight or anything afterward?"

"No."

"You were at the Porthole Club that night?" Crippen cut in. "You played a show, yes?"

"Yes. But I didn't see any fight. Or see anyone die, thank God."

"Was it a shooting?" Shane's face lost colour. "How did it happen?"

"The victim was thrown through a plate glass window." Rowe shook his head in mournful dismay. "Piece of glass severed an artery in his spine. He bled out onto the sidewalk."

Tilda felt the tall detective's eyes fix on her, watching for a reaction. He folded his hands. "What time did you play?"

"About ten. I was supposed to play later but the first band bailed. So I opened."

"What time did you leave?"

"I didn't notice the time. An hour after that. Maybe a little longer."

"So eleven, eleven-thirty." Rowe unfolded a notebook and consulted a page. "But you spoke with the assailant?"

"Excuse me?"

"You were seen talking to the assailant."

"I was? Good God. I had no idea."

Crippen almost sneered. "You don't remember talking to him?"

"I talked to a lot of people that night. But I didn't see the fight so I don't know who you're talking about."

"Well who is this guy?" Shane blurted out.

"We don't know. That's why we're here."

Shane darted his eyes from one detective to the other. "Then how do you know Tilda talked to the guy?"

Rowe dipped his shoulders. "Some of the people there said you spoke to him, Mrs. Parish. Do you remember everyone you talked to that night?"

"Most," she said. Then her eyes narrowed. "What did he look like?"

"White male," Crippen said, without consulting any notes. "Six feet, dark hair. Twenty to thirty years of age."

"That could have been anyone," she said. "Anything more specific?"

"Not at this time. The people we spoke to all gave contrary accounts of what he looked like. Some said he was ugly or deformed, others said he was attractive."

"Were they talking about the same person?" Tilda looked at one officer, then the other. "If that's the description, then I may well have talked to the guy. Or assailant, whatever."

Detective Rowe gave an apologetic shrug. "It happens. People remember what they want to remember."

"Of the men you spoke to," Crippen asked, "did any of them seem aggressive or angry? Anyone spoiling for a fight?"

"No."

The tall detective's face soured, as if personally insulted by her answer. Tilda guessed that Crippen was the tough cop to Rowe's friendly one. It was easy to see how that routine would work. The harsh grimace of disappointment in Crippen's eyes made Tilda want to sit up and tell him anything he wanted to hear. She didn't know why, she just did.

Be careful, she thought. *Take it slow, don't blurt anything out.*

"So you didn't see the fight, is that right?" Crippen laced his tone with a dose of scepticism. "Didn't see or hear anything?"

"I packed up my gear and went out to the car." Panic was swelling up inside. She pushed it back down, fighting to keep her own tone even. "I must have missed it."

Detective Rowe gave her a tired smile, seemingly satisfied with her answer. Crippen was like a dog with a bone. "And then what? You drove straight home?"

"Yes. Well, no..." She scrambled, not anticipating this.

Shane leaned forward. "You didn't get home till late."

She fired a lethal look at him. Shane stammered, confused at her frostiness.

"Where did you go?" Rowe asked. Crippen leaned in, straining his ear in her direction.

The eyes of the three men fixed Tilda to the spot. Despite having just showered, a bead of sweat trickled its way down the small of her back. "I went for a drive. Down to the lake."

"A drive?" Crippen leered, as if he'd found the thin edge of the wedge.

"It was hot. And the market stank. You know how it gets in the summer. I wanted to cool off."

"Where along the lake did you go?"

"Ireland Park. Bottom of Bathurst. You know the one?"

Detective Crippen looked ready to pounce, call bullshit on the whole thing but his partner stood, squeaking his chair back.

"Okay. I think that's all for now," Rowe said. He produced a card and placed it on the table. "Thanks for your time. If you think of anything, anything at all, give us a call."

The officers went out the front door, Crippen stealing one last look back at Tilda before climbing into an unmarked Crown Vic.

THE hollering started as soon as the officers were out the door. The lies followed.

Shane stood in the kitchen, eyes goggled wide. "What the hell is going on?"

"Someone got hurt." Tilda lingered at the front door, watching the police unit drive away. She was in no hurry to face what was coming.

"Hurt? Some guy gets killed where you're at and you don't think to mention it? What the hell?"

"Stop yelling." She turned and scanned the living room, the hallway. Molly and her friend must have fled upstairs. "I didn't know about it."

His voice grew louder. "Look at you. You don't even care—"

"Lower your voice, damn it." She turned and fled into the kitchen. "The whole neighbourhood will hear."

"That you're worried about? Tilda, we just had two cops here. Questioning you. And that one cop didn't believe a word you said. How can you brush that off so easily?"

She dropped a pot into the sink and ran water into it. "What do you want me to do, cry?"

"Yes! Some reaction," he spat. "Jesus. You have a fit over the stupidest things, like an overdue bill or the lawn needing mowing. But this, being grilled by cops over someone's death you shrug off like it's nothing?"

"Don't get so dramatic, Shane." She pulled up the notched cutting board, the big knife. She wanted something to keep her hands busy, keep her back to him. "You make it sound like I had something to do with it."

Shane dropped the volume, exasperation supplanting anger. "Who are you? And what have you done with my wife?"

She ignored the sarcasm, staring into the contents of the refrigerator but seeing nothing. The neverending question of what to fix for dinner. She felt his grip on her elbow.

"What happened last night?"

She shook his hand off. "I told you."

"Some guy gets killed where you had a gig. You show up full of bruises like you got beat up? Tilda, tell me what happened."

"I did!" She hurled the celery onto the counter. A cup rattled. "What do you want? Some drama? A good story?"

"I want you to be honest with me."

"You think I'm lying to you? You think I'm just, what, making all of this up?"

His hands went up, palms out as if showing that he was out of ammo. "I didn't say lying. But you're holding back. So take a breath and tell me what happened."

Her cheeks puffed in a long sigh and folded her arms. Stalemated silence crept across the kitchen floor. She turned away, gathering up the cutting board. "I told you what happened. Believe me or don't. Your choice."

"Answer me!" His voice boomed off the tiles.

Tilda dropped the big knife, letting it clatter into the sink, and then marched out of the room.

His stomped after her. "Where are you going?"

"Fix your own damn dinner." She slipped on her shoes and pushed through the screen door to the porch.

Molly and Zoe straightened up, perched on the wicker lounger. Zoe's eyes immediately dropped to her lap but Molly gaped at her mother with big, almost cartoonish eyes. No pretence that she hadn't heard every word.

Tilda felt her anger wither away against the sheer power of her daughter's gaze. "I'm going for a walk," she announced and hurried down the porch steps to the street.

19

Paper wings

WHERE ELSE WAS SHE GOING TO GO? Dusk was just settling in but even with the waning light she had a hard time retracing her steps back to Gil's building. Entering the maze of alleyways was like stepping into some otherworldly barrio, sidestepping the broken glass and limp condoms. She held her breath against the stench of maggoty garbage and piss marinated in stale summer heat.

She pounded his door. No answer, no sound of anyone rumbling around inside. She yanked the handle but the door was bolted. She had a stupid thought to leave a note on his door like she used to do. Back when Gil was... well, still Gil, she would leave nasty notes on his door when he wasn't home. *I dropped by to fuck your brains out*, she'd scribble, *but you weren't home so I humped your neighbour. We are so over!* She'd tape these little valentines to his door for his neighbours to titter over. Gil never saw the humour in it.

If she had a pen, she could draft another love note.

Go back to being dead. You're messing up my life.

Love, Tilda.

How cruel that would be. But there was something about his locked door that irked her to irrational fury. How like him to be unavailable when she needed him.

She took a step back and mulled her options; wait here in the hall or turn around and go home. Both lacked appeal. Back when they were still together, Gil used to keep a spare key hidden on the top of the door frame. Would he still? The lintel of the door was too tall to reach. Searching the hallway, she found an old paint can and used it as a step. Fingers trailing through the dust over the lintel and there it was. A key. Pushing the can aside, she unlatched the lock and went uninvited into Gil's flat.

Dark as all get out. She called his name, tossing it into the void but nothing sounded back. Knees knocking into furniture, she groped her way to the window and drew back the heavy curtain. Ambient light from the dusky sky allowed her to see the logistics of the space, crazy as it was. The furniture and shelves and crates made little sense in terms of living space, no areas marked out as rooms. Then again, Tilda supposed, he doesn't actually '*live*' here, does he? Her eyes picked out a few candles on a table, along with a box of matches.

The quivering light from the tallow multiplied against the bank of dried up aquariums, the small flame reflected in the dirty glass. Her eyes fell to an old stereo stacked up on metal shelves. Tall speaker cabinets flanked both sides and a dusty armchair was set before it, as if Gil had recreated that old JVC ad of a listener being blasted by sound. She knew there was no electricity but hit the power button anyway. A dead click. Racked above the sound system were shelves of vinyl and she picked through the record sleeves. Floyd, The Replacements, Violent Femmes, Sleater Kinney. Stuff they used to listen to, as if Gil had recreated their old record collection. One sleeve, caught her eye and she pulled it out and studied its cover. The Gorgons first record, *Bombs Away*. The photo on the back cover showed a much younger Tilda, flanked by the band, each face a study of posed defiance or indifference. How old was she in this picture, twenty-six? Just kids, posturing for the camera with childish displays of world-weary cynicism. How silly it seemed now. Why were they so eager to grow up back then? Why was that bored indifference deemed so cool, as if they'd seen it all when they'd barely tasted anything of life? It seemed like such a waste of time now.

She pushed the record back into the stack and poked through more of the shelves. Tucked behind a chainsaw was a familiar sight; the old homemade flamethrower. They had torched a few of Gil's paintings that last night they were together. Remembering that, she threaded her way through the clutter to the back where the paintings were propped against the wall. Was it too vain to look at these? She didn't care if it was and leafed through Gil's renderings of her. Some were meticulous in their execution, others slapdash and hurried, as if Gil had attacked the canvass in anger. The expressions varied too. In some, Tilda appeared demure or serene but in others she sneered or glared at the viewer as if in accusation of some crime.

At the back of the stacked frames she uncovered one that didn't show her at all. She plucked it out and tilted it towards the candlelight. It was ghastly. Three figures against a backdrop of darkness, their blasted-looking faces barely human. Pale as fish bellies, the faces hung like brittle paper stretched taught over their skulls. The eyes were black hollows, pinpricked with a dark red glow. Their mouths hung open as if aping Munch's famous screaming figure, the collected maws no more than dark wounds in their faces, punctured by sharp yellow teeth. Terrifying and lurid, almost obscene in the revulsion it stirred in Tilda. She wanted to hurl the picture away but couldn't tear her eyes from it.

These obscene wraiths were not some fantasy from Gil's imagination. They could only be one thing and a shudder pulsed through her at what these monsters were.

"Don't look at that."

Gil hovered at the edge of the candlelight. He took the frame from her hand. "Why are you looking at that?"

"Is it them?" Her eyes ping-ponged between him and the painting. "The coven?"

"I forgot about this. I should have burned it."

"They're repulsive."

"They're not human."

She watched him slip the picture into the end of the stacked frames. "But they used to be?"

His head bobbed gently. "A long time ago. The longer you exist as one of them, the more you change, becoming less and less human."

"But you don't look like that."

"I'm a baby compared to them," he said. "The old ones go back two, three hundred years. Colonial era. You survive long enough, this is what you become."

"How can you even look at them?"

"You learn to deal. Your intolerance for things diminishes after you've died." His shoulders popped in a shrug. "You know that thing about vamps and mirrors? It's kinda true. They hate them."

Her eyebrow arched in disbelief. "They don't cast a reflection? Come on."

"Of course they cast a reflection. But they avoid mirrors at all costs because they can't stand seeing what they've become. The price they've paid for cheating death. Kinda like what's-his-name in that Oscar Wilde story, with the portrait. His sins and decay only showed on his painting, not the man. You want to scare the shit out of a vamp? Hold a mirror up to one."

He laughed but Tilda made no response, no noise at all. "Til, you all right?"

"No. I'm not."

"What is it?"

"I need some air." She straightened her back. "Let's go for a walk."

THEY meandered out of the alley and onto the side streets, stepping around the pools of light cast from the streetlamps. She told him about the police coming to her house, about how the man he tossed through the window had died later in hospital.

"I had no idea," he said. "That guy was an asshole but I didn't mean for him to die. I'm sorry you got grilled by the cops. Did they believe what you told them?"

"One did, one didn't." She folded a hand over her belly but it did nothing to quash the sick churning within. "I still can't believe that poor man died."

He didn't respond. Hands in his pockets, as if they were discussing the weather. Didn't he care or was he just letting her get it all out? Tilda couldn't tell and her brain felt too fried to sort it out. There was more she needed to get out. How conflicted she felt about him, about being with him the night before. As wonderful as it had felt and as hungry as she was for more, she couldn't stomach the queasy residue it left at betraying her husband. How seasick this whole thing made her and how she couldn't go through with it anymore.

That was the verse she had scripted on the way to his place. She had it all drafted in her mind and rehearsed. A firm resolve to lay down the law and do the right thing, no matter how much it hurt. But scripts are flimsy things, as brittle as the resolve that conjured them, and created solely to be broken, adapted, shredded. Walking next to Gil, close enough to touch him, that carefully plotted script had shredded long before they had even left his building. Small bargains were scratched up. One more block, and then she would lay down the law. Just around this corner. Just past these pedestrians.

They sauntered out of the market, a slow shuffle past College Street and north into the outer fringe of the Annex and still her declaration remained stifled in her throat. Jesus Christ, she thought. It's now or never. "Gil, we need to talk."

"Check it out," he said, turning bright eyes on her. Whether he hadn't heard or simply ignored her, she couldn't tell. He wagged his chin at the buildings lined up on their west flank. "Do you remember this street?"

The street looked unremarkable. A mix of Victorians and four-squares, buttressed with three story walk-ups. An auto garage that had been there since forever. Tilda shook her head. "What about it?"

Pointing out a grey brick building two doors up, he said "Sicky Vikki's apartment. Our dream place."

A head-smack of recognition. Sicky Vikki was an adorably deranged friend of theirs famous for hair-brained schemes and fevered art projects. She changed careers the way other people changed underwear, flirting from music promotion to gallery owner to set design, often leaving a trail of wreckage and burned bridges in her wake. Sweet and generous to a fault, Vikki's true vocation was narrowly escaping disasters that would have ruined saner people.

Vikki also had a magic touch when it came to finding gem apartments, always snatching up these lofty spaces with tons of room for next to nothing. At a time when everyone they knew lived in overpriced dumps, Vikki was sniffing out charming and spacious finds that left all of them green-eyed. With this building, Vikki had outdone herself, landing the entire top floor of an old tenement for peanuts. Her decorating style ran to the insane, somewhere between Dali and Japanese kitch, which appealed to both Tilda and Gil. A step outside the north window, the adjacent flat roof had been transformed into a massive patio.

Best of all, Vikki was moving out. After tracking down another sweet deal down on Queen, she had offered the place to them. In their two years together, Tilda and Gil had never shared a place and Vikki knew they were holding out for just the right space. "Ta-da," she had told them, waving her hand over the apartment. She was moving out in two months. If they wanted it, they could move in first of October.

They were over the moon, already making plans and figuring out how they would use all that space. There was enough square footage for Tilda to have a huge rehearsal space and for Gil to turn another room into a studio. The accident of course had deep-sixed all those plans.

Standing on the sidewalk, Gil looked up at the third floor windows. All dark. "Whatever happened to Vikki?"

"She had this massive breakdown," Tilda said. "Couple years after you died. She just melted down and her parents came and got her. I think she was hospitalized at one point."

Gil whistled. "Is she still at her parent's?"

"Oh no. She recovered, moved out west. Last I heard, she was a realtor. Married, three kids."

"I wonder what kind of palace she's living in now."

"I'm sure it's fabulous." Tilda studied the building before them, trying to gather her thoughts and screw up some courage. She needed to level with Gil but kept letting the opportunities to do so slip away. Do it now, she scolded. Now or forever.

"Let's go have a look," he said, striding towards the building.

"What? We can't just walk in."

"The place is empty." He reached back for her hand and guided her to a side entrance. The door was locked. He slammed his shoulder into it and the bolt splintered away.

Three flights up, the apartment was stuffy and smelled stale. Tilda found a lightswitch while Gil opened the windows to air the place out. Their footsteps echoed off the bare walls as they toured each empty room. No furniture or debris, just a little dirt swept into tidy piles in the center of each room, waiting for a dustpan.

"This was supposed to be our first place together," he said.

Tilda wandered into the kitchen. The stove had been removed, leaving an outline of clean paint against a dirty wall like a ghost image. It made the kitchen feel like a tomb.

Gil came up behind her, slipping his hand around her waist. "Do you think we would've been happy here?"

"I don't know." She slipped out of his grip and crossed to the window. "We'll never know."

"I think we would've been." He leaned back against the wall and slid down to the checkerboard patterned floor. "We had so many plans for this place. Rooms for both of us to work in, that huge rooftop for a deck. It's a shame really."

"That's life." Tilda looked down at the street below.

"That's death," he countered. He folded his hands in his lap and looked up at her back. "Do you think we'd still be together? If the accident hadn't happened?"

She shrugged without turning around.

"Come on, we were meant to be together."

"I can't answer questions like that, Gil. I hate 'what if' questions."

His eyes narrowed to slits. "You okay?"

Tilda nodded. A dog was barking somewhere below on the street.

Gil snapped his fingers. "Didn't we leave a mark here? We carved our initials into a door frame or something. To mark it as ours. Do you remember?"

"No."

He shot up to his feet. "I wonder if it's still here. Let's find it."

"I don't want to," she said.

"Why not?"

"Because. I don't want to talk about the past anymore. Or what might have been. Things have changed but you don't seem to realize it. You live in the past."

That blew the wind from his sails. "It's all I got, Til."

Silence crept in. Then the dog outside started up again. Tilda turned halfway. "We can't do this anymore."

"Do what?"

"This. Us," she finally blurted. "I just can't do it, Gil. The guilt is too much. And it's not fair to Shane."

She watched him lean his head back against the wall and close his eyes. She didn't know how he'd react but this wasn't helping. She should have known he wouldn't react at all and leave her guessing.

When his eyes opened, he said "Don't do this, Tilda."

"I'm sorry. But it's not right and it's eating away at me." She groped for something to ease the blow, grasping the first thing that came to mind and immediately regretted it. "We can still talk and spend time together. We just can't, you know, be lovers."

Gil's laughter boomed through the empty kitchen, loud and cruel. "What, we can still be friends? Gimme a fucking break."

"Don't get nasty."

"You're breaking up with me?" he guffawed. "Now? After twenty years?"

"Oh, don't be so bloody stupid."

He was suddenly on his feet, inches from her. "You can't do that. I still love you. That's never changed. And I know you love me too."

She seethed. He could be so obtuse. "What am I supposed to do? I'm married. I have a daughter. A family!"

"I know, I know," he rumbled. "And I'm sorry about your husband but I loved you first. You were mine before he came along. It's not like we broke up."

"No. You died. And I was destroyed."

"And I've spent all this time staying away. But I can't anymore." He gripped her arms and bent low to search out her eyes. "Don't turn me away now. Not after I found you again."

She pushed at his hands but had no strength to get free. She hated that weakness, hated the tears welling up unwanted in her eyes and her frail whisper for him to stop. He pulled her into him. How was she supposed to fight this? "I don't know what to do anymore. What's the right answer here?"

He whispered back, telling her things that lovers always say. That they would figure it out, find a way. How all that mattered was that they were together. The stuff that young people say, when they're young and stupid as bricks and are convinced that they're the only ones who have ever felt this way. It was past it's sell-by date and they both knew it but he kept breathing it into her ear and she kept listening to it. Believing it.

Who was the bigger fool?

Tilda shivered, her arms quivering around his waist. She assumed it was the last of the sobs shuddering out of her system but it wasn't. Her flesh goosed, prickled cold. The temperature was dropping fast.

"Shit." He pulled away.

"What's wrong?"

"They're here."

"Who?" Her first thought was the police.

Gil crossed to the window and cocked his head to listen. He sniffed the air. The fear in his eyes was something she hadn't seen before.

"The coven."

20

Stand by your man

HE SIGNALLED FOR HER to be silent, took her hand and ran for the door. Every step creaked loudly under her feet as they spiralled down the stairwell. Gil on the other hand, seemed to make no noise whatsoever. A dull thud echoed overhead from the apartment they were just in. The scrape of a door flung open. She hustled, almost knocking Gil down.

They gained the landing, Gil reaching for the exit but then stopping cold. He flattened his palm against the door as if feeling for a fire on the other side but it was the chill he determined. She could feel it too and when he snatched his hand back, her stomach dropped. Whatever they were, they were clearly outside the door. She cast about in a panic, saw another door and pulled Gil by the hand.

He shook his head. No.

"The basement," she hissed. "Come on."

There was no other option. He popped the cellar door open and they fled inside. The light from the stairwell blew out as the door shut and Tilda was blind. A tug on her hand, leading her down more steps. Gil whispering to watch her step. Soft light glowed up ahead, a dirty bulb pushing back the pitch. They descended into a cavernous boiler room and he pulled her along, ducking under old steam pipes. Moving further into the gloom.

He stopped short before a door in the far wall. Old and sealed shut.

"Where does it go?" she hushed.

"Steam tunnel. It leads out into the university campus." A rush of stale air blew against her face as he cracked the door open. But he didn't pass through. A foul smell exhaled from the tunnel and Tilda gagged until he eased the door shut again.

"Damn it."

"Don't tell me..."

"They're in the tunnel." He retreated for the stairs. "Come on."

A scuttling noise issued from the way they had come, descending towards them. Tilda winced as his hand crushed hers. Gil snapped his head around like a bird, as if willing some other exit to appear.

The door to the steam tunnel cracked, dust billowing the air.

He yanked her fast across the room. A square metal panel under the stairs, tall enough for a child. A service access with a louvered vent in the door. He flung it open and Tilda felt herself being shoved inside.

"Wait," she said. It was even darker inside the access door. She didn't want to go in.

"Not a sound." He pushed her inside. "Don't even breathe, or they'll destroy us both."

She folded her legs into the cramped space and the panel door slammed back into its frame. The darkness was total.

Light spilled in through the panel's louvered vent, allowing Tilda a partial view of the boiler room outside. Gil scissored over the massive pipes, moving quickly away from her hiding spot. Leaping onto an enormous elbow joint, he folded his legs up under him and sat quiet. As if he'd come for the view.

Tilda strained her eyes but nothing seemed to happen. Just Gil perched on the steampipe like a commuter waiting for a bus. Then the smell leeched through the vent and she pulled back in revulsion. A stench of decay and death unlike anything she had ever encountered. It smells evil, she thought.

She heard them scuttling in from the darkness and when they shambled into the light she clamped her palm over her mouth to keep from screaming. Like the figures in the painting but more repulsive because they moved. Pale wraiths with dark hollows for eyes and ragged pits where their mouths should have been. They moved with a strange twitch and jerk as if their joints were rusting dry. They closed in around Gil like a deputation of nightmarish spastics surrounding some bedraggled fugitive.

Gil remained still, watching them press in but said nothing.

Two of the wraiths hissed at Gil like cobras. Others snarled or popped their teeth like rabid dogs. Another made odd clicking sounds, as if its jawbone was misaligned.

Gil spoke to the things before him as if he understood their hissing and clicking. Tilda strained her ear to the vent to listen.

"No," Gil said. "That's bullshit."

The pale figures twitched their heads atop their necks, their jaws articulating with that awful clicking noise.

"Where am I gonna go?" Gil spat with contempt.

One pointed a thin finger at him, an accusation sputtered in a snarl.

"Yeah. I've been avoiding you," Gil said. "Why would I hang around? You make me sick."

A pale hand clutched at him. Gil pushed it aside. "Don't bullshit me about loyalty. You know that I am. And you know I'll come if you call. That doesn't mean I'm gonna nest down with you every morning."

Another snatched at Gil's collar as if to throttle him. Gil spat in its face and shoved it back to its brothers. "Don't fucking touch me."

The hissing grew louder, the wraiths twitching more as they became agitated. Two of them stepped aside to make room for another, this more nightmarish than the last. Not so much inhuman as completely alien and the others scuttled around him in deference. Even Gil lowered his eyes as it sklathed in.

The stench of the things grew worse, rolling in waves through the vent into Tilda's face. She had to turn away to keep from gagging. Covering her mouth, she looked back through the louvers, unable to keep her eyes from the awful things assembled out there.

The tall spectre hissed at Gil, its slash of sharp teeth snapping. Gil averted his eyes, the way one does before a sovereign, and shook his head in response.

"What does it matter?" Gil said. "I do what you want. You know where I am. What the hell does it matter if I don't nest with the rest of you?"

The sovereign lashed out, fast as a rattlesnake, and snatched Gil by the hair. It threw Gil to the floor and began pummeling the mutineer with its fists. The others piled on, kicking and beating Gil mercilessly.

Tilda bit the scream back down her throat. She couldn't see Gil, only the monsters swarming over him. Were they killing him? The bastard things shrieked in a frenzy but she heard no sound from Gil, no cries or pleas for mercy. When a gap in the swarm opened, she caught a flash of him on the floor, curled tight into a ball to protect himself from the blows.

The frenzy waned. The tall one clicked and the others backed off, fresh blood on their claws and faces. Gil unfolded his limbs with a loud groan. He got to his feet slowly, clothes torn and face bloodied. Beaten back into the pecking order, he kept his head down and his mouth shut.

The wraiths gibbered and twitched, agitated from the mob beatdown and hungry for more. The chieftain snarled for silence and curled its arm, waving something forward. A fresh noise echoed through the boiler room; a whimper and a sob. Tilda strained to see, wondering if one of the things held a frightened dog but there was no dog. Two people were hauled into the center of the room. A young man and a young woman, their eyes crazed in terror as they were pushed down and forced to kneel. Street kids, like the squeegee punks who clean windshields for spare change. The woman begged to be let go while the man just cried, as if he knew already knew what was coming.

"Wait," Gil barked. His eyes shot for the vent where Tilda hid and then quickly looked away. "Don't do this. Not here."

The others screeched at him, the smell of another frenzy crackling the air.

The woman spun her head towards Gil, catching sight of him for the first time. The only one in the room who appeared human, she dove for his knees like a life preserver. Begging to be let go, her pleas coming so fast and urgent that she clicked back into her native Quebecois. Even the young man had stopped crying, looking to Gil with childish eyes of hope.

The monsters pressed in around the pair, like convulsives from some alien shore eager for violence. Gil stepped back, shaking the crying woman loose. The coven snatched up the couple and tore their filthy clothes from them until the two were left naked and cowering on the cold floor. Their sunburned arms and necks etched stark against the white flesh of their exposed torsos. The boy cried anew, whimpering the Lord's Prayer through a string of tears and snot. The woman simply shut down, curling onto the floor with a blasted sheen glazing her eyes.

The room went quiet and all Tilda could hear was the sound of water dripping from some dark corner. Then a sharp click as the sovereign dipped its pale face towards the captives.

The coven pounced.

Shrieks of terror and pain as the wraiths swarmed the boy and girl like piranha. Tilda's heart stopped, watching the monsters feed. Blood sprayed across the room, splattering even through the panel vent with an ejaculate of gore. She jerked back, wiping the blood from her face like it was poison. The victims cried out for help and for Jesus and for their mothers. Tilda clamped her palms over her ears to block out the unending torment of their screams.

The screaming ended. She chanced a look through the metal vent. The monsters were on their hands and knees, rolling in the gore like dogs. Only Gil remained standing but his gaze was transfixed on the bloodspill and Tilda watched in horror as he succumbed, dropping to his knees to join his fraters in the filth. She turned away, stoppering her ears against the obscene sound of the feeding.

She couldn't stop shaking. Couldn't slow her heart from clanging like a fire bell in her chest. It thrummed so loud in her eardrums she feared that those things would hear it. She tried to remember the Lord's Prayer but couldn't recall anything past the first verse.

Our Father, who art in Heaven,

Hallowed be thy name,

yadda yadda yadda...

She lowered her hands. The awful sounds had stopped. She peered through the vent but the things were gone. So was Gil. And those poor kids. The room appeared to be empty. But she wasn't ready to chance it and she waited a long time before making another move.

The panel scraped as she eased it open. Nothing rushed at her, no monsters roared out from the dark to eat her. Tiptoeing slow over the tangle of steam pipes, the urge to sprint for the exit was primal and difficult to restrain.

Then she saw the blood.

Pooled into black puddles on the floor and spray-painted against the walls. Dripping from the ceiling. It was everywhere. All that was left of the couple was wet gristle and bone scattered about the room. Small pieces, torn asunder.

There was no way around the gore and she was forced to step in it. Something crunched under her heel and she looked down. A molar in a puddle of blood. She doubled over and retched.

Staggering on, looking for the way out, she spotted the door that Gil had said was a steam tunnel. Ajar by an inch, the stench wafting from the breech.

Ignore it

Find the stairs

Get out

A synapse misfired. She reached for the door and pulled it back, scraping it across the floor. The stink rolled out over her. The wretched things were inside, huddled on the floor in a tangle of limbs. The coven, coiled up in a nest like a ball of wintering snakes, as still as death.

Her throat stitched seeing Gil tangled amongst the others, as unmoving and ossified as the rest. One more wretch among the repugnant filth.

The hair on her arms bristled to attention at the horrid sensation of being watched. Eyes on her. The tall one, the rector of this blasphemous cabal, reposed like a dead fish amongst the others but its eyes were slung open and fixed on Tilda. Clouded with cataracts and blank without iris or pupil, the dead eyes stared without blinking or moving. Was it awake or sleeping with its eyes open? It didn't stir but the thing seemed to stare right through her.

Tilda backed away, groping for the stairs. She bolted up the steps two at a time until she burst through the exit door. She ran for the lights of the street, desperate for a cab but the street was arid. No cabs or traffic of any kind. She ran west, feeling her knees jelly under her but spurred on by two thoughts.

No more. Never again.

21

Gouge away

MOLLY SHUFFLED INTO THE KITCHEN to, once again, find her father alone at the counter and her mother absent. This was becoming a habit. "Where's Mom?"

"In bed." Shane splashed milk over cereal, getting more of it on the counter than in the bowl. "Sit down and eat. We're running late."

She glanced at the clock. "Is she okay?"

"She's sick."

"Oh. Is that why she's being so weird lately?"

"Here, catch." He slid the bowl across the counter to her like a saloon-keeper. It sailed over the edge and splattered across the floor. Molly yawned.

"Damn it!"

"Smooth move," Molly said.

"You were supposed to catch that."

"I don't catch anything before eight 'o clock." She watched him cram something nasty looking into a sandwich-baggie. "What is that?"

"This? This is a new umbrella," he barked. "It's your lunch, goofy."

She turned her nose up. "Peanut butter?"

"You love peanut butter sandwiches."

"I can't bring peanut butter to school," she clucked. "I'll kill half the student body."

"What? Oh, right." He turned to the coffeemaker on the counter. It sat quiet and still instead of gurgling and puffing. "What is wrong with this damn thing? Is it broken? Doesn't anything in this house work?"

Molly crossed to the counter and pressed the power button. Shane had done everything but that. He groaned at his mistake. Molly turned and headed back upstairs. "I'm going to get dressed."

"Make it snappy," he shouted after her. Looking down at the mess of cereal on the floor, he cursed and went to get the broom and continued cussing as he picked pieces of broken bowl from the milky mush. Although annoyed at the mess, the focus of his cussing was directed upstairs where his wife lay hidden under the covers. She hadn't even looked at him when he'd tried to wake her, pulling the blanket over her head and asking to be left alone. When he had opened the drapes to let in the sunlight, she had barked at him to keep the room dark.

She's just tired, he told himself. She's going through a big change right now. Giving up music, taking on the new job. Give her time. She'll be back to normal soon.

He chewed over these excuses to mollify what was poisoning his guts like an ulcer. A sour, evil little thought that he couldn't shake no matter how many lame excuses he gnawed on.

She's fucking someone else.

Your wife has grown tired of your sorry ass and this boring existence and found someone else to fall in love with. Someone younger and better looking. More fun to be around, more exciting and better in bed.

The flimsy handle of the dustpan cracked from squeezing it so hard. Like a little Dutch boy with his finger in the dyke, once he took it away, the flood was unstoppable. It seemed ridiculous. Tilda wouldn't cheat on him. She wasn't like that, wasn't that kind of woman.

Still.

He dropped the dustpan and beelined for the hall table where his wife's handbag lay. The one he'd gotten her for her birthday. It was wrong and petty and paranoid to go snooping but he dug into it anyway. He didn't even know what he was looking for. A motel receipt? Love notes? Condoms? Nothing of the sort was excavated from her bag. Keys and loose coins, old lipstick. He thumbed her phone on and scrolled down the list of calls. Home, work, a few friends he recognized. No strange numbers or names.

See, you idiot? You're being paranoid. He dropped the phone into the bag and went back into the kitchen, scolding himself for being so foolish. That settled the matter. He just wished that the slow burning ulcer in his guts would let up.

IF she stayed perfectly still, it didn't hurt so bad. In the scramble through the boiler room, she'd scraped her arms and banged her shins, adding to the bruises already marring her body. And now they were hurting and there was no position she could find where something didn't ache.

She hadn't slept. Every time she closed her eyes, her mind flashed onto those two people, naked and prostrate on the floor. Their cries for help and the absolute awful sound of those things as they tore into them. Even after seeing all that, the aftermath of it, it was still difficult to believe it was real. That those monstrosities were not some nightmare conjured up from a fever but were real. Things that moved and lurked in the same world as she did. Monsters that preyed on the weak while the rest of the world carried on oblivious.

The door unlatched. Molly came in and sat on the edge of the bed. "You okay, mom?"

Tilda didn't move, keeping her back to the girl. "No. I'm sorry."

"Don't apologize." Molly looked at the drawn curtains. "It's so dark in here. Do you want me to open the windows?"

"No. I want it dark."

"Do you want an aspirin or something?" Molly reached over to touch her mother's brow.

"Don't do that," Tilda snapped, shrinking away.

"Okay."

"I just don't want you to get sick too." Tilda coiled up tighter. The last thing she wanted to do was see her daughter's eyes. "I'm fine. I just need some sleep."

"You guys had a pretty big fight last night, huh? Dad's acting weird too." No response came from the mound of blankets. Molly twisted the hem of her shirt in her hands. "What did you two fight about?"

"You don't want to hear all that stuff, honey." Tilda turned her head slightly. "It wasn't about you."

"Maybe I need to hear it," Molly sighed. "I hate when you guys hide stuff from me. I'm not a kid anymore. You don't have to protect me from anything."

"I know."

"Then what's going on? You haven't been yourself lately. What's going on with you?"

Tilda had to bite her lip. The girl knew something was wrong and of anyone in the world right now, Tilda wanted to tell her the whole thing. Would Molly despise her for what she had done? Probably. The girl was very black-and-white about things, given to extreme positions that only the very young and inexperienced were privileged to. Save the planet, stop the war, give up oil. There were no grey areas, no complications. Her daughter would be sickened if she knew what she had done.

Tilda raised her head to find the bedside clock. "You're going to be late for school, honey."

"Fine." Molly stood and turned for the door. "Keep your secrets."

SHANE lingered at the door, waiting for his daughter to get her butt into gear. Molly sauntered out with her school bag dragging across the floor in an apathetic dawdle meant to infuriate her old man. A practiced antagonism that was as much a part of their routine as brushing their teeth but this morning was different. He didn't say a word about her lackadaisical pace.

Shane looked out over the street and avoided his daughter's eyes, shame-faced at having searched through his wife's purse and phone. He had even opened the laptop and scanned through her email. At once relieved to find nothing unusual but peeved for not uncovering something incriminating to justify his suspicions. For once he was grateful for Molly's dawdling pace. How would he have explained what he was doing if his daughter had found him scouring her mother's things like some paranoid creep?

"What's the hold-up?" Molly asked, standing by the truck while he wool-gathered on the stoop.

Two blocks before the school, he pulled the Nissan to the curb so Molly could walk the rest of the way. Still embarrassed by existence of parental units.

Molly unlatched her door. "See ya."

"Hey." Shane touched her elbow. "Do you think your mom's okay?"

"She's sick."

"Besides that. Is there anything going on with her that I don't know about? Or I'm not seeing?"

Molly shrugged. "Who knows? Maybe it's just one of her phases."

"Phases? What phases?"

"You know, her weird blue periods." Molly tilted her head, as if to level with him. "They come and go. Remember two Christmases ago when she moped around like a zombie?"

Shane watched the street, trying to recall the details. "Yeah. What was that about?"

"She finished that last record, remember? She spent four months bitching about how hard it was going and then when it was done, she was depressed it was over with. Schizo-artist shit."

"Language," he reprimanded.

"Well what else do you call it?" She saw the concern in his eyes and softened her tone. "She'll be all right. Just give her time to snap out of it. Or buy her some Xanax."

"Thanks, smart ass. Get your butt to school."

Molly swung out of the vehicle and slammed the door. Shane watched her walk away and then looked at his watch. Already late for work. He shifted into gear and spun the wheel hard. Instead of continuing north towards the office, he swung the truck around and drove for home.

SHE had just begun to drift away. With the house empty and silent, Tilda finally found a position that didn't hurt and her mind slowed, sleep gratefully wearing her down. She floated in that half-life between states but something clawed her back, pushing slumber away. She rolled over, causing a fresh stab of pain down her shin and then her eyes caught something out of place.

The antique chair in the corner, the one no one ever sat in, was occupied. Its occupant no more than a dim outline in the darkened bedroom. She propped herself up on one elbow, squinting at the form. Gil? Had he crept inside after everyone had left?

"Who is he?" the silhouette asked.

Not Gil. Shane. Sitting in the dark. Watching her.

"What are you doing?" Tilda rubbed her eyes at the bedside clock. "Did you forget something?"

"Who is he?"

Something wasn't right. Shane didn't move. He didn't hit the lights or open the drapes. He just sat there, lobbing questions in the dark.

"Who's who?"

"The man you're screwing."

Everything went instantly numb. Her brains, her limbs. This wasn't happening. She was dreaming, she decided, and lay back down.

The antique chair was a remnant from Shane's mother's house. Beautiful but badly used, Tilda had always meant to refinish it. She watched it sail across the room and splinter against the wall with a boisterous crash.

"ANSWER ME!"

She jerked upright. Looked at the broken chair legs. "What is the matter with you?"

Shane charged across the floor, his face red. "What's the matter with me? My wife is cheating on me, that's what's wrong, Tilda! So pardon my fucking outrage!"

"You're being ridiculous." Dropping back down, she turned away. "Leave me alone."

"Then what is it, Tilda? You're out all night long, acting weird, the cops show up. What the fuck!" He paced the floor, his tone turning cruel. "Are you going through a crisis? You upset because you're over forty now like the rest of us? Did you misplace your 'authentic self'?"

She screamed at him to go away.

He snatched up the blanket and flung it back. Tilda coiled, exposed.

"Good God." He gaped at the bruises and scrapes hatched up and down her body. "What the hell did he do to you?"

"Get out!" Tilda swung off the bed and shot to her feet. "Get out, get out, get out!"

Shock registered across his face. "What did you do?"

What little rage Tilda had left was running out. She bolted for the bathroom before it all tipped over into tears.

He seized her arm and threw her back onto the bed. She scrambled for the other side but he tumbled onto her, pinning her down. His eyes were manic and bloodshot as he hovered over her. "All this time, I've been telling myself to be patient with you. To give it time cause you're going through something tough. Giving up your music career. She'll come around, I keep telling myself. Stand by her. And all this time, you're fucking someone behind my back!"

She turned away from his snarl. "Get off me!"

"What a fucking joke? Did you have a good laugh at me, honey? Sweetheart?" Spittle flew from his clenched teeth. "Was it worth it?"

"No! It wasn't like that—"

"All this time I been begging you to fuck me, being gentle, being patient. And you're out giving it up like a whore." Shane bounced up to his feet and tugged open his belt. "No more."

She squirmed away, her whole body hiccupping in sobs. "Is that what this is about? Then go ahead. I don't fucking care!"

He pushed her down into the bed, forced her legs apart. Skin scraped as he pushed into her dry. He pounded hard as if to punish her but he was already losing steam and then he went limp inside her.

Shane pulled away and his face twisted, souring up with tears. He slid to the floor with his pants around his knees and his face hidden. Tilda curled into a knot.

The hitching noise of their sobs harmonized in the dead air before tapering off into sniffles and panting.

Shane slumped over, unable to look at her. "Why?"

"I'm sorry," her voice cracked.

"Who is it? Tell me that much at least."

"What does it matter?"

"It matters."

Was there an answer to this? Tilda sat up, staring at a wedge of sunlight splitting the drapes and wondered what possible reply would satisfy him. Any name would do, really. All he needed was a target to focus his rage on. Brad Pitt. Nick Cave. Vladimir Putin.

It just fell out of her mouth. "Gil."

"Gil who?"

"Dorsey."

She watched his brow crinkle, trying to pinpoint the name in his memory. It eluded him like a slippery fish and then he looked at her. "I know that name."

Stupid. She'd said too much. Tilda swung her legs over the side but the thought of standing seemed impossible.

"Gil Dorsey. Why do I know that name?"

She lifted up on shaky knees and tottered clumsily around the bed.

Grasping at straw after straw, Shane finally snapped his eyes on her. "Wait a minute. Isn't that the guy you went out with before we met?"

"Yes."

His forehead rippled again in confusion. "But that's the guy who died."

Tilda bumped the doorframe as she teetered into the bathroom. "Yes," she said and then closed the door behind her.

22

All the pretty horses

SHE DIDN'T EMERGE FROM the bathroom until she heard the slam of the front door. Leaning into the window, she watched the Pathfinder drive away and then crawled back into bed. Her hands were shaking but worse than that was the nauseous loss of footing, as if gravity had been switched off. Shane knew the truth, or most of it, and there was no going back. He wouldn't understand and he would not forgive. Her betrayal would break him like a twig, along with their marriage and nothing would set it right.

What had she done? She had dropped a grenade into their life and watched it detonate. Why was she thinking of forgiveness or reconciliation? She had no right to expect it, having forfeited everything.

No relationship is ever truly equal in the strength of its clutches on the other. If she could admit the truth, she always knew that Shane's love for her was the stronger knot than hers to him. And this would kill him. In some dim corner of her heart, Tilda had always harboured a cold suspicion that she needed Shane more than she actually loved him. Had the situation been reversed, she could have dealt with it. Of course it would hurt and trust, once broken, takes a lifetime to rebuild, but she could get there. She could deal with his infidelity if she had to. Shane was a different story. Cut to the quick like this, he might never recover. He may never want to.

And Molly? Good God, how could she face her daughter if the girl finds out?

Rumbling under all of this was the horrors she had seen the night before. Those obscene things, the coven. She couldn't shake the images from her eyes. Gil, the victims, the blood. The whited eyes of that abhorred chieftain staring right through her. Had it seen her?

How could Gil be one of those monsters? He didn't look or act anything like them. And yet when the blood was spilled he prostrated like the rest to feed.

Tilda flung the sheet aside and sat up. She had to get out of here. Hiding in the dark was just making the images worse. She needed sunlight. A walk, fresh air, anything. She padded to the bathroom and ran the shower. She avoided the mirror. The last thing she wanted was to look into her own eyes or see the scrapes and bruises on her body. Stepping under the scalding jets, she remembered what Gil had told her, how the vampires detested mirrors because they couldn't stand to see what they had become. Her hand went automatically to the bite wound on her breast. Is this how it starts? Was she any different?

Thirty minutes later she was out of the house, her wet hair dampening the back of her shirt. The unrelenting sunlight felt warm and antiseptic on her skin. It was five blocks before she spotted a payphone. The local Crimestoppers number was displayed below the push buttons. She dialled and informed the person who answered that a murder had occurred last night in the Spadina and College area. Unable to recall the exact address, she described the building as a sooty grey-brick two doors north of College. She told them to check the boiler room. When the dispatcher asked if she wanted leave her name, Tilda hung up.

SHANE sat at his desk with his eyes on the screen but he may as well have been on the moon. Nothing made sense and he couldn't understand how his co-workers just went about their day like nothing had happened. They gossiped around the coffee machine and dissected last night's baseball game. The phones rang and people buggered off for an early lunch. How could they not see that it was all bullshit? How could they just carry on the same insipid conversations while the whole world had turned to shit overnight?

Their obliviousness galled him and he hated them for their happy fucking lives. Like they deserved their smug contentedness. Their callous nonchalance was like lemon squeezed on a papercut.

How could she do this to him? Hadn't he always been there for her? Hadn't he supported her every step of the way in her career, through the good times and the tough times? And truth be told, the tough months far outweighed the good ones. Did she hate him? Had Tilda just taken him for granted, figuring him to be a doormat that she could walk all over knowing he'd always come back for more?

Maybe you brought this on yourself.

Shane startled at that little voice suddenly nagging his brain. His eyes darted about to see if anyone else had heard it. Of course he hadn't caused this. He'd never been un-faithful to Tilda. He didn't treat her badly or hit her or any-thing.

But you've been drifting from her, becoming distant. You even withhold your affection to punish her.

He thumped his desk to silence that evil voice, causing a few of his co-workers to look his way. Maybe some of that was true, he argued back silently, but that wasn't cause for her to take their marriage and flush it down the toilet. Was it?

All this time he'd been making excuses for her odd be-haviour. What a chump. And then, as if he hadn't had his guts kicked in enough, she had salted the wound by telling him that the other man was her old boyfriend. Her dead old boyfriend. What was he supposed to do with that? Was she losing her mind or did she layer that on just to be cru-el? Tilda seldom talked about him but he had always known that she had loved him. That his death had screwed her up bad. In the really dark moments, Shane suspected that he and Tilda wouldn't have met if that son-of-a-bitch had never bought the farm.

Fuck him.

Fuck her too.

When he came up for air, Shane squinted at the big wall clock as if unable to read its hands. He had lost two hours inside his own head and had accomplished absolutely nothing at his desk. His phone blinked with waiting messages, emails piled atop one another in his inbox. It all seemed so pointless right now, this shit called work that was shovelled onto his desk so he could dump it onto someone else's desk later.

He turned off the monitor and got to his feet. Stuffed a couple of folders under his arm in a pretence of taking work home and headed for the door.

The receptionist looked up as he swept past her. "Shane, if you're making a coffee run, I'd kill for a latte," she said.

"I'm going home." He muttered, stabbing the elevator button again and again.

"Oh. Not feeling well?"

"Family emergency," he said, then cut for the stairs.

"TILDA!"

No answer. Shane took the stairs two at a time and pushed the bedroom door open. The bed was unmade and the drapes still closed. She wasn't here.

"Goddamnit." He had scripted this perfect speech on the drive back and there was no one to deliver it to. With the target of his anger absent, all the pent up rage and speechifying curdled in his guts with nowhere to go.

Fine. Play it that way.

Hammering back down the steps, Shane stomped through the kitchen and down into the basement. The cat, perched on the window sill, listened to the banging and crashing echoing up from the cellar. It watched Shane clomp back up the stairs, dragging an enormous suitcase behind him and then watched him bang it all the way up to the second floor.

The suitcase landed on the unmade bed and Shane unzipped it. Then he opened a dresser drawer and started tossing clothes in.

IT was her day off but Tilda ended up at work. After wandering through the park and meandering along Queen, she didn't know where else to go. She needed to talk to someone, and the best candidate for a patient ear and sound advice was Sarah. Cutting down to Richmond, she hoped to steal her away for a cold drink.

Sarah, bless her heart, quickly twigged to the dark cast of her friend's face and grabbed her bag, leaving Anne-Marie to hold down the fort. They snagged some iced tea and cut across to the park.

"Okay, I'm all ears," Sarah said as they settled onto the grass under the shade of immense elm. "Spill."

Tilda tripped over her words, fumbling about for a way to begin. Sarah touched her knee and told her to just state it as simply as possible. Tilda wiped her eyes and opened with the fight she had had with Shane and backtracked from there. She omitted Gil's name, referring to him as simply 'an old boyfriend', along with the darker, confounding details about the coven. Everything else, including the fight that resulted in a man's death and being questioned by the police about it, Tilda laid bare as simply as possible. Winding down, she threaded back to the fight with Shane and the implosion of her marriage.

Sarah set her cup onto the grass. "Wow. You really fucked up."

Tilda bobbed her head in agreement and wiped her raw eyes.

"It's okay," Sarah shrugged. "Everybody does."

"What does that mean?"

"Everybody cheats," Sarah stated plainly, as if discussing the weather. "At least once."

"Oh stop. I'm not asking for justification for what I did. I just need to get it out."

"Honey, look at me. Everyone steps out somewhere along the way. And I mean everyone."

"I don't believe that for a minute."

"Oh, not everyone will admit it. But they have." Sarah slurped the last of the tea. "Everyone who's stayed married has. You know those old couples you see on TV on Valentine's Day? Talking about how long they've been together and the inevitable question about the secret to a long relationship? They did. That cute old man banged his secretary and that adorable grandmother had afternoon trysts with tall, dark and handsome down the block. They'll deny it of course. Once it's over, they run back to their spouse and convince themselves that it never happened. But they did it."

"Everyone? That's ridiculous."

"Why is that so ridiculous? You don't stay truly, madly, deeply for twenty years. Or even ten years. There's loneliness in the happiest of marriages. And everyone's human, everyone gets get weak or desperate or foolish. Every couple that's managed to stay the course are the ones smart enough to know where to draw the line."

"What line?"

"They stepped out, had a fling, scratched that itch. But they were smart enough to pull back before they got too mixed up in it or got caught. A moment of clarity, after the fun was over, when they realized exactly what they were risking. Before they got burned, they went back to their husband or their wife with a renewed sense of devotion or gratitude. That's their big secret, all those cute old fogies celebrating forty years together. They knew when to quit."

Tilda looked out over the park. A picture postcard of young couples walking hand in hand. "You honestly believe that?"

"I do. Hell, I'm surprised it took you this long to do it."

"You think I'm a skank?"

"No. You're a musician. You've been on the road, on tour, surrounded by other musicians. I'm surprised it hasn't happened before, that's all."

Tilda squared her friend with a sharp look. "You've cheated before?"

"I told you about Frankie, remember? But there was someone else a couple years ago."

"Who?"

"Does it matter?" Sarah watched a dog patter by. "Let me ask you something; do you think Shane has ever cheated on you?"

She didn't hesitate. "No. Never."

"How would you know?"

"I just would," Tilda sighed. "He's not good at keeping secrets. No poker face."

"Maybe," Sarah conceded. "But I doubt it. He's a good looking guy. I've seen women bat their eyes at him."

"So what if he has? Does that mean I'm owed a fling? Or it excuses what I did?"

"No. It just means you're both human and everybody needs to get off their high moral horse about it."

A Frisbee whizzed over their heads and bounced off the trunk of the elm tree. A young man with tattoos across his neck ran after it. "Sorry," he said and ran off again.

Sarah stretched out on the cool grass. "So who is this mystery man?"

"Just an old boyfriend," Tilda said. "Not someone you know."

"Must be a really old beau if I don't know him. Do you love him? Or is this just an itch being scratched?"

"It's complicated."

"Wrong answer. This is an itch. Scratch it and then wise up. Move on."

"I never stopped loving him. All this time... " There was more but wrapping words around it was too hard and she fell quiet.

Sarah groaned. "Jesus, Tilda. Where's he been all this time? Why weren't you with him before?"

"Like I said. Complicated."

"He's married."

"I wish it was that simple."

Sarah sat up, stymied for a response. They watched the people strolling past them and then Tilda saw her friend check the time on her phone. "You better get back. Thanks for letting me bend your ear."

"What are you going to do?"

"Dunno. I don't want to go home."

"You're welcome to bunk with me for a few days if you want. Let this cool over before you go back."

"Thanks. That's sweet but it wouldn't fix anything."

Sarah brushed the grass from her palms. "You want my advice, go home and fix this. Shane will be devastated. Men don't do well with this. He'll moan and yell and crucify you with guilt but eventually, he'll come to accept it. And there's nothing you can do but take your punishment. There's no shortcut here. But you both have too much at stake to let it fall apart over something like this. Take your lumps, be patient and fix this." Sarah leaned in for a hug and got to her feet. "Love you," she said and walked away.

Tilda waved back. "Ditto."

THERE is something about Kensington in summer that draws the crazed and deranged to it like blowflies around a carcass. A bedraggled blowhard stood in the middle of the street, blocking traffic and venting his personal tragedy to the cars honking at him. "Look at my life!" he screamed. "Somebody's gotta pay!"

After the park Tilda had wandered east, mulling over the problem. By the time she reached the market, a plan had started to take shape. She'd arrange for Molly to go a friend's house, cook up a fancy dinner for her husband and have it out with him. The plan was simple; tell Shane everything. About Gil and his return, about the coven and the whole mess she had tangled herself up in. It would sound crazy, just blurting it all out in a spew of events but she didn't care. Gil wouldn't like it either, revealing his secret, but she couldn't afford to keep secrets anymore. Not from Shane. She was sick to her stomach with secrets. The only way out of this mess was to flush it all into the antiseptic light of day.

As difficult as that would be, the harder part would come after that. She would have to be honest with Shane and admit that she still loved Gil. Had, in fact, never stopped loving him. But here was the kicker; that didn't mean she no longer loved Shane. That hadn't changed. She loved them both and she couldn't cast Gil out of her life now any more than she could leave Shane for Gil.

The clarity of it almost stung, and Tilda realized that she hadn't been honest with herself either. Caught in a trap, assuming that it had to be one or the other. She loved them both and the truth was she wanted both. Selfish, greedy and maybe even vain but there it was. Why couldn't she have both men in her life? Why did it have to be one or the other? It wasn't like she had fallen out of love with her husband or that her marriage had failed. The circumstances were beyond strange and that meant that any resolution would have to be equally strange.

What if they could work it out? Shane would reject it at first, dismiss it as crazy and refuse to play along. But Shane wasn't obstinate or prideful. He was actually very empathetic, easily seeing both sides of an argument. Given the option of dissolving their marriage or simply making a little room for someone else, Shane might come around. He might want to take a lover in that circumstance and her heart nettled with jealousy at the mere thought but she could deal with it. Neither of them were starry-eyed kids with rigid ideals of love and fidelity anymore. The idea of compromising, of adjusting to a new reality rather than blowing it all up, seemed tangible. It would hurt, it would be difficult, but it wasn't impossible.

It could be downright European of them.

The lightbulb moment of compromise cheered her for a moment, basking in its optimism before it dissipated like any other happy moment. As her mood sifted back down to earth, so did her gaze until it snagged on a handbill pasted to the side of a trashbin. A photocopied missing persons poster showing a blotchy picture of a young woman. A homemade one, not the official kind the police issued. Tamara Mladavic, age 22. Last seen in early May. The contact info consisted of a single phone number. The woman in the picture didn't smile, a street-tough attitude in her posture.

There seemed to be more and more of these missing persons notices all the time. Small town kids from across the country drifting into the city only to live under a bridge or join the hidden caste of homeless. A shadow society that everyone drove past on their way to somewhere else. 22 year-old Tamara was just one more unwashed face added to that shambling crowd and now she was gone, missed only by a very few. Missed by someone who cared enough to look for her. She could have been the young woman in the boiler room. These were the people the coven preyed on. The powerless and the faceless. Who would miss them besides others of that same ghost class? Those perversions could feed with abandon and no one would be the wiser.

"God damn you."

Tilda startled. The old religious woman hovered nearby, her face shaded under a straw hat. An immense silver cross dangled from a chain around her neck, like some born-again rapper. Clutched in her white gloved fist was the homemade cross, fashioned out of pineboard sticks and duct tape. "God damn you," she said again.

Tilda froze. The same woman she and Gil had run into fleeing the scene of the Porthole. She had cursed Gil that time but now her curses were aimed squarely at Tilda herself.

"What do you want?" Tilda snapped. She was not in a tolerant mood.

"You damned." The old woman clucked her teeth in schoolmarm disapproval. "Like that other one. Lake of fire. You and him. Burning."

"Please. Go pull your schtick on someone else."

"Him and the others." The woman wagged her chin to her left, as if those in question were just around the corner. "I see them. In the dark. Bad people."

Tilda straightened up. "You've seen them?"

"They think I can't see but I see." The woman nodded, then pointed her wooden cross at Tilda. "You one of them now. God damn you."

"I'm not one of them," Tilda barked. The old woman flinched and swung the cross up, slapping it across Tilda's arm. Her hangdog face withered in disappointment, clearly expecting Tilda to burn at its touch.

Tilda snatched the cross away, snapped the flimsy thing in two and threw the pieces to the ground. "Stay away from me."

23

Demon host

SHANE MUST HAVE FORGOTTEN to latch the sidedoor when he left. It was unlocked when she came home. Tilda dropped the groceries onto the table and splashed cold water over the back of her neck to dispel the scorching walk home.

Molly would be home soon. She'd ask the girl to call Zoe and ask if she could have dinner with them. If Molly asked why, she'd simply say that she and her father needed to talk. Molly would leave it at that, having no interest in her parent's problems.

Then she'd start dinner. Seafood paella, Shane's favourite. A bottle of red to chip away the glacier that would inevitably ice across the table between them. It was a lame ploy, trying to soften him up with a nice meal but she couldn't think of any better tactic. Sometimes clichés worked.

She unpacked the vegetables she'd bought, tossed the seafood and chorizo into the fridge and put on some music. The Rattlesnake Choir seemed to fit her mood. Just forlorn enough to keep her motivated without breaking down entirely. She opened the bottle of wine, poured half a glass and started to prep. With her hands busy, her attention focused on a singular task, a small measure of relief came to ease the churn of thoughts in her mind. Maybe, just maybe, this was going to work.

The twang and lurch of the music abruptly stopped. Tilda turned to find Shane killing the power to the kitchen stereo unit. "You scared me," she said. "I didn't hear you come home."

A second glance told her that he hadn't left the house at all. He looked dishevelled and distracted as if he'd just woken up. His eyes were bloodshot. She assumed he'd been crying but the minute he spoke, it was clear that he'd been drinking. "What are you doing?" he asked.

"Getting dinner started. Are you all right?"

"Terrific."

Tilda dried her hands. "Shane, I'm going to make dinner for the two of us. Molly's going to go to a friend's house for a while and then we can talk. Okay?"

Shane leaned back against the wall. He didn't seem angry or even upset. Defeated maybe. "Don't bother."

"I know this has been rough but—" She grasped at some way to placate him without igniting another powderkeg. "We're going to talk this through, okay? Just let me get Molly sorted and out the door."

He guffawed, as if she'd said something funny.

She turned the music back on and went back to the sink. "Why don't you go lie down for a little while. Just don't drink anymore."

The music cut out again. Shane ripped the unit from the shelf and hurled it into the wall. It clunked to the floor, leaving a broken pockmark in the sheetrock. It was turning out to be a red letter day for masculine assertions of power. "You don't get a say anymore. Turn off the water."

She turned the faucet. This clearly wasn't going to go as planned. She looked at the mess on the floor. "Feel better?"

"Nope." He stepped into the hallway, waving at her to follow. "This way."

She followed him out to the foyer. Shane wagged his chin at the big suitcase waiting at the front door. "I packed your things."

Tilda blinked at the luggage. He couldn't be serious. "What for?"

He sighed, as if too tired to explain. "You're leaving."

"Okay." She levelled her tone, needing to talk him down from the ledge. "Before we do anything drastic, we need to talk this through."

"No, we don't. You have to leave."

"You're kicking me out?" she sputtered. "You can't do that."

"This is how it works." He swung the front door open. "Cheaters leave. The cheated stay."

"This is ridiculous. We haven't even talked about it."

"Jesus, Tilda. You always wanna talk when it's time to act." He kicked open the screen door, snatched up the suitcase in both hands and hurled it down the porch steps. "Go."

"Oh, cut the melodrama, Shane, and be an adult for once."

"Stop. You can't talk your way out of this one. Just leave."

She couldn't move, her feet frozen to the hardwood. A sickening sense that if she walked out that door, she wouldn't ever be coming back.

"Mom?"

The timing of it. Molly stood at the bottom of the stoop, plucking the earbuds from her ears. She looked at the suitcase on the flagstone walk then up to her father. "What's going on?"

Shane looked at his daughter then back to his wife. "You wanna explain it?"

The thought appalled her. She still couldn't move, couldn't breathe.

Molly waited for an answer, the earbuds dangling from her hand. "So this is it, huh? The big break-up? I'm surprised it took this long."

Shane stared down at the slat of the porch floor and didn't say anything. Tilda gasped for oxygen. The cat slipped past both of them and nuzzled the girl's ankle. The whole family assembled.

Molly picked up the cat and nudged the suitcase with her foot. "So? Which one of you is leaving?"

Like duellists waiting for the other to blink, neither adult moved. Tilda felt her chest about to burst open all over the porch. Walking out seemed impossible but standing here was too excruciating to endure any longer. Her heels unglued from the floor and she walked past Shane without looking at him.

Stopping at the bottom of the porch steps, she couldn't even look at Molly. "I'm sorry. I can't explain this right now."

"I'm not asking." Molly pulled the telescoped handle of the suitcase so her mother could roll it away. "Where will you go?"

"I don't know."

"Call me later. Let me know where you are."

Tilda took hold of the suitcase handle and kissed Molly's cheek. Then she walked away.

SHE considered going to Sarah's place to take her up on her offer. For all of ten seconds. Taking a cab west, she rolled the big suitcase down the byzantine alleys to the grey brick building behind Chinatown. The door was locked but the key had been returned to its hiding spot so she let herself in. Clicking the door shut behind her, she called his name but there was no response. Was he ever here?

Groping her way to the central table, she found the matches and struck one. No candles on the table but there was a kerosene lantern with a note sticking out from its base. She lit the wick and the lantern's light pushed the shadows back and she read the note.

Running low on candles. Try this.

G

She smiled at his note, at the banal message jotted there.

She dropped onto the couch like a dead weight. She hadn't slept in a day and the fight with Shane had exhausted her. Tucking her feet up, she laid her head down and closed her eyes. Just a few minutes of rest and then she had to figure out what she was going to do.

When she opened her eyes, Gil was sitting on the floor with his head tilted back against a cabinet. Tilda pushed herself upright and shivered, a chill ripping down her. "What are you doing?"

"Nothing. Watching you sleep."

"Don't. It's creepy." She stifled another shudder. "How long have I been asleep?"

"An hour." He rose and retrieved a blanket from a chair and draped it around her shoulders. Then he took his place on the floor again. "I wasn't sure you'd come back."

"I didn't know where else to go."

He inched closer. "Why?"

"Shane knows. We had a fight."

"Ah." he said. "I'm sorry. How bad was it?"

"He kicked me out."

"Ouch. Are you okay?"

"No. I'm not."

"Stupid question."

Gil crawled forward to kneel at her feet. He slung his arms over her knees. "I've been thinking. About us. About what to do."

"I can't think about that right now."

"We should leave. Get out of this city."

"Leave?" Her eyes wide with incredulity. "And go where?"

"Anywhere." His hands gripped her tighter. "We could go west, out to B.C. Or south, down into the states. Some place where the coven won't dare come after us. Then we can be together. Just the two of us."

Tilda rubbed her temple, feeling a headache settling in. "I can't do that."

"Yes you can."

"No. I can't just abandon my family."

His eyes lit hopeful. "Molly can come visit us."

"Gil, stop. You're asking too much."

His face clouded. "Shane. You still love him."

"Of course."

She felt him retreat by an inch. She touched his chin. "This is complicated, Gil. You gotta understand."

"I know, I know," he said, peevish and dissolute.

His hand closed over hers. Tilda looked down at his raw knuckles. The blue veins spidering under the white flesh and the bruised colour of his fingernails. She pulled her hand away.

He tilted his head, trying to lock onto her eyes. "What is it?"

"Those things last night." Tilda shuddered at the memory. "They killed those two people."

Gil's hand remained in her lap, waiting for hers to return. "I'm sorry you had to see that."

"They were just kids. The same age as us when we met. And those monsters tore them to pieces." Her eyes rose to his, painted in cold horror. "And you took part."

This time his eyes broke away. "I didn't have a choice. Not without making them suspicious. They might have found you."

"I know but still... those kids are dead. I can't just pretend it didn't happen." Tilda launched off the couch. "This is what you do. You feed off people."

Gil watched her pace back and forth but said nothing.

"Am I wrong?" She stopped pacing. "Have you ever killed someone?"

"Yes. Three. I've killed three people."

"Three? In all this time, just three?"

"I learned how to take only what I need without killing anymore," he said.

"How can you do that?" Tilda shivered, eyes hateful. "How can you live with yourself?"

"Don't judge me." Gil rose to his feet, his face darkening. "Live through this and then you can judge me. Not a moment sooner."

A muffled honking sounded from the street below, filling the silence in the room. Gil crossed to the window and looked down. Then he laughed. "I tried to kill myself once. More than once. Couldn't do it."

"What happened?"

"I sat on a rooftop and waited for the sun to come up. But I choked at the moment of truth and ran when it started to burn. Life, even one as monstrous as this, is better than no life at all."

She chewed her lip. "Would you have died from that? Sunlight?"

"Yeah. Like a bonfire. It's a gruesome way to go."

"As bad as being eaten by a vampire."

"Don't get nasty, Tilda. I didn't ask for this."

"No," she said coldly. "You just go along with it."

"What do you suggest I do? Call the police? Try to stop them?" Gil leaned his brow against the pane glass. "I thought about destroying them once. I had a plan to burn them in their nest while they slept. I even had a couple barrels of kerosene set in place to do it."

"Why didn't you?"

"I think they knew what I was up to. They started moving around. They've got nests all over the city. But the main one is under the university campus. Remember the steam tunnel in the boiler room? There's a whole labyrinth of steam tunnels under U of T but underneath those is a network of older tunnels, all connecting to a central vault under Knox College. That's the main nest, the oldest one. I had snuck down a few kegs of kerosene, thinking I could rig up a trap."

"Why didn't you go through with it?"

"They broke up into smaller cells in different places every night, instead of the one central nest. My plan was a one-shot deal. I had to get them all in one go. If any of them survived, they'd hunt me down. God knows what else they'd do."

Tilda slid down to the floor and hugged her knees. "This is a nightmare."

"Yes it is."

He studied her for a moment but, with her hair cascading over her face, he couldn't tell if she was crying. He crossed the floor to her. "I'm sorry I completely fucked up your life like this, Tilda. I should have stayed away."

"Don't say that." She clutched his hand. "I just don't know what to do right now."

"Stay with me," he said. "You'll be safe here."

He drew her close and Tilda let herself be held. "I'm so tired, Gil. I can't think anymore."

"Then close your eyes."

She felt his arms curl under her and he lifted her up and carried her to the bed. She nestled back into his chest and he coiled around her like a cocoon. A faint flush of longing as her body reacted to his but they lay still and after a while, she drifted off.

SHE stirred and reached out for him but the bed was empty. Sitting up, she scanned the room. Nothing moved.

"Gil?"

Stale humid air. Nada mas. Where did he go?

She slid off the bed and waited for the dizziness to pass. The lantern was a small glow and the darkness of the room was disorienting. How long had she slept? She tiptoed to the couch for her bag but it wasn't there.

Then a noise. Odd and out of place.

"Gil?"

A scraping clatter cut the silence on her right. Nails on plasterboard. Then a hiss on her portside, like a snake in the dark.

Tilda uttered his name again but she already knew it wasn't him.

That awful hissing. So vile and inhuman.

The wraith floated up from the pitch, its pale flesh limned in the lantern light. Its maw gaped up and down like some prehistoric fish, ready to eat her. The other one reared up in her periphery, its claw slashing the still air.

24

Heads will roll

YELLOWED NAILS CUT INTO her arm, drawing blood. Tilda recoiled at its touch and scrambled away. The thing's claw clicked as it snapped after her like a pincer. She dove behind a wobbly wooden shelf, rattling its contents to the floor. The thing shambled forward and she pushed the shelf over, toppling it onto the vampire.

The second wraith slammed her to the floor, locking its cold grip around her throat. Up close, its face was even more repulsive. The lifeless eyes and blackened mouth. A sewer rot stench billowed from its maw into her face. A dark tongue prodded out between the sharp teeth like some perverse moray.

Tilda convulsed and clawed at it, kicking out like she was on fire. The wraith pressed down with its weight, writhing on top of her and Tilda could feel her mind shut down at its horror. This isn't happening. This isn't real. When she felt its black tongue on her cheek, instinct kicked in and she lashed out, driving her thumb into its eye with everything she had. It shrieked and she pushed harder. The eyeball popped like an egg and something wet spurted onto her palm. It jerked and coiled up, clutching its ruined eye.

Tilda scuttled away in a panic, colliding into furniture but moving fast, putting distance between herself and that thing. She could hear it thrashing and shrieking behind her. Trying to orient herself in the room, she hazarded a guess where the door was and bolted. The other one sprang up to block her escape as if it had shot straight up out of the floor. Its jaw clicked as it snapped its teeth.

She backpedalled searching for a weapon, anything to fight back with. There was nothing. The wraith sprang and she kicked at it violently but it kept coming. Its lamprey-like mouth gaped open and bit into her stomach, shaking savagely like a wolf on a lamb. She pounded it with her fists but the vampire was clamped fast like a leech and would not let go. Its teeth were sharp and its spittle stung like venom.

She screamed Gil's name.

Gil was there, dropping out of darkness onto her attacker.

Slamming a knee into its back, he yanked back the thing's head but the teeth remained clamped. Gil dug his fingers into its mouth and pried the monster's jaw open. When Tilda slipped free, he pried the mouth open wider and wider until the jawbone snapped off in his hand. Black blood gushed forth and the thing shrieked in torment with its jawbone flapping loose. Tilda twisted away to avoid the dark vomit of blood from the monster's broken mouth. Gil was unrecognizable, the rage twisting his features into something demonic. The wraith flailed at them both with its ragged claws. Gil slammed the thing into the wall of aquariums in a catastrophe of broken glass. It flailed and flopped in the splintered shards.

The other one came from behind. It slammed into Gil like a truck, propelling him into the shattered aquariums. It shoved his face into the broken glass again and again. Gil broncoed the thing from his back and spun about, his face hatched with bloodied lacerations. The vampire launched at him again, chomping at Gil's face like a crazed dog.

Tilda scrambled for something to bash the monster's skull with when a trinkling of glass sounded on her left. The jawless one lurched at her, its face and limbs prickled with glass. Her groping hand found a metal candlestick and she broke it over the thing's head. It stumbled drunkenly and fell to one knee.

A cacophony of noise thundered around her as if a bull had been set loose in the room. She lost sight of Gil and the other wraith. Then an otherworldly shriek sounded from the dark. A window exploded, something dark sailed clean through the pane. When Gil appeared, his mouth and chin were foul with blood. His eyes on fire.

The shard-encrusted wraith slashed clumsily at Tilda. Gil kicked it down then rifled a shelf and came back with a hatchet. He planted a boot on the thing's head and swung at its neck with the short-handled axe. Two powerful swings before the vertebrae snapped and the monster's head rolled free. Its legs jerked and kicked as if trying to run away. Gil spat on the carcass and kicked the severed head across the room.

Tilda stammered between racking breaths. "Where's the other one?"

"It got away," he said. "Or most of it did."

He nodded at something on the floor. A pale forearm lay among the broken glass, chewed off at the elbow.

HOW much horror can the mind endure before it snaps? A bloodied stump of an arm on the floor and a severed head booted across the room. Tilda felt the ground flip-flop under her. When the wound on her stomach flared hot and stinging, she doubled over and hit the floor.

Kneeling over her, Gil saw the blood seeping wet through her shirt. He pulled away the material to find puncture wounds below the navel, leaking blood in a slow pump. He flattened his palm over the wound and felt the blood pumping hot through his fingers. Crossing the floor, he tore apart a shelf for the gauze hidden there. A roll of medical tape.

Her eyes were white, the pupils rolled up. He smacked her cheek and called her name, barking at her to wake up.

Nothing changed. He slapped the gauze over the bloodied gash and taped it into place. The smell of her blood tweaked his nose, the particulate iron and hemoglobin, her hormones. The saltiness of it. Tilda's essence distilled down into a scent that made his mouth water and his heart beat faster. His erection immediate and aching. He wagged his head like a dog to shake it off, pushing down what was boiling up fast.

He smacked her cheek and shook her hard until her pupils swung back into place and her eyelids fluttered as if dusted.

Vertigo see-sawed the earth under her. Tilda clutched his arms, convinced she was dying.

"Easy. I'm right here. I got you."

"Oh God this hurts."

"You got bit. Just relax."

Horror burned hot in her eyes. "It bit me? Oh Christ, Gil... "

"Don't tense up like that. Be still. The wound's bandaged, the bleeding's stopped."

She closed her eyes and breathed through it. Her memory jolted and she recalled giving birth to Molly. Her midwife coaching her to just breathe through the pain. It hadn't worked then either.

"How bad is it?" She struggled to sit up, clawing back the gauze to see the wound.

"Stop." He pulled her hand away but the damage was done. The wound pumped fresh as the gauze peeled away.

"Am I infected? Am I going to become one of those things?"

"You have to die first before that happens. But you're bleeding again."

"Jesus this hurts. Can't you get it to stop?"

"I don't know how. Not the normal way."

"What's the not-normal way?"

He bit his lip in hesitation and then slid out from under her. "Lie back," he said. Then he popped the button on her jeans and yanked the waistline down. Slid between her legs.

"What are you doing?"

"There's something in my saliva. A coagulant. Lie still."

She laid her head against the floor and stared at the ceiling. Breathe, she reminded herself. And then she felt his lips on the wound, his tongue lapping at the fleshy spot below her navel. She lifted her head and saw his eyes roll over white.

Tilda had a smell and Tilda had a taste. It was there in her sweat and on the back of her neck and the soft tissue of her thigh. But in her blood, both were amplified to an intoxicant that detonated his brain. He lapped her up, greedy for more and his erection ached and he shuddered and laid his head against her belly with a low growl.

Tilda exhaled a long sigh. The pain receded instantly, like a candle being snuffed. She reached down and ran her nails over his scalp, unsure of what had just happened. "It's gone."

He grunted, as if winded.

"Gil…"

"What is it?"

"Did you just come?"

"Yes." He looked up at her with a guilty smile. "Couldn't help myself."

She ran her fingers along his cheek. "That's weird."

"Yup. Does it bother you?"

It should have but it didn't. All that mattered was that the wound didn't burn anymore and the weight of his skull against her belly felt good. Quiet bliss and then she felt his hand on her foot. His grip was too hard, the fingernails cutting into her skin.

"Easy. You're hurting my foot."

His head came up. "I'm not touching your foot."

They both looked down. The severed arm clutched her ankle, its fingers scuttling up her leg like a hermit crab. Tilda kicked it off in a panic and scrambled away. The severed limb thudded against a wall and she heard its nails clicking on the floor, scratching away in the dark.

Her skin crawled. "That's revolting. How can that thing move?"

"The rest of it's still alive." Gil's face instantly dropped, eyes bald with fear. "Oh shit. It got away."

Tilda didn't follow but the fright in his eyes was contagious. "Will it come back?"

"No. But it saw you here. It'll tell the others."

The coven will know about her, she thought. And how Gil broke their law. "What will they do?"

"They'll kill us both."

"You have to hide," she said. Another thought stopped her heart. "They don't know who I am. They wouldn't be able to find me. Will they?"

His face clouded. "The one that was here knows your scent. He could track you down, lead the others to you."

A cold thought bit her marrow. "To the house? To Molly and Shane?"

He had barely nodded and Tilda was on her feet, sprinting for the door.

"Tilda, wait."

"No! Not if those things are going to the house. We have to stop them."

"I can't fight them all, Tilda."

"Then we have to get Molly and Shane out of there. Hurry!"

Tilda rabbited through the door, her heels pounding the steps two at a time.

DUSK had painted the underbelly of the clouds pink, striking in its clarity against the outline of the streetscape. Night coming fast on its heels. Tilda hurried down the alley maze without looking back. Gil appeared alongside her and took her hand.

Traffic was light for this time of day. Tilda scanned the street. "We need a cab," she said but the only taxi in sight was occupied, its toplight switched off.

"Forget the cab," he said.

Music blared out over the street, a heavy bass rattling the windows nearby. Its source was an electric blue Toyota Sirrocco, pristine and without a scratch. Two young men sat inside the idling vehicle, vacantly watching the street and making no attempt to hide the weed passing back and forth.

Gil squeezed her hand and marched for the car. He yanked open the driver's door, startling the young man behind the wheel. "I need your car."

"The fuck you doin', asshole?" The orange-tanned driver sneered. "Don't touch the fucking car."

Gil yanked the young man from the driver's bucket like a blighted potato and threw him over the hood of the next car. The companion shot out, his sculpted eyebrows raised in shock, but his posturing wilted as he approached Gil. High as he was, he sensed that something was not right, that the pale man before him was not trouble to be messed with. He backed off, fanning his arms and cursing but it was all bark.

"Get in," Gil said to Tilda without taking his eyes from the two men.

They climbed into the running vehicle and Gil pulled into traffic, clipping the bumper of the car parked in front.

"Can you turn that shit off?" He nodded at the instrument panel, the rumble of the bass all but shirring the meat from their bones. Tilda stabbed the panel and killed the music.

Gil stomped the accelerator and then clutched, geared up. "Shit. I haven't been behind the wheel in years. Maybe you ought to drive."

"Just go." Tilda turned to peer out the rear window, expecting to see red flashing lights chasing them.

The engine growled and the exhaust rumbled under them. When the traffic slowed, Gil swung out into the oncoming lane and forced his way through a red light. Tires screeched and horns bleeted as they bullied through the intersection. Tilda clutched the Jesus grip as he swerved past the crawling traffic, swiping the side-mirrors from a handful of parked cars. Maybe she should have driven after all.

His driving was aggressive and erratic, leaving a cacophony of honking horns in their wake but it worked. They swung onto Neptune Avenue and Gil threw the car up onto the curb and cut the engine. Tilda ran for the house.

The Pathfinder was parked out front but the house was dark. Her heart clenched as she bolted for the sidedoor. Were they too late?

Don't think that way. Just find them.

She burst into the kitchen. Dark, the only light coming from a dim bulb under the hood fan. Fleetwood Mac was blaring throughout the house. The stereo that Shane had wrecked earlier remained broken on the kitchen floor, its cables splayed across the linoleum.

"Molly!" Tilda shot down the hallway. "Shane!"

The living room was dim, lit by a low wattage lamp. The figure in the armchair didn't move. All Tilda could see of Shane were his legs sprawling out from the easy chair. Her heart pumped into her throat, fearing the worst. "Shane?"

Shane didn't look up as she stepped into his periphery. Slumped back, the easy chair facing the turntable and a tumbler in his hand. A bottle of Glenlivet sat on the table and a mess of vinyl records scattered at his feet. He swished the ice in the tumbler. "You forget something?"

Her knees wobbled. "Where's Molly?"

"She didn't want to be here."

Tilda dialled the big volume knob to zero. "Where is she?"

"Spending the night at Zoe's." He would not look at her. "It's funny. She's more pissed off with me than you. Ain't that a kick in the pants?"

"Shane, listen to me. You have to leave. Go get Molly and go somewhere."

"Why are you still here?"

She knelt down to his level, forcing him to see her. "I know you're angry but something's happened. It isn't safe to stay here right now. Pack a bag and get Molly and go."

"Why, so you can have the house to yourself? Get out."

"Listen to me!" She knocked the tumbler away and it clunked across the floor. "You and Molly are in danger."

"Hoopdee-doo. Like this shitty situation could get any worse." He turned the volume back up and then took the scotch by the neck and stood the bottle on his knee. "My house, my rules. My Alamo."

Tilda lowered her head, hashing her brains for some way to get through to him in his state. Stone sober, her reasons for leaving sounded absurd. What story could she concoct to convince him now?

"She's telling you the truth."

The voice grumbled up behind them and Tilda's gut ran cold. Gil stood in the doorway, leaning up against the jamb. "You're not safe here. You need to get your daughter and find somewhere else to spend the night."

Shane's jaw just hung there, eyes piebald, trying to process what he was seeing. His gaze rolled slowly from the intruder to his wife. "You brought him here? Into our home? How cruel can you be?"

The confusion and pain in his eyes was unbearable. "Shane... " she uttered. It was all she could think of to say.

Shane launched out of the chair with the bottle tight in his fist. Winding up like a pitcher he hurled it at the interloper. "Get the fuck out of my house!"

Gil ducked the spinning missile. It sprayed him with scotch as it dented the wall and clattered to the ground. Wiping the mess from his face, he glanced up to see Shane charge at him like a toro.

Shane slammed the homewrecker into the wall. Locked his hands around his throat to crush the bastard's windpipe. His teeth gnashed at every obscenity he could muster. "Cocksucking-son of a bitch-piece of shit-faggot!"

Gil grimaced but he made no move to stop the man from trying to kill him. "Let go of me."

"Stop it!" Tilda pulled Shane off but her husband was a rigid column of rage, unstoppable and superhuman.

"Fucking kill you motherfucker." Shane's eyes glassed out in hatred, lost to reason and his snarls reduced to a single word, 'kill', uttered over and over like a mantra.

Gil's slammed him away. Shane caterwauled back into the Lazyboy and he and his chair toppled over. The Fleetwood on the turntable jumped and the needle skipped from *Dreams* to the chorus of *Go Your Own Way*.

Tilda shrieked at Gil to stop and rushed to Shane.

Shane wheeled to his feet with one hand clutching his ribs. Tilda reached out to help him up but he pushed her away and squared his eyes on Gil. A lopsided grin on his face. "Round two, asshole."

Gil raised his palm. "No more."

"You wrecked my life. My family. You think you can get away with that shit?" Shane lurched for the fireplace and rattled the poker from its stand, brandishing it like a weapon. "There's a price to pay, asshole. And I'm gonna flay it from your hide."

"Enough!" Tilda stood between the two men, arms outstretched like a referee. "Both of you."

"Get out of the way, Tilda" Shane snapped.

"No." Tilda motioned to the weapon in Shane's hand. "Put that thing down."

Gil turned away, no stomach left for fighting. "This is hopeless."

"Don't you turn your back on me," Shane barked. "Step into the light, asshole! Let me see your face."

Tilda blocked his way. "Put the poker down."

"No," he snarled at his wife. "I wanna see his face. Or do you wanna bullshit me some more about this being your dead boyfriend!" He stepped around his wife and barked at the figure skulking in the shadows. "Face me, you son of a bitch! Have the balls to look me in the eye."

Gil obliged, stepping into the thin light of the lamp.

Shane's eyes crinkled in confusion, the weapon in his hand falling to his side. He had seen pictures of Gil, old snapshots that Tilda kept in a box along with other Polaroids from her life before they were married. The man standing in his living room was the same as the one in those old snaps. He looked to Tilda. "What the hell... This is some kinda sick joke."

"It's not a joke," she said.

The record on the turntable came to an end. The arm swung the needle back to its cradle with a clunk and the turntable shut down. The room went silent.

Gil spoke softly. "Shane, the circumstances are weird. But for what it's worth, I'm sorry you got hurt in all this."

Shane flinched as if stung. Something about this man uttering his name flushed blood to his eyeballs. He charged, swinging the iron at the bastard's skull with enough power to crush it like an egg.

Gil dodged and the poker cracked his forearm as he blocked the strike. He grabbed for the iron but Shane was too fast. He pivoted round and smacked the rod square onto his enemy's ear. Gil dropped to one knee, his ear split in two and blood trickling fast down his neck. Shane was already winding up for another swing when Gil lashed out.

Gil rocketed forward and stove Shane's head into the wall. He heard Tilda screaming but it was all white noise now. He pinned Shane's neck to the sheetrock and his lips curled back over his sharp teeth.

All Shane saw was a leering devil face, teeth gnashing an inch from his nose. Things clarified in an instant. Long dead Gil Dorsey was neither ghost nor hoax. No shared spectral mirage; he was something far far worse.

Tilda pushed herself between them and Gil backed off. Shane slid to the floor, clutching his bruised throat. She knelt before her husband. Shane recoiled at her touch then gripped her arm in a vise. "Stay away from him, Tilda. He's fucking evil."

"Easy," she cooed. "Take a breath."

He clamped onto her wrist. "He's not human, Tilda... "

"I know what he is."

"No, you don't! He's a monster. What have you done? You brought this monster into our lives? Our home?" He pushed her away as if she was diseased. His face caught somewhere between terror and revulsion.

Tilda shivered. The flesh on the back of her arms goosed at the chill but it wasn't just her husband's disgust that brought on the shudder. The temperature in the room had dropped suddenly, fogging her breath in a vapour.

The single lamp winked out, as did the ambient light from the hallway. The whole house going dark at once. Shane and Gil both disappeared in the pitch.

"Gil?" she pleaded. "What's happening?"

She heard his footsteps creak the wood floor. Then his silhouette framed up against the light in the picture window.

"They're here," he said.

25

Scream Dracula, scream!

THE HOUSE ACROSS THE STREET went dark, the lights flicking off like a power outage. The house adjacent to it blacked out. Standing at the picture window, Tilda watched the streetlights of Neptune Avenue wink out one-by-one like blown out candles.

"The whole street's gone dark," she murmured.

"What the hell?" Shane crossed to the wall switch and flicked it up and down but no light came. "Who's they?"

Tilda lurched for the phone. Stabbed 911 into the keypad. "I'm calling the police."

Gil locked the front door. "They won't get here in time."

"Who's out there?" Shane barked, enraged at being ignored.

"Dangerous people," Gil said. "Do you have a gun?"

"A gun? No, I don't have a gun. Who are these people?"

The dispatcher's voice crackled over the phone, asking for the nature of the emergency. Tilda stifled the panic in her throat and blurted out that she was in danger and needed the police immediately. Hurry, hurry, hurry.

"Stay calm, ma'am." The dispatcher's voice was tinny and dispassionate through the receiver. "What is your address and how many people are with you?"

"I'm on Neptune Avenue. Number twenty-seven. There's three of us here."

"Do you know who these people are?"

"No. They tried to kill us earlier."

"Are there any children in the house?"

"Yes. No. My daughter's not here. Are you sending someone?"

"The police are on their way—"

Noise broke over their heads. The tinkle of shattering glass followed by a thud from the upstairs bedroom.

Gil looked at the ceiling. "They're in the house."

"Oh God," Tilda pleaded into the phone. "Please hurry. They're inside now."

"Son of a bitch. Who the hell is this?" Shane marched for the stairs.

Tilda grabbed his arm. "Don't go up there."

"And let them just break in? Screw that."

"Listen to her, Shane. You don't want to mess with them." Gil took the phone from Tilda and set it down on the table without hanging up. The dispatcher's voice crackled on like the buzzing of a housefly.

A new sound, the racket of more breaking glass but this time coming from the back of the house. The snap of wood as the backdoor was blown in.

"Goddamnit!" Shane paced in frustration.

Tilda clutched at Gil. "What do we do? Should we run?"

"No. Stay together. If we can hold them off until the police come, we'll be okay. The coven will scatter when they hear the sirens."

"Coven?" Shane blanched. He dug his cellphone from his pocket and activated the tiny flashlight. The thin beam arced over the door leading to the hallway. Nothing moved. He swept the light across the floor until he found the fireplace poker he'd lost. He scooped it up, held it high. "Who are these assholes?"

"That's what we need." Gil reached for another fireplace tool but found only the dustpan. Snapping the pan away, he handed the iron rod to Tilda. "Aim for the face. The eyes, if you can."

Their breath misted in the throw of the tiny flashlight. The walls ticked and creaked around them as the temperature dropped. A rumbling underfoot, as if a subway train was blasting through the cellar. The floor rattled, the walls shook. Picture frames dropped from their hooks and crystal tumbled from the shelves. The whole house was under attack, as if the nightmarish things outside wanted to shake the structure from its roots and plow the walls in.

"Jesus Christ." Shane jawed the air in disbelief.

And then it stopped and the house stilled. A pane of glass tumbled from the cracked sideboard and chimed against the floor.

Tilda reached for Gil. "Are they gone?"

"No." Gil nodded at the cell in Shane's hand. "When they come, flash that light into their eyes. It will blind them."

Shane froze. "Do you hear that?"

A low scratching sound, impossible to pinpoint its source. Shane aimed the light at the hallway. There was nothing there but the grating noise grew louder. Closer.

"Shane," Tilda whispered. "Look up."

He swung the weak beam up. The thing overhead scrabbled across the ceiling like some demented crab. Its wretched face gibbered at them, black drool stringing from its diseased lips.

The flashlight fell to the floor. The vampire dropped onto Shane, flattening him. He screamed out in terror, a sound his wife had never heard until now.

Tilda swung the rod, cracking it against the monster's back. Zero effect. It pushed Shane down and popped its lamprey teeth, drizzling dark spittle across his face.

Gil kicked it off, tumbling the thing away. Its pale eyes radiated hatred but its shriek of betrayal was cut as Gil attacked it, stomping its head underfoot until the skull imploded in a balloon-burst of gore like a blighted pumpkin.

Something shot out of the dark and freight-trained Gil into the wall.

Tilda ran to help him, the iron swinging up, but a dark shape erupted from the floor and its withered scarecrow face gibbered at her. She swung hard but the thing batted the weapon away and smacked her to the ground. Her back walloped flat to the hardwood, knocking the wind from her lungs. The wraith curled back its dark lips and lunged at her throat.

It stopped when the cold iron pierced its skull. Shane speared the poker through its ear. It tumbled leeways off Tilda, poisoned blood spraying from its eardrums. Shane threw his shoulder into the thrust, driving it further in until the wraith twitched and flopped like a spastic.

Tilda flailed away from the geyser of blood and rolled to her feet. Shane set his heel against the thing's skull and jerked the weapon free. "Are you hurt?"

"No." She scanned the darkness. "Where's Gil?"

Shane cursed. The crashing, thumping row of a struggle filled the air but all Tilda could see was the monstrosity charging at them from the hallway. And then another, crab-walking across the ceiling towards them.

Tilda dove over the sofa to get away, felt its claw rake her shin. The sofa lifted clean off the floor as the thing tossed it from its path. It roared at her and Tilda kicked out. She backed hard into one wall then slid into another. Cornered, the wraith closed in.

Her flailing hands bumped the framed mirror above her and something Gil had said hitched at her memory. She wrenched the mirror from the wall and swung it before her like a shield. The vampire reared back like a spooked horse, twisting away as if blinded.

It worked. The thing slithered this way and that to avoid its reflection but Tilda adjusted the angle and pressed forward. It hissed and flailed to get away and as she pushed on, the thing backed right into Gil.

Gil ducked its flailing claws, snatched up the iron rod Tilda had dropped and plunged it hilt-deep into the monster's ribs. It bansheed in pain and lashed at his head. Gil plucked the weapon free and stabbed it again and again in rapidfire blows that painted blood over the walls and opened the thing's chest into a wet wreckage of gore. The monster flopped to the ground and steam billowed up from its twisted shape. Tilda turned away from the noxious stench that issued from it as the undead thing putrefied before her eyes into a bubbling mass of inky filth.

The flush of victory was quashed short as Tilda watched two more of the coven drop from the ceiling. One roared at her like some hellish primate and this time she was the one backing away, the mirror shield barely keeping the thing at bay. She glanced at Gil only to see him swarmed by two others.

Chaos erupted on her left. Shane was backed into the far corner, swinging the poker madly to keep another vampire at bay. The wraith seemed to be toying with him, waiting for Shane to give out in exhaustion.

Shane cried out for help, his voice raw with panic.

Gil, across the room and outnumbered three to one, called her name.

Pierced into an impossible choice of whom to save, Tilda froze up. Gil. Shane. The horrid little voice in her head woke and rubbed its hands at her dilemma.

This is what you get for thinking you can have your cake and eat it too.

Who's it going to be?

"Tilda!" one of them screamed. She couldn't tell them apart anymore.

Gil could handle himself, she decided. It was the only way. Shane was failing and the monster was already batting him around like a cat with a mouse.

Driving the one before her away, she ran to help Shane and already knew the choice was wrong. Either choice would be wrong. She shrieked at the thing menacing her husband and it spun to receive a face full of mirror and shrank back. Shane broke the poker across its eyes. It flailed, clawing the air blind while averting its reflection.

She heard her name ring out again. Surrounded by three shadowy wraiths, Gil lashed out madly to drive them back but was losing ground at every step. A fourth and then a fifth shadow dropped into the fray and Gil stumbled and it was all over. He fell to one knee and the coven pressed the advantage. The things swarmed in and Gil vanished in a void of ragged cloaks and ripping claws.

As Gil was lost in a writhing scrum, one wraith remained apart, observing. Its countenance haughty, more ravaged and alien than the rest. The rector of this godforsaken clan of monsters. Tilda felt her heart stop as the chieftain raised its dead gaze from the chaos to lock onto her own widened eyes. Its dark lips curled back in a pervert's leer of anticipation.

Caught offguard, the blinded vampire before her struck out in a wild swing and shattered the mirror. The glass fell in a twinkling mosaic, the frame splitting. The thing gnashed its teeth and Tilda flung back defenceless.

Shane batted for the thing's head, putting all he had into his swing. The vampire took the blow, blood squirting from its ears. It lashed out on the backswing and hurtled Shane into the wall. The impact shook the house and Tilda watched her husband slip to the floor like a broken puppet. He didn't move.

A ringing sound stung her ears, growing louder and louder until she realized it wasn't a burst eardrum but a police siren. Red lights flashed in the picture window, strobing the walls scarlet. The coven, illuminated in the blinking light, retreated like cockroaches.

Where was Gil?

Slumped on the floor in a bloodied heap. His eyes wheeled drunkenly until they landed on Tilda. He reached out for her. Tilda dove for his outstretched hand but the wraiths sunk their claws into him and, for the second time in her life, Gil Dorsey was dragged away from her. The coven slithered back into the darkness with their prize and vanished one by one. Gil's fingernails raked down the hardwood, flailing at something, anything to latch onto but there was nothing and then he too was swallowed up by the shadows.

The front door crashed open, two uniformed officers storming into the room. One held her palm over the butt of her holstered weapon but the other gripped his service issue in both hands, sweeping the barrel over the room.

He lowered the sidearm when he saw the woman on her knees in a mess of broken glass, her head hung low and her shoulders wracking in sobs.

"Ma'am?" The officer spoke softly, careful not to spook the distraught woman.

The first officer thumbed on her flashlight and swept the beam over the catastrophe of the family room. It appeared as if a cyclone had spun everything in the room and flung it against the walls.

"Holy cow," she said.

TWO more police units joined the first at the scene, crowding onto the curb and spinning their strobing lights into the branches of the trees. The ambulance arrived shortly afterwards, the paramedics rushing a gurney into the house. The neighbours crowded around on the sidewalk and craned their necks when the paramedics wheeled Shane Coleman into the back of the ambulance.

Tilda sat on the front stoop, pressing a towel to her bloodied knee. A third paramedic looked her over, gently prodding her and asking if this hurt, did that.

A plainclothes officers approached the stoop and nodded a hello. "Ms. Parish. Are you all right?"

She looked up. Detective Crippen hovered over her. Tilda looked around for his partner, the chubbier man who was nicer but Detective Rowe wasn't there.

Detective Crippen looked up at the gaping mess of the broken picture window and whistled as if impressed. "Jesus H. What happened?"

26

Do you know how to waltz?

"WHO ATTACKED YOU?"

Tilda sat under the fluorescents of Interview Room B inside the new 14 Division building of the Toronto Metro Police. Detective Crippen sat across from her with his big hands folded neatly on the table between them. He wanted to know who had broken into the house and assaulted her and her husband.

Tilda rubbed her eyes, trying to conjure up some answer that would satisfy the police detective. *They were vampires, officer. A whole bunch of them. They live in the sewers. And they kidnapped my undead boyfriend. Did I mention he was a bloodsucker too?*

Detective Crippen sat patiently, still as granite. His much friendlier partner, Detective Rowe, was nowhere to be seen. Apparently Crippen had abandoned the whole good cop/bad cop tactic and gotten straight down to brass tacks.

The paramedics had treated her at the house. Mostly cuts and scrapes but they were concerned about the ravaged marks on her stomach. Tilda had insisted it was fine but did ask them to bandage it up properly. When the detective returned, she told them she needed to phone her daughter.

Molly was safe and sound at Zoe's house. Tilda explained what had happened and that her father had been taken to hospital. Despite Tilda's insistence that her dad was fine and it would be best if she stayed where she was for the night, Molly insisted on going to the hospital. When she hung up, she asked the detective for a police car to pick up her daughter and take her to the hospital. Crippen said he'd be happy to and, if she was feeling up to it, they would escort her over to 14 Division for a discussion about the night's events.

She had tried to get out of it, saying she was too exhausted and all she wanted to do was see her husband. Detective Cripped was having none of it and asked if she needed a hand walking to the car.

Interview Room B consisted of a small table that was bolted to the floor and two moulded plastic chairs. The lighting was harsh, giving the room the claustrophobic feel of an incubator.

Detective Crippen offered a watery smile. "Did you know these assailants?"

"No," Tilda said.

"What did they look like? How many were there?"

"Six or seven. The power was cut, so it was dark. I didn't get a look at any of them."

"Of course." Crippen varnished his tone with a thin wash of sarcasm. "So these people just came out of nowhere and broke in? Laid siege to the house like Vikings on a bender and you have no clue as to why they targeted you and your husband?"

"It was so dark, they could have been Vikings. Or ninjas, I dunno."

Crippen leaned forward, as if he'd caught the scent to something juicy. "Do you want to know what I think?"

"I'm all ears." She couldn't help returning the bad attitude.

"I think those attackers were the homies of the dude you and your boyfriend killed at the bar last week."

"Homies?"

"Compadres," Crippen said. "Posse, gang, bros. Whatever culturally appropriate term you want to use to designate the associates of the deceased man."

Tilda studied the detectives hands splayed out on the tabletop. They were clean and void of calluses or marks, the nails neatly trimmed. She wondered if he had them manicured. "That's quite a theory. But I already told you, I don't know anything about that man's death."

"Ahh, see..." Crippen raised a finger. "That's where the theory finds it legs. I found a witness who not only puts you on the scene when the man was assaulted but states that you were with the assailant who shoved the victim out the window."

"We've already been through this. Your witness is wrong."

Crippen grinned, flashing pristine white teeth. "No, I think he's dead on. You know why I think that? Because he liked your music. He said you sounded like... Damn, who is that singer?" Here Crippen snapped his fingers, trying to recall a name. "That skinny English woman from years back. Lanky, real weirdo... Ugh."

Tilda watched the detective rack his brains but didn't offer any suggestions. Finally, another fingersnap. "P.J. Harvey! That's it!"

She reared back. "Harvey?"

"Yes!"

"And that makes him right?"

"Sure. That, and the fact that he thought you were hot."

"Golly. Great witness, detective."

"But he is, Ms. Parish. You know why? Because no guy who liked your music *and* thought you were hot would finger you on the scene." Crippen's face fell by a degree. "Poor choice of words, but you know what I mean."

"Maybe he had too much to drink."

"That's always a possibility. But he was sober enough to remember your date that night. The witness even helped our sketch artist draft up a likeness." The detective plucked a sheet of paper from his jacket pocket and unfolded it. He flattened it on the table and slid it across. "Pretty good, huh?"

It was. The sketch artist had captured the angular frame of Gil's face and the unruly fall of hair over the eyes. The mouth and nose were off, generic and unremarkable in their rendering. Tilda flattened the paper against the tabletop. "So this is my boyfriend, huh?"

"This is the man you were with that night. So, who is he?"

"Is this a joke? Because if it is, it's a cruel one."

"No jokes here, Miss Parish. I'm just trying to get to the bottom of this."

Tilda tapped a finger on the sketch. "You're right. I do know this man. His name is Gil Dorsey. And he was my boyfriend. For a time."

Detective Crippen leaned forward, eager to kill this case and drag it home. "I see. And where would I find Mr. Dorsey now?"

Tilda slid the picture back. "Bottom of Lake Ontario."

The detective's mouth went oval in surprise but no sound came out.

"Gil died seventeen years ago," Tilda continued. "In a car accident that took his life and left me in the hospital for a month."

Tilda had been allowed to keep her bag with her in the interview room and it sat on the floor under the table. As Crippen's face darkened, she plucked the bag into her lap and found her wallet. She dug through its flattened bills and creased receipts until she found a small photograph. Old, its edges frayed. She snapped it onto the table like a playing card. "Here," she said, squaring the photo alongside the sketch. "That's him."

Crippen scrutinized the face in the photograph and then studied the sketch and went back to the photo. The smug vestige of triumph drained from his eyes.

"Whoever your witness is, he has a nasty sense of humour." She nodded at the photo. "You can keep that picture if you want. Now, I need to go to the hospital and see my husband."

THE night sky clouded over, hiding the few visible stars, and after a while, it began to rain. Tilda watched the raindrops collect on the windows of the police cruiser as it prowled along College Street. Detective Crippen had arranged for a uniformed officer to escort her to the hospital and Tilda experienced her second ride in a police unit in the same night.

"You okay back there?" The officer turned her head towards the backseat but kept her eyes on the road. Officer Whittaker had introduced herself with an easy smile and completely non-judgemental demeanour, for which Tilda was grateful.

"I'm fine, officer," Tilda said. "I just have a lot on my mind."

"I hear that," the uniform replied. "Sometimes you want to switch your brain off but it just races on, worrying about everything. Call me Jenny, by the way."

"Thanks, Jenny. I'm Tilda."

"Pleasure." Officer Whittaker bopped her horn to alert the driver in front that the light had turned green. "How do you like our Detective Crippen?"

Tilda shrugged, unsure of how to respond. 'Utter asshole' was probably not the best description to employ given the company. "He seems tough. Kinda snarky too."

"He is that. Freaky-smart, you know. But he's fair."

"That's good to know."

Rain patted the roof with a light drum and Whittaker turned her attention to a call coming over the squawk box. Tilda settled back and wondered if Gil was dead.

For a second time in her life, he had been snatched away by monsters and her heart stung at the thought of what might happen to him. According to Gil, the most sacred law of this hellish coven was secrecy and Gil had broken it. For her. Would the coven destroy him or just punish him? Either thought clenched her heart like a coronary.

Constricting her heart even tighter was the cold realization that there was absolutely nothing she could do about it. The coven could be hidden anywhere. She was outnumbered. They were fiendish, inhuman monsters. And now that they knew about her, they would be return to kill her too.

And then there was her daughter and husband. If what Gil had told her about the ruthlessness of the coven was true, they would also be targeted. Simply by association.

Shane would be safe for the moment inside a hospital. Of that she was sure. A hospital was too busy and too bright for them to risk any assault on the place. Molly had been driven to the hospital in another prowl car and most likely escorted straight to Shane's hospital bed. She was safe for now but what about after? What happens after the uniformed officers like Whittaker say goodnight and leave them on their own?

Molly couldn't stay at the house, that much was certain. Sending her back to her friend's house wasn't an option either. Zoe lived eight blocks away and Tilda was certain that those degenerate wraiths would sniff her out. She needed to get Molly out of the city. But to where?

Tilda rooted around in her bag for her phone. She scrolled down the list of contacts for a number that, under normal circumstances, she was reluctant to dial.

"You making a call?" Officer Whittaker snagged her reflection in the rearview mirror.

"Is that okay?"

"Sure." Whittaker reached for the console. "Let me just turn down the squawk-box so you can hear."

Whittaker toggled back the volume of the police radio to a civilized decibel of squelch. Tilda thanked her and thumbed down the list and hit a number. Listening to it ring, she steeled her nerves against the prospect of asking her mother-in-law for a favour.

OFFICER Whittaker sensed Tilda's rising tension as they pulled up to the hospital and offered to go with her inside. Tilda was grateful. Hospitals were unpleasant under the best of circumstances and having spent a month in one at the age of twenty-four, Tilda hated being within spitting distance of one. The officer's calm presence helped her keep it together. At least until they located the room Shane was in. The sight of their daughter sitting alone by her father's bedside struck Tilda as the saddest thing she had ever seen. She would have collapsed had Whittaker not taken her arm.

"Okay, catch your breath." Whittaker led her to a chair in the hallway and made her sit. "You might want to take a minute before you go in."

"I'm okay. Just took me by surprise, seeing that."

"Course. But they're both okay." Whittaker nodded then stole a glance inside the room. "How old's your daughter?"

"Thirteen."

"She looks like a strong kid. Watching over her dad like that."

"She is." Another wave threatened to choke Tilda into tears but she breathed through it and then got to her feet. She reached out and touched the officer's arm. "Thank you, Jenny. You've been very kind."

"I'll be out here if you need anything."

Tilda thanked her again and went into the room.

MOLLY turned at the sound of the door clicking open, saw her mother and then slumped back down in the chair. Tilda tiptoed inside and placed her hand on her daughter's head. She felt Molly's hair and the shape of her skull and fought down the urge to squeeze the girl in a bear hug. "You all right?"

Molly shrugged. "I'm not the one in a hospital bed."

Shane looked remarkably peaceful under the thin hospital sheet. His eyes were closed, his hands folded neatly over his stomach. A split on his cheek had been closed with two stitches but other than that, he appeared unmarked.

"How is he?"

"He says he's fine," Molly said. "Dad, you awake?"

Shane opened his eyes, registered Tilda standing there and then closed his eyes again. "I'm awake."

Molly stood and shuffled to the door. "I'm going to find a Coke machine."

The door clicked shut. The girl's absence left a vacuum in the room. Tilda didn't move. "How do you feel?"

"Like shit," he said without opening his eyes.

Tilda took the chair. "I'm sorry, Shane. I never meant for any of this to happen."

"I don't care anymore."

Tilda leaned back and the weight of exhaustion smothered her like quicksand. Everything around her lay in tatters and she hadn't a clue as to how to fit the pieces back together again. Maybe they never would.

Shane opened his eyes and stared up at the tiles on the ceiling. "Those things that attacked us. Gil's one of them, isn't he?"

"Yes."

"Why did they attack us?"

"Because of me. Because I know they exist."

He didn't react to this news. "And now I do. Will they come back?"

"You're safe in here. There's too many people in here for them to try anything."

Shane tried to sit up but winced at the pain and settled back down. He waited for the dizziness to pass. "We gotta get Molly somewhere safe."

"Lie still." Tilda rose and straightened the sheet over him. "I got it figured out."

"How?"

"Your mom's on her way. She's gonna take Molly back with her until it's safe."

Surprise lifted his eyes. "That must have been an awkward call. What did you tell her?"

Sylvia, Shane's mother, had never warmed to Tilda. Even after the birth of her only grandchild, Sylvia regarded Tilda with cool suspicion. "I told her that you and I were having problems and we needed time to sort it out."

"Okay. Good. Molly will be safe out in Wasaga." Sweat beaded up over his face and he seemed spent.

Tilda smoothed the hair from his brow. "What did you tell Molly?"

"That a bunch of crackheads busted in," he gasped. "The rest of it, I pretty much told her the truth."

Tilda looked at the door. "I have to talk to her."

"You're gonna get a blast of it. Don't lose your temper on her."

"Okay," she said, and went to find her daughter.

27

Far too young

MOLLY WAS IN THE LOBBY, curled up in one of the stiff-backed chairs while the injured and the disturbed shuffled around her like phantoms. Tilda slowed her pace as she came up behind the girl, a lump of ice forming inside her heart.

While she screwed up her courage for what was coming, she saw Molly turn to the dishevelled woman next to her and whisper something. The woman was older, her hair a frayed tangle of grey and she was overdressed for the season. Possibly homeless. The old woman reached out and pressed something into her daughter's hand. Tilda's dander shot up, scolding herself for leaving Molly alone in a busy hospital waiting room.

"Honey?" Tilda came around the bench and stopped short when she laid eyes on the old woman.

The same old woman who rambled around the market with her home-made cross, admonishing sinners to come to Jesus. The same voodoo woman who had tried to burn her with the same wooden cross that rested in the old woman's lap.

"Molly, what are you doing?" Tilda put a protective hand over Molly's shoulder, claiming territory. She turned a cold eye on the old woman. "Is this woman bothering you?"

"It's okay, mom" Molly said. "We were just talking."

The old woman looked up but her eyes held none of the scorn she had flung at Tilda earlier. If anything, the woman looked sad. She stood and took up her flimsy cross, muttering something Tilda couldn't decipher, and ambled off to find another seat.

Tilda looked her daughter over, as if searching for an injury or mark. "What did she say to you?"

"The usual stuff. About Jesus and being saved," Molly replied. "How's dad?"

"Angry."

Molly brushed lint from her knee. "He has reason to be."

"He told you."

"Yes," Molly said in a cold tone. "How could you do that to him?"

Tilda closed her eyes. "Honey, what I did was wrong but sometimes... sometimes things happen and you have little control over them."

"That sounds like an excuse. Did somebody put a gun to your head? You didn't have a choice?"

Tilda tensed her jaw muscle. Steeling herself for this conversation, she'd anticipated a lot crying on her part. What she hadn't foreseen was the seething she could barely restrain at being called out by a child.

"If you love someone, you don't cheat on them." Molly folded her arms, indignantly righteous in her moral stance. "Simple as that. And if you do cheat, you don't get to whitewash it with excuses and justifications. Don't you love dad anymore?"

"Molly, what I did was wrong. Without a doubt. I own that. But not everything is black and white. It isn't always love or hate or right versus wrong."

"Right. Because you're *such* a complicated person. Tilda Parish, the tortured artist."

"Stop it."

Molly's tone had carried over the room and now heads bobbed up to see what all the fuss was about. The injured and the sick and the gravely disturbed, all roused from their stupor and hoping for some spectacle to alleviate the excruciating boredom.

Mother and daughter clammed up, mortified at the unwanted attention. Neither made a peep until the walleyed gawkers lost interest and fell back asleep.

Molly twisted a length of beads in her hand. "This other guy. Do you love him?"

"Don't ask me that."

"Are you and dad having problems?"

"No. That's the crazy part, nothing was wrong. I mean, we had our fights and nothing's ever perfect but there's nothing big, nothing really wrong. But still, this happened. Or I let it happen and now I've destroyed everything. And now I don't know what to do."

"Fix it," Molly said.

"It's not that simple, honey."

"Sure it is. Just make it right. Whatever you have to do, fix it. At least try."

"I can't. Aren't you listening to me?"

"Yes you can. Is there another option here? Is it worth it?"

"Of course it is."

Molly shrugged again. "Then you don't have a choice. Just fix it. Or burn in hell."

"Burn in hell?"

"You know what I mean. Deal with the consequences." Molly sighed. "That old lady put all that Jesus talk into my head. Got biblical."

Tilda looked out over the room and pinpointed the old woman standing near the entrance. The woman gazed back, watching Tilda, before turning to the automated doors and shuffling out of the hospital.

Tilda's gaze swung back to her daughter. "Did she give you something?"

"This." Molly unfurled a rosary bead from her clenched hand. A small brass crucifix dangling on the end of it. "It's kinda pretty in a Goth way."

"Why did she give you that?"

Molly shrugged. "She said it was for protection. I guess it will save my soul." Molly stood and patted her mother's hand. "I'm gonna check on dad."

"I'll catch up." Tilda watched Molly cross to the elevators, then she hurried for the exit.

Taxis bumpered up along the front curb, clogging the hospital entrance. Two police officers dragged a man with a bloodied face into Emergency. Tilda caught sight of the old woman halfway up the block, hobbling away on crippled knees. She turned when Tilda called out to her.

"Wait," Tilda panted as she caught up. "Why did you give my daughter that rosary?"

The old woman's face soured with scorn. "To save her."

Tilda snatched her arm. "You know what those things are. How do I protect my daughter from them?"

"Trust Jesus," the woman chuffed, as if the answer couldn't be anymore obvious.

"Please. I need something more."

"There is no more." The woman pulled her arm back. She dug into the grimy folds of her clothing and produced another cross. This one about the size of a fist and made of brass. She held it out for Tilda to take. "Trust Him or trust nothing."

Tilda looked down at the cross but didn't touch it. In those old scary movies, the cross had potency only if its bearer held faith. Tilda had none. An avowed atheist in her youth, Tilda became spiritually starved in her thirties but remained wary of most religions. Now that she was in her forties, she was simply lost. "They're going to come after my daughter."

"Take it." She pressed the brass into Tilda's hands and then turned away. Five limping paces and then she stopped and looked back. "Fire," she grunted. "Everything burns. Even them."

She shambled away, leaving Tilda alone on the sidewalk.

OFFICER Whittaker waited for Tilda at the nurse's station on Shane's floor. After Molly had said goodbye to her dad, the officer walked the two of them down to where she had left her patrol unit and drove Tilda and her daughter home.

One uniformed officer was still on scene when they pulled up to the house and Whittaker nodded to him as they came up the walk.

"Holy cow," Molly sputtered at the state of the family room.

The power had been restored and almost every light in the house was switched on. One crime scene technician stood in the wreckage of overturned furniture, snapping a few last photographs. He waved them through, telling Whittaker that he was finished.

"Okay, upstairs." Tilda took Molly's arm and steered her towards the stairs. "Let's get you packed. Take enough clothes for a week."

Molly looked up the staircase. "Are you sure it's safe?"

"I'm coming up." Tilda followed her up the stairs. Everywhere she looked she saw the after-image of the coven inside her house, hiding in every shadow or crawling the ceiling like beetles. She wasn't about to let her daughter out of her sight for a second in this house.

Whittaker followed them up to the second floor, which Tilda was grateful for, checking Molly's room first before leaving the girl to pack. They walked through the rest of the rooms and then crossed into Tilda's bedroom. The window was blown in, shattered glass flung across the bed. Dark blemishes of filth and soot trailed from the window sill to the floor.

Whittaker looked up, following a second trail of filth running overhead. "Jesus. What did these creeps do, crawl across the ceiling?"

Tilda feigned ignorance. She tugged the hem of her shirt, looking at how torn and dirty her clothes were. "I need to change."

Whittaker turned to go. "I'll wait in the hall."

"Don't bother. I'll just be a second." Tilda said, rifling through a drawer. Truth was she simply didn't want to be alone in the room.

Whittaker leaned out the broken window and looked down into the backyard. "Do you have somewhere to stay tonight?"

"Molly's grandmother is coming to pick her up and take her back to Wasaga. I'll stay at a friend's place."

"Good." Whittaker thumbed on her Maglite and swept the beam over the yard. "You know, it's kinda funny me getting this call."

Tilda shimmied into a clean pair of jeans. "What's funny about it?"

"I'm a fan. I've seen you play half a dozen times." Whittaker offered a sheepish smile. "Last time was the Mariposa festival, couple of years ago. Your stuff's on heavy rotation on my iPod."

"Oh. Well, thanks." Taken aback by this news, Tilda wasn't sure what to do with it. "How come you didn't say anything before."

"I dunno. I guess I didn't want to sound like some geeky fan. Even though I am." A shade of pink flushed the officer's cheeks. "Hell, I even went back and found your earlier stuff with the Gorgons."

Over the last twenty-four hours, Tilda hadn't given music a second thought. Too busy dealing with this uncanny situation and trying not to get killed by a nightmarish pack of ghouls. Her old life, her music career, had faded so far into the background that it felt like someone else's life. A book she had read a long time ago. She almost asked Officer Whittaker if she hadn't mistaken her for someone else. "Thanks," she said again, almost apologetically.

"It's been a while since you put out a record. You working on anything new?"

"No," Tilda said. There was the rub. She rummaged through another drawer. "There won't be anymore new records."

"You mean it's all digital now? No CDs or vinyl?"

"No. I quit music. Quit writing it, quit playing it. Finito."

Whittaker's expression went from confusion to crestfallen. "Jeez. That's too bad."

"No. It's just life." Tilda took a breath, feeling marginally better in clean clothes. She desperately wanted to shower but would have to make do with scrubbing her face. "Sometimes you have to let go."

Molly appeared at the door, letting her overstuffed backpack thump to the floor. "I'm finished." She surveyed the damage in her parent's bedroom. "Whoa. This room too?"

TILDA'S relationship with Shane's mother had gotten off to a shaky start and pretty much stayed that way, even after Molly was born. In fact, it had probably gotten worse. Although she had never verbalized her feelings about her daughter-in-law's career choice as musician, Sylvia made no attempt to hide her disapproval of it. Given that foundational rift between them, Sylvia positively despaired about how her granddaughter was being raised. To make up for it, Sylvia Coleman spoiled Molly every chance she got and, to Tilda's mind, seemed to go out of her way to 'correct' Molly's upbringing.

Tilda used to seethe over it. Shane would shrug and say "What do you want me to do? She's a grandmother."

Sylvia, who hated Toronto for its lack of parking and rude denizens, pulled up onto the curb and honked the horn. Whenever she came into the city, Sylvia fully expected to be robbed, shot, raped, assaulted or spit upon by all the gun-toting gangbangers or serial-killing perverts she was convinced were lurking behind every corner. She stayed inside her car and locked the doors until someone came out. To her relief, the first person she saw was a police officer.

When Tilda came outside, she found Sylvia deep in conversation with Officer Whittaker about the vileness of the city and how she'll never understand why people chose to live in this godforsaken sewer. To her credit, Whittaker was accommodatingly good natured about the whole thing, giving Tilda the impression that she endured this line of complaint all the time.

"Thank you so much for coming, Sylvia" Tilda said. "I'm sorry to drag you away from home in the middle of the night."

"Anything for Molly." Sylvia hugged her granddaughter then told the girl to load her things in the car. She turned back to Tilda. "I stopped by the hospital to see Shane."

"Is he resting?"

"No." She looked past Tilda to the house. "But he was damned tight-lipped about what happened here."

"It was just a break-in. These things happen."

The woman looked ill at the very thought. Of any emergency to call about, this one had been the worst, confirming for all time Sylvia's opinion of the cesspool in which her granddaughter was being raised. "It's nightmarish. Just standing here gives me the creeps."

"Well," Tilda hummed, "I'm grateful you can take Molly."

"How long can I keep my granddaughter?"

"The rest of the week? I think it'd be best for Molly to stay away until we can fix things up."

"Let's make it two weeks. I've made plans."

Typical Sylvia, taking a mile when a centimetre had been offered. Tilda forced a smile. "Well, there's school."

"She can miss it. The girl's smart as a whip." Sylvia leaned in for a slight brush of a hug and scampered back into her vehicle before she was gunned down in a drive-by.

Molly came around to say goodbye. "Will you be okay?"

"That's my line. Don't worry about me. Have fun with your grandmother, okay?"

"We always do. Listen, don't do anything stupid. Okay?"

Tilda leaned back in surprise. "Why would you say that?"

"I dunno," Molly said. "I told you to fix it but...within reason."

Tilda swept the girl up and squeezed her tight. "I love you. Be good for Grandma." A kiss on her daughter's cheek and then the girl ducked into the waiting car.

Tilda wiped away the inevitable tear, grateful she'd held off until Molly was away. She heard Whittaker come up behind her.

"Your mother-in-law's a real hoot," Whittaker said.

"That's a nice way to put it."

Whittaker hooked a thumb into her belt. "Okay. That's one squared away. Now, what do we do with you?"

Tilda blew the bangs from her eyes. She didn't have a clue.

28

Your love glows in the dark

OFFICER WHITTAKER REFUSED TO abandon Tilda, insisting on escorting her safely to a friend's house. Tilda was grateful but she just wanted to be alone, even here inside the house with its broken windows and strange scorch mark left on the floor. Realizing the police officer wouldn't be swayed, she traipsed upstairs to pack a bag.

She sat on the bed and listened to the crickets chirping in through the catastrophe of the window. If the coven suddenly returned at that moment to finish the job, she wouldn't have cared much. Her husband hated her and her daughter could barely hide her disgust. Everything had been blown to smithereens. Gil was dead. Again.

The prickly feel of déjà vu was downright sinister, grieving over Gil a second time. How cruel. As ecstatic as she had been when he miraculously came back to her, she never imagined that she would have to go through it all over again and be left mourning. It wasn't fair. How cruel could God be to allow that? Better still, how could He allow those monsters to exist? Perverse abominations to everything under the sun, to God and nature alike. Her mistake, she grasped, was thinking that God existed or cared. She'd assumed it had to be one the other.

Fix it.

Molly's words kept buzzing at her with gnat-like irritation. But there was nothing left to fix, nothing that could be glued back together in any form. So what was the point? It would almost be easier if those monsters burst in to finish the job.

Was Gil dead? He had told her that the coven destroys traitors. He didn't say kill or execute or murder. Destroy. Torn apart and ripped into little pieces. The flash images, once conjured up, refused to go away, refused to stop looping in her mind. She could almost hear him screaming.

Almost...

Then a shudder hit. A full body jolt that flensed her muscles as if she'd been electrocuted. Her hands went numb while her veins surged hot and bristling through her frame. The wound on her breast flared and stung and flared again.

Gil wasn't dead. Gil was alive. Or still undead, or whatever the hell he was.

It made no sense, no tangible reason beside this flux of hot and cold, this throbbing where his teeth had cut into her. Her grief was premature. Gil wasn't dead. He was still out there somewhere.

It's in the blood. Her veins had been contaminated with his and now some bizarro bond stretched between them on a gossamer tissue of heat and stinging nettles. He wasn't dead. The sensation was as acute as torture and as strong as revenge.

What now?

The question aligned into a neat order in her brain but her heart was already tapping out the answer in Morse code. Fix it. Find Gil and get him out. A tug of war, the push and pull between mind and heart. How could she save Gil?

Was it worth it?

Yes.

Then go down there and get him

Just waltz down into the subterranean nest of a coven of vampires and demand they hand him over to her? It's suicide. They'd destroy us both.

Then burn them, like the old voodoo woman advised. Torch them like cockroaches.

How?

The nagging little voice in her head whispered the answer. That same cringing screech that delighted in wreaking havoc with its doubts and sober second thoughts suddenly changed its tune and provided a plan. Suicidal maybe, but sitting here in useless despair was the surer death.

A means of entering the nest had already been shown to her. A weapon to keep the vile things at bay was available. A little planning was needed, that's all.

That and the small detail of getting shed of the police officer waiting for her downstairs.

"ALL packed?" Whittaker watched Tilda descend the staircase with a duffel bag slung across her shoulders.

"Almost," Tilda said, turning towards the kitchen. "Just a few last minute things. I'll meet you at the car."

Whittaker nodded and went out the front door. Tilda lugged the bag down to the basement and hit the light. Shane's woodshop smelled of pine and tungst oil. Dropping the duffel onto the bench disturbed a fine layer of

sawdust that powdered everything in the room. Rifling
through the cupboard, she brought down Shane's big Maglite and tested it. It worked but the light flickered so she
unscrewed the base and let the batteries spill over the
bench. She slotted six fresh ones into the tube, replaced the
cap and tossed the big flashlight into the duffel. A roll of
duct tape followed it. She rummaged through the metal
cabinet until she found her husband's hunting knife. A six
inch blade with a sturdy handle tucked inside a leather
scabbard. This went into the bag, along with a pair pliers,
even though she wasn't quite sure what she needed them
for. It just seemed like a practical tool to have.

One last look over the woodshop, trying to think of anything else she might need. A spindle of wood lay chucked
in the lathe, ready to be turned and she idled a thought to
making wooden stakes to bring along too. She doubted any
of those things would sit still long enough for her to hammer one into its decrepit heart so she hit the light switch
and went back upstairs.

She found her cell phone and changed into a sturdy pair
of running shoes. Stuck a couple of hair bands into her
pocket and threw a pair of gloves into the duffel before
zipping it up.

"YOU can pull over here."

Whittaker pulled the cruiser to the curb on the south side of Dundas Street and looked with some dismay at the hideous block of tenement housing off their starboard side. "Your friend lives here?"

"No, up there." Tilda nodded to the opposite side where Kensington's one-way fed into the corridor. She pulled the door latch. "I can walk from here."

"Hang on. I can drop you right at the door."

"Then you'd have to go all the way around. No point." Tilda stuck out her hand. "Thank you, Jenny. For everything."

"My pleasure. It's not everyday I get to help out a musical hero." Whittaker took her card from her pocket, scrounged up a pen and wrote something on the back. She held the card out to Tilda. "That's my cell number. If you need anything or remember anything more about the attack, call. Or if you just want to talk."

"Thanks. That's really kind of you."

The officer fixed Tilda with a stern look. "I mean it, Tilda. You've been going on adrenaline for the past twelve hours and you're gonna crash. That's when the reality of what just happened is going to hit you like a ton of bricks. Don't be shy about calling when it does, okay?"

Tilda felt her throat catch at the woman's earnestness. "I will. Thank you."

She lingered a moment before climbing out and retrieving the duffel from the back. She ducked down to wave goodbye. Whittaker lingered until she saw Tilda cross Dundas and thread her way up the narrow street. When Tilda was out of sight, she put the cruiser in gear and pulled away.

TILDA glanced back over her shoulder. When the police unit was gone, she started running. Winnowing through the maze of alleys and shortcuts to the grey brick with the darkened windows. The hallway was empty, the door to Gil's flat closed but not locked. Tilda wondered if there were other tenants in the building and, if there were, what they must have made of the intense racket coming from the third floor space earlier when the two coven members had tried to kill her. Ideal neighbours, she thought, the kind that don't complain even when the undead lay siege to the adjacent flat.

They might also be dead, she considered. Slaughtered by the coven before they came after her.

She dug the flashlight from the bag and pushed into the flat. Crunching over a floor of broken glass, she trained the Maglite beam over the shelves, searching through the tangle of bric-a-brac for the one thing she needed. There, at the back of the second shelf, hidden behind a chainsaw.

The flamethrower.

Gil's arts-and-crafts project of incendiary destruction. Some of the black finish had flaked off but it appeared to be undamaged, the tall can of butane still loaded in the frame of a caulking gun. She tried to remember how it worked. The wick extending off the front needed to be lit. The BBQ lighter fused to the carriage clicked uselessly before it fired and lit the wick. She pointed it at the ceiling and squeezed the nozzle. A blast of angry bright flame erupted in a straight six-foot roar of dragon's breath. The cobwebs drifting from the ceiling sparkled as they burned and smoked into nothing.

Nasty piece of work. A tiny smile tugged up the corner of her mouth.

She rifled the shelf for any backup cans of fuel and came away with two fresh rounds to be loaded into the flamethrower. She toggled back the loading arm and unseated the can from the gun and shook it, feeling its weight. A quarter full, maybe less. The thought of having to reload in the midst of those things was unnerving so she tossed the spent can and loaded in one of the spares. Test-firing the fresh supply of pressurized fuel evinced a clean seven-foot blast of fire. Her smile widened at the added distance. The more real estate she could keep between herself and those monsters the better.

Blowing out the wick, she laid the weapon on the floor and ransacked the shelves for anything else that might be useful. Gil was such an odd packrat that she half-hoped to find a gun amongst all the junk but none appeared. There was, however, a wood-handled machete. The rusty patina mottling the blade only made the thing look cruel and devastating. She tossed it into the duffel bag.

Clamping a hair elastic in her teeth, she tied her hair back into a tight ponytail to keep it out of her face. She tightened her belt by one notch and then unwound and retied the laces of her shoes to keep them from slipping off if she had to run.

She prayed it wouldn't come to a dead run. She didn't have the knees for it anymore.

The last bit of business required the duct tape. She tore off strips of it with her teeth and lashed the Maglite to the undercarriage of the flamethrower. The end result wasn't as snug as she'd hoped but the flashlight held, throwing its beam in whichever direction she aimed the blowtorch.

The weapon was loaded into the duffel bag along with the extra can of fuel and then zipped closed. Tilda slung the strap over one shoulder, adjusted its weight and then quit the flat.

THREE blocks north to the building where she and Gil had once dreamed of living. The same building where she had witnessed two young people die at the hands of the coven. Tilda shouldered open the side door and it gave way with a dull scrape. The dim hallway and then the stairs, two flights down to the decrepit boiler room. Nothing had changed since she'd last been here. No yellow police tape left behind, no sign that the police had been here at all. They had ignored her call, probably dismissing her as a crank. Across the room, nestled under an alcove was the door to the tunnels. Its riveted metal surface was laced with cobwebs as if undisturbed for ages.

She slipped the duffel to the floor and zipped it open. The machete slid under her belt at the small of her back. She lifted the flamethrower out and slung its strap over her shoulder. The Maglite clicked on, shining its powerful beam across the stagnant puddles on the concrete floor. She took out the second butane can but had no place to carry it. The duffel was too bulky to carry through the confined space ahead. She didn't want it dragging or getting in the way. Scrounging up the duct tape, she tore off two strips and taped the backup can to the one loaded in the frame. It looked kind of badass, she thought, like a double-barrelled flame tosser.

Two clicks on the lighter and the wick ignited, a bright birthday candle extending from the business end. A test pull on the trigger and flames spewed forth, leaving a sooty mark on the metal door.

Her hand gripped the handle and the door cracked open with a pop, as if vacuum sealed. The throw of the flashlight lit up a dusty floor and brick walls that inclined overhead in a gentle archway. Beyond that, darkness.

Tilda blew out her cheeks and tried to slow her heart from rabbit-pounding inside her ribs. It wasn't too late. She could still turn around and go home. Take the phone from her pocket and dial Whittaker's number. Explain the whole unexplainable mess.

Speak now or forever hold.

Gil was still down there. She could feel that much. Was it worth it?

Tilda ducked under the low slung lintel and disappeared into the tunnel.

29

Wave of mutilation

THERE IS DARK AND THERE IS PITCH. The powerful flashlight cut through fifteen paces of stygian ink but no more. The tunnel ahead was a solid wall of darkness, concealing whatever godless thing slithered within it. The fluttering wick of the flamethrower cast a glow up over the arched ceiling and the stale air was humid and smelled of dirt. Tilda's jaw ached from clenching her teeth so hard, fighting down the overpowering instinct to get the hell out of this cramped space and sprint back the way she came.

The tunnel went on and on. A straight path with no exits or deviations but Tilda still couldn't shake the sensation of getting lost, as if each step diminished her chances of ever finding her way out again.

Go back. Give up. He's dead anyway.

Just

fucking

RUN

Then the darkness expanded up ahead as the tunnel bisected another channel. Tilda inched forward, straining her ears to hear anything beyond the crunch of her own heels on the grit floor. Nothing.

This second tunnel cut perpendicular to the one she travelled. Aiming the light to her left and then her right revealed nothing but more tunnel and three options. Port, starboard or straight ahead. There was no sound to indicate which path lead to the coven but a bad smell wafted up around her. She sniffed at it, found the stench venting in from the tunnel on her left and followed it.

Ten paces on and the grade of the floor dipped, angling deeper underground and the smell growing stronger along with the descent. A foul rank somewhere between sewer gas and something dead left out to rot. It left little doubt that she was on the right path.

Up ahead in the darkness, something moved. Tilda froze and sighted the beam on a pale mass flopping across the floor. It reared its head at her, revealing two milky pupil-less eyes. The thing flopped and jerked like a landlocked seal and it took Tilda a moment to make out what she was seeing. The vampire had no legs, just bloodied stumps that scissored uselessly behind it. The left arm was chewed off at the elbow and the thing clawed the floor with its one remaining arm, pulling itself along with an obscene flopping motion.

To her horror, she recognized this dismembered member of the coven. The same one that had attacked her at Gil's flat only to hurl itself through the window sans arm. The vampire clawed the air as she approached but it posed little immediate threat being little more than a torso. How had it ended up in this state? A fresh wave of horror came when she hazarded that the thing had been punished. It had fled back to the coven, bringing news of Gil's betrayal and her existence before leading the others to the house. The creature had been punished for letting Gil escape. Stripped of its robes and crippled with a double amputation, the revolting thing was left to slither off on its own. When it snarled, she could see its maw of broken teeth. It had been defanged.

If the cabal of monsters had done this to its own loyal acolyte, what would it do a Judas like Gil?

The pale thing snatched at her foot, raking its nails on the cold floor. Tilda aimed the flamethrower at the creature but then turned it aside. She didn't want to alert the others to her presence in their lair by torching this one. She slid the machete from her belt and wound back, bringing the rusty blade down on the flopping leech. Its neck cleaved open, the blade chinking on the bone, and dark blood spilled foul into the dirt. It shrieked and Tilda swung again, cutting its cries short. The head thumped to the stone and the shorn legs jittered in a spastic running motion, as if it sought to outrun its own demise.

Tilda looked at the bloodied machete in her hand, surprised at her own handiwork. Two days ago she would have been sickened at what she had just done but now she felt nothing. At most a residual hatred for the abomination at her feet. Pressing the flat of the blade against the dead thing's ribs, she wiped the machete clean and slid it back into her belt. Then she went on, moving down the gentle grade of the tunnel and further into the damp earth.

THE rancid stench grew stronger the further down she travelled until the tunnel came to an abrupt end. The arched ceiling opened up into a low slung space not much wider than the tunnel that fed into it. No exit, no corresponding tunnel. Old ironwork machinery rusted in a heap to her left and dusty oil drums tilted in the grit to her right. Coils of cable and rotten crates cast about. Condensation beaded off the brick wall and a musty fungal smell assault-ed her nose.

Nothing more. She had taken the wrong path. Tilda cursed, ready to double back but then she stopped to scan the room one more time. Why was the stink of the coven so strong here, the temperature so cold? She stepped over a twisted length of trestle and swept the beam of light over the walls.

Hidden behind one of the oil drums was a hole in the brick, dark like an open wound in the earth itself. She knelt before it and felt a draught of air wash over her, the stench coming from the breach in the wall. Cobwebs wafted on the foul breeze.

They were down the hole, she realized, and backed away. The dark breach in the brick was no more than three feet in diameter. She'd have to crawl through.

No way in hell was she going to crawl inside that foul darkness.

Training the lightbeam into the aperture revealed noth-ing. A sucking black hole from which nothing returned. Tilda set her knees against the cold floor and dropped her chin to her clavicle. It was too much. Too far, too fucking frightening. She had tried. She was already drafting an epis-tolary apology to Gil for abandoning him.

"I can't do it," she whispered.

Fix it, said the grating little voice that never slept. *Fix it.*

She inched forward on her hands and knees to the opening. Three deep gasps and then she held her breath, as if bracing for a dive into cold water, and crawled in.

The space was tight, scraping down on her back and pressing in against her arms. Dust and filth rained down from the ceiling of the confined space, into her hair and sticking to the sweat on the back of her neck. The beam of the flashlight bounced and flared but showed nothing, its light simply eaten up by the darkness. Her heart jackhammered against the raw terror of becoming stuck in this suffocating tomb and she wanted to scream but then her fingers latched onto an edge.

The burrowed passage ended at a lip and she shimmied through, tumbling out of the canal like some ashen newborn birthed into a world of darkness.

Tilda grunted as she hit something hard and slid down a slope until she crashed against what felt like a bed of dry sticks. A rustle and crack as she hauled herself upright, the slur of dry wood crunching around her. Sweeping the light down, she saw that the rustle was not kindling but bones. Dry and brittle, splintering against her weight. The entire floor of was a field of dry bones, picked clean and left to petrify in the dark in some hidden ossuary. Thousands of them.

She scrambled to get out, to find some patch of dry land where her feet didn't slur the tinkling bones under her. A ledge appeared before her where the floor rose up and Tilda vaulted out of the pit onto solid ground.

She strained her ears but the only sound was that of dripping water. Casting the throw of the flashlight revealed the floor, a mosaic inlaid into stone and barely visible under the grit and soot. Columns rose up, vaulting overhead where they vanished in the darkness. All else was pitch where the maglite could not penetrate. The space was big and cavernous and, Tilda shuddered, it felt like a church.

She moved past a column, the crunch of her shoes on the grit too loud by far. The stench so strong it made her eyes water. Something wet dripped onto the crown of her head and Tilda swung the light up.

The coven hung above her. Suspended upside down, their wretched faces flaring in the lightbeam.

And all at once, their eyes opened.

The faces twisted up in hatred. Their lamprey mouths of teeth hissed and the first one dropped, opening its arms to receive her.

Tilda pulled the trigger and blasted fire into its face and it went up like a torch. It hit the ground and shrieked and rolled as it burned. Another flew at her. She throttled back and fired.

A second vampire went down in a roil of flames and a third knocked Tilda sideways before being immolated at point blank range. It bolted away as if it could outrun the flames, a fireball on two legs, and collided into its brothers and they too were swatting at the fire that licked at their mildewed rags and kicked their burning frère away.

Nails ripped down Tilda's shoulder and she blasted another and kept the pressure on, torching everything within range and the shrieking of the burning monsters overpowered the roar of the flamethrower. The coven withdrew, backing away from the flames in a gallery of hissing faces and popping teeth. Four carcasses flopped as they burned until they stilled and now a quartet of bonfires pushed back the darkness of the coven's lair.

All but one of the creatures retreated. The tall rector of this coven of monsters stood his ground and fixed Tilda with pupil-less eyes of molten hatred.

Tilda swept the weapon to his direction but toggled back the flames and met his stare. "Where is he?"

The rector didn't move, didn't blink.

Gil had said that most of these monsters were so old they didn't speak anymore, communicating in some nonverbal way. It was possible that this tyrant didn't understand a word she'd said. Still, how could it mistake her demands? She triggered a blast of flame and barked again. "Where's Gil?"

The rector swiveled its grotesque head a quarter turn to the right. The wall of gibbering and bobbing vampires parted like gates opening and something took shape in the new light of the burning bodies.

He was lashed to a column. Head down and drenched in so much blood that he looked painted. The flesh of his chest and arms were scored with wounds and wet flaps of skin hung loose, exposing muscle tissue and bone to the stale air. Iron spikes had been driven through Gil's palms, crucifying him to the stone pillar.

Her stomach dropped at the sight, knees threatening to buckle under her. What had they done to him? The filthy things had strung him up like a piece of meat and flayed him alive. She was too late.

"Cut him down."

No one moved.

Tilda snapped the flamethrower up and torched the nearest creature. It screamed and tried to hide behind its brothers but they kicked it away and Tilda kept the pressure on until the thing blazed up and fell over.

"Cut him down!"

The tyrant dipped his chin in a slight nod. The coven members shambled over Gil and cut away the thick rope from his ankles and plucked free the iron from his palms. Gil tumbled down and flopped onto his belly and lay as still as a corpse in a lye dusted trench.

Tilda poured on the flames, driving them away from the prone figure on the floor. The filth gnashed their teeth in retreat. She knelt over Gil and rolled him onto his back, her hands coming away slick and red. His eyes were open but there was no pupil, no fixed point. His ribs were still, no faint rise or fall.

Oxygen rushed out of the space and the only sound was the pop and crack of the bonfires. Tilda smoothed the hair out of his eyes and bent close to his ear. She told him that he couldn't go, that he had to come back to her. Now.

The body jerked under her and a wet rattle issued from his throat. Gil's pupils dropped and swam drunkenly, clicking an f-stop against her features. Tilda clutched him, as if she could stop him from slipping away again.

His voicebox cracked. "Til?"

"I'm here." She pulled him up. "I'm here."

His eyes reeled, trying to comprehend what he was seeing, where he was. The underground nest and the perverse figures shuffling around them. Tilda smack in the middle of the coven, fifty-two feet below the surface. Also out of place were the bonfires blazing around them, casting warmth into a place where light never touched.

He gripped her arm, smearing blood over her skin. "How did you get here?"

"Get up," she said.

"I don't think I can stand."

"Yes you can." She hooked an arm under him and lifted. "Get up now."

He creaked and fumbled to his knees, pain shooting hot at every move. He stared at the object in her hand with its candlewick guttering until he made sense of what she was holding. The name of the object had simply dropped out of his memory and he groped around to find it again when a burst of flame roared out of the business end in a great arc.

The wraiths inching forward caught a facefull of fire as Tilda hazed them back. She drew a bead on the rector, who again refused to withdraw. "I'm taking Gil out of here," she spat at him. "And you will leave us alone. I'll keep your secret but if I smell any of you within a mile of my family, I'll expose you and bring every cop in the city down on your little fucking clubhouse. Do you understand me?"

The despot didn't respond. Whether he failed to understand or refused to capitulate was anyone's guess.

"Tilda..." Gil wheezed.

"Gil, make him understand."

"...behind you."

She spun just as one wraith sprang from its brothers and she torched it but its momentum propelled it on all the same and she kicked it down, blasting it again until it blazed up into an inferno.

The others hesitated, articulating their jaws with that awful clicking sound.

"Lean on me." She draped his arm around her, felt his weight drag her shoulders down. "Watch our backs." Another blast of the fire and the coven parted. They hobbled back toward the entrance, Gil craning his neck behind him.

When they came to the edge of the pit, Gil all but fell into the bones. The dessicated femurs and ribslats rattled like kindling as he regained his footing. Tilda fired a warning blast and dropped in beside him and they waded through the bonefield of nameless remains.

When Gil stumbled and fell to one knee, she saw the wraiths dropping into the pit after them. She snatched his arm and dragged him, Gil caterwauling drunkenly and then one creature sprang, vaulting off the edge towards them.

Tilda brought the weapon up fast and fired but no flame issued forth, the can hissing dry. She throttled the trigger piece again and again.

Empty

empty

and still empty.

A guttural howl of victory went up from the filth as they surged forward like sharks on chum.

30

Blister in the sun

THE FIRST MONSTER TACKLED HER, buckling Tilda at the waist and sprawling her into the pit of bones. Her hands pushed in a frenzy to keep the snapping teeth from her locking onto her face. A sudden tug at her back and then she felt a geyser of cold blood douse over her. The machete blade appeared an inch from her nose, sunk into the decrepit neck of the creature. It jerked taut as if electrocuted then fell limp. Looking up she saw Gil pull the blade free and boot the carcass off of her. Then he turned to face the oncomers.

Tilda racked back the lever arm on the flamethrower and spun the dead can out. With the backup canister taped to the empty one, she snapped the seal and flipped it over, seating the fresh supply into the body. Jamming the arm back in, she fired blind into the horde of undead things rushing at Gil.

One went up with a whoosh and another ignited into a ball of flames and flailed against its fraters for help but the others knocked it away like some malignant thing. The acrid reek of charred flesh stung Tilda's nose but she kept the pressure on, a steady stream of dragonbreath until the hateful things backed away.

Gil swung the machete clumsily, the strength of his attack blunted by blood loss and massive trauma. She pulled him away and clawed up the slope towards the breach in the wall. The way out of this hellhole.

"Go," she said. The breach in the wall was narrow. One at a time.

He shook his head. "No. You first. I'll hold them off."

"You can barely stand. Go!" Tilda shoved him forward and then put her back to the wall. The coven rattled through the bone pit, fanning out below her at the base of the slope. She swept the air with another blast of flame but there were too many to keep at bay at once.

Chief amongst the rabble was the rector of this dae-monic cloister, wading through the bones, its eyes fixed on her and her alone.

Gil disappeared into the gap. The wraiths clawed up the slope towards her. She fired the air one more time and then clambered into the fissure. The space was tight, barely enough room to work her elbows as she clawed and wrig-gled through. She pushed the flamethrower ahead of her and shimmied her weight in a peculiar slither, her legs kick-ing uselessly on the other side of the wall.

"Gil!"

The wick of the thrower guttered before her but beyond it there was only darkness. She called his name again. Why wasn't he there? Had he collapsed or was something wait-ing for them on the other side?

That's when she felt something clamp over her ankle. Tighter than a tourniquet, it tugged hard, dragging her back out.

Her scream burst her own eardrum as it boomed around that cramped space. She wedged her elbows against the dirt walls, dug her fingers into the earth to anchor her-self but she kept sliding back in some infernal breech birth. The flickering wick went out, plunging her into darkness. She felt teeth clamp onto her calf and bite down.

Then pressure on her wrists. A grip. Gil's voice in the dark, telling her to stop screaming. He pulled her forward but the teeth in her calf sunk deeper. An obscene tug of war, Tilda pulled apart over an infernal line of demarcation. Forward into Gil or backwards into Hell. She could hear Gil snarling against the strain and she muled out with her good foot, kicking like she was on fire. The lamprey mouth barnacled on her leg tore free, the teeth scraping down her ankle before she shot forward, ejected from the burrow hole.

She tumbled onto Gil and they sprawled over the floor of the small anteroom. Gil snatched up the flamethrower and aimed it at the crawlspace. A pale face appeared, slithering after them and he toggled the nozzle and spewed fire into its horrid visage.

"Hurry," Tilda hollered, already pulling at his arm.

"Wait." He tossed her the device and turned to one of the oil drums standing guard near the wall. He spun the cap off and pushed the drum over and a viscous fluid gurgled from the spout, pooling across the gritty floor.

He snatched up a smaller canister and knocked the cap off of it too. Pushing her ahead of him. "Go."

They ran up the incline of the tunnel. Gil falling once and then twice as he staggered to keep up, emptying the canister as they ran and twice Tilda doubled back to haul him up and pull him along.

The canister emptied before they reached the intersecting tunnel and they could already hear the coven pouring out into the anteroom below, knocking the debris out of their way.

Gil limped to a stop, wheezing. "Torch it."

Tilda judged the distance from their position to the lateral tunnel up ahead where they could dive for cover from the blowback of the inferno she was about to set off. Gil reeled, losing blood from almost every pore. "Can you run?"

"Throw it, Tilda. Before it's too late."

"You'll never make it in time. Run up ahead and take cover."

"Torch it!"

She could already see movement at the far end of the tunnel, figures slithering in the dark. The wick of the flamethrower guttered and she tossed the weapon in a soft underhand. It arced through the air and clanked to the floor. Flames crackled up the trail of fuel and snaked furiously down the passageway.

They ran headlong and heedless and didn't look back. The next tunnel closing fast when they heard the explosion and Tilda felt the heat at her back as the fireball chased them up the incline, eating everything in its path.

Gil was staggering and she seized his hand to pull him along and light filled the archway as the fire found them out. She dove for the bisecting tunnel, scrambling for cover behind the damp brick wall and yanked Gil after her. She wasn't fast enough. The fireball swept over him, searing the flesh on his back as it ate all the oxygen into it and Tilda gasped for air, gulping heat into her lungs.

The fireball thundered over them and then petered out quickly, leaving wisps of greasy black smoke in the air. Smaller fires kindled up around them as the air rushed back in to fill the vacuum and Tilda chomped it down. The taste of ash burnt her tongue and seared down her throat.

Gil lay face down in the grit. His back was charred and carbonized like a piece of over-grilled meat. He didn't move.

"Gil," she whispered. "Gil, look at me."

His hand crawled into hers and held tight. His jaw racked up and down, trying to speak but the only sound it made was a wet rattle. His pupils dilated and his mouth corkscrewed in pain and then he closed his eyes to it all.

A sound hooked Tilda's ear, rising above the crackle of the various fires around them. Hellish screams of anguish echoed up from the way they had come. Banshee wails of pain sounding over them in that echo chamber of sooty brick. The sound of the coven, in what she prayed were death throes.

"Can you walk?"

A grunt with no recognizable syllable.

"Try."

She saw his jaw clench over the pain as she helped him up. They hobbled forward in a brittle sidestep and Tilda felt his body trembling under her like an injured dog. Her own muscles quivered and she didn't know how long she could keep him upright before she would give out.

She made for the first tunnel, backtracking the way she had entered, but Gil tugged her sideways, nodding to the intersecting passageway. They limped along in the dark, Tilda blind in the gloom and she cursed herself for not tearing the Maglite from the torch before tossing it away. Groping in the dark, Gil guided her along, steering her through the corridor. His weight sank onto her with each step and she strained to stay upright, unsure of how long she could keep either of them vertical.

His wrist was slick and her grip slipped and Gil slid away, dropping to his knees with an unearthly groan. Tilda winced and grimaced to haul him back to his feet. They shambled on in this manner for some time, Tilda straining her ears for the sound of anything coming up behind them but there was no sound, nothing above her own panting and his grunting.

He pulled her to a stop and let go of her, leaving her stranded in the dark. Then a rattling click, metallic and sharp. Light split the pitch as a door creaked opened and Tilda's retinas burned against white light. She groped her way through the door like a blind woman, pulling Gil after her.

THE blinding light was no more than a low watt incandescent bulb frosted with dust. The room they filed into was storage space, an archive of sorts with dusty boxes reposing on metal rack shelving. A faint whiff of must and damp newspaper. Tilda scanned the room for an exit. Gil slid down the wall to the floor, legs splayed out before him. Under the steady glow of the incandescent, she could see the extent of his injuries. There was nary a patch of skin that wasn't painted in blood. His flesh had been flayed and bit and cut and ripped open. His entire body was scored with the dark hatchings of trauma. A sucking chest wound and snapped ribs gelled in dark blood, as if the coven had tried to dig Gil's heart out with their bare hands.

Tilda felt her brains short-circuit for some way to help him. He needed surgery. He needed a hundred surgeries. "Oh God. We need to stop the bleeding."

A deep rupture on his stomach split open and ropy intestines bubbled out in a slow ooze. His hand shot over it, like some unseemly blemish to hide from a girl on a first date. Gil wheezed and then his eyes rolled over white, chin dipping to his collarbone.

She smacked his cheek. "Wake up. Don't you pass out on me. Gil!"

His eyes wheeled about crazily but could not lock onto hers. "Tilda," he slurred. "I think I'm fucked."

"No, you're not. But I don't know how to stop the bleeding." She scanned down the wounds. Too many to count, she didn't know where to start or what to do.

He followed her eyes, tracking the panic that was growing fast in them. "That bad, huh?"

"You've looked better." Shaking herself free, she turned and ransacked the shelves for towels or cloth or a first-aid kit. Anything to cover the worst of the leaking wounds but all she unearthed were soiled rags. She cursed and flung them away.

"Don't waste your time."

"No," she said sharply. "Don't talk like that."

"Okay. Then don't waste mine. Cuz they're ain't much left."

She just had to look harder, that was all. Sweeping whole shelves to the floor, she tore the room apart but there was nothing here. She stopped her ransacking but was afraid to look back at him. This wasn't happening, she thought. Not now, not after all this. When she finally turned around, she saw his chest glisten red as it heaved up and shrank down.

Think, damn it. Gil was a vampire, like the others. He fed on blood. He'd lost a massive amount of it at the hands of those monsters. He needed more. Simple as that.

"You need blood." She scurried back and crouched over him. She thrust her forearm out and set the soft flesh of her inner wrist to his lips. "Take mine."

Gil tilted his head away. "No."

"Do it! Take just enough to heal up. Or enough to walk out of here." She took his chin in her hand and turned his face to her. "You can't die on me. Not a second time. Do it."

She pressed her wrist to his bloodied lips again. Just below the epidermis throbbed the arteries, both radial and the ulnar that pulsed her hot blood. The red and white cells, the platelets and the haemoglobin. Both banquet and sustenance, a feast and an aphrodisiac. All he had to do was bite down and pierce the skin and it would gush out over his tongue and geyser into his throat. So simple and primal. Even a mindless leech could understand the task required.

He pushed it away.

Anticipating the pain, Tilda's eyes shot open when the pain didn't come. Confusion flashed hard in her eyes, then frustration. "Do it. As much as you need. Just heal up."

"No."

"You have to." Was he insane from the blood loss? She dug into his gaze for some sign of delusion or death wish, found neither. "I don't know what else to do. Please."

"Help me," he said.

"I'm trying to!"

He took her hand and squeezed tight. "Upstairs. Help me up the stairs."

She clasped his arm and pivoted back on one heel, hauling him to his feet. "Where."

"The roof," he said. A sliver of a smile on his lips. "Help me get to the roof."

THE sky overhead was grey and rainclouds hunkered so low that Tilda could almost reach up and touch them. To the east, the sky was clearing and the clouds broke apart as their undersides burned orange from a sun almost risen.

The building was deserted and they were undisturbed as they limped and reeled up the stairwell to the access door at the very top. They came out onto a flat square of rooftop covered in clear stone gravel. Tilda drew in great gobs of clean sweet air but the bitter ashen taste in her throat would not go away and she was terribly thirsty.

She looked over the edge to the street below. Trying to orient herself from this angle was difficult and it took a moment before she determined that they had resurfaced into the old building in the crescent on the edge of the university campus. Two blocks from their dream apartment.

Gil hobbled to the western lip of the roof and all but collapsed onto the gravel. The bleeding hadn't abated and a trail of dark blood drizzled across the stones from the door to the roof edge where he crumpled. Leaning back against the flashing, he drew up his legs and cantilevered his elbows atop his knees. "Do you see smoke?" he asked.

Tilda swept the eyeline of the old buildings and treetops. There, to the north, a twisting funnel of black smoke coiled up from some unseen origin to meet the rainclouds above. She pointed. "There."

"Where's it coming from?"

"I can't tell. Somewhere on Saint George." She looked down over the edge. A sheer drop to the potholed laneway below that made her dizzy and she took a step back. "Do you think they're all dead?"

"I don't know. Let's hope so." Gil leaned his back against the dull metal and considered her question. The fire in the lair had been massive. Total. Had it incinerated them all? Even if one or two had escaped, the coven itself was destroyed and, like herd animals, the creatures could only thrive in numbers. Alone and adrift, a solitary wraith would crumble under its own outcast loneliness and the depravity of its existence. Tribe mentality, without the tribe, would not be enough to survive. It would starve to death or become desperate and be caught, snapping the sacred law like straw and exposing itself to the rational daylight world.

They had held him captive for almost two decades. A lifetime, or rather, he considered, a deathtime. How old the coven itself was, he didn't know. The rector had held his secrets close but Gil suspected the monsters went back to the time of the first European settlers. Had the coven come with the earliest French and English pioneers or were the wraiths already on this continent, waiting for them? He didn't know. He no longer cared.

Regardless of whether they were all destroyed, he was now shed of the hateful things. All that mattered now was his escape and Tilda. Always Tilda.

He opened his eyes and saw the wreckage of his body and the blood pooling underneath him and he looked away. Filled his view with her. "Come here," he said. "Sit beside me."

Tilda eased down slowly onto the gravel. Everything seemed to hurt. Her bad wrist most of all, flushing hot and tender as if the bones were grinding against one another. She'd gotten away relatively unscathed, she thought, compared to the man from her past.

"Let's go back down," she said. "Where it's dark."

"No."

The dark blood pooling around him soaked through her jeans and she gaped at the volume of it and wondered how it still seeped out of him and where it was all coming from. His breathing was laboured, like a coal-miner on his deathbed, and his hand was back on his split belly holding his guts in.

She had expected tears but her eyes were dry. Too dehydrated to cry, she thought. She swiveled her head to him. "It doesn't have to be this way. We can go back down. Find some other way."

His hand raked the gravel and found hers. "I want to see the sun come up."

"It's not fair." It sounded childish to her own ears but she didn't care. It was honest.

"I know."

Blackbirds dove through the air above them and barnswallows chittered mindlessly from the wires. The wail of sirens could be heard, growing louder.

His head tilted away and he spit blood onto the stones and turned back to see the east. The horizon washed pink and orange. "How long has it been since that night? The accident."

"Seventeen years."

"A nightmare." His voice croaked, an effort just to speak. "But it was worth it. I got to see you again."

She pulled her hand away to cover her eyes. The little hydration left in her system welled up and was falling now. "I can't do this, Gil. I can't just watch you die."

"Yes you can."

She could already feel warmth on her skin. It was happening too fast and there was so much she wanted to say but no coherent words formed in her mind or on her tongue. This wasn't fair. No one should have to endure death twice.

"Are you scared?" A silly thing to ask.

"Terrified," he said. He tried to lift his arm but there was no strength left to do even that. The best he could do was to unfold his fingers. "Will you hold my hand?"

She folded her hand over his and tried not to wince as the skin of his palm peeled away like rotten fruit. His fingers flensed at her touch but squeezed back. He said "I already miss you."

"Then don't go."

"This should have happened a long time ago."

"I love you," she said.

He opened his mouth to say something but the clouds shifted in that moment and the first ray of sun unfolded over his face. His face, his beautiful face, darkened to char instantly and the first lick of flame parted from his lips like another tongue and then the fire was total. He erupted into flames.

The heat of it slammed into her. Her hand remained clenched in his and she watched her own flesh burn. When it came the pain was diabolical and she pulled her hand away but his blackened fingers would not let go.

The flames ate her hand. She twitched and jerked it free. Gil's fingerbones popped apart and the carbonized phalanges fell to the gravel.

She coddled her burning hand into her chest to douse the flames and when she looked down her palm bubbled up in blisters. Turning it over, the blackened skin split across the knuckles, exposing the bone beneath it.

Gil burned away, a dark silhouette inside the rippling Halloween orange of the flames. His head shifted back and the jaw dropped open and then he didn't move again.

The pain was total and it snipped her breath. She was going to pass out from it. She was going to die alone on this rooftop from the naked pain but she didn't want to die. Clawing the phone from her pocket, she fumbled and dropped it onto the stones and scooped it back up. The screen lit up and the last number she thumbed into it displayed on the little screen. Above the digits was the name.

Whittaker

31

Lift your skinny fists like antennas to heaven

WHEN SHE AWOKE IN the hospital, Tilda Parish remembered nothing. Her short term memory a black hole, the edges of it rendered hazy by pain killers. Opening her eyes to a soiled patch of a ceiling tile, she held only a dim understanding that she was in a hospital room. The reason why escaped her completely. Another car accident? She faded in and out, seeing nurses enter to adjust this or that. A doctor with a smug tone, an orderly taking away an untouched breakfast tray.

The pain, unlike her memory, was acute and constant and localized wholly around her left hand. It was elevated and bound in burn dressing, the wound beneath it a mystery. When a nurse came to change the dressing, a sheet was draped over the arm to block Tilda's view, maintaining the mystery of the wound. Tilda tried to move her fingers and a new, startling pain raced up her arm and that was when her memory came back, as if jolted back into place by a bombshell of pain.

The coven and the fire, the rooftop and the warmth of the rising sun.

Gil, eaten alive by the flames.

This time there would be no coming back. He was well and truly gone and for the second time in her life, Tilda lay in a hospital bed contemplating Gil's death. The déjà vu was eerie but the grief was manageable. Hell, she was an old hand at it now. Her fingers tingled and she looked at the gauze wrapped over the hand, hiding it like a prize waiting to be revealed. Under normal circumstances, her mind would be racing ahead, imagining the extent of the damage and how it would affect her but the pain killers kept her brain flaccid and calm and after a while, she slept.

A tug on her hand woke her and she saw a doctor gingerly peeling away the burn dressing. He said hello and asked her how she was feeling, just as the last of the dressing came away, some of it sticking to the flesh with stringy tissue. That first glimpse of the mystery was too much, the boiled-looking skin and patches of charred flesh. The angry rawness of it made her turn away.

She fixed her eyes on that brown water stain on the ceiling tile and kept them there. The doctor told her that the burn was severe. In a calm monotone, as if discussing weather or engine trouble, he explained that she had suffered a third degree burn and that the reticular dermis had been damaged. Skin grafts would help to restore the surface of her hand to an extent but her motor skills and mobility would be severely limited. Over time, she may learn to grasp simple objects, a tennis ball perhaps, but that would be the extent of it.

The doctor droned on but Tilda stopped listening. What was the point? They should have just amputated the damn thing, instead of leaving it to mock her. When the doctor finally left she closed her eyes again, suddenly loathing the sight of the water stain above her. She didn't bother opening them when she heard someone else enter the room. Another nurse come to poke and torture and drug her with meds.

"That looks nasty."

Officer Whittaker stood in the doorway with her hat in her hand. She offered up a hesitant smile. "How are you feeling?"

"Like shit."

"Sorry." Whittaker crossed to the bedside. "Silly question."

Whittaker studied the bandaged hand and how Tilda's frame tapered to almost nothing under the thin hospital sheet. "What happened?"

"Is there water in that cup?" Tilda tried to swallow but her tongue was paste and a faint ashen residue lingered. She sipped the straw as the officer brought the cup to her lips. "Have you called Shane? Or Molly? Do they know I'm here?"

"I saw Shane yesterday." Whittaker set the cup back onto the table and refilled it from a pitcher. "It was kind of convenient you two winding up at the same hospital. He was just being released, so I told him you were here."

"Did he come see me?"

Whittaker turned the hat in her hand and looked into the band as if some answer was proscribed there . "No. He went home."

Tilda didn't move. That should have hurt but it didn't. Whether it was the meds or a limp sense of finality, she didn't know. Logically, she should have been furious or heartbroken but she felt neither. She had made this bed and here she was lying in it.

Whittaker shifted her stance, creaking the leather of her thick belt. "I'm sorry."

"Don't be. What about Molly? Does she know?"

"I don't know. I didn't call your mom-in-law. I don't know if Shane did or not." Whittaker sought out Tilda's gaze and held it fast. "Tilda, what happened?"

"I'm not sure. It's all kinda foggy." Not exactly a lie. The details and chronology were a jumble of hazy snapshots. "Did I call you?"

"Yup."

"What did I say?"

"You said you needed help. You told me where you were and said to hurry. Then the line went dead."

"What happened then?"

"I gunned for the location you told me, the old building in the round-about on Spadina," Whittaker said. "I was only a few blocks away when you called. There was a fire call on the campus."

"A fire?"

"In the Knox College building. Damn thing went up in a massive blaze. Four alarmer."

Tilda tried to picture the building but couldn't remember which one it was. It must have been above the lair. "How did the fire start?"

"Who knows? Those old buildings, it could have been anything. The fire forensics crew will be pulling overtime on that job."

Tilda nodded, as if this was common knowledge. "So I called you. Then what?"

"I tore off to the building in the crescent and ran up to the roof. You were passed out on the gravel, not moving and your hand was still smoking. I thought I was too late. I radioed for an ambulance and carried you downstairs myself. The paramedics pulled up just as I got you out the front doors. They took care of you and I humped it back up the stairwell."

Tilda tilted her head. "Why?"

"There was another body on the roof, but there was no saving that one. It was still burning."

The bitter taste of ash returned. "Who was it?"

Whittaker shrugged. "No idea. There was nothing left of it. I grabbed a tarp on the way back up and threw it over the body to douse the flames. It just crumbled. When I pulled the tarp away, there was nothing but ash. Damndest thing too. I've seen bodies burned before and there's always bones left behind. This? Nothing. Powder, that's it."

The image of that drifted up in Tilda's mind. Ash floating away on the breeze.

"Tilda," Whittaker cleared her throat. "Who was on that roof with you?"

Her eyes floated back to the stain on the ceiling tile. She had neither the strength nor the brains to lie anymore. "His name was Gil. He died a long time ago."

The police officer regarded her coolly and Tilda could almost read Whittaker's thoughts, trying to determine if she had lost her mind or was simply babbling in a medicated stupor.

"That's going to cause a stink if I put that in my incident report," Whittaker said.

Tilda raised her good hand and rubbed her eyes. Her skin felt oily and she suddenly wanted a shower. "Then I don't know who it was. My memory of that night is really scattered. Can you put that in your report?"

"For now, but you have to promise me something. When you're feeling better, you have to be straight and tell me what happened. Deal?"

"Okay."

"Good." Whittaker smiled and crossed to the chair by the door. A plastic shopping bag rested on the seat and she held it up. "The clothes you were brought in with were pretty much destroyed, so I stopped by your house and grabbed a few things. Hope that's okay."

"Thank you," Tilda said.

Whittaker dangled the bag on a finger then settled it back onto the chair. "They're here when you're ready to go home."

Tilda sat up and swung her legs over the side. Waited for the dizziness to pass. "I'm ready to go now."

"Hold on. I meant when the doc says you can go home."

"I don't care what he says. I have to get out of here." Tilda held out her hand. "Will you pass me those clothes."

FITTING Tilda's arm into a sling, the doctor prattled out a dozen reasons why it was too early to go home but Tilda ignored them all and got dressed. Pressing her luck, she asked Whittaker for a lift home. The officer sided with the doctor but saw that Tilda was prepared to walk all the way home if she had to. Shaking her head, she pushed the wheelchair through the lobby and out to the sidewalk. Tilda breathed in the smell of fresh rain on old concrete.

As Whittaker cruised down College Street, Tilda looked out at the people on the sidewalks. Hovering outside of restaurants with cigarettes in their hands or filing into the gelato shops that peppered the strip. It all seemed so normal and routine and Tilda felt an anaesthetized disconnect from all of it. These people going about their business, falling in love or breaking someone's heart, drowning in debt or bitching about their car insurance, all without a hint that under their feet glided sharks waiting to eat them up.

"Busy night," Whittaker said, breaking the silence.

"It's like nothing ever happened."

The radio squawked, police jargon that Tilda couldn't decipher and Whittaker lowered the volume. "You know, that offer still stands. I got a couch you can crash on if you're not up to going home yet."

"Thanks." Tilda smiled. "But I need to get home."

Whittaker nodded solemnly and drove on. "Not to pry or anything, Tilda, but do you know what to expect when you get there?"

"No. I don't. But I still have to go."

The congestion on the street cleared away and within minutes the police unit wheeled onto Tilda's street and pulled to the curb opposite the house. The yellow police tape was gone and a length of plywood had been squared into the broken picture window.

"Thank you." Tilda climbed out and bent down to the open passenger window. "For everything."

"Don't thank me yet," the officer said. "I still need answers about how you got hurt. I'll drop by in a couple days and we'll go over it again. Get some rest, okay?"

The prowl car pulled away and Tilda looked up at her house with its faded brick and parched front lawn. It looked a little forlorn with its patched-up window, like a smile with a tooth punched out.

The front door was unlocked and noise leeched from the kitchen. The dull clink of utensils against china. Tilda tiptoed inside.

Shane and Molly sat at the kitchen table, eating but not talking. Take-out cartons steamed on the table, the aroma rich and heady. They both looked spent, glumly going through the motions of chewing, joyless as monks at their cold gruel. Blissfully unaware of another presence in the room.

Tilda shifted her weight and the old floor creaked under her heel. Shane and Molly looked up, forks frozen halfway to their mouths. The surprise washing across their faces dropped to an unfamiliar wariness.

Unsure of how to respond, Molly looked to her father for a cue. Shane slid the tines of curried chicken into his mouth and lowered his eyes back to his plate.

Hard as a fist to the breadbasket, Tilda took it in the guts. As unwelcome as a cockroach in her own home. Running away right now would be so easy that her wobbly knees stiffened, anticipating a bolt for the door. She shushed her frayed nerves to be still.

Molly lowered her fork. "Mom. Shouldn't you be at the hospital? What are you doing here?"

Trying to patch up my family, she screamed on the inside. *Can't you see that? I know I screwed everything up but let me fix it. Let me try.*

Tilda cleared the hook in her throat. "I'd thought you'd still be at Grandma's. Did she spoil you rotten?"

The chair squeaked back as Molly shot up and came around the table. Tilda blinked in disbelief when her daughter caught her up around the waist. A tight embrace was the last thing she expected.

Molly leaned back. "Why didn't you call so we could come get you?"

"I just had to get out of there."

"Sit down." Molly led her mother to a chair at the table opposite to Shane, then buzzed across to the cupboards. "Did the doctor say you could leave or did you just book it?"

Tilda looked up at her daughter with no small blast of amazement. Gratitude even. "I'm fine. I want to know how you're doing. Did you and Grandma go down to the beach?"

"You booked, didn't you?" Molly set plate under her mom and clattered a fork beside it. "What did the doctor say about your hand? Will it, you know, be okay?"

"It's burned pretty bad but... we'll see."

"Don't be stoic, mom. How bad is it?"

Tilda grasped at some way to flip the conversation or allay her daughter's concern but the effort required was an Everest. She sighed and decided to simply come clean. "It's useless. I can't even feel it anymore."

Unprepared for the frankness, Molly spooned lentils onto her mother's plate. "I'm sure they can fix it up. Not right away but over time, with some physio. You'll be back to flipping off stupid drivers just like before. Playing guitar."

The instinct to dismiss the truth was suddenly and powerfully ridiculous. Who benefited? Not a soul at this table. "It's all but dead, honey. No more flipping the bird, no more guitar. Nada."

Too harsh. The brute force of it rippled across the table like spilled water, dripping cold into everyone's laps. Molly rigored, stiff as a shop window dummy, and once again looked to her father for a cue or a reaction. Anything.

Shane took a napkin and wiped his mouth, finally raising his eyes to meet his wife's. But his gaze was cool and Tilda could decipher nothing in it.

As ever, Molly was pinned down in the crossfire like a bead jerked taut on a string. She got up and came around the table, kissed the crown of her mother's head and left the room without another word.

The charge in the air dialled up to fill the vacuum left behind by the third party. Shane pushed his plate back.

Tilda felt her hand throbbing so she propped the elbow on the table to keep it raised. And then squared Shane up. "Are you not speaking to me?"

Shane tilted his head like a dog at a strange noise. "What do you want to talk about? Your infidelity? Or maybe our joke of a marriage. Your ex-boyfriend maybe or those things that attacked us? The state of the house?" He snapped his fingers. "There's a neutral topic. Home repair."

"Stop. I don't have the energy to fight." It felt silly having her bandaged hand pointed towards the ceiling but it eased the throbbing. Hard to be serious when you look like an eager pupil with a perpetual question for the teacher but she took a breath and gave it a shot anyway. "Do you hate me?"

He took his time before answering, letting the question just hang there. "No," he said finally. "I don't. I'm still angry. Furious, in fact, but I don't hate you."

The noose slackened, the hangman's grip easing back on the trap lever.

"Okay." She took another breath. "Where does that leave us?"

"Where is he?"

"Gone."

Shane reached for his water glass but it was empty. "For good?"

"Yes."

He seemed satisfied with the answer but she couldn't be sure. Shane had never been a mystery to her and was thus always easy to read but something had changed and he sat across from her like a stranger at a dinner party. The wariness and distrust were to be expected but beyond that lingered a sudden and deep unfamiliarity between them. Tilda had put it there and she knew that she would have to build the bridge back to it.

The word 'purgatory' flickered through her mind. The Catholic in her was never really dead and like those things that slithered in the dark, it resurrected itself to haunt the present.

"For what it's worth, I still love you. That didn't change." Tilda lowered her hand to the table. "Never will."

"Good," he said.

With her hand horizontal, the throbbing returned so she folded it back into its sling.

He caught her wincing. "What is it?"

"My hand. Starting to hurt."

"Did they give you something for the pain?"

"It's in my bag."

Shane stood and went to the stool where her bag lay. He came round to her end and placed two pills on her plate, pushed her glass of water closer. "Take these."

Her good hand shot out, like it had a mind of its own, and gripped his before it left the table. She held on and squeezed but could not think of a single thing to say.

Shane tugged his hand away but held his eyes where they were.

"You look pale," he said. "Eat something."

32

Walk through this world with me

THE SEIZURE CAME OUT OF NOWHERE, snapping Tilda from a dead sleep. Every muscle jerked and coiled so hard it left her breathless and panting like a dog. When the second wave hit, the constriction of her muscles was so violent that she feared her molars would crack.

They had ended the night so peacefully. More peacefully than she had had any right to hope for. It had been awkward; cautious and hesitant as she and Shane orbited around the other as they brushed their teeth and got ready for bed. As polite as strangers. Lying in the dark he asked if she wanted another painkiller and they spoke a little about Molly and then said goodnight.

Tilda lay there in the darkened bedroom, looking up at the squared patch of light thrown from the street onto the ceiling. Feeling the warmth of his body under the sheets, Tilda wanted to curl into him and rest her cheek between his shoulder blades. To wrap her arm around him and beg him to understand. Her good hand slid forward to touch Shane's back and he didn't shrink away. She settled for that. It was more than enough for now.

The jarring spasm destroyed all that. It felt as if she'd been stabbed with a live electrical cable, the voltage frying through her and working her muscles like a dead frog in science class prodded into a post-mortem flinch.

Her belly rumbled up in a sloshy gurgle. At first it felt like hunger, suddenly and powerfully ravenous but it flopped on a dime into a nauseous churn that sent her running for the bathroom. It came up fast and she threw up violently, eyes clamped shut and watering. When she opened them she saw blood in the toilet bowl and more of it splattered across her hands, the tile floor. Another retch and something solid came up and knocked against her teeth as it chucked out. A lung or her spleen, she didn't want to know.

The tile was mercifully cool against her skin as she slipped to the floor. By now a pulsing headache scrambled her thoughts and something like fire snaked through her veins in what she imagined to be a junkie's death.

Her gauze-wrapped hand lay flat on the tile before her face. Why this was happening? A bad reaction to the medication they gave her at the hospital? No. All they had administered were painkillers. Another guess flitted around the periphery of her mind but she dismissed it as panic, the headache frying her brain cells.

Prone on the bathroom floor, she stayed as still as possible and waited it out. Counting to three, she clutched the rim of the vanity and pushed up to her feet to wash the mess from her hands and rinse the goddawful taste in her mouth.

Don't look in the mirror

Who can avoid a mirror? The blind and the insane maybe. The rest of us too weak and too vain to avert our needy gaze. Lot's wife looking wistfully back at Sodom.

Tilda's eyes watered again at the figure in the bathroom mirror. As pale as snow, her flesh startlingly so against the dark blood on her mouth and chin. Her eyes didn't look right. They too were pale and cloudy, as if the colour of the iris had bleached out. And when her jaw fell open, there was something terribly wrong with her teeth.

Blood, so dark it was almost ink, stained wet through the cotton of her T-shirt. Her breast, where Gil's teeth had sunk into her. It had never healed and was bleeding fresh. Lifting the shirt revealed purpled flesh over the whole breast, spidery traces fingering out across her sternum. *Infected. Spreading fast.*

Her knees buckled, the floor hard as it came up fast to smack her. She coiled up, tugging her knees under her chin.

Didn't she have to die first? Isn't that what Gil had said? You die and then on the third night you come back. Or was that just some stupid movie she had seen? The pain inside her skull suddenly receded, pushed back by the sensation of her nose burning. The smell of blood. A warm body lying asleep and helpless in the next room.

And now she was crawling on hands and knees like an animal through the bathroom door and over the hardwood towards the bed. She couldn't stop, her limbs ignoring her mind, obeying only the hot scent in her nose. She tried to scream, to warn Shane to run, to get Molly and get out but her throat constricted, disobeying her will along with the rest of her. Trapped inside this prison of her body as it scuttled across the bedroom floor, her mind wept but even her tear ducts wouldn't obey.

This can't be happening, she thought as her hand gripped the coverlet of the conjugal bed. Shane lay still under the sheets, turned away towards the wall. She could feel the heat coming off him. She could hear the beating of his heart, pumping blood to his sleeping limbs. Her fingers touched his shoulder and he stirred, rolling over towards her. A fold in the pillow had left a crease in his cheek and his mouth was open. He looked peaceful and oblivious to the threat that loomed over him.

Seeing his face snapped Tilda like a fist hard across the mouth. She saw herself hovering over him, a moment away from whatever evil inside her demanded she do. Even in this moment of lucidity it was still driving her forward, pushing for her to take him.

Turning away was like fighting a gale force wind, she had to lean into it. Gaining the hallway, she stumbled and crawled the rest of the way to the stairs. The awful thing inside reared its head again, sniffing the air and pushing her for what lay behind the door across the hall. Her daughter's room.

Tilda pushed back, throwing herself down the stairs where she banged and tumbled and splayed across the landing. Stymied, the push in her veins backed off and she made it as far as the kitchen. She had to get out of the house, away from her family. But to where?

Reeling into the kitchen, she sensed something shuffle in the darkness. She wasn't alone. Something darker than the shadows shifted and hissed. She could smell it now, the sharp tang of charred flesh mixed with the stench of something long dead.

The thing in the corner opened its eyes and before she could make out its silhouette in the dark, she knew it was the rector of the coven. It had survived the flames and come for her. Even now, it raised its burned arms wide to receive her like a wayward daughter.

She had no strength left to fight and Tilda's stomach turned. It was so unfair; Gil was gone but this obscene wraith endured. The repugnant hatred the thing stirred gave a little strength to her hand. If there was any justice in this world, she could at least take the thing with her when she died.

It hissed as it slithered in and Tilda spat in its wretched face.

IN the summer months, Shane woke with the sun every morning. Had done so since he was a boy, stirring from sleep the moment the first rays touched the window no matter how heavily draped. He used an alarm clock only in the winter when the sun rose late but by May, he had no use for it.

This morning was no different than any other. What was out of place was the potent smell of smoke drifting in through the bedroom window.

The panic was instant. Fire. He reached out to wake Tilda but she wasn't there. Springing up, he rushed to the bathroom but it was as empty as the bed. Where was she? He ran into the hallway in his boxer-briefs and banged open his daughter's door. Molly was no morning person, grouchy and slow to waken, and Shane didn't have time to be gentle. He shook her twice and then simply dragged her out of bed and down the stairs.

Rushing past the window, he saw the smoke. The fire, thank God, was outside. The backyard.

He hollered Tilda's name over and over but no response came, the hallway and kitchen both empty. Dropping Molly into a chair, he threw open the back door and raised a hand against the roiling wave of heat that greeted him.

A bonfire raged in the dewy grass of the yard. Dangerously close to the garage, the air rife with floating cinders that rose up and winked out. He couldn't tell what was burning, there was just a dark mass silhouetted inside the bright light of the flames.

The grass under his feet was still wet with dew where the sunlight had yet to reach it. It felt odd, the heat on his chest and the chill on his feet.

Molly appeared in the doorway, squinting against the glow of the fire. "Dad, what happened?"

"Call nine-one-one!"

"Where's mom?"

"I don't know! Get the phone and go out the front!"

Molly darted back inside for the cordless but, disobeying her father, returned to the backdoor. She watched him dart for the garden hose as she called for help. Later, she wouldn't remember anything she had said to the dispatcher on the line.

Shane barked at Molly to search the house while he unspooled the garden hose and opened the spigot. The bonfire was localized but the flames were already roasting the drooping boughs of the willow tree and licking dangerously close to the garage. The thin spray from the hose would be useless against the fire itself so Shane directed the water around it, dousing the garage and the willow and the lawn to prevent it from spreading.

When Molly appeared at his side, she held a small fire extinguisher in her hands, the one kept under the sink. Swapping it out, he gave her the hose and told her to soak the ground around the flames. Yanking the safety pin from the nozzle, he blasted the blaze with a dust cloud of potassium bicarbonate. The flames hissed and roiled and he kept the pressure on, holding his breath against the white cloud and didn't let up until the canister ran dry.

He waved the dust away until he could peer through the haze to see what had incinerated in his yard. Charred and blackened, the limbs materialized in the dissipating fog. An arm, carbonized to charcoal, lifted straight up to the sky. The fingers curled into a claw. He blinked at it stupidly, unable to process what his eyes were seeing.

"What is it?" Molly pressed up behind him to see.

Shane dropped the canister and pushed her away, railroading the girl back into the house before she could see anything. He prayed she hadn't seen anything.

The cloud of bicarbonate and greasy smoke shrouded the yard in a ghostly wash. Shane waved it away as he returned to the mess, a few flames yet licking up around the dark mass. Staring down at the charred remains, Shane felt his brain shut down at the identity of who this was. It can't be her, he thought. It just can't. While his mind rejected the idea, his body seemed to grasp the truth as his knees threatened to buckle under him.

It was then that he noticed the garage door was ajar. He pushed it open, the interior folded in deep shadow. Squinting into its inkiness, something shifted there, coiled up against the far wall.

"Tilda?"

It was her. Folded up into a ball on the floor, her face hidden under the tangled fall of hair. He rushed to her but she flinched at his touch as if he'd hurt her. Her arms were dark with ash and soot and she kept her face hidden.

"Tilda, what happened? Are you hurt?" He ran his hands over her but found no sign of injury beyond some bruising and a few scrapes. He swept her hair aside and straightened her chin. "Tilda, look at me."

Her eyes wheeled crazily in their sockets before coming back to earth. The bandaged dressing on her hand was filthy and loose, the gauze trailing out across the concrete floor. When her eyes clicked into recognition at who was holding her, Tilda curled into him and buried her face into Shane's chest.

"You're okay," he said over and over as he pulled her to her feet. "Let's get you out of here."

She leaned into him, unsteady on her feet but balked when he eased her towards the door. The sunlight blasting through the door was almost white against the darkness of the garage and she didn't want to go. "No," she said.

"It's okay," he cooed. "I promise. Just walk with me."

She didn't want to go but she had no strength left to anchor herself and Shane strong-armed her to the door. The sunlight touched her skin.

Nothing happened. She didn't burst into flames, didn't shriek and burn under its rays. It simply warmed her bare arms and face after the cool damp of the garage. Her hand wrapped around his waist and she leaned into him.

The garden hose at their feet was old and leaked from a split washer. Cold tap water sprayed out in a thin line that misted over the remains of the bonfire. Tilda gazed down at the darkened mass of cinders and charred limbs. Shane told her not to look as they limped back towards the house.

When the carbonized hand that reached for the sky finally crumbled in on itself, there was no left in the yard to witness it.

Three weeks later

THE MYSTERY GUITAR HUNG FROM A PEG on the garage wall, untouched and gathering dust. It was the only ornament on the naked soundproofed walls, the old gig posters and handbills long since torn down leaving only clean patches of white against an outline of faded paint. The archival history of Tilda Parish was gone and the only trace left were these ghostly after-images of where they had hung.

Tilda sat at the bench underneath the slung guitar, her good hand on a keyboard before her. A cable trailed out from the instrument to a speaker monitor behind her.

She'd found the keyboard at Orbiter Music, walking in on a whim four days ago looking to purchase an instrument. Assuming she was looking for a guitar, Travis reminded her that her old Rickenbacker was still hanging from the wall on a commission ticket but was surprised when Tilda had said she wasn't interested.

"I'm done with guitars," she'd said. Her left hand was still cradled in a sling and she saw his eyes dart to it but she was tired of explaining its appearance. "I'm looking for a keyboard."

They didn't have a lot but he led her through the shop to the few keyboards they did have. She found a Yamaha that looked badly used up but sounded fine when she tested it out. "I'll take it," she said.

"It's good to see you back, Tilda. You falling off the wagon?"

"No. Not really," she said. "Just exorcising a few last ghosts."

The 'few last ghosts' was a complete understatement. The melodies and riffs were drifting up all the time and she couldn't stop them coming. Like a musical form of Tourette's, the stuff just blurted out on its own at the most inconvenient or embarrassing times. Exorcism was a practical solution; get it out, craft out the song so she could put it aside and get some peace. A musical trepanation. Drill a hole into the skull to let out the demons and get some re-lief.

Like most plans, it flopped. At first anyway.

She couldn't play guitar anymore. Her burn-ravaged hand was useless, unable to curl around a fretboard much less form chords. A keyboard was the compromise. She could work the keys with her good hand and, if needed, could bonk a few keys with the thumb of her wounded hand. It sounded like hell at first but bullheaded practice is the only way forward. After a while, the botched key strikes improved to the point where she could lay down the basics of a song. Sing quietly overtop the racket she made with the synth.

Trepanation proved to be effective. One song after an-other was hammered out, relieving the tension in her head. Exorcised into strings of notes and lyrics scrawled on scrap paper, the demons were let out and she could breathe again. She had hoped the relief would help her sleep but there were still nightmares to contend with. They didn't disrupt her sleep every night but when they came, the nightmares were raw and terrifying.

Post traumatic stress. Understandable, considering what she had gone through. Songwriting had always been a form of meditation for Tilda, one that calmed her mind and al-lowed her to center herself. Without it, the stark dreams of the coven, their faces hissing from the darkness in the underground nest, would have driven her insane.

The tyrant of the coven had survived the fire and come for her that awful night. Seeing the hatred in its eyes, she was sure was going to die but the thing was weakened and her own hatred gave her strength. Burned by the flames into a horror of charred flesh, the wraith was slow and clumsy and she kept its teeth at bay as they tumbled outside. It gibbered and clawed at her. She had scooped a brick from the garden and broke its teeth with it. Dawn was already chasing the night back and when the sun came up, she knew that it would die, not her. Crumpled into a wreckage of limbs in the grass, the rector had tried to crawl away into a shadow but Tilda dragged it back and when the sun came, it burned.

It had been three weeks and still nothing would grow in the patch of earth where it had burned. Tilda had swept away the ash, turned the earth with a spade and laid down fresh soil and grass seed. Nothing grew there now, not even weeds, leaving a bald swath in the yard.

She had fled the sunlight when she felt it singe the back of her neck and shoulders. She hadn't needed to. The infection or curse or whatever it was was gone. Whether it had run its course like any other infection or it was linked somehow with the death of the coven leader, she didn't know. All that mattered was that it was gone.

No other wraith had appeared after that. The coven, it seemed, was destroyed in the fire.

Detective Crippen had visited once, asking the same questions. A fishing expedition but he left empty-handed. Officer Whittaker had dropped in too. The first visit was official, asking Tilda how she had been injured, how she had ended up on that rooftop. Tilda told her that she couldn't remember, lying that she was suffering memory loss from the attack on the house that night. Whittaker let it go at that. The police officer had visited twice after that but these had been social calls, popping in with Starbucks or a pint of blueberries from the market. Whittaker, bless her heart, was concerned about her recovery and Tilda found herself enjoying the officer's company more and more. A new friend.

"How's Shane?" Whittaker had asked during her last visit. "He seemed kinda tense last time I saw him."

"He's okay," Tilda had said. "At least he says he is."

"Is everything back to normal with you two?"

Tilda took a moment before answering. "No. But it's slowly moving that way."

"You guys have been through a lot. Give it time."

That was the plan. There had been no grand gestures. No reaffirming their commitment nor renewal of vows or any of that schmaltzy stuff. There was still tension and a wariness around one another but they slipped back into the old routine with alarming ease. The ice was slowly melting and things seemed to get a little better every day. Shane was making an effort to share some of her burden, even making dinner a few nights since she came home. Small gestures but there seemed to be genuine tenderness behind them. For that she was grateful and he in turn seemed grateful for any kind word or thoughtful gesture.

Neither she nor Shane were big on showy displays so it was enough for now, this slow waltz around each other in a gradual decay of orbits.

They had gone out to dinner twice. It had been pleasant but awkward as well. Once the safe topics of conversation (Molly, work, the house) had been exhausted, there was a silence when the topic of their marriage or the recent past had drifted to the surface. In a strange way, it was almost like they were dating with all this shy clumsiness. They hadn't had sex in almost a month, the idea seemed too precarious to float for now. Tilda hoped they could get over that hump soon. It had simply been too long.

The keyboard buzzed as it came out of the monitor and she tuned the levels until it evened out. It was odd playing one-handed but it felt right when it hit her heart before it resonated in her brain the way music should. Like she had explained to Gil that night.

Did she miss Gil? Without a doubt. With an ache so acute it left her feeling cored out on the inside. But it wasn't debilitating; she'd had seventeen years of practice dealing with it. Old hat, the scar tissue on her heart growing back with breathtaking speed. She mourned him now, she would always mourn him. In her darker moments, she would project ahead to old age and a doddering mind. Whose face would flicker in her senile mind, Shane's or Gil's?

Tweaking the levels on the keyboard, a thought occurred to her and she tested it with a few notes. Expecting it to sound terrible, she was surprised at how the notes flowed on keys. She had only ever played Gil's song on guitar but the piano brought a whole different feel to it. The tempo needed adjusting to the new instrument but that was simple. Banging out the first notes again, she calibrated the new tempo and started from the beginning, her voice jutting the lyrics between the keys with an eerie precision. It worked. When it was over and the last note hung in the rafters of the garage, Tilda let up a tiny laugh. She had played this song three times in '96 and then buried it for almost twenty years. In the last two months, she had played it more than half a dozen times. It still held power.

A voice hollered in through the door of the garage. Shane, announcing that dinner was almost ready. She hit the power switch, shutting down the keyboard and walked out of the cool garage to the bright light of a July sun.

Shane stood before the barbecue, a retro dome on tri-pod legs. Old school charcoal glowing hot and sizzling three slabs of angus cut. He set the tongs aside, smiled at Tilda as she emerged from her studio and snapped the caps from two bottles of Tankhouse.

She smiled back. "How are the steaks coming?"

"Ten seconds from perfect," he said, clinking the neck of his bottle against hers.

"What can I do?"

"Sit your butt down and get hungry." Anticipating her protest, he cut her short and shooed her on. "Hush. Go sit."

The picnic table was set with plates and cutlery and a pitcher of ice water over a gingham throw. Molly stepped out of the backdoor with a bowl of salad she had made. Tilda watched her daughter fuss the plates and weight the paper napkins under the cutlery.

Tilda peered into the salad bowl and smiled up at her daughter. "That looks yummy."

"It's tart. I overdid it on the garlic." Molly looked up at her dad. "You said two minutes. Are we eating or not?"

Shane brandished the tongs like a magic wand. "Patience, kiddo."

Molly doled the salad onto the plates. "I liked what you were playing out there."

"Thanks."

"Me too." Shane brought the steaks to the table and they all sat down. "Is that a new song?"

"No. That's an old one." Tilda smiled at her daughter. "Older than you actually."

"You should play it more," Shane said. "It sounds really good."

Tilda watched her family tuck into their plates. The picnic table sat in the shade of the big willow tree but the sun filtered through its tendril boughs and dappled them with drops of sunlight. Tilda's heart clenched a tiny bit as she gazed at the two of them, remembering how lucky she was.

"Nah," she said. "I think I'm done with that song."

BY THE SAME AUTHOR

Bad Wolf
Pale Wolf
Killing Down the Roman Line

ABOUT THE AUTHOR

Tim McGregor is a novelist and screenwriter. His Bad Wolf Chronicles series is available in print and ebook form. His produced films can usually be found in the discount DVD bin. Tim lives in Toronto with his wife and children.

timcgregor.blogspot.ca

CPSIA information can be obtained
at www.ICGtesting.com
Printed in the USA
LVHW011751290621
691473LV00009B/1175

9 780992 040314